THE MONTANA MARSHALLS

RUBY JANE

BOOK FIVE

SUSAN MAY WARREN

SDG PUBLISHING
A division of Susan May Warren Fiction
Minneapolis, MN

Ruby Jane
Montana Marshalls series
ISBN-13: 978-1-943935-38-3
Published by SDG Publishing
15100 Mckenzie Blvd. Minnetonka, MN 55345
Copyright © 2019 by Susan May Warren

For more information about Susan May Warren, please access the author's
website at the following address: www.susanmaywarren.com.
Published in the United States of America.

For Your glory, Lord

Prologue

Aw, York just knew this would happen.

Knew he should never have come home. Knew that if he set foot back in America, he'd end up in the back seat of a covert CIA SUV, winding through the back hills of Washington State with a guy who had probably figured out that York knew his secrets.

A guy who wasn't going to slow down to question him, but rather was simply searching for a good place to dump a body.

York's body.

Ex-CIA agent York Newgate hadn't imagined exactly this scenario—the one where he left behind the woman he loved, where he never really got to say goodbye, where somehow the happy ending he'd grasped for a wonderful, disbelieving second slipped through his fingers—but he had known, without a doubt, that the CIA would find him.

After all, he knew their tricks.

Knew they were tenacious. And that the driver, former officer Alan Martin, dressed in a suit, with close-clipped dark hair and a pair of aviator glasses, had no intention of "questioning him down at headquarters."

Liars, all of them.

And York had been one of the very best.

Maybe he deserved this.

"So, taking the shortcut back to DC?" he said now, his knees jammed into the passenger seat in front of him.

Martin glanced at him over his shoulder, not even allowing a smirk at York's attempt to point out the obvious—they were traveling down a remote highway in the middle of the Okanogan-Wenatchee National Forest.

"I saw a great hike to Bridal Falls a couple miles back. Maybe we should stretch our legs?" York said.

No response.

They'd flex-cuffed his hands behind him, but he could get out of that easily enough. He just needed them to slow down. Last thing he wanted was to take a header off the side of the road, end up in a metal crumble at the bottom of the mountain.

But maybe that would be better than what Martin had planned for him.

York should have put up a bigger fuss at the hospital, but frankly, he'd been so startled by the sight of Martin, a fellow CIA contact, showing up to arrest him, he'd simply conceded.

And of course, RJ's family was there, with all her protective brothers who formed a sort of wall around her. The last thing he wanted was a reason for them to dislike him more.

So he'd gone with Martin, quietly. *Nothing to see here, folks.*

The minute Martin and the other thug he'd brought for backup had locked York in the back seat, the churning in his gut started.

He looked out the window at the thick tangle of pine and underbrush. The sun had dropped behind the mountain, leaving long, jagged shadows along the road.

Yep, they were looking for a place to end him and make him disappear.

Forever.

Sorry, RJ.

The other goon hadn't spoken, not once, but York bet if he did, he might find a Russian accent emerging from his mouth. The man had "Russian-street-fighter-named-Igor" written all over his scarred mug.

Wow, he'd been all kinds of stupid when he didn't send Martin an uppercut, kick Russian Thug, grab RJ's hand, and run for the hills.

"So, I'm assuming you haven't booked us a cute little Airbnb in the woods?"

"Enough, York," Martin snapped.

"We're not on a CIA holiday at all, are we? This is some off-the-books field trip."

Martin's jaw tightened.

Yes, that made sense. After all, Martin had been working off the books for some time now. Ever since—

Martin slammed on the brakes as he came around the turn.

York barely had time to catch himself on the seat, his hands already loose in the cuffs.

Martin swerved the car into a scenic overlook, the first deserted pull-off they'd come to.

Oh good, now came the fun part.

Martin got out, walked around the car, and opened the passenger door. "Get out."

Right. York noticed Igor got out too. So maybe this was more of a tussle than an execution.

York kept his hands behind him, no need to give away the fact that in about two-point-three seconds, as soon as Martin took a step closer, he was going to slap away Martin's gun, grab his wrist, jerk him forward, and land his knee in his gut a second before he slammed the palm of his hand into Martin's face, hopefully breaking his nose.

Then he'd round on Igor and redirect the fist headed toward York's face, roll, and cut off his breathing with a side-handed hit to his neck. Maybe lock Igor's arm into an arm bar and shove him into the ground before Igor had a chance to figure out what was happening.

York would grab the keys from a bleeding Martin, get in the car, and return to RJ and their happy ending.

But none of that went down quite like he hoped because just as Martin made to grab York by the lapel to haul him to the edge of the overlook, a voice emerged from the trail nearby.

"Hey! Can you help me?"

Oh no. York wanted to turn to the kid—maybe early twenties and wearing an Oregon Ducks football jersey—and shout, *Run!*

7

He wasn't fast enough. Ducks spotted Martin's gun and froze. Igor grabbed the kid.

And the what-ifs flashed through York—grab the gun, turn it on Martin—but right then Martin shoved it against York's head. "Good try. Hands up, York."

York raised his uncuffed hands. Aw— "Let him go. He's just a kid."

Igor pushed the kid against the hood of the car. A long metal cross hung down from a leather lanyard around his neck. And the kid must have played football because he had the name Mack on the back of his jersey. He wasn't too keen on Igor holding him down either.

"Let me up!"

"Martin—he's not a part of this," York growled.

Mack wasn't listening to his hostage negotiator because he jerked back in a move he might have seen on *Lethal Weapon* and—hey, it worked!—connected with Igor's nose.

Good kid!

Igor's nose exploded in a spray of blood. He shouted, and then, of course, smashed his fist into Mack's face.

The kid spun and dropped like an anvil. Didn't move. A pool of blood leaked out from where he'd hit the ground.

Martin stared at Igor. "*Seriously?*"

York's moment was gone. Because he couldn't leave the kid here to die—

A car drove by, slowing as if to pull into the overlook.

No, please—

From behind, Martin shoved the gun into York's neck. "Get back in the car."

Not. A. Chance.

The car was pulling in, a car top carrier on the top, a couple of children's bikes strapped to the back.

Shoot. York moved toward the SUV.

Igor had grabbed Mack and dragged him to the SUV. Mack dropped like dead weight into the passenger seat behind Igor, and York had a sick feeling.

York glanced at Mack as he got in behind Martin. The kid's

eyes had rolled back into his head, his skin pale.

"Gimme your hands," Martin said and York complied, Martin's gun still on him. Igor came around and flex-cuffed him again.

Aaaand, here they went again.

Martin got in at the wheel and pulled out, spitting gravel.

Yeah, the next stop would be the end.

"You didn't have to kill the kid," York said.

"He's not dead," Martin said, but York reached over and pressed a finger to his carotid artery.

Maybe, maybe not. York couldn't tell, but he did get his hands on the kid's lanyard and ripped it with a hard yank from his neck. "I beg to differ."

Martin glanced in the rearview. "Don't touch him."

York gripped the cross in his hand. Looked like something he might make at camp—a couple of nails soldered together. And the lanyard would free him.

Thank you, kid.

York wound the lanyard through his flexicuffs at the wrist, caught one edge of the cuffs, then clamped the ends of the lanyard between his teeth.

"Hey!" Igor shouted and York dodged a cuff to his head.

A couple sawing motions and York was through the cuffs.

"Stop him!" Martin shouted as he went around a curve. He nearly hit a car off to the side.

York exploded. He stabbed the long end of the cross into Igor's neck as the thug came over the seat, hitting the carotid artery. Blood gushed as Igor grabbed his neck, gasping.

RJ, hang on. I'm coming back to you.

York snaked an arm around Martin, held him against the headrest, the bloody end of the cross next to his neck. "Stop the car."

But Igor was thrashing, grabbing for the wheel, or maybe just help, and Martin had to shove him off. Which made him swerve hard. He banked off the guardrail, over the center line, toward a wall of mountain.

And into the oncoming lane.

Just then, around the corner, a semi appeared, big grille,

wide load, and oh, that would make a splat. York leaped forward and grabbed the wheel, wrenching it over hard.

The force turned the SUV, screeching, spinning, around, slamming York against the door.

Right about then, something cold and hard sliced across his side. Maybe the cross, still gripped in his hand.

The SUV smashed against the semi, careening it toward the edge of the road.

York grabbed the door handle and jerked it open just as the car hit the guardrail.

The car went airborne, spinning up, over the edge.

York felt himself tearing out of the door, slipping into the air, his body flying.

Then the world twisted around him as he fell and fell into the tangled forest below.

1

R uby Jane Marshall wasn't a runner. Normally.

Usually, her SOP was to hunker down and hide. Like a rabbit, her little heart pounding in her chest, seconds away from a heart attack.

But as she stood in the kitchen of the rowhouse in DC, sirens haunting the autumn night air, a voice screamed in her head that sounded a lot like York's.

Run!

The blaring unsettled the Mayfair neighborhood, lights flickering on in nearby townhomes, and she had five minutes—maybe less—to track down a serial killer.

A killer whose victims included her boss, Sophia Randall.

And maybe the man she loved, York Newgate, although—nope, she wasn't going there.

She simply refused to accept the idea that York could be dead. Not when his body hadn't been conclusively identified.

So running wasn't an option. Nor hiding. Not until RJ tracked down Sophia's notebook and maybe her laptop computer. Anything that might give her a fresh lead on Sophia's death, give her a clue as to why her boss would have been in Seattle.

And most of all, how she ended up in the sights of a Russian assassin.

RJ darted out from shadows behind the fridge where she'd momentarily planted herself when she heard the first mourn of a siren. Of course they'd be coming for her because she *wasn't* a supersleuth or even an action heroine. More like a glorified secretary with the B&E skills of a third grader.

To get into Sophia's place, RJ had broken a window on the ground floor. Climbed in over a plant, which now littered the sofa with its dry-as-dust remains, and tracked her footprints across the formerly white carpet of the guest room and up the stairs to the kitchen and living room area.

Oh, she was definitely going down for this. Jail. Prison. And orange *so* washed out her complexion, clashing with her dark hair and blue eyes.

But desperate times called for crazy actions and…

What would York do?

He was still in her head, those blue eyes looking at her like she could save the world—or maybe just *his* world.

She bumped into a table in the dark and reached out to right the wobbling lamp—

The crash raised gooseflesh and she froze again. She was going to leave a raccoon trail of evidence through Sophia's apartment. But it wasn't like Sophia was around to press charges.

Not since she'd died four weeks ago.

Don't. Think. About—

RJ blew out a breath, trailing her hand down the hallway toward the first door on the right, Sophia's office, working off the scant memory of a casual dinner party a year ago.

Please let Sophia have left behind her journal, the one she always carried, old-style, to jot her thoughts.

The journal had to be here. Vicktor Shubnikov, the police detective in Seattle who headed up the investigation, had been kind enough to give her a list of the evidence found at the crime scene.

No journal in Sophia's possession. Just her body, a lot of blood, and evidence of a struggle.

At least her boss had gone down fighting.

Hopefully the journal led to clues about how she ended up in a hotel room in Seattle, her throat slit, clearly having been tortured.

Don't. Think—

RJ drew in a breath and brailled the wall inside the office door. She found a light switch. Flicked it on.

Hello, neighbors. Maybe they would think Sophia had returned.

The sirens faded, and for a moment, she heard her breath, heavy in her chest. Maybe she *hadn't* triggered an alarm...

Still, she needed to add some giddy-up to this snatch and grab.

The tiny office was palatial by DC standards, containing a standing desk, a credenza, and a bookcase. The entire townhouse, a three-story walk-up brownstone, had been renovated in the revived trendy, early-eighties' style—muted gold fixtures, dark wood floors, shaggy white rugs, and cool white driftwood furniture. The office overlooked the lush garden alleyway that ran between the homes.

A deck led out from the office and ran the length of the unit.

She opened the credenza and began to sort through it. Bills, papers, folders, and a printer. Nothing that resembled Sophia's small gray journal.

On the black desk, a dust ring framed the outline of a laptop computer, probably confiscated by a CIA sweep. Another fine wisp of dust over the top of the desk suggested they'd been here some time ago.

Opening the desk drawers, RJ riffled through pens, a checkbook, and leafed through the duplicate pages. She found an entry for a piano tuner, another for the Great Frame Up, a local picture framer. The office sported a few photos of friends and family, but Sophia was single, so no shots of her on a beach with a cute man.

On the wall, however, hung a picture of the astrological clock from Prague's Old Town Square. The picture stirred memories of the last time RJ had been in Prague. She'd been meeting with a man named Roy who had sent her on a trip to Russia and ignited this whole fiasco.

The fiasco in which she'd found herself on the lam through the former Soviet Union, dodging the FSB and Interpol, suddenly named as the lead suspect in the attempted assassination of

General Boris Stanislov.

Ex-CIA operative York Newgate had pulled her out of hiding, kept her alive, and secreted her out of the country. Of course, that only led to more trouble when the *real* assassin turned his sights on RJ and then her foster sister, Coco, and then, of course, York. Which only caused Ford, her Navy SEAL brother, to completely overreact and stage his own rescue attempt, one that nearly got him killed.

She could take care of herself. Really.

Nothing in the desk, and RJ stared at the picture.

Maybe…

She pulled the picture off the wall, looking behind it. No safe. No secret compartment. So much for her super CIA analyst skills.

After checking the back of the picture, RJ replaced it on the wall.

She flicked off the light.

RJ had personally searched Sophia's CIA office after VP candidate Senator Reba Jackson had cleared her of the assassination charges. No journal in the small office overlooking the Potomac either.

So, either her murderer had taken it, or Sophia had left it here in her home.

RJ took the stairs up to Sophia's bedroom and turned on the bedside light. The nightstand held a vitamin container, a Kindle, still charging, and some lip gloss.

She gave a scant search through the closet and bathroom, looked in the hall linen closet, and stood in the hallway, heart thumping.

The sirens sounded again, this time closer.

C'mon. *Think.*

She was out of leads. But she desperately needed to track down Sophia's killer if she hoped to find York. Or at least his killer…

No. He had to be alive.

RJ refused to believe the body identified at the accident scene, burned and unrecognizable, belonged to her York.

Of course, the CIA denied even arresting him. Denied knowing the two suits who had dragged him from the hospital in cuffs. Their bodies had also burned in the car accident that had charred the vehicle.

She wasn't stupid—she could spot a cover-up when she saw it. After all, she'd seen every episode of *Alias*.

And somehow—she didn't yet know how, but she'd figure it out—entangled in it all was a Russian assassin named Damien Gustov. An assassin who had followed York from Russia to America.

In her worst fears, Gustov had York. Was torturing him the same way he had Sophia—

Sirens. Nearly deafening, and RJ had a minute, tops.

She came down the stairs and headed for the family room. Light bathed the room as she flicked on a lamp to reveal a leather sofa, fireplace, bookshelf, and an upright piano. A cursory glance at the shelf revealed nothing.

A stack of books on the piano held a lamp. She searched through the books and accidentally hit a number of the piano keys.

Oops. Although…a couple hadn't hit, leaving a dull thud where a note should be.

Piano tuning. She remembered the duplicate check. Clearly someone hadn't done their job.

Or…

RJ pulled the books off the piano top and opened the lid.

There—inside, lying on the strings—the weathered gray journal, the corners fraying as if Sophia had brushed her thumb against them too many times, thinking.

RJ grabbed it and shoved it into her inside jacket pocket. Zipped up the jacket.

Red lights flashed through the front windows.

She turned off the light.

Yeah, she should run.

Now.

Clearly the front door was out, so she slipped out onto the deck.

Second story. And below her was the patio, a hedge, and a

not-so-sweet landing.

Oh, where was her inner Sydney Bristow when she needed it?

RJ's hands slicked as she threw her leg over the edge of the railing—probably smart cops would run around back, but all the townhomes were connected, so maybe she had a minute or two—

Her hands slipped, and she let out a scream, her grip sliding down the rails to the bottom.

Her legs dangled, maybe eight feet from the patio.

Okay, she just had to let go and drop.

Let. *Go.*

Her hands gripped the bars, frozen, and, see, this was why she wasn't a superspy.

Hiding. So much better.

"Just let go!"

The hiss emerged from the darkness, and for a second, the guttural whisper raked up her fragile hopes— "York?"

How had he—except he *always* showed up when she needed him the most—in the middle of an alleyway in Moscow, on a train, just in time to save her from a stabbing, and even in Seattle, when she walked in on a dead body.

Of course he'd show up now.

"Just let go, sis!"

She gasped as hands touched her ankles.

What? *"Ford?"*

"Yes—c'mon!"

She released one hand, turned and reached for his shoulder, and let go with the other.

He caught her easily of course, his arms thick from hours of SEAL PT. He was dressed in black, wore an earpiece and night vision goggles, and now grabbed her hand. "Run!"

"How—"

"Not now!"

Then they were fleeing down the boulevard between connected rows of townhomes, in and out of puddles of light. He pulled her into an alcove and planted her beside him. "Shh!"

Her heartbeat could give her away, but she said nothing as two figures darted past them, toward the home she'd just escaped.

"What are you—"

He put his hand over her mouth, turned to her ear, just a whisper. "Stay on my six."

Huh?

Then he grabbed her hand again and took off.

They ran across the yard, through a narrow walkway between units, and out into the opposite street.

A van sat parked under a cherry tree and the door opened. Ford pushed her inside. He climbed in after her, pulled the door shut, and they streaked away.

The van's seats had been removed, so she scooted back along the wall, trying to find herself.

"Hey, RJ."

RJ stared at Scarlett, the petite brunette who had been Ford's SEAL team communicator, sitting in the passenger seat.

Next to her, in the driver's seat, sat Ford's teammate Trini, a large, dark-skinned man from Trinidad. He drove as if on a casual Sunday drive, his fingers tapping on the window.

"I don't—how did you—"

"Tate told me what you were up to," Ford said, pulling off his earpiece.

How did Tate, her overly protective bodyguard brother—okay, they were *all* overly protective—know where she was? Or what she was doing...

"Wait...he's working with Vicktor in Seattle, isn't he?"

Ford had pulled off his night vision goggles. Ran a finger and thumb across his eyes, then blinked. Looked at her. "I don't know. I just got a text from him with this address that said you were in trouble and that you needed an exfil."

She stared at Ford, her eyes adjusting to the darkness, the DC neighborhoods outside the van's back window sentried by the gnarled limbs of barren cherry trees, their leaves turning to dust in the autumn air. She was surrounded by brick homes, manicured yards, tidy lives.

She'd had a tidy life, once upon a time.

A tidy, safe life where no one needed to rescue—or exfil—her.

"I had everything under control."

Ford's mouth tightened around the edges. Even in his all-black attire, she could make out his too pensive pale-green eyes.

See him unmasking her lies.

Except it wasn't a lie.

She got them into this mess.

She was going to get them out.

Besides, "You, better than anyone, should know that when people try and rescue me, they only get hurt. Or..." And she looked hard at him. "Killed."

Then, with the accuracy of a knife to her heart, Ford took a breath, looked away.

Virtually agreeing.

She deserved that.

Pulling out Sophia's journal, she ran her thumb along the frayed corners.

Yes, she might have started this whole nightmare. But she was going to figure out how to end it.

Without anyone else she loved getting hurt.

I will find you, York.

Please, please be alive.

◆

Monday nights usually didn't get that rowdy.

Even at Jethro's, the only tavern in Shelly, a tiny town in the shadow of the Cascade Mountains of Washington State. The tavern-slash-craft brewery located on Main Street saw mostly well-attired locals who came in for their Freaky Fries—crispy steak-cut fries slathered in sour cream and cheese—and a pint of amber beer fresh from the kegs in back.

But on Mondays, the tavern turned into a sports bar, the two giant flat-screens over the bar tuned to *Monday Night Football*.

And tonight, the Seahawks versus Vikings.

Jethro didn't have to even ask Mack to stay late after the kitchen closed to make sure none of these jersey-wearing fans got out of line.

Because Mack would do just about anything for his boss.

Mack glanced through the crowd, looking for trouble as he wiped up a puddle and grabbed an empty mug.

Especially since the Vikings were up by a field goal, two minutes left, with Wilson under center. And at least two of the spectators in the crowd were wearing Vikings jerseys.

In the middle of Seahawks country.

That took brass.

He was also keeping his eye on a couple broad-shouldered tough guys bumping against each other at a high top, his instincts nudging him.

Not that Mack had any idea where he'd gotten those instincts. They seemed embedded in his bones, along with the knowledge that should something go south, he probably knew how to handle himself.

Or maybe not, because he'd been pretty worked over when he arrived in Shelly. He didn't remember much about how he'd gotten here, which was bad enough, but when Jethro Darnell had found Mack huddled under a tree in Riverwalk Park, the wound in his side had already started to pus and burn, infection setting in.

A couple more days and it might have gone septic.

Mack had been shivering, running a fever, but in his gut he knew—just *knew*—that going to a hospital would be deadly. For someone. Probably him, but…something about hospitals had raked up his defenses.

Jethro had taken him to his pub and sewn up his wound with the steady hand of an Army medic and probably his many years as a bar owner. The cut separated Mack's flesh along his ribs, nearly into his gut, and combined with the hematoma just above his ear, he looked like he'd survived a plane crash.

Jethro asked him a couple questions which Mack honestly couldn't answer. Then he'd fed him and let him bunk in the vacant upstairs apartment until he could find his feet again, basically keeping him alive, feeding him, and then employing him.

Giving Mack time to figure out…well, who he was.

A month later he still hadn't figured it out.

"How's the game—oh my—" Raven Darnell had come in

from the patio area where a fire flickered in the firepit and more spectators sat at high tops watching the outdoor screen. She wore a tight blue-and-silver Seahawks shirt, put her hands on her hips, and stared at the screen over the bar, her mouth a tight line.

He followed her gaze. Third and ten, one minute left.

Yeah, it wasn't looking so good for the Hawks…

Wilson hiked the ball, dropped back—

Mack winced as Wilson went down, sacked.

He shot a glance at the Vikings fans in the back. One was pumping his fist, shouting in a sea of furious Seahawks.

Down, boy.

"Aw, shoot. There goes another twenty bucks," Raven said.

Mack grinned and held out his hand. "I don't know why you keep betting against me."

"I believe in my Seahawks. That's what a true fan does…" She slapped a twenty, probably out of her tip stash, into his hand.

Mack liked her. She stood maybe six inches shorter than him, her dark hair pulled back into a sloppy ponytail, her lips a deep red to match her fingernails, although the paint was chipped on the ends. She played her guitar and sang on open mic nights, her voice a deep, smoky alto, and had dreams of making it big as a country music star.

He had a feeling she was just sticking around to help her old man.

Her brother's picture, the one in his Army Ranger uniform, hung on the wall behind the bar. Grinning, holding his weapon, the Afghani mountains in the background.

A war hero cut down before his life really started.

No, Raven wasn't going anywhere, even if she was discovered.

The bar crowd began to close out their tabs, and the next time he looked up, the place was nearly empty.

Even the Vikings fans had left, and he hoped he'd given them a bill. Maybe—shoot.

Mack wasn't a waiter, that much he knew. He let beers warm on a table, forgot to bring out food under the warmer, and too many times found customers holding out their water glasses as he walked by.

He could pour beers, however, and…

Well, there was that one night about a month ago when he'd spotted a couple college-age guys lurking around the back entrance and decided to stick around as Raven cleaned up.

Raven had let him walk her all the way to her car.

Since then, she'd been ultra-friendly. Started betting on the games with him.

Technically they were still open, so he left the door unlocked but turned off the Open sign.

The night shadows played off the eclectic vibe of the tavern. Tall barrels served as the base to high top tables, beer kegs lined the back wall with copper piping running along the ceiling, and Edison lights hung down like starlight from the painted black ceiling. The floor was original to the warehouse—a work-worn hardwood—and the walls red brick. The bar had been made from scrap copper, the stools handmade by Jethro, simple wood, also painted black.

The man had put his life into this place after he'd lost Ace to the Taliban.

Outside, the fire in the pit had died, the crowd that had been watching the game dispersed. Mack would have to go out there and get the glasses next.

"Hey, tough guy, are you interested in sticking around for the Riverwalk Open Mic tomorrow night?"

Raven stood at the bar, washing by hand the mugs for the mules. She looked up at him.

Something about her stirred a memory inside him, the way she laughed, a feisty edge to her persona. He liked down-to-earth, loyal women.

At least, he thought he did. He picked up a tray and began to clean the tables, piling up glass and copper mugs. "Who's playing?"

"Besides me? There's a guy doing a bunch of Neil Diamond covers, I think."

"Who?"

She looked up at him. "Seriously? You don't remember Neil Diamond?"

He made a face. "Should I?"

She laughed. "I dunno. Maybe not. He was sort of a big deal in my dad's era, but you're definitely too young for that—how old do you think you are?"

He added a plate of half-finished fries to the tray and headed for the back. "I don't know. Twenty-nine?"

"Oh, dude, you wish."

His mouth made a tight line, not sure if she was kidding. Probably not. He caught his reflection in the window of the freezer door.

Forty, maybe, given the lines around his eyes. He had blond hair, no gray, but a weird scar along his neck that had given him pause, but it was covered now by his beard. His head injury had finally faded, although the deep bruise still darkened part of his head.

And the wound in his side had stopped aching. Which meant he couldn't be that old—he'd bounced back pretty fast. His body had, at least.

His mind, not so much.

The only thing that seemed to linger from his past was his accent. He'd tried to ping it, and decided it sounded more British than Aussie. When he googled it, in conjunction with amnesia, he discovered that speech patterns were part of muscle memory, along with knowing how to walk, and couldn't be erased with trauma.

So, in short, he wasn't from around here.

Mack set the dishes into the sink and began to spray them off to put in the dishwasher, loading them onto the rack.

"Here's the rest," Raven said, coming in beside him. She set another tray into the sink, then loaded it into the automatic dishwasher and turned the machine on. "So, Neil Diamond?"

He looked at her. "Are you…are you asking me out?"

Her mouth opened, just slightly, and he was a cad, until—

"Um, yes. I think so." She flashed a smile at him.

He expected more of a response, something inside him that might stir to life. Feelings, if not memories.

Nothing.

Still, she *was* pretty and he liked her, so, "Okay."

She grinned, reached out and touched his arm. "I know you don't remember anything, Mack, but maybe you don't have to. Maybe you get a fresh start." Then she winked and headed back to the dining room.

A fresh start. He mulled over the words as he loaded another tray. The previous tray came out of the machine on the far side, the dishes clean and dry, so he retrieved it, and started putting the dishes away.

Over the last month he'd spent hours searching for anyone with the name Mack missing in Washington State, his age, his build. Then Oregon and Montana, and finally the United States at large.

Found three men, none of them matching the mug he saw in the mirror. Two his age, one younger.

Apparently, he'd dropped off the planet.

Or, possibly, his name wasn't Mack. But it was the only scrap of information still lodged in his brain when he'd flagged down a trucker four weeks ago on Highway 2 headed east. He didn't know why, but he'd gotten off at Wenatchee and picked up another ride, this time headed north. The driver, a recent college grad with his wife, had parents in Shelly and talked about the place with such fondness Mack ended his trip here.

Mack wanted a life that he could talk about with fondness. Anticipation. And while he hadn't a clue what life he'd left, the wounds on his body told him that maybe he didn't want to return to it.

So yeah, a fresh start sounded good. With Raven, at least for one night under the stars listening to Neil Diamond covers.

Honestly, the artist's name did sound familiar.

A crash sounded from the other room. "Did you drop something?" He opened the dishwasher and pulled out the clean, steaming tray. "Raven?"

He picked up a couple glasses with a towel, set them on the rack—

Another crash.

He dropped the towel and headed toward the front room.

"Are you o—"

Raven stood in the main room, her arms pushing hard against the chest of a man who had his arm around her neck, shaking her.

"What the—?" Mack's shout turned the man. Then memory clicked in and yes, he'd also seen him a month ago.

Raven's ex-boyfriend. A man named Teddy, if Mack remembered correctly.

"Let her go!" Mack advanced on the man, but Teddy grabbed Raven's arm and pushed her through the door, out into the patio area.

Oh no, he wasn't getting away. Mack wasn't sure where the rage came from, the sudden heat that boiled into his veins, but as he pushed through the door, he didn't stop. Not when the guy turned, held Raven in front of him, threatening her. Not when the assailant picked up a poker out of the fire, the one used to stir the embers into the dark sky, pointing it at Mack. And especially not when Mack grabbed Teddy's arm, bent it away from Raven, and smashed his fist full into Teddy's face.

Mack shunted Teddy's feeble attempt to smash him with the poker, squeezing his wrist so hard the poker fell away onto a chair cushion, then he kneed the man in his gut, pulled his head down, and kneed him again.

Blood. So much of it that it filled the cracks of the patio as Teddy went down shouting, writhing, Raven screaming in the background.

Somewhere in there, Mack found himself and turned to her. She was staring at Teddy, back to Mack, and then—

"Who are you?"

Mack stared at her, blinking hard. Adrenaline ratcheted his heartbeat to high, his entire body buzzing.

Teddy moaned.

Then something of sanity grabbed hold, and Mack stepped back. Looked at Teddy.

The man held his face—his nose destroyed, his lip split, maybe missing a couple teeth.

Oh.

"Are you okay?"

Raven's question, and Mack looked up, thinking Raven was headed for Teddy, but she came up to Mack and backed him away from Teddy, her hand on his chest. "You're bleeding." She pointed to his side.

He looked down and only then felt the heat scurry into his side.

His movements might have reopened the wound. Raven drew up Mack's shirt, completely ignoring Teddy, and yep, the stitches had reopened.

Now, wow, the pain burned through him. He grabbed her wrists. "Just leave it—"

"You need a hospital—"

"*I* need a hospital!" Teddy shrieked. He was on his feet.

Mack grabbed his shirt and directed him to a nearby chair. "Just sit down, Slick. You had it coming."

Raven shoved a wet bar towel in Mack's hands and he gave it to Teddy. "Call 9-1-1," Mack said to Raven.

"I already did." Jethro had come out of the bar. He'd been in the back office doing the books, last Mack knew, and now emerged with the look of murder as he stared at Teddy. "I told you last time you showed up that if you ever came back—"

"Daddy. It's okay."

"It's not okay," Mack said. "He had his arm around her neck."

And with that, he had to step in front of Teddy to keep Jethro back. He might be in his early sixties and completely gray, but he was lean and bore the movement of a man who still worked out.

Teddy got up, a little wobbly.

"Don't even try to run, kid," Mack said quietly. "You can sit on the sidewalk outside to wait for the cops." Mack glanced at Jethro. "I'll wait with you."

"Me too," said Raven. "I probably need to give a statement, make sure you don't get into trouble."

Mack frowned at her.

"Anyone who handles himself like that has a past," she said quietly.

He drew in a breath. But, yeah, that's what he was afraid of.

Very afraid.
So much for fresh starts.

2

M ack couldn't shake the sense of déjà vu.

The police chief had hauled them all down to the station to record their statements. Now, with the moon high, the night dark, his entire body still buzzed with the eerie sense of familiarity, an old memory lying under his skin.

Like he'd spent time in a police station or being questioned.

They hadn't arrested him, but he felt like a criminal all the same. Because behind the veil of his blank memory, he knew, just *knew* in his bones that he had done something—or many somethings—very, very bad.

"Are you okay?" Raven glanced over at him from the driver's seat of her Ford Focus as she pulled into the parking lot of the pub. Her father's truck sat in its place behind the back door, near the dumpster. She parked beside it. "You're awfully quiet."

Mack had been drumming his fingers on his knees and now flexed them and glanced over at her. The lights from the lot shone down on her, her blue eyes soft.

"I'm fine."

How could he tell her that the moment the police had arrived he'd fought the urge to bolt? Who but a criminal had that reaction to a cop?

"I'll bet you're wondering why Teddy…well, why he attacked me tonight."

"You don't have to talk about it."

"Yes, I do. It helps me sort it out." She blew out a breath. "I

27

met Teddy when I was a freshman at WSU. He played baseball, was super popular, and when I met him, he was so nice. Attentive. He gave me gifts and came to my open mics. He was sweet and tried hard…but he had a temper. He blew up at me for the smallest of reasons…usually not because of me but something else. And then he'd apologize and do his best to fix it."

"That's called emotional abuse, by the way."

She nodded and turned off the car. "I know that now. Then, I thought there was something wrong with me. I started to do everything I could to make him happy…"

The memory of Teddy's hand on her throat tightened a fist in Mack's chest. "Did he physically hurt you when you were dating?"

"He pushed me a couple times. Grabbed my arm hard, once."

Mack should have hit him harder. More.

"I broke up with him twice before I realized that I had this weird addiction to wanting to please him. I'm not sure why—maybe because I thought I needed him. That I was better with him."

"What was he doing here tonight?"

"I don't know. He texts me every once in a while, and some-times…I don't know. I fall for it. I text him back. I try and be nice. It's probably my fault he showed up here—"

"It's not your fault he attacked you—"

"I know. When he showed up last time with his friend, he left right after you walked me to the car. Tonight, well, he was so nice and said he'd missed me, and for a long minute, I fell for it. Then he told me that he didn't care that I'd left him, that he'd take me back, and I thought…what was I doing? That girl—the one who let him hurt me—she's gone. Or at least, I want her to be, so I told him to get out, and he just…flipped." She looked at him. "I know I deserve better than that, but sometimes I have a hard time believing it, you know?"

He did know. Deep inside, although he hadn't a clue why.

Just that, at his core, he knew he probably didn't deserve anything good. And his instincts tonight only confirmed it—during and after the fight.

But Raven wasn't him. Wasn't the kind of person who let

rage fuel her, who was so easy with her fists that she didn't let pain slow her down. So, "Why don't you deserve better, Raven?"

She made a face, shook her head, looked away.

Okay. He drew in a breath. "We often don't see ourselves the way we are."

"No duh, Superman." She looked back at him, and it seemed her eyes were glistening. "You were a hero tonight."

"A guy ended up in the hospital because of me."

"It was about time."

Yeah, okay, he could agree. "Still…"

"Made you wonder where you got those skills, right?"

Mack said nothing.

"I've never seen him so angry as tonight." She smiled. "Thank you for what you did." Her hand slid to his arm. "I'm glad my dad found you."

Oh. His heart thumped at the expression on her face. "Raven—"

"I know you're trying to figure things out, Mack. But you have a place to stay here, as long as you need it. And…I hope you'll stay."

He wasn't planning on going anywhere, but her words settled into his bones.

Whoever he'd been in the past, he didn't want to be him anymore. And maybe, if he was careful, he never had to be again.

Maybe he could be a guy who deserved a happy ending.

"You don't have to go in," she said quietly. "My dad is still here. He'll probably spend the night on his sofa in the office…" She licked her lips. "You could come back to our place and we could, um, talk…"

Oh yeah, she had *talking* on her mind. And frankly, he wasn't far from wanting a long conversation either, but even as the thought swept in, something like shame followed it.

Hmm. So, he might be a criminal, but apparently he wasn't the kind of guy to take a girl home for the night either.

Interesting.

Mack put his hand on hers, held it a moment, then slid it away. "Thanks, but I'm beat. See you tomorrow?"

Although Raven gave him a nod, a smile, a hint of disappointment hued her eyes. "Okay, Slugger. See you."

Mack got out and stood back while she drove away, then headed into the pub's back entrance.

A light shone from the office just off the kitchen, and he walked past his apartment entrance and stopped at the open office door, knocking on the jamb.

Jethro looked up, his readers down on his nose. He reminded Mack of that British actor who'd played James Bond—Daniel Craig. Lean, no-nonsense, and the fact Mack could even remember that made him wonder just how selective his memory might be.

Maybe he was hiding his identity from himself.

Jethro looked up and pulled off his glasses. "So, how'd it go?"

"Raven gave her statement, and with yours and mine, they released me. Teddy is at the hospital—has a broken nose."

"Good thing you came out when you did. I would have brought my shotgun," Jethro said as he turned in his desk chair. "I never liked Teddy, but I tried to be nice to him. My mistake. I should have told Raven from the beginning that he was bad news."

The metal desk and tall filing cabinet took up one wall of the office. A bookshelf on the other, filled with supplies, books, old promotional giveaways, and every manner of clutter, suggested the man had little time to organize his life.

The old sofa shoved against the far wall only confirmed it.

Jethro's pub was his entire life. That, and Raven.

"Why didn't you like him?" Mack asked.

"Fatherly instincts, maybe. I tend to know if someone is good stock—it's a gift."

Mack didn't want to ask him—

"I knew right off that although you had been through something, I could trust you."

He didn't want to disagree, so, "Thanks for that."

Jethro pointed to his head. "Anything coming back upstairs?"

Mack picked up a picture of Ace and Raven holding a stringer of fish. "Naw. Just shadows." He put the picture back on the shelf. "I do have this one recurring dream of being on a train, but I don't know where it is. And people are speaking a foreign language, and I understand it, but when I wake up, I can't remember what language it is."

"Maybe you were in the military. The way you handled yourself tonight, I wouldn't doubt it."

"Maybe."

"I could ask Jimbo down at the station to do me a favor and run your prints."

Mack stilled.

"Or not," Jethro said. "Sometimes a man needs a fresh start."

Is that what he needed?

"I'll think about it," Mack said. "I was thinking I probably don't want to overstay my welcome."

Jethro's mouth tightened, as if he might be deciding whether to disagree.

But if he was a criminal, the last thing Mack wanted was to bring trouble into Jethro's and Raven's lives. So, yeah, hitting the road might be exactly what he should do.

But not tonight. "Shouldn't you be home in bed?"

"The Harvest Festival is coming up in a couple weeks and I need to order for it…"

"I can help you figure it out if you want—in the morning. Go home and get some shut-eye."

Jethro considered him, then nodded. "Okay. Probably be good for someone to know how to run the place if I go down."

Oh. Um. That wasn't… "I think Raven's a better choice…"

"Oh, Raven. I know she thinks she's helping me—and she is. She's a joy in my life. But she has school to finish and dreams to follow. She can't stay here waiting bar and tables for the rest of her life." He slid his glasses back up. "And don't you start making her fall in love with you or she'll never leave."

Mack's eyes widened. "I'm not—she's—I mean, she's fantastic and beautiful and—"

"Aw, breathe, son, I'm kidding. I know you're not a player. Clearly you're either blind to all the women who make passes at you every night or you're not interested. But should you decide to get interested, well…I'm not saying you need to go to therapy, but at some point, you need to wrestle with who you are, and I just want you to be clear of that before…aw, it's probably too late after tonight…"

He probably didn't mean it as a slap, his voice gentle. But Mack drew in a breath.

"I respect your daughter, Jethro. I promise to…well, I agree. I'd love to fall for a girl like her. But frankly, she probably needs a better man than a drifter who doesn't know his own name. And someone who isn't sticking around." There, he said it, despite the burr it stuck in his chest.

Jethro let out a long breath. He didn't have to nod.

"See you in the morrow, boss." Mack headed upstairs to the one-bedroom apartment, the conversation stirring inside him.

Sometimes a man needs a fresh start…

It's probably too late after tonight.

I hope you'll stay…

The apartment was sparse, with brick walls, a soaring ceiling with exposed pipes, and a cement floor. Furnished with a futon sofa, an old table and two chairs, and a bookcase, Ace had lived here the year before he'd left for the military. He'd left behind a couple *Star Wars* paperbacks, his Nintendo machine, and an ancient television.

The bedroom had no windows, but the main area overlooked the lake, the stars sprinkling it with glitter. Mack cracked the window, letting in the cool autumn air. He liked this little town, with its wineries, festivals, farmers markets, and relaxed lifestyle.

Regardless of who he'd been in the past, the small town hearkened to a place inside him now. No, not a terrible place to lose his past and reinvent himself.

Call home.

But how could he live with not knowing who he was?

He took a shower, sloughing off the night's craziness, and when he crawled into bed, the light on the bedside clock read after 2:00 a.m.

Mack fell hard into slumber, and the dreams found him again. On a train. Red vinyl seats, the clank of the tracks familiar.

He sat with a woman. Dark hair, blue eyes. Pretty, and he knew her.

He just couldn't remember her.

She got up and walked out of the compartment, and he followed her.

Down the hallway and out into the area between cars. She stood in the darkness, her hair blowing in the wind, the pine scenting the air, smiling at him.

Yeah, he knew her. And in his dream, he loved her, heat stirring in him as he reached for her.

She morphed right in his arms into a man. Someone he also recognized but couldn't name—blond—and he held a knife.

Mack grappled with the man, his blood pumping in his ears, grunting as he grabbed for his wrist.

He missed. The knife slashed his side, and he groaned, his voice dislodging him from his dream.

He fell back into it, however, just as the man's fist came at his head.

Then the man was flying off the train, falling into the free, down and down and—

Smoke.

Mack sat up, the smell slight enough for him to wonder if it might be part of his nightmare. Sweat slicked his body, his heartbeat thundering.

Definitely smoke. He threw off the thin sheet and headed toward the main room.

Orange light flickered, a reflection in the window, and he looked out. Nothing lakeside—wait—

Fire. Coming from the patio area, the blaze reflecting off the buildings, back into his loft.

What—? He grabbed his shoes, a T-shirt, and pulled on his jeans, buttoning them as he went down the stairs.

Stopped.

The fire had engulfed the office area.

Turning, he headed back upstairs to his fire escape.

He pulled the ladder down from the ceiling, climbed it and accessed the roof panel.

Landing on the roof, he ran over to the edge to get a good look at the fire. Smoke billowed up from the patio and the back entrance and had worked its way into the building.

The fire stairs latticed the back of the building and Mack scampered down, kicking the last section free. The flames bit at him as he jumped the last six feet.

He backed away from the building, the flames licking up to the second floor.

The sprinklers hadn't cut on. Which meant that maybe the fire department hadn't been notified. He was scanning through his options when he spotted—oh no, *Jethro's truck.*

Mack stared at the entrance, now overcome with smoke and fire. No—*no*—

Mack took off, cutting through the alleyway and emerging to the front entrance.

The flames engulfed the side of the building, smoke blackening the inside.

Sirens blared—maybe the fire alarm finally kicked in, but it did nothing to dent the smoke.

"Jethro!" The man wasn't standing on the street and Mack knew—just *knew*—that he'd fallen asleep on that ratty, flammable sofa.

He picked up a boulder from the landscaping in the front and hurtled it through the door. Glass shattered, and he used another rock to slap out the biggest pieces.

Smoke gusted out, the fire rolling along the ceiling with the influx of oxygen.

He gulped a breath, ignored the sirens blaring in the back of his head—and on the street—and launched into the darkness.

His memory led him through the room, dodging tables and chairs as he stumbled toward the back.

The heat blistered his skin, watered his eyes, and when he reached the bar, he crouched behind it, reaching up to run the water. It splashed hard into the sink, and he grabbed a bar towel and wet it, throwing it over his head.

Alcohol was flammable. That thought lodged in his brain as he picked up the water nozzle from the bar and shot it toward the opening to the back.

The smoke cleared, turned white, and he plunged into the kitchen.

The fire had slowed as it hit the tile, the stainless steel, but beyond it, in the back that led to his stairs, the fire roared, an inferno.

"Jethro!"

The office door was closed. Mack kicked it and it slammed open.

Jethro lay on the sofa, his eyes closed.

Please—

Mack pressed his hand on his chest. Still breathing, but barely.

"Jethro—wake up!"

Nothing. Mack put the wet cloth over Jethro's head, leaned over, and pulled him up, hoisted him onto his shoulder, fireman style.

Please God—give us a way out.

And the fact that he even thought to lift a prayer rooted inside him.

So maybe he was a man of faith.

Before his criminal ways, of course.

The flames licked at the door.

Mack took off into the hallway, running hard through the kitchen, out into the dining area.

Flames blurred the ceiling, roiling over each other.

He set Jethro down behind the bar, picked up the water hose, and sprayed him down. Then grabbed another towel and sprayed himself.

"We're not dying today, old man."

Then Mack again lugged Jethro onto his back, stood up, and fled for the door.

———

"I am not in over my head." RJ stalked to her picture window, looking out into the darkness, her own reflection staring back at her. She'd lost weight over the past few weeks, circles hanging in shadows under her eyes.

Behind her, on one of her high top chairs, Scarlett sat, her leg crossed, paging through Sophia's journal.

Ford wasn't so calm. "Are you kidding me?" He held a bottle of water and stood up from where he'd been leaning against the wall of RJ's kitchen, following her into the family room of her tiny condo. "And get away from that window."

The words jerked at RJ, mostly because it sounded exactly like something York would say.

She pulled the curtains. Not quite the palatial townhome of her boss, RJ still had nice digs. On the second floor of a walk-up just off the Beltway. She'd had to pull some strings to get into the rent-controlled building.

She missed her life, the one where she wasn't accused of a terrible crime.

Then again, her old life hadn't included a man who'd made her feel brave and smart and beautiful.

She wrapped her arms around her waist and turned to face Ford. He was still dressed in black but had taken off his hat, his gloves, and looked mostly like a normal guy with his short dark hair, pale-green eyes. Except for the fact that Ford never seemed to completely relax, a coiled energy always buzzing off him.

She got that. Felt it. Possessed the same restlessness. "No, I'm not kidding you. You seem to forget that I can fend for myself."

"What part of you nearly getting killed in Russia, a couple times, and being hunted by an international assassin says *fending for yourself?*"

"Ford!" Scarlett looked up from the journal, and he shut his mouth.

Just in time because RJ had never slapped her twin in her entire life, but…oh—shoot. Tears bit her eyes and she swallowed them back. "Fine. Okay. But the last thing I want is someone I care about getting hurt trying to save me. Besides, I was ten seconds away from getting away on my own."

He considered her. Took a breath.

Fraternal twins, of course, but he still seemed to be the other half of her soul, possessing the same desire to prove himself.

Or maybe that just came with the territory of being a Marshall.

Nevertheless, he nodded and took another drink of his water. Wiped his upper lip. "Sorry, sis. You probably were. Just about took out my heart to see you go over that balcony."

Hers too, but she just shrugged as if she was exactly the action hero she had attempted to be.

"How did you find me? Seriously—what, do you have a tracker on me? A drone following me?" She shot a look at Scarlett, who glanced up at the word *drone*.

Scarlett had manned the drone for Ford's SEAL team during many of their ops. "I think you'd notice a drone," she said, smiling.

"I know. But it's still creepy—you showing up out of the bushes."

"It's what I do," Ford said, draining the water. "Slink around the bushes."

"Hardly," Scarlett said, her gaze on him, warmth in it.

An ache went through RJ.

Wow, she missed York.

She looked away.

"Listen," Ford said. "All I got was a text from Tate who told me to get over to that particular address. That you were in trouble."

"And you *just happened* to be in town, out of everywhere in the world."

"Jones, Inc. is in town for a fundraiser," Scarlett said. "Ford and Trini flew in for the weekend. I think Ham is trying to recruit Trini."

Hamilton Jones, the owner of the private global SAR team and a multimillionaire of GoSports Gyms, had also been the guy who'd accompanied Ford on his field trip to Russia to "save" her.

"How is Ham?" RJ asked.

Scarlett looked again at Ford, drew in a breath.

"What?" RJ said.

"Nothing. Just…well, apparently Ham has a life nobody knew about. And someone from his past he'd very much like to find."

RJ walked past him, into the kitchen. "Don't we all."

Silence. She opened the fridge and pulled out an orange. Late-night crimes always made her hungry. For a second she had a memory of sharing tea with York in his safe house in Moscow.

She had to stop thinking about him.

Or not. Because *someone* had to obsess enough about his disappearance to find him.

She closed the door and walked to the counter, digging her thumb into the center of the orange to work off the rind. Ford was leaning forward, his hands on his knees, tapping the empty bottle on his leg.

Scarlett was still paging through the book.

"What?" RJ put a long peel on the counter.

Ford sighed. Looked over at her. "You need to accept it."

She froze. Looked at her orange.

"Don't—"

"He's gone, RJ."

Her hand tightened around the orange. "He's not—"

"His body was found in the crash."

"It wasn't him!" She looked up at him, very close to hurling the orange at his head. But his eyes were glistening as if he might be in real pain for her, and it made her draw in her breath. Swallow. Her eyes, too, filled. "It wasn't him. They couldn't identify the remains."

Ford's mouth clenched around the edges.

Her voice cut low. "Besides. I'd know." A tear dripped down her cheek, hung at the edge of her jaw. She met Ford's eyes. "I'd know. I'd feel it."

Ford drew in a breath.

Scarlett pressed her hand over RJ's. Nodded. "I felt the same way when Ford went missing. I just knew he was out there."

Oh. Scarlett was referring to the horrible night she and his team and RJ and her brothers searched for Ford after a storm. While he'd been fighting not to drown.

One night was nothing compared to one month.

"The coroner in Seattle sent the remains to the CIA in hopes they had York's DNA on file," RJ said quietly. "Until then…"

"Tate said you went through all the surveillance camera

footage at the hospital the day York was arrested," Ford said.

"I got a good look at the two goons who arrested him. He even recognized one of them—called him Martin. They said they were from the CIA, but my contacts at the CIA have no record of them. Vicktor said he thought that they might be from the Russian mob. He was cross-referencing them with all the known Russian mafia thugs in the area," RJ said. "But then again, I don't know what to think. My boss said she suspected there was some rogue faction inside the CIA trying to cause problems between the US and Russia, so maybe they took him. And, maybe her."

"Except the Bratva tried to kill you in Russia," Ford said.

"And York had a nearly lethal go-round with a couple goons a few weeks later. Of course they'd be out for revenge." She swallowed. "But he's smart. And tough. He wouldn't just... I mean, that SUV went off the road at a high rate of speed. Who knows what was going on to make that happen."

The car that the highway patrol had discovered burned down to the metal on the side of a mountain.

Even she couldn't see how he'd survived.

But she believed it with every ounce of strength she possessed.

"Ham thinks that the Bratva is behind the assassination attempt you were blamed for," Ford said.

"It's because General Stanislov is a moderate. They want General Arkady Petrov in—he's a hardliner who wants to turn Russia back into a superpower. War means weapons, weapons mean money, and the Russian mob is at the center of it all."

Ford shook his head. "I still don't know how you got involved in all this."

She didn't want to suggest the reasons that came to her head. Like her need to prove that she too could save the world.

Apparently that reason was simply part of her gene pool.

"The bottom line is, York was taken by someone posing as the CIA—maybe even part of this CIA faction. Maybe even in league with Damien Gustov, the assassin who framed me, who tried to kill me and Coco, and who probably killed my boss, Sophia Randall. And if I can just find a link between Sophia and Gustov—any clue as to how she got to Seattle, then maybe I can find Gustov."

She took a breath, and Ford filled in the rest.

"And find out what happened to York."

Close enough. She nodded. Broke the last peel off her orange. Then she met Ford's eyes. "He's alive, bro."

Ford nodded, an unfamiliar compassion in his eyes.

"I got something," Scarlett said into the silence. She set down the journal. "Sophia was investigating a near bombing in Alaska that involved presidential candidate Senator Isaac White a few months ago."

RJ vaguely remembered hearing about it right before she left for Europe to meet Roy, her contact, the one who had sent her to York.

"Randall has an entire entry about the bomber. Apparently, the CIA got ahold of his computer. One of the things they found was a membership to a dating site. MyAmore.com."

"A dating site?" RJ ate a wedge of orange. "Coco found a bunch of emails from a dating site on the information she recovered from Gustov. I tried to find a connection between the names, but I got nothing."

"Sophia wrote down a phone number next to the site." Scarlett turned the journal around. "And circled it."

Indeed. Circled and starred and ran a balloon cloud around it.

"Yikes. Holy clue, Batman. Can anyone say, Call me?" RJ reached into her drawer and pulled out a flip phone. Dialed the number and pressed Enter.

"What. Are. You. *Doing?*" Ford rushed toward her and grabbed her wrist.

Oh, he had strong hands. She dropped the phone on the counter. "What are *you* doing?" She jerked her hand away.

"You can't call that number—"

"Why not?"

It was ringing. Ford scooped it up and pressed End. "Because what if—well, what if this is how the killer found her? Tracked her call—"

"It's a dating site!"

Ford just looked at her.

"Okay, maybe I should call Vicktor and see if he can track Sophia's phone calls and find a connection to this number."

"That's a plan I like," Ford said. He picked up the flip phone. "What is this, anyway? A burner phone?"

She lifted a shoulder.

"Oh brother." He flipped it shut. "Sis. I know you've always… well, I know I'm not the boss of you, but please, *please* stay out of trouble."

She stared at him.

His mouth tightened. "Not a chance, huh?"

"York isn't dead. And I'm going to find him. So you can tell Tate, or whoever has put a tracker on me, to lace up their tennis shoes."

Scarlett smiled as she slid off the high top. "Yeah, she's your sister, Ford."

He rolled his eyes. Took Scarlett's hand. Then he looked at RJ. Paused. "I'm here if you need me," he said quietly.

"I know," she said just as softly.

"Okay then." He kissed her cheek and headed for the door.

She closed and locked it behind them, then swept the journal off the counter, bringing it to the sofa.

Read through Sophia's handwriting about a man named Akif, including the typical profile of a man brainwashed, poisoned by the ideology of a deranged leader. Sophia had drawn an arrow from Akif to a bubble cloud with the Bratva sketched in the middle. And from that, another arrow to a set of question marks.

As if someone, or some group, might be controlling the Russian mob.

Hard to believe, but maybe.

RJ traced her finger across the number.

Looked at her phone.

First thing in the morning she was calling Vicktor.

Maybe hopping a plane to Seattle.

She picked up the remote and turned her television on to CNN.

Then she pulled her knitted afghan off the end of the sofa, lay down, and closed her eyes.

Sometimes it just helped to hear other people in the room. Then she didn't have to listen to the questions deep in her heart.

Oh, York. Where are you?

3

Y ou've had quite the night, son."

The words came from the tall man standing by the nurses' station. Chief of Police Jimbo Reynolds. Mid-fifties, balding, and with an aura around him that said he knew this town, its people, and all of it was under his protection.

He was Jethro's best friend and the second on the scene standing beside Mack as they watched the brewery burn.

The Shelly fire department had arrived first, just in time for Mack to emerge from the building, nearly on fire himself. They grabbed him and Jethro and pulled them away from the flames, and then one of the firemen administered oxygen.

Mack had sat on the sidewalk across the street, watching as the EMTs revived Jethro. He'd wanted to weep when he saw the man start to cough, as the EMTs bundled him onto a board to take him to the small hospital in town.

Mack had refused to go—he was fine, thanks—and instead watched as the firemen battled the flames that crawled up the side of the building, into his apartment, and chewed away at the roof. The fire ate the wooden rafters but spared the brick and mortar, and by the time the dawn dented the pallor of night, nothing but smoke and char remained of the inferno.

The building might not be a total loss, but Mack didn't relish giving Jethro a report. He'd stayed until the fire chief, a man with years lined in his tanned face, produced what he thought might be the culprit.

"I found this poker in the burned remains of one of the patio chairs," he said and showed it to Mack.

Right. The poker Teddy had used. The one Mack had shaken from his grip.

The one that had fallen on the cushions, left there to smolder.

Clearly not his fault, but it felt like it as he'd headed to the hospital.

There, an ER nurse had spotted the blood on his shirt, his blackened face, a rasping cough and practically dragged him to the ER.

Now, Mack sat on the end of a bed in the ER, waiting for the all-clear to leave after getting checked over by one of the docs.

And of course by Jimbo, who hadn't moved from his spot across the hall, just in case—what—that Mack might make a run for it?

"Yeah," Mack said in response to Jimbo's comment. "I was sleeping when I woke to the smell of smoke." He took a sip of orange soda, still trying to clear his throat.

Jimbo nodded. He wore a pair of jeans and a black T-shirt with the letters SPD on the breast. "And that's when you went outside."

"Had to take the fire escape. I saw Jethro's truck and realized he hadn't gone home."

The nurse came by. "I'm just waiting for the doctor to sign off on your release, Mr. Jones."

Jones. He'd picked that name because, well, it felt ironic. Not that he meant to keep it, but, well, Mack Jones seemed like an okay moniker.

"So remind me where you're from, Mack?"

Yes, he knew this kind of questioning, circling back to earlier questions to see if he made mistakes.

Hopefully he remembered all his answers. "Seattle."

"Mmmhmm. I used to live there. Whereabouts?"

And shoot, he didn't know Seattle well, so, "Actually, I spent a lot of time overseas. I just lived there shortly. Downtown." He had a vague memory of the piers, and even oddly Pike Place. "I worked downtown, in the market. Slinging fish."

Sounded like something he'd do.

"And how'd you get to Shelly?"

That was trickier. Because if Mack said he woke up on the side of a highway, bruised, bleeding, and not sure how he got there— "I needed a change. Got a ride from a couple friends who said they liked this little town."

"What friends?"

He did remember their names—a young couple visiting for the weekend. They'd taken pity on a guy walking along the highway. He couldn't believe that the fact that he'd looked freshly dragged behind a car hadn't given them pause. They'd even tried to drop him off at the hospital, but he'd opted for the town park. "Taylor and Sienna Bart."

Jimbo nodded, said nothing, but Mack could see his wheels turning.

And right then he nearly said it, nearly confessed that he didn't actually have a clue who he might be, and would Jimbo be willing to run his prints, because maybe, just maybe, he wasn't a criminal on the run, or even a military fugitive.

Maybe he had a family, people who loved him, a job as a... fireman?

Then the nurse came back with his papers. "The doctor is a little worried about your wound in your side—it seems to have reopened. He wants to see you back here in a week."

Jimbo raised an eyebrow, and the last thing Mack wanted was for the cop to get a look at an injury that, even to Mack's eyes, looked like a knife wound.

As if he'd been in a serious fight.

Setting down his soda on a nearby cart, he signed his discharge papers—Mack Jones—and slid off the bed.

"Mack!"

Raven's voice echoed down the hallway, and he turned to see her striding hard for him. She wore a pair of yoga pants and an oversized T-shirt, flip-flops, her dark hair down and wild as she broke into a run toward him.

For a second, a memory flashed, or maybe just another round of déjà vu. Dark hair. Someone running into his arms.

Then, he barely had time to brace himself before she barreled into him, her arms around his neck. "Are you okay?"

He caught her hips, just to make sure she didn't bang anything else loose, then eased into her hug. She smelled good—cottony and warm—and something about holding her felt right and easy and familiar.

Or at least, he wanted it to be.

She leaned back and caught his face in her hands, settling her blue eyes in his. "Dad's going to be okay because of you." Her eyes filled, and she whisked away a tear. "You're a hero."

"Oh, I don't think—"

"Jimbo said that if you hadn't pulled him out..." Her hand covered her mouth. "Anyway, it's a good thing you didn't take me up on my offer."

A tentative smile, and he glanced at Jimbo, but he had his phone out, so, "I guess so."

She wiped away another tear. "He wants to see you."

"Sure." He glanced at Jimbo, who looked up at him.

"See you 'round."

Mack wasn't sure how to take that, but he let Raven slip her fingers through his and pull him down the hallway of the small, twenty-five bed hospital.

"They said he needs to stay for a while, under observation, but..." She turned to him. "He's already talking about rebuilding." She stopped outside his door. "I don't know if we should encourage him. He's not young, and this is a big job—"

"Hey," Mack said, turning her. "I'm not going anywhere. It's going to be okay." And he didn't know why he said that, the words just spilling out. But her face lit up and she nodded.

"Thanks, Mack."

Jethro was sitting up in his bed, wearing an oxygen mask, his face cleaned. Mack, however, probably still wore the dark soot on his face, his arms. He needed a shower and a strong cup of coffee. Or two.

Jethro reached for the mask, pulling it aside. "Hey there."

"Put that back on," Mack said. But he met Jethro's hand, shook it. "You okay?"

"I'm fine. Throat's a little sore." He held the mask just above his mouth, not quite obeying, of course. His eyes searched Mack's. "I knew God had sent you here for a reason. He works out all things for good."

Mack stilled.

"Mack—?"

The words boomeranged in his head, old voices tumbling down from a top shelf. *According to His plan.*

"Get him a chair, Raven."

Mack felt Raven's hand on his arm, and he looked over at her, not quite seeing her.

You're going to be fine, son. In time, you'll see the victory of the Lord in this.

He took a breath, and the voice vanished.

"Did you remember something?" she asked.

"I..." He looked at Jethro. "I don't know. A voice, maybe. Romans 8:28. That's the verse you're referring to, right?"

Jethro raised an eyebrow. "You know the Bible."

Maybe he did. He slid into the chair. "It was just a voice." Mack took a breath. "Anyway, I don't know about God, but I do know that Raven says you want to rebuild."

"I've been wanting to remodel for years." He glanced at Raven. "I could build a stage."

"Dad, the place is still smoking—"

"Sometimes you have to burn down the past in order to get a fresh start." Jethro's eyes flashed, and he looked at Mack. Oh. Their conversation from hours ago about him leaving.

Jethro glanced at his daughter standing behind Mack, then back at Mack, and smiled.

So maybe the man had changed his tune.

"We'll see," Mack said. "I need to get a shower and some shut-eye." And that's when it hit him.

He had nothing. The meager belongings he'd managed to scrape up, including a change of clothes, had turned to ash.

Nice.

"Come home with me," Raven said, as if able to read his mind. "I think we still have some of my brother's clothes..." She looked at Jethro, who nodded.

And the gesture swept warmth clear through Mack's body.

Before he could protest, Raven had him by the hand again and was pulling him out of the room.

The sun had cleared the horizon, sent a golden trail through the windows at the end of the corridor. She didn't release his hand even as they stepped out into the sunlight.

Jimbo was standing on the curb, surrounded by a handful of press, giving a statement.

"Uh oh," Raven started, but her warning came too late as one of the videographers spotted him. He turned the camera on him as a reporter pushed a microphone in his face.

"Mr. Jones, can you tell us how it feels to know you saved the life of a Medal of Honor recipient?"

What? He looked at Raven. She wrinkled her nose. "Sorry."

"You think?" He looked at the reporter. A woman, short blonde hair, mid-twenties, a little fire in her eyes. "I…I'm just glad I was there. Right place, right time." He glanced at Jimbo, wondering what he'd said.

"Will you be staying on to help them rebuild?"

"C'mon, Mandy, that's too much," Raven said. "He just survived a fire."

Mack glanced at Raven, frowned. Then, "Yes, of course. Jethro's pub will be back in business ASAP. In fact, we'll still have a booth at the Harvest Festival, so make sure to stop by."

Now it was Raven's turn to frown. But Mack tugged her hand and headed out into the parking lot, hopefully in the direction of her car.

"Seriously, the Harvest Festival? That's two weeks away."

"Hopefully some of the beer in the kegs survived the fire."

She dug out her fob and clicked the door open. Then she turned to him, over the top of her car. "You're really going to dig in, help us rebuild?"

He looked past her toward the lake, the fire of the morning sun burning its way through the green-platinum waters, the rumple of mountains along the far horizon. *Burn down the past…* He met her eyes, warm in his. "I told you, I'm not going anywhere."

She grinned, and it could almost gulp him whole with the sunshine in it. "Then we're going to need pancakes."

———————◆———————

There was something magical about the morning hours in D.C. The way the sunlight streamed through the fading pink flowers of the autumn-blooming cherry trees that lined RJ's street. The quiet of her neighborhood, the nip in the air that dissipated into the day.

It all conspired to hint at a hope that RJ desperately wanted to lean in to as she sat on her front steps and laced up her shoes.

Hope that she'd seeded into Coco's smart brain.

The fact that her soon-to-be sister-in-law had also been awake this morning in Seattle, at the very early hour of 3:00 a.m.—three time zones away from D.C.—told her that neither of them wanted-ed to admit the probable truth.

York really was dead.

And Damien Gustov, Russian assassin, was loose in America.

Or maybe that thought, along with the nightmare of York being burned alive in the mangled SUV, had only driven RJ out of bed to fire up her computer just as the dawn cracked through her blinds.

Coco was probably just catnapping beside the hospital bed of her son, Mikka, still in his induction phase of his leukemia treatment. So far he hadn't suffered any infections or seizures from the cocktail of chemo drugs injected into his system, but he'd had two painful intrathecal injections and had already lost all his hair.

"What are you doing up?" RJ said when Coco responded to her ping and answered her video chat request.

Coco moved into the hospital bathroom, only the computer screen glowing on her face. She looked tired, her hair growing out red at the roots and now pulled back into a messy ponytail. She wore one of Wyatt's Blue Ox hockey practice jerseys and a pair of leggings and leaned back against the tiled wall, drawing up her legs, the computer beside her on the floor. "Mikka was sick right before he fell asleep. I'm exhausted, but I can't stop watching him, making sure he's breathing okay, checking for seizures." She scraped her hands over her face. "Your mother is coming by in the morning to relieve me."

Wyatt had purchased a loft apartment near the hospital for family members to stay while his son underwent treatment.

"Where's Wyatt?"

"In the next room, sleeping on the lounger. He has PT in the morning, and his hip is getting better. He's leaving for a pre-season game in Nashville against the Predators tonight. I wish his coach would put him on the Injured Reserved list but he wants to keep him on the active roster. Last week it nearly wrecked Wyatt to leave Mikka. I rarely see him cry, but he was losing it when he got on the bus."

Yes, well, he'd waited five years to find out he was a father. He didn't want to lose another moment. But RJ didn't say that.

Coco had her reasons for keeping her son's existence quiet.

Namely, her high-profile father whose identity could put Coco and Mikka under a shadow of danger.

Another reason why Wyatt didn't want to leave their sides.

"How is Mikka?"

"So far, it looks like the chemo is working. He's going into remission, which means he'll be ready for the second stage of treatment and maybe a stem cell transplant." She offered a wan smile. "We have good doctors. And prayer."

Yeah, prayer. RJ hadn't exactly looked up for help. Maybe... except she seemed to have plenty of backup, thank you, Ford. And Tate. And Wyatt and... "So, I have a question..." RJ didn't exactly know how to broach the topic but, "Last night—"

"That was me." Coco made a face. "Not entirely, but yeah, I set up the tracker. Wyatt and your brothers asked me to set up a GPS to track your phone and...well, he put two and two together when he saw you casing Sophia's place two nights ago. He told Tate, who told Ford, who was in DC, and Ford was supposed to intercept you before you went into the house, but...are you okay?"

RJ just stared at the computer. She wore her pajamas and sat cross-legged on her sofa, the computer on her lap, and just about gave in to the urge to slam down the cover. "You *what*? Put a *tracker* on my phone?"

"It's because your brothers are all freaking out about you leaving the ranch—especially after, um, well…"

"After what happened to York. They think he's dead."

Coco's mouth made a tight, solemn line.

"And that Gustov will come after me."

Coco lifted a shoulder. "Gustov's gone dark. I've been looking for him all over the internet—even that dating site he's hooked into. Nothing. No activity. He's vanished."

And yes, that put a wrinkle of fear under RJ's skin. But she wasn't going to live her life looking over her shoulder.

Or having her brothers come to her rescue. "Listen, Coco. I get it—but you gotta turn that thing off. I don't need to be babysat."

Coco drew in a breath.

"Now. I'm not asking."

"Wyatt is going to throw a conniption."

"I'll deal with Wyatt and Ford and Tate and Knox and even Reuben."

"Speaking of Tate, he's back in town. Glo is on vacation in Cannon Beach. He's staying at Wyatt's flat. Says he's planning on talking with Vicktor in the morning about the shooting."

"Any news on the wedding? Maybe something small, and soon?"

"I don't know how. The election is only a month away. Senator Jackson is going to make sure her only daughter's wedding is the event of the season at the estate in Nashville."

"I meant yours, silly."

"Oh." Coco lifted a shoulder. "It's hard to think about that with Mikka being sick."

Sure, RJ understood that.

"But according to Tate, Glo has been pestering him to set a date. I'm not sure why."

RJ knew why—because the man she loved tended to get into trouble and she didn't want to waste one more day waiting for the rest of their lives to start.

In case it didn't.

The thought thickened her throat. RJ swallowed, looked away as her microwave beeped. "I'll be right back."

She'd probably nabbed four hours of sleep, at best, given her late hour last night. Doctoring her coffee, she then returned to the sofa. "Coco, I actually need your help. I found Sophia's journal, and in it, a phone number that might lead to her contact in Seattle. Can you run a trace on her number and match it to the one I found? And then see if you can connect the number to a name?"

"Of course." Coco's secret abilities—and her job when she lived in Russia—were her black hat hacking skills.

RJ read off the number. Coco leaned over her computer, clearly working her magic. "By the way, did you ever verify the information Kobie gave us about Jackson?"

Alan Kobie. The bomber who'd kidnapped Coco, strapped a bomb to her, and used her as leverage to try to tell the world some crazy story about VP candidate Reba Jackson and her involvement with a Chechen warlord, maybe even some collusion with Russia.

The fact that Coco said his name without a tremble in her voice spoke to how she'd managed to free herself and triumph over evil.

Evil seemed to keep winning, however.

"Kobie said she took a covert trip to Chechnya two years ago, but I scoured her travel history. She did take a humanitarian trip to Chechnya ten years ago, when she was a freshman senator, to tour refugee camps, but…nothing recently."

"He probably lied," Coco said. "He just had a vendetta against the government for abandoning his brother to the jihad camps. He said his brother was a POW there."

"His brother was one of the bombers who tried to kill Glo and later her mother, the VP candidate in San Diego," RJ said. "So, apparently some of his jihadist conditioning took."

Coco nodded. "I got something. Sophia Randall called this number twice. Once for a minute, then a week later for three minutes. The number called her back five days later for four minutes, then again two days later for forty-nine seconds."

"When was the first call?"

"The day before you went to Russia."

"She went missing right about then."

"Maybe she was under the radar. It looks like all her calls took place while you were escaping Russia, but the return calls came shortly after you returned. Maybe around the same time."

"Except Damien Gustov was still in Russia, trying to find you, for at least another month."

"And you never heard from her after you got back?"

"My calls always went to voice mail."

Coco looked up and RJ heard Wyatt's voice at the door. "Just a few more minutes. We're looking into something."

Wyatt settled down next to her, half his face appearing on the screen. "You're not staying out of trouble, sis."

"I had everything under control, Wy."

His mouth pinched.

"I don't need you guys hovering."

"Says the woman who was accused of an international crime, had to escape a foreign country, and walked in on a dead body."

"I was cleared of any crime, and the dead body was planted so I'd walk in and find it."

"Which just sends warm fuzzies through me." Wyatt ran a hand around the back of his neck, his brown hair growing longer in anticipation of hockey season. And his many photo shoots, probably.

"You guys completely overreact."

"Overreacting would be making you wear an ankle monitor. Maybe confining you to house arrest," Wyatt said.

"I'm a trained analyst!"

"You're our only sister! And the youngest, and we're only trying to do what Dad would want us to do—"

"Leave Dad out of this."

"Hardly. We all know you've always tried to keep up with us because you didn't want Dad to see you as weaker, someone to be rescued."

She drew in a breath. "I'm not weaker. And I don't have to be rescued—"

"Yet. Or should I say again?"

"Wyatt!" Coco said.

He looked at Coco. Back to the screen. "Sorry. I'm clearly tired. And edgy and—"

"Being a jerk," RJ said. "Just because you went to Russia and saved Coco's life doesn't make you the only one who can save the people you love."

He drew in a breath. Swallowed. "Sorry. I know. I'm just... I'm—we all—are worried about you."

"Clearly. But I'm fine." Her throat tightened, and she clamped down against the lie. "Just fine."

He nodded. "Okay. Just promise me not to do anything crazy."

"Oh, like running off to a foreign country to save—oh wait, I did that. And so did Ford. And you—"

"I'm going back to bed."

Coco was grinning as he kissed her on the cheek.

"I love you, sis," Wyatt said. He got up and walked out of the shot.

Coco reached out with her leg, and RJ imagined her toeing the door closed. "He means well. And he wants to do what he thinks your dad would do. He's been reading your dad's Bible, and it's made him want to be more connected to your family."

"He did miss out on a lot with his hockey career."

"I'm searching the GPS on both phones."

"How long has my mom been there?"

"A couple days. Got a hit—both phones were in Seattle three months ago, near the same cell tower. And there are no more calls from Sophia's phone after that."

"Might be when he took her. But why would he hold her for a month?" And RJ didn't want to answer her own question. "And if Damien was chasing you across Russia...who took her?"

"And if someone else, not Damien, killed Sophia, did that person also grab York?"

RJ finished her coffee. "I have a call in to a man named

Crowley who York knew at the CIA. I'm trying to track down the guys who took him. They say they don't have him, but…"

Coco met her eyes. "If he's still alive, we'll find him, RJ."

If… "He is," she'd said softly, her eyes burning. She couldn't give in to the alternative.

Coco nodded. "I'll see if I can track down an owner for the phone. I gotta get back to Wyatt."

"I'm going out for a run to clear my head."

Coco had pressed two fingers to her lips, then the screen, and RJ had mimicked it, then shut her computer.

Now, ten minutes later, she sat on the front steps, the morning air sweeping into her nose, her body.

Prayer. She hadn't really considered that God might be willing to get involved. But if that's what it took to find York…

Please.

She got up and started at an easy pace down the sidewalk. The morning sun just lipped the roofs of the townhomes and condos in her area. A few neighbors were out walking dogs, a couple more running, and she raised her hand to the former Marine who lived across the street. He wore his blond hair short, not an ounce of fat on his body, and it reminded her so much of York, she quickened her pace.

York, with those blue eyes she couldn't seem to forget, nor the way he kissed her, as if, when she was in his arms, he forgot the man he was, became the man he wanted to be. He'd even told her that.

She liked—okay, loved—the man she knew, despite the things he'd done, the man he'd been.

That man had also been the one who'd saved her life.

At the corner, she stopped to wait for the light. Beside her, a limousine pulled up, then slowly turned right on red.

Stopped in front of her.

Before she could react, the back door opened, and a man stepped out, grabbed her arms. "CIA," he said, flashing his I.D. "Come with me."

"What—why?"

He didn't answer her. Instead, without a pause, he pulled her inside the vehicle.

The door shut on her scream.

She sent her palm into his jaw hard enough for him to whoof out his breath, then rolled back and kicked him, center mass. He let out another grunt as he fell back.

She rolled over, clawing for the door—

"Stop!"

The voice jerked her around, her attention to the man seated on the back seat. Thin, with salt-and-pepper hair, he wore a suit and now held his hand up—either to her, or her assailant, she didn't know. But his gaze fell on her and held fast. "I'm here to help."

"Help? With what? Kidnapping?"

He gestured to the seat. They still hadn't moved from the curb, and she glanced out the window in the hope her neighbor had seen her abduction. She could use a former Marine right now—

York was a former Marine.

Oh, she had to stop going to him for help. To anyone for help.

"Please, sit down. We need to talk."

She narrowed her eyes.

"I'm Director Tom Crowley. You've called my office about thirty times." He flipped open his identification for her.

Oh. She bit her lip and slid onto the seat. "Uh, thanks for taking my call?"

He smirked and put away his I.D. "You are persistent, Miss Marshall."

"Where's York? I know your men took him."

His smile fell. "Actually, no, they didn't, and to cut to the chase, I don't know where he is. If he is dead, or alive. And, if he's alive, I'd like to find him too."

"I'll bet you would," she snapped.

He frowned at her.

"He told me that you warned him never to return to the US. After, well…after…"

"After I said he got my daughter and grandson killed."

56

Her mouth tightened.

He swallowed, looked away from her, a flash of sadness on his face. "I shouldn't have blamed him for the evil that is in the world. He did everything right. I was grieving, of course. And angry." He looked back at her, and his eyes glistened. "Of course York is a hero. But he also is dangerous."

She looked at him.

"Not to us—to the rogue faction of the CIA that is hunting him."

Her eyes widened. "So it's true."

"Yes. My team has been rooting them out for a year, trying to find the power broker who's at the helm, one of a handful across the globe who is trying to cause international unrest."

"Why?"

"War leads to weapons which leads to money which leads to power."

"Were they behind the assassination attempt on General Stanislov?"

"Yes. And possibly the attempt on Senator White in Alaska. Sophia was on my team, looking into a cell of sleeper agents."

Oh.

"She was investigating a dating site that we believe activates the sleeper agents."

RJ managed to keep her expression still. But, "Was it called MyAmore.com?"

He raised an eyebrow.

"My, um, sister and I found emails sent to a user of the site."

"Can you forward them to me?"

She nodded.

"And while we're at it, did you find Sophia's journal when you broke into her house last night?"

Her eyes widened.

"We tried to keep the police away when the security alarm was triggered, but they responded to the 9-1-1 call from the neighbors."

Oh. "I suppose you're tossing my house right now."

"It would be easier if I could just make a call."

She made a face. "It's in the bathroom, behind the sink."

He nodded at the goon who'd taken her and he took out his phone.

She sighed. "Do you think York is alive?"

"I don't know."

"He was picked up by a man named Martin. He recognized him."

Recognition registered on Crowley's face. "Really?"

"Who is he?"

"He used to work for the agency. He left shortly after York did and has been off the grid ever since. We thought he might have been connected to York's cover being blown, but we weren't sure. And York killed the informant, so..." He glanced at the driver. "Take a drive around the block."

They started to move. "If Martin took him, a good bet is that he thought York knew something that could incriminate him."

And right then, York's voice swept into her head. *I have a feeling that if the CIA knew I was here, I might be in trouble. I have too many secrets.*

"Do you have any idea what that might have been?"

"I don't." Oh, maybe she'd answered too quickly. But really. "He never told me."

"Miss Marshall. You work for me, remember?"

"I worked for Sophia."

He tilted his head.

"No, I don't know anything. But I think York did know something. And Martin took him."

The way Crowley's jaw tightened swept heat into her eyes, cotton into her throat.

"You think he's dead."

"Martin did wet work for the agency," Crowley said simply.

She looked out the window. They were pulling up at the corner again.

"This is where your investigation ends, Miss Marshall. You're in over your head and I don't want you to get hurt."

She'd heard that before. She reached for the handle.

Felt a hand on her arm.

Looked at Crowley.

"I'm sorry for your loss," he said quietly. "We had our differences, and he had his faults, but at his heart, York was a patriot."

She swallowed, nodded. "Sorry for your loss too."

He blinked, as if the words hit him.

She got out, and the limousine pulled away.

Down the street and across from her condo building, a van also left the curb.

Her Marine neighbor was standing on his doorstep, watching. She lifted a hand in greeting as she ran back to her condo, up the stairs of her building.

She shut the door behind her, her heart pounding.

The place hadn't been completely destroyed, but the sofa cushions were askew, a kitchen drawer opened.

She walked into her family room and sat on the sofa. Picked up the remote.

Voices. Just something to tell her she wasn't alone.

That this wasn't over.

It couldn't be over.

This is where your investigation ends, Miss Marshall.

She flopped back, barely listening to the CNN reporter list off her two minute around-the-nation report.

Who cared who turned 101? And yes, the mudslide in California was tragic, but no one had died. And she tuned out the blurb about the lifesaving actions of a man who saved a Medal of Honor winner. She leaned up and pulled off her shoes—and caught the shot of the man on the screen, just coming out of a hospital.

Wide shoulders, blond hair, blue eyes. And sure, he was covered in soot and smoke and wore the shag of a tangled, dirty beard, but...

Her heart stopped.

York.

"Mr. Jones, can you tell us how it feels to know you saved the life of a Medal of Honor recipient?"

Mr. Jones?

"I...I'm just glad I was there. Right place, right time."

The voice slid under her skin. Right place. Right time.
Yep, that was York all right.
Oh, she knew it. She *knew* it!
RJ pulled her pillow to her face and let herself weep.

It was a slow, dismal rain, the kind that poured darkness into his spirit as Tate pulled into a parking garage opposite the sleek black-and-gray brick building of the Seattle Police Department, West Precinct.

He just needed answers.

Needed to know what to look for.

Needed to make sure no one got ambushed by a serial killer or long-range sniper on his watch as lead security for Gloria Jackson, daughter of VP candidate Senator Reba Jackson.

Because, frankly, last time had been way, way too close.

Tate squeezed his Ford Taurus rental into a space, got out, and ran up the ramp to the sidewalk, holding a magazine over his head as he dashed across the street through the drizzle to the lobby.

The lobby was sparse, with white marble and tall, clear pillars showcasing historical artifacts from the SPD's history. Tate easily spotted his target.

Detective Vicktor Shubnikov. Military-short dark hair, the stance of a cop, and he wore the expression of a man who knew how to size up trouble as he stood near one of the pillars, arms folded, waiting.

He didn't blink at Tate. But then again, he already knew Tate's story, had already fielded his plethora of phone calls.

Already knew that Tate wanted to put his fist into the stone wall he was getting from the Feds in the investigation of the assassination attempt on Senator Jackson—the *second* attempt.

No, the second attempt that Tate *hadn't seen coming*, hadn't caught until it was nearly too late.

He didn't want to be blindsided by a third.

"Hey, Vicktor," Tate said as he met his hand. Vicktor stood

the same height as Tate, but had a few years on him.

"Sorry to drag you into the station," Vicktor said, only a hint of Russian accent burring his voice. "But I thought it would help for you to see the evidence board. The SPD is working with the FBI on the investigation, but you should know, we're getting the same cold shoulder."

"Thanks. I'm not sure how the secret service expects me to protect Glo without all the information." He followed Vicktor down the corridor to the stairs.

Vicktor swiped his pass, and the doors unlocked. Tate followed him up the flights to the second floor.

"How is your fiancée?" Vicktor asked.

Vicktor had met Glo Jackson, country music singer, a month ago after the shooting on the pier during one of Jackson's rallies.

"She's fine. Just came off a month of gigs for NBR-X, the professional bull-riding event she and the Yankee Belles play for. They have a break now until the NBR-X national finals in November."

The stairwell door opened to a hub of quiet activity, workstations equipped with computers, junior detectives on the phone, a few sharing conversation as they drank coffee. Tate followed Vicktor down the hall to his office.

"I'm surprised you left her alone," Vicktor said as he opened his door and gestured Tate inside.

"She's at a private house in Cannon Beach this week, holed up with her bandmates, writing songs. And the place is heavily guarded. My man Swamp is on it."

Vicktor's office window overlooked a sleek skyscraper that housed on its ground floor a Starbucks and a soup-and-sandwich place. The other three walls were filled with massive whiteboards littered with written notes as well as photographs of people, maps, buildings, and a timeline.

Vicktor offered him a chair.

"That's okay. I think better when I pace," Tate said.

"So, where do you want to start? The shooting or your missing—or dead—friend?"

Oh, York. His *sister's* missing or dead friend. But because she was obsessed with the idea that her boyfriend-slash-action hero was still alive, that made it Tate's problem too.

"Is RJ in contact with you about her search for York?" Tate asked.

"And her dead boss, Sophia Randall," Vicktor said.

Tate didn't know much about the case—admittedly he'd been too wrapped up in protecting Glo. But he had been alert enough to pick up Wyatt's call last night about RJ getting in over her head. He'd texted Ford, who happened to be, providentially, nearby.

Saved him from getting on a plane. Or better, calling *Knox* to get on a plane. Since his big brother had taken over the gig as director of livestock for NBR-X, he had left the ranching in Reuben's hands, and frankly, stayed clear of most of the drama happening with RJ and Ford and Wyatt.

But if Knox knew RJ was in trouble...yeah, it was probably better Ford was in town to intercept his twin. Which, according to Ford, was all about said dead boss.

"Do you think Randall was involved in the potential assassination of the VP candidate?" Tate asked.

"Are you sure the VP candidate was the target?" Vicktor walked over to an aerial map of Piers 62 and 63, just a couple blocks from Pike Place Market on the harbor.

Tate joined him, seeing that day in his mind. The pier had been sectioned off for the event and a giant battleship brought in for backdrop. A banner of presidential candidate Isaac White and VP candidate Reba Jackson flanked the side of the ship, the words *For a Safe Tomorrow* written below their faces.

Tate could still smell the brine mixed with oil that lifted from the water, feel the chill of the day on his legs as he'd watched Glo get ready for her warm-up song—she had taken to singing "God Bless America" before all her mother's events.

"We had extra security that day. They were lined up along the street, everyone was being checked. And still, Kobie got in," Tate said, referring to the bomber who'd used the fame of Tate's NHL hockey-star brother to wheedle his way into the event.

"The bomber used your brother to get him onstage, right?"

"Yeah. Wyatt showed up behind the screen and told me that

if he didn't tell the world that Reba Jackson was some kind of Russian spy or traitor or something along those lines, that Coco would be killed. Wyatt was supposed to read a statement, but before he could, shots were fired." He ran his finger along the long pier to the buildings along Alaskan Way. "Maybe from here."

Vicktor was nodding. "That's a long, long shot."

"With wind. So it would take someone with skill. Which is why York thought it might be a Russian assassin by the name of Damien Gustov. York was pretty sure he was working for the Bratva—the Russian mob."

"I know who they are," Vicktor said, and of course he would. Because Vicktor had spent fifteen years working with the FSB before he immigrated.

"Were you able to get surveillance video from any of these buildings?"

"Unfortunately, those are all high-end condos. And we're not even sure if the shots came from there," Vicktor said.

"Did you get ballistics from Kobie's body? York thought he'd shot him, but he couldn't get an angle."

Kobie had been shot while trying to flee the chaos.

"York surrendered his weapon to the FBI. We haven't been privy to their results."

Which left Tate right back at nada. No leads, no hint of who might have killed Kobie and nearly his brother.

Had tried to take down the VP candidate.

Tate took a breath, shook his head. "So we have no idea who, really, was shooting that day."

"Or their intended target."

He hated this with every cell in his body.

"Sorry," Vicktor said, clearly reading him.

"So, any news on York's death?"

"Just the preliminary forensics report." He walked over to his desk, sat down, and pulled up something on his computer. "According to the autopsy—which, by the way, was inconclusive on the DNA evidence of your friend—there were three bodies, all male, burned in the crash."

Tate walked over to the window. Watched a bicycler wearing a rainsuit ride up to the Starbucks in the rain. "According to RJ, the CIA has no record of anyone from their office arresting him."

"We have another lead, or maybe just an interesting problem."

Tate turned, leaned against the window ledge.

"There's a tourist reported missing that same day, a college kid named Jason MacDonald. Twenty-one, about six foot, played second-string football for the Ducks, went by Mack. He was on his way to a family reunion at Stevens Pass. Never showed."

"And?"

"His car was found at a pull-off near the Tye River hike on Highway 2. The vehicle York was traveling in was found three more miles down the road. There's a sharp turn, and the car tore through the guardrail, and went down the mountain. It's doubtful anyone could have survived, even before the fire."

"You think this kid might have seen something—"

"I dunno. It just…it's just bothering me."

Tate got that. The same way he kept waking in the night with the sense of doom in the middle of his chest.

As if someone he loved was about to die.

"What about the semi that reported the crash?" Tate asked.

"The driver just saw them swerve and go off the road. He had to wait until he could get to a pull-in before he could stop, about fifteen miles down the road. So it was some time before the authorities arrived. And by then, it was all over."

Tate straightened. "Well, my sister is convinced that he's still alive, so…I don't know." He walked over to Vicktor's massive board. "Is this the woman who RJ found at the hotel?"

Vicktor returned to the board. "Yeah. Sophia Randall. Age forty-six, single. She was never reported missing, technically, but RJ says she went off the grid about six weeks before her body was found. Coroner found evidence of long-term confinement—dehydration, ligature scars, and even old bruises."

"She was beaten."

More pictures outlined the bed where RJ had found her body, her neck slit. Even more showed an array of the room and pictures of people from what looked like surveillance camera shots.

"There was a card left on file for the hotel, but of course it was stolen, so we have no idea who really paid for the room. And no record of her checking in. There's a supply entrance in the back of the building, and it looks like the camera was switched off. But we did manage to capture three unidentified people on a different camera who didn't come through the lobby."

Vicktor pointed at three pictures taped to the bottom of the board.

Tate stilled, then took a step closer. "I know this one." He pointed to a photo of a lean, tall man with closely cropped dark hair, wearing suit pants, his white shirt rolled up beyond his elbows. He had high cheekbones and the look of higher education in his demeanor. He carried a gym bag, his face half turned away from the camera.

But it was enough. "That's Sloan Anderson," Tate said tightly. He took another step closer. "He worked for Reba Jackson—he was her assistant campaign manager until he was fired."

"Why was he fired?" Vicktor asked as he untaped the picture and retaped it near the top, between the murder case and the shooting.

"Because he tried to have me beaten to death," Tate said quietly.

Vicktor raised an eyebrow. "Oy. Why?"

"I don't know. We never had a heart-to-heart. He took off before we could apprehend him. Clearly has some avoidance issues."

Vicktor stared at the board for a moment, then, "You were on the pier that day, right?"

"For the campaign event? Yes, I was behind the screen for most of the time, but I helped chase down Kobie."

Vicktor traced his finger along the pier. "How far behind him were you?"

"I don't know, a few steps…why?"

"Have you ever stopped to consider that the target that day wasn't the VP candidate…but maybe it was you?"

4

If you want to be a Shellian, you have to do this, Mack."

Raven straddled the picnic table bench, far enough away from the stage of the pavilion for him to hear her teasing voice over the music playing. The Tuesday night open mic event in Riverwalk Park was hosted by Mystical Pizza, the local gourmet joint located across the parking lot from Jethro's.

Overhead, the sky had turned a deep, inviting dark blue, the stars starting to wink, and if he didn't still feel and smell like ash, Mack might have thought this was a date.

Maybe it was a date. After all, Neil Diamond was in the lineup.

He'd nearly forgotten about his words to Raven, yesterday feeling like it might be years in the past after the night's events and today's work. Mack had spent the day cleaning and hauling away debris with what felt like half the town of Shelly—volunteers from local businesses and even Jethro's church, the Shelly Community Church. By the end of the day, they had the building cleaned out, the salvageable pieces of furniture tucked away in storage, the copper tanks drained of beer, the unburned kegs removed to a nearby cellar, and pictures taken for insurance.

That's how they got it done in a small town.

He'd never leave if he had the choice.

Mack looked at the open box of pizza. "Why is it called Firecracker?"

"Because along with Italian sausage and pepperoni, it has jalapenos, sriracha, peperoncini, red bell peppers, and garlic. Oh, and pineapple," Raven said.

So, not a date then.

"I brought spearmint gum for dessert."

Or, maybe?

She dug out a piece of pizza and handed it to him on a napkin. He took a bite. "Oh, yeah, that's hot."

"Right?" She grinned at him, her gaze warm. She'd spent most of the day cleaning with him, the other parts of it on the phone with her father, who came straight from being discharged to supervise the transportation of the kegs. One of them went to the firehouse as a thank-you gift.

But somewhere in there, Raven had gone home and cleaned up so that when he arrived later with Jethro, she was sitting on a high top stool in the kitchen, smelling fresh and clean, wearing a cutoff jean skirt, a tank top, a flannel shirt tied at the waist, and cowboy boots.

She was tuning her guitar and looked up, a little hope in her eyes when she said, "Are you still going to come out and hear me sing tonight, Mack?"

What was he going to say? No? "Love to."

He'd taken a shower and didn't know what to say when he found a pile of clothing on the bed. Jeans, a couple T-shirts, some button-downs, tennis shoes, and a jacket.

Ace's things.

Mack felt a little weird pulling on the jeans—surprisingly a good fit—and a white button-down. But at least he had something to wear. He'd picked up a few more essentials at the grocery store yesterday on the way back to Raven and Jethro's place—underclothing, a toothbrush, deodorant, a razor. He shot a glance in the mirror— he hadn't shaved in a month and had acquired a decent reddish-blond beard—and decided he liked it, so he put the razor away and returned to the kitchen.

Maybe he'd keep the beard to go with his new persona.

Jethro's gaze hung on him only briefly, a double blink, as if seeing a ghost as Mack entered the room. Then he smiled. "Stay out of trouble."

Raven had slid off the stool, shaking her head. "You can

come too."

"I need to sketch out some plans."

Mack had stood by the man today as he'd walked through the debris, listening as Jethro talked through the changes he'd make.

Perhaps that's how someone lived through trauma—by moving ahead, keeping their face forward to the future. Seeing a tomorrow in their mind's eye that was better than what they left behind.

Raven had driven, and they'd picked up the pizza before bringing it to the park. Now, the night stirred around them with music. A crowd was assembled in front of a small amphitheater, sitting on chairs or other picnic tables.

"This looks good on you," Raven said, tugging on the center of his shirt. "It was Ace's church shirt. He only wore it when Mom made him."

"I'll try not to spill pizza on it."

"Ace would be thrilled, believe me. Mom, not so much."

"What happened to your mom, if I can ask?" He caught a piece of cheese before it dripped off his chin.

"She had cancer. It was quick—found out in August and she was gone by Christmas. Ace was a senior in high school. I was fifteen. Since then, it's just been us."

"Sorry."

"Thanks. How about you? Are your parents still around?"

He just stared at her. Took a breath.

"Oh, wow. Sorry. I'm sorry. That was a stupid question—"

"I don't think so. I…it feels like they've been gone for a long time. But…" He lifted a shoulder. "I don't know."

"Is it weird, not to remember anything?"

He finished the pizza and wiped his fingers. Just one of those was enough. He looked around at the crowd, at the darkness beyond. "It is. I mean, I could know anyone out in that crowd and not know it, right? And I could have been anyone. A doctor, a fisherman, a park ranger."

"A firefighter?"

He grinned. "Maybe."

"My dad thinks you were in the military, the way you handled

68

yourself with Teddy. And the way you got him out of the fire. You're pretty coolheaded."

"Or just too dumb to know when I'm in trouble." He winked at her.

She laughed again, her hand going to press her hair behind her ear, and that's when it hit him again.

A flash, a memory, something so familiar—

Then it vanished. But he drew in a quick breath.

"You okay?"

He nodded.

Shots cracked the air.

His body erupted, pure adrenaline, and he leaped toward Raven, pulling her down, his arms around her, his body arched over hers in the grass.

"What the—"

"Stay down," he snapped.

More shots, crackles, and he looked for the source.

"Firecrackers, Mack. It's just kids." Raven pushed on his shoulders, scooting out from beneath him. "But thanks for the protection."

Kids. Of course.

And now he realized what an idiot he looked like, tackling her.

Worse, eyes raked him as he got up, helped her up. "I got your skirt dirty."

She dusted off her bum. "No, it's just grass. But I gotta go onstage soon. You… going to be okay?" She said it like he was a real head case, softly, worried.

"I'm fine."

Her mouth made a line as she smiled. She squeezed his shoulder and picked up her guitar.

Nothing to see here, folks. He tried to ignore the onlookers as he watched her pick her way through the crowd.

Maybe he had been in the military. He'd just *reacted* on instinct alone, and what kind of person did that?

A person used to being shot at.

Sheesh.

Raven took the stage to the cheers of a number of locals, maybe more, and as she warmed up her guitar, she leaned in to the mic. "I want to thank everyone who came out to help us clean up Jethro's today—and especially our foreman, Mack Jones. Mack, I don't know where we'd be today without you."

He just nodded, hoping the darkness hid him.

"I'm going to do a cover tonight from one of my favorite bands, the Yankee Belles. This is their first hit. I hope you enjoy it."

She stepped back, began to strum, and when she came back, it was armed with that smoky tone that added heat to the night.

She met him on a night like any other
Dressed in white, the cape of a soldier
He said you're pretty, but I can't stay
She said I know, but I could love you anyway...

It seemed—and maybe it was simply because he still felt eyes on him—that Raven stared straight out at him when she sang, her voice deep and husky and vibrant, and if he let it, it could touch him.

Find his bones.

Could he love Raven someday? Maybe. She was sweet and hardworking and determined—never mind beautiful—and seemed exactly like the kind of girl he could love.

So they started their own love song
Found the rhythm and tone
He said he'd never found anyone
Who made him want to come home

Mack looked beyond the stage to the boats, white upon the water. Why he'd decided to flee to here, and from what, he couldn't know.

But here, yes, he was safe.

He was Mack Jones, local hero.

She belted out the chorus, her voice beautiful and strong.

She...don't wanna cry,
But she ain't gonna fall for another guy.
It's too hard to be apart
Not after she's waited for...one true heart...one true heart...

Yes, Jethro was right—she could make it big if she wanted. This town and, frankly, Mack were too small for her. She needed a bigger world with a guy who had a real future.

Not one who always felt eyes on him, watching him, whether they were or not.

He said I'm leaving, baby don't cry.
No, Stay with me, please don't die.
Always, forever, together, with me
She lay in his grass, clutching eternity.

Raven dropped out the guitar for the final chorus, her voice sweet, haunting, lingering.

She...don't wanna try,
It's too hard to fall for another guy.
But you don't know if you don't start
So wait...for one true heart...one true heart...

Then she stared out into the audience.

At him.

His heart just stopped. Because in the silence right before the thunderous applause, he heard it.

The voice he couldn't place, the one on the train and in his dreams.

The only promise you have to make to me is to not let go of the guy who saved my life.

He closed his eyes, willing the face to come to him, a piece— *please*—of his past.

It faded, leaving only his heartbeat.

He opened his eyes. Raven was striding toward him, grinning, holding her guitar case. She set it on the picnic table as he got up.

"So, what did you think?" She took his hand, drew him toward herself.

Oh.

"It was amazing."

Her mouth tugged up in a smile. And then, before he could stop her, she lifted herself up on her tiptoes and kissed him. Full on the mouth, her hand clenching his shirt.

He couldn't move, his heart thundering. She smelled so good, her lips soft, her body close to his, and a wave of desire swept over him, something that had nothing to do with her touch and everything with being wanted and needed and...belonging.

His breath trembled out, and she leaned back even as he made to bring his arm around her.

"Too soon?" she whispered.

He swallowed, then nodded. Oh, he wanted to like her. Wanted to belong here. Wanted to...be the guy who deserved her song.

Only who was the guy in the dream? The one who'd saved a life?

To whom did he belong?

Maybe it didn't matter. He touched her face with his fingertips, not sure what to do.

"It's okay, Mack. I'm not going anywhere either." Then she winked and picked up her guitar. "Besides, you need a breath mint."

He laughed and took the guitar from her grip.

But again, the eyes followed him as he walked her to her car.

———◆———

RJ tried not to tremble as she stood on the porch of the River-walk B&B, an old house parked right next to the riverfront—the first lodging she could find when she hit town earlier today.

York was alive.

Very much alive by the looks of the kiss between him and the girl singer who'd crooned one of the Yankee Belle's songs at him like he might be her long lost love.

No…that couldn't be right.

It might not even be him. The man wore a beard and looked leaner than she remembered York being. Didn't everyone have a doppelgänger?

But not everyone leaped from their perch to tackle an innocent bystander when a firecracker bit the air.

RJ, too, had jumped. Because it had sounded like gunshots. Clearly, she was still suffering from a little PTSD.

So, when she spotted the takedown, her instincts—and yes, hopes—reignited.

They had died earlier when she'd seen him get out of the car, trek over to the pizza joint, and emerge later with a large box. Such an ordinary activity for the superhero man in her mind, but she, too, had shared a pizza with him before. In Russia. Right after she was told she had to escape via the Trans-Siberian railroad.

Then, York had told her about his life, those dark blue eyes on her, and she'd felt safe and a little powerful, and it might have been the first time she realized she could love this mysterious, dangerous man.

So, no, she hadn't been entirely sure it was York across the park eating a pizza, until the takedown confirmed it.

"Ma'am, can I get you anything?"

The voice of the waitress dragged her attention away from the white Ford Focus as it pulled away from the curb. She sat on the porch of the B and B at a tiny wicker table on a wicker chair, nursing a cup of coffee, still warm but overcooked in the pot in the kitchen.

RJ had arrived in town just as the sun dropped in the jagged horizon in her rearview mirror. Shelly was a beautiful little hamlet secreted away in the middle of Washington State, nestled along the shores of a deep blue lake.

Paradise.

She'd like to run away and hide here too. If that's what York was doing.

What *was* he doing?

The Riverwalk B&B was a remodeled 1910 two-story house

with four bedrooms, a wraparound porch with white wicker and green rocking chairs, and a living room decorated lodge style with a grand stone fireplace.

The kind of house that said old wealth and family legacy.

Safety.

Now, RJ looked over at the proprietress, a pretty, slender woman with long dark hair named Darcy, who ran the place with her husband, Micah.

"No. I'm…I'm done." RJ handed the cup and saucer to the woman and drew in a breath to stop the shaking.

But inside, she might be coming apart.

Really. What was going *on*?

"Your room is ready anytime," Darcy said, her gaze warm. "What brings you to Shelly?"

"The scenery," RJ said, getting up.

"Yes. It's gorgeous this time of year. Where are you from?"

RJ drew in a breath, not sure what to say. Finally, "Out east."

In fact, it had taken her roughly sixteen hours since this morning's news flash to find a flight, rent a car, and drive east from Seattle through the mountains. Sixteen hours and still it was only pushing 8:00 p.m.

She could sleep for a year.

Because, really, she hadn't slept in a month already.

"Say," RJ said, glancing out at the park, "did you hear that woman singing earlier?"

Darcy was wiping the table. "That was Raven Darnell. She's a local. Her father owns Jethro's, the place that burned last night. She's good, right?"

She nodded, all truth. "And this Mack Jones guy she mentioned?"

Darcy lifted a shoulder. "Some guy they hired a month ago. Not sure where he's from, but he seems like a good guy. Apparently, he saved Jethro's life in the fire."

Of course he did.

"I drove past a burned building on the way in, just a block away."

"That's the one. The town volunteered all day to help with

cleanup. If I know Jethro, they'll rebuild."

RJ tucked that information away and headed upstairs as another crooner took the stage.

Her bedroom overlooked the park. But it wasn't a terrible place to hide out as she spied on York—a queen bed with a soft white cotton cover, a table and two straight chairs, a white-painted fireplace, and a quaint bathroom with black-and-white checked tile and a clawfoot tub.

She debated running a bath and instead climbed onto the bed and pulled out her phone.

Her mother picked up on the second ring, and RJ wasn't exactly sure why she'd dialed that number, but for some reason her mother was the only one in the family who didn't hover.

She didn't need her brothers to swoop in and—

"Hey, honey, how are you?"

And that's all it took. "I found him, Ma. I found him." She drew her legs up to herself and wrapped an arm around them.

A pause then, "Um—"

"York! He's here, in a little town in Washington State—I just saw him."

"Is he okay?"

Outside a female voice had taken over, was singing Diana Ross's "Ain't No Mountain High Enough."

"I don't know. I...yes. He looks fine. Not hurt at all."

"Oh?" And her mother said it appropriately, with question in her tone. Because her mother had been there when York found them in the hotel room, a dead body on the bed. Had seen the way he'd grabbed up RJ, held her, so much panic, so much relief in his embrace that his feelings could have been written in headlines.

Her mother had probably even seen the way he'd kissed her in the fish market not long after, like he not only missed her but...well, maybe *needed* her.

Maybe loved her.

So then, "Yeah, but...he's with this other woman."

Silence. "I don't understand, RJ. What—?"

"I know. I don't know what's going on!" RJ could imagine her mother, maybe in the apartment in Seattle that Wyatt had purchased, with its wide windows that overlooked the Sound, sitting in the darkness watching the lights play over the dark waters. Her hair would be up in a jumble of brown curls, and maybe she'd still be wearing her jeans and a T-shirt, or maybe already changed into her yoga pants and an oversized shirt, one of their father's old flannels.

Gerri Marshall had become the foundation of the family, someone who knew how to weather the storms her children stirred up. "How did you find him?"

RJ didn't know what she'd do without her mother's wisdom. "I saw York on the news—he'd saved some guy from a fire, and it made a round-the-nation brief this morning."

"So naturally you thought it was York and hopped on a plane—"

"Ma! It *is* York. He's alive."

"Honey."

"Okay, it might not be him—he is wearing a beard and looks a little leaner than York, but Ma, you should have seen him. Some fireworks went off and he nearly shot out of his skin and tackled this girl next to him. I've seen him do that before."

"I'm sure you have."

She could almost see her mother's smirk on the other end.

"Ma—"

"RJ. I know you loved York—it was clear from the moment you returned from Russia pining for him. But could your hope that he's alive be clouding your vision here? Didn't you say he was with a woman?"

RJ let go of her clench around her legs and got off the bed, walking to the window. Her light was still off and the sky arched a deep blue over the reflection of the lake, stars blinking down on it. "Yes. He was with a woman."

"As in, *with*?"

She drew in a breath. "She kissed him."

A pause, then, "York was in love with you, too, RJ. No one could miss that. If he was still alive, don't you think he would have contacted you? And he certainly wouldn't be kissing someone else."

RJ pressed her hand on the window. "What if he couldn't? What if he's undercover? The woman called him Mack Jones. Doesn't that feel like an undercover name?"

Another pause.

"Okay, don't say it. I know I've been watching too many episodes of *Alias*. But still, Ma—maybe he had to come here, had to change his name, had to—I don't know—fake his death?" The thought caught her up. "Maybe he's faking the entire thing."

"RJ—"

"Ma. I have to find out what's going on—"

"What if...and I'm not saying this is him, but didn't you say that York wanted to leave his life and start over?"

Her mother's question came like a slap, something bright and hard and—

"Oh."

True. He'd told her that more than once.

Fact was, the man in the park didn't look at all like the man she'd known a month ago, the spy who had saved her life.

This man looked like a lumberjack. Or at least a mountain hipster.

Maybe he wasn't York.

Or at least the man she knew.

Maybe he *was* trying to leave his world behind.

Leave *her* behind.

She closed her eyes.

"Honey, I'm not saying York wanted to leave you. I know he loved you. That's why I don't think this could possibly be him. But—"

"But I have to find out." She walked back to the bed, sat on it.

A sigh. "How are you going to do that? If it is York and he's undercover..."

"Right. Okay so...apparently there are volunteers helping with the cleanup of the building that burned. So maybe tomorrow I show up with a shovel."

"That's my girl."

"That's why I call you. You believe in me."

"Of course I do."

"Wyatt and Ford and Tate think I'm in over my head."

"They're your brothers."

"Not my babysitters."

Her mother laughed.

"Ma, it's not funny. I don't want them getting hurt—"

"I think they'd say the same about you."

"It makes me feel incompetent."

"You might consider letting it make you feel loved."

Oh.

"Your father would be proud of you."

She drew in a breath. "Would he? I don't know. I think he probably wanted me to get married, stay on the ranch…"

"You father's heart was for you to be exactly the woman God created you to be. He was protective, sure, but he saw your desire to keep up with your brothers. That's why he taught you to ride and shoot and do all the things he knew you wanted to do."

"I miss him."

"I do too. No one will ever replace your father."

A beat, then, "Even Hardwin?"

She hadn't exactly been against her mother dating the rancher-slash-banker next door, but the thought still unsettled her. Felt weird to think of her mother in the arms of anyone but her father.

"I don't know. Hardwin is a good man. And I might be falling for him. But he can't replace thirty years of raising a family and building a life."

"Maybe he can be a new season. Not a better one, but a different one." RJ could hardly believe the words emerged from her mouth. Still, her father had been gone for over five years.

Her mother made a noise, not quite of agreement, but…

"Ma?"

"I think he wants to marry me. I'm just not sure if I want to bring more change to our family…or give my heart away again. It's…well—"

"Terrifying. Because how do you know he's a good man? A man you want to trust with your life?" Huh. Sounded a lot like the questions her mother might ask her.

78

But she'd trusted York with her life. More than once.

"You just know, I think," her mother said. "Right?"

Yes. "I know this man is York, Ma. And tomorrow I'm going to find out exactly what's going on."

"You go get your man, honey."

"Thanks, Ma." RJ hung up and stared out the window at the moon waxing down onto the lake, a spotlight in the darkness.

Oh, please, let it be him.

Tate was going to die before Glo could get him to the altar. She knew it in her bones. And frankly, her nightmares.

"You should tell him." Kelsey Jones sat cross legged in front of a fire table on a teak deck chair, holding a glass of cabernet sauvignon, the night behind her fractious, as the Pacific Ocean threw itself onto Cannon Beach.

Dixie, their bandmate, was walking out of the house, holding a bag of pita chips and a bowl of hummus. She wore her blonde hair back in a loose bun, a pair of yoga pants, and a Yankee Belles T-shirt. She set the food on the table. "No, she shouldn't. Tate is already freaking out about the idea that she—*we*—could get killed onstage. Or at some political function. Or even at the coffee shop. Sheesh—I'm surprised he didn't stay this week, just to hover."

"He's doing his job, Dixie," Glo said. But yes, Tate had gone nuclear with his protection since the shooting in Seattle.

Maybe his heightened anxiety had rubbed off on her. She'd stopped sleeping and more than anything she wanted this political race to be over.

To marry Tate.

To stop living in fear.

Hence why Kelsey had suggested their songwriting getaway. That and a spa day complete with facials and pedicures and a massage. Distraction as a method of coping.

And they'd picked up wedding magazines, one of which sat open on Kelsey's lap. She turned pages under the glow of twinkling Edison lights hanging from the portico.

The house was the private vacation home of a friend, and yes, they'd spent nearly a week of delicious privacy beachside. Glo had begun to hear her voice—the poetry inside—after spending months giving sound bites and speeches for her mother, then racing off on the weekends to fulfill her NBR-X commitment with the Yankee Belles.

Even her bones felt thready, shredded, fatigued down to the marrow. And probably that's why her demons so easily found footing.

Namely, a man named Sloan Anderson. Or at least the specter of him rising in her nightmares.

Dixie sat down on another teak chair. "So, you had the dream again?"

"Second night in a row. But this time I was in a wedding dress—"

"You have wedding on the brain," Kelsey said. "You should elope, like Knox and me. As soon as the season officially ends, we're off to Hawaii."

"And what about us? Or your brother?"

"I haven't talked to Ham in ages." Kelsey flipped a page in the magazine. "For all I know, he could be off saving the world in Europe. And you guys see us all the time... Sorry. Knox said we could have a pretty wedding at his ranch, but...I don't know. I think I want it to be just me and him."

"The ranch would be a pretty place to get married," Glo said. "But my mother, I'm sure, would want to make a big thing out of it."

"Why does your mother always get her way?" Dixie said.

"You've met her, right?" Kelsey said. She reached for a pita chip.

"She's planning a huge to-do, but if it's up to her, we won't get married until she's into her second term as VP. But then we'll be gearing up for her presidential run, again, and..." Glo picked up one of the magazines, started to page through it. "In the dream, I'm in a wedding dress, and we're standing at the altar, and when the preacher gets to the part asking for objections, Sloan stands up. And he has a gun, and he turns it on Tate, and then…then I wake up."

She had the attention of Kelsey, who put down her chip, and Dixie, who had leaned forward in her chair. "You think Sloan is in love with you? And wants to stop the wedding?" Dixie said.

Glo looked at her. "*No.* I think Sloan tried to have Tate beaten to death in Vegas! And for the life of me, I can't figure out why. But he escaped before we could find out why, and I can't help but feel like he still wants to hurt Tate."

Silence. The flames flickered, no sparks, just orange and red flares against the darkness. The air carried the edge of autumn, not quite brisk, but cool and laden with the smells of loam and the salt of the sea. "I'm terrified that he's going to finish what he started."

"You can't carry that fear around inside you, Glo," Kelsey said. "It's going to eat you up, paralyze you. Trust me, I know." Kelsey *did* know—after being brutally beaten and left for dead as a teenager, fear ruled her life. It had taken her over a decade to crawl out of that trauma. To live in freedom.

"We promised to not keep secrets from each other, but telling him about my stupid dream is just going to freak him out more. And frankly, Tate already seems spooked."

"About the assassin?"

"About *marriage.* Yes, he asked me to marry him, but every time I talk about setting a date, he sort of evades the subject. Do you think he…well, maybe he doesn't *want* to get married?"

"Glo," Kelsey said. "Tate has been crazy about you since the day you met in San Antonio. Trust me, he wants to marry you. It's just…timing, right?"

She drew in breath. Nodded. "You're right. It's just…you know when you feel like something is too good to be true and you're just waiting for the catch? Marrying Tate feels like I won big."

"And now you're waiting to fall hard," Kelsey said. She set her magazine on the table. "Glo—"

"I know it isn't true."

"No, you don't," said Dixie. "But you're *hoping* it isn't true."

She picked up her glass of wine. "We all hope it isn't true. That when something good happens, it's because we deserve it. Or because fate likes us. But the fact is, the sun shines on the good and the bad. And so does the rain. You have to believe that no matter what happens, you're going to be okay. That God's grace is enough."

Lights flickered on the horizon, probably boats at sea, almost pinpricks against the fabric of night.

But what if God's grace wasn't enough?

She didn't voice her thought, just let it simmer in her brain as Kelsey and Dixie began to discuss their current song. Kelsey was humming a tune into her phone. Dixie had her eyes closed, as if imagining the harmonies on her fiddle.

Glo stared out into the darkness and tried not to let Sloan creep into her thoughts.

Her cell buzzed on the table. Tate's picture appeared on the screen.

She picked it up and answered. "Hey, handsome." Getting up, she walked off the deck, along the semi-lit pathway to the beach. In her periphery, she noticed Swamp moving too, a shadow of Tate-assigned protection.

"Hey. How's the songwriting going?"

The ocean was still working out the last itches of the storm that had come through a day ago, froth edging the waves. The wind rushed through the tall seagrasses behind her.

"We hacked out a couple songs, but mostly we're just…unwinding. How's Seattle? Did you get any answers from Vicktor?"

She sat on the beach, digging her feet into the gravelly sand.

A pause, and something in it felt dark and pregnant. But, "No, nothing really." His voice, however, sounded distant.

"Tate?"

"The FBI is stonewalling him about the shooting, too."

Oh. Maybe it was just his frustration bleeding out. "So, no idea who the shooter was."

"RJ still thinks it's the Russian assassin, but why would the Russians want to kill your mother?"

"I don't know. But if she is in league with the Russian

mob—which is crazy talk—then why would they want to kill her?"

"I don't know. But I'm going to stay here and hunt around a few more days. And my sister just won't give up the idea that York isn't dead. She nearly got caught breaking into a townhouse last night, hunting down a lead."

When you loved someone…

Glo took a breath. "I don't blame her. I…I wouldn't want to lose you."

"You're not going to lose me, Glo."

"Yeah, well, Rambo, you're not exactly Mr. Run-from-Danger." She kept her voice easy, without the tremor that threatened to rattle out.

"Nothing is going to happen to me. I'm more worried about you."

"I'm fine. I'm sitting on the beach, staring at the stars."

He made a humming sound. "Me too. I'm sitting on Wyatt's balcony. He's got this hip loft that overlooks the Sound. And right now, there are about a hundred million stars in the sky, although I'll bet your view is better."

"It would be with you in it."

She could almost hear his grin. "Ditto." He was probably dressed in his off-duty attire of jeans, a T-shirt, and flip-flops. Probably smelled good, too, a hint of the morning's aftershave still on his skin, a dark five-o'clock shadow skimming his chin. In her mind, she slipped onto his lap and put her arms around his shoulders. Leaned in to his strength.

Yes, Tate would be just fine. He was a former Ranger. A survivor.

Not a guy Sloan could take down easily.

"I had this crazy dream that Sloan found you and killed you," she said softly, surrendering to the need to tell him. "I know—crazy. Probably just residual PTSD. And of course the daily reminder in the news of Mom's 'near miss' a month ago in Seattle."

He sighed.

"And I might be a little bit jealous of Kelsey's plans to elope next month."

"Knox and Kelsey are planning to elope?"

"Maybe *we* should elope." She meant it as a joke.

"Maybe we should," he said quietly. "I wouldn't mind being able to keep watch over you all night long."

Oh. Heat filled her to her bones.

"It was a lot easier when we slept in the same tour bus."

"Along with the rest of the Yankee Belles and Elijah Blue."

"Still. Knowing you were on a back bunk, knowing that anything that came through the bus would have to go past me to get to you…yeah, Vegas, here we come."

She laughed. "You can't go back to Vegas, and you know it." Because last time he was in Vegas, he'd nearly been beaten to death by a Russian mob thug named Slava.

Apparently the Bratva had a playing card with his picture on it.

And there went the happy warmth. She blew out a breath.

"Okay, fine. Atlantic City. Or maybe we just get a license and fly out to the ranch. Make it easy."

Make it easy.

"With my mother, nothing is easy, but…"

"Glo Jackson, I love you. And I'm going to marry you. You set the date. Sooner than later. I'll be there."

Silly tears edged her eyes. "Come back to me. I miss you."

"Just a couple more days."

"Please stay out of trouble, Rambo."

"Glo." His voice had turned low, almost a hum under her skin. "Nothing is going to happen to me. Or you. And I am going to marry you. I promise."

She drew in his voice, let it settle inside her.

But yes, she was going to set the date.

Before her nightmares came true.

5

M ack just needed a mission, a game plan, a strategy. A villain to fight.

Like the fire that wanted to destroy the livelihood of the man who'd saved his life.

Mack had woken up, galvanized behind a goal. Maybe he'd been an engineer in his previous life because he appreciated a plan with workable tactics to get a job done.

As Jethro had described it, Mack could almost see the finished pub with its gleaming cedar and pine boards, the reworked copper bar, the industrial pipes.

But probably he'd been a criminal engineer because Mack had again woken in the middle of the night, sweat slicking his body, having grappled with his nightmares.

Having killed someone in his dreams.

He could probably live without waking with the residue of guilt, shame, and even horror in his soul.

The sunrise over the lake at Jethro's house helped him shake it off, find his purpose. The deck overlooked the platinum expanse of Wapato Lake, the mountains rumpling the far side, the dawn bursting with rays of orange and red into the turquoise sky. A touch of autumn hung in the air, the scent of loam and the faintest rub of smoke in the breeze.

"The past just won't leave you alone, will it?" Jethro greeted him from where he sat in his rocking chair, wearing his pajamas and a ratty green robe, leather slippers, and his spectacles down on his nose.

Mack had helped himself to fresh coffee and cupped his other hand around his mug as he slipped into the rocking chair beside Jethro. He stared at the sunrise. "So, Medal of Honor?"

Jethro glanced at him. "It's just something that happened."

"It's who you are."

"It's what I did. Who I am is how I live every day." He leaned over. "What do you think of this?" Jethro slid his notebook over to Mack's lap, a hand-drawn sketch of the inside of the new and improved Jethro's.

Not a bad drawing either. "Is this the brick wall along the inside of the building?"

"Yes. Let's turn the bar so that it runs the length of the building. We'll add a few more flat-screens behind the bar and lengthen it, but that'll give us a full view of the patrons and the patio."

Jethro leaned over and pointed to a space in the back. "We'll put a stage here, for open mic nights. That way the crowd will have to go all the way to the back to hear the music, and leave room for more restaurant guests in the front."

"And big picture windows here?" Mack ran his finger where the wooden wall had been, the one they'd cleared yesterday. The second floor had been held up by massive steel beams, which had survived the fire.

"I want those kind of doors that open to the outside, onto the patio. Bring the outside in. Maybe we'll even move the open mic out there in the summertime."

Mack looked up at Jethro, whose eyes shone. Nothing of quit in this guy. "You need to get this drawn up by an engineer so we can get an estimate."

"No need. It's all up here." Jethro tapped his head.

"Still, a blueprint helps. So I know how to build it right."

And yes, Mack had said that deliberately, but why not?

He wanted to stay. To help. And maybe even let himself fall in love with Raven.

Shoot, last night had been…well, it could have been a fiasco, the way he hadn't responded to her kiss. But she hadn't mentioned

it the entire ride home, and Jethro had been in the kitchen with a
cold cup of coffee, waiting to talk repairs when they came home.

He wanted to belong here, to this town. And maybe even to
this family.

Jethro grinned at him, then slapped the notebook on his
knee. "What'ya waiting for? Daylight's burning."

An hour later Mack found himself standing on the sidewalk,
hot coffee in a travel mug in his hand, surveying the burned shell
of the pub in the morning light, seeing Jethro's vision.

Yes, tall windows with *Jethro's* painted on the front, and that
long copper bar shined up and expanded. The big copper beer
tanks along the back, with a glass wall separating the brewery
from the pub. A wooden stage, the cement floor washed and
restained, and those tall windows overlooking an expanded patio
area.

Raven got out of her car and came up beside him. "The
pastor of our church just texted. He's coming over with more
volunteers to help today."

"Good," Mack said and took a sip of his coffee. "We have a
lot of cleaning to do."

She wore a black T-shirt, her hair up, and short shorts with
hiking boots, and looked about twenty-one years old.

He felt forty, or older.

Maybe that was the reason he just couldn't seem to let his
heart move in her direction. He probably had fifteen years on
her, at least.

Raven looked past him, and he turned to see a Caravan drive
up, a few people climbing out of it.

One of them arrowed straight for him, early thirties, wearing
a smile, a clean blue T-shirt, and a pair of work pants.

"The pastor?"

"Caleb Brown. He's young, single, and energetic."

Indeed. Mack met Caleb's hand. "Hey."

"Quite the thing you did the other night, Mack—hope it's
okay if I call you Mack?"

Mack had a crazy retort in his head, something like, *Go ahead
and be creative*. It didn't matter what he called him.

But maybe it did. Especially if he was truly embracing Mack Jones.

"No problem, Caleb."

"Jethro is a beloved member of our congregation. Put us to work." Caleb glanced behind him, and Mack noticed a number of other vehicles had pulled up. Helpers were emerging from their cars, many of them retrieving brooms and mops from their trunks, all of them in work attire.

Huh.

"Such a shame. I'm glad he's rebuilding. He makes the best Reuben sandwiches," Caleb said. "And I like to watch the game here, sometimes."

Mack just nodded. "Today's project is to clean the smoke off the massive brick wall."

"I'll see if I can rustle up some gloves, masks, and brushes," Raven said. "And I'll put a call in to the Shelly Hardware Store to see if they can mix up some TSP solution for us." She walked away as she pulled out her cell phone.

"What a tough break." Caleb turned to stare at the building. The fire had eaten away the wooden exterior of the building on the sides and the front as well as charring the second-story apartment. The remainder of the building was made of cement, having been a former Mobil gas station and later a used car dealership. Mostly it was sooty and dirty and needed a good scrub so that they could get down to figuring out what was left.

"Jethro's had a number of bad breaks in his life. Coming out of Desert Storm should've been enough, but then his wife gets cancer and dies. He lost Ace shortly after I arrived here. Such a man of faith, even in grief. And now this."

Caleb looked at him. "You saved a pillar of the community when you went into that fire after him, and we're all very grateful."

Mack didn't know what to say. Instincts had driven him into that building.

The instincts of someone accustomed to running into trouble.

Except maybe he did have an answer. "Yes, well, Jethro is a good man. He sure helped me out."

Pulling out a pair of gloves from his pocket, Caleb said, "So, where are you from? Jethro says that you just sort of showed up one day."

Mack also donned his gloves and headed toward the building. "Seattle. And before that I think I did a lot of traveling."

Caleb raised an eyebrow. "You think?"

Mack laughed, and it sounded a little too high even to his own ears. "I mean yes, I did do a lot of traveling."

They entered the building. Without the charred beams, the place just looked dark and sooty, the floor black, the walls shadowy. Smoke embedded the core, and although he hadn't really noticed the smell before, now it lodged inside him, something oddly, even painfully, familiar.

So, a criminal engineer firefighter.

Caleb was looking around at the wreckage. "I suppose Jethro has big plans for this place."

"Yes. He stayed up late last night drawing and coming up with a plan."

"It'll be beautiful," Caleb said. "Probably better than before. That's what fire does. It burns away all the chaff and stubble down to the core, and only then do you see what it's made of. See its true strength and value."

The words nudged something inside Mack, and he looked at Caleb. "'See, I have refined you, though not as silver; I have tested you in the furnace of affliction.'"

Caleb frowned. "Isaiah 48:10. I didn't know you were a man of the Bible."

Neither did he. "I guess so." But even with his easy shrug, more verses stirred inside him. *The crucible for silver and the furnace for gold, but the Lord tests the heart.*

He could almost hear himself, a younger version, reciting the verses. *But he knows the way that I take; when he has tested me, I will come forth as gold.*

The last one came with a different voice. *And we know that in all things God works for the good of those who love him, who have been called according to his purpose.* Deep, soft and sure, settling into his bones.

It left him momentarily wrung out.

Caleb to the rescue. "The fire is supposed to burn away everything but our faith and character."

"And what if nothing remains?" Mack asked, his gaze away from Caleb.

"Then you rebuild with new materials, the kind that last despite the flames." Caleb clamped a hand on his shoulder.

Raven came in carrying a bucket of water and a brush. "Delivery from SHS," she said. "Brushes and cleaning solution and masks and gloves."

He looked past her and spotted a teenager unloading supplies from the bed of a truck, a Shelly Hardware Store logo on the side.

"Tony is a local member of our congregation as well," Caleb said and headed outside to help.

"And Annie is bringing over donuts," Raven said.

Yes, Mack very much wanted to belong to this town.

"Where do I get started?"

He turned toward the voice and found a woman addressing him. She wore her long brown hair down, a T-shirt, and a pair of jeans and looked at him with eyes so blue, for a moment he couldn't move.

Impossibly blue, the color of the lake at twilight. And even as he stood there, something reached out and wrapped around him. A feeling different from the verses, something almost violent and raw, and he gasped.

She raised her eyebrow, a smile stealing across her face.

"Grab a brush from the truck. You can start on the walls." Raven had come up beside him. Put her hand on his arm.

The woman's mouth opened, but he nodded, suddenly aware of how much alike they looked. Dark hair, blue eyes, but Raven was a little more petite. And younger, maybe by a couple years. More, Raven had an innocence about her that this woman didn't possess. In fact, she radiated an earnestness, a sense of confident urgency about her that felt a little unnerving.

Maybe that was it. Clearly the familiar vibe was simply the resemblance and the fact that he oh so very badly wanted to recognize someone.

He turned back to the woman, and for some reason, he held out his hand. "My name is Mack."

He searched her face for a hint of recognition, something—

She looked at his hand, then took it, frowning. "Um, you can call me Sydney."

Sydney. Nope, not the slightest nudge. "Thanks for helping today. The church congregation is really nice to help Jethro like this."

She offered a slight smile, nodding. "Yep." She held his hand for a moment too long, and he took it away. Then she drew in a breath. "Okay," she said and walked away.

Weird.

People had brought in ladders and brooms and now set up the ladders, climbing up them to start washing the walls. Others attacked the cement floor. Mack joined them, grabbing a brush for the floor.

Voices raised in a cappella song, a hymn that, oddly, he knew.

Turn your eyes upon Jesus...Look full, in His wonderful face,

And the things of earth will grow strangely dim...In the light of His glory and grace.

Caleb came up beside him. "Hey, since you're sticking around, probably we should recruit you for the big game next week."

"What big game?"

"Main versus Lakeside."

Mack just looked at him.

"I can't believe Jethro hasn't mentioned it. He's one of the troublemakers who sets it up. It's a big all-town softball game we hold every year right before the World Series during Harvest Festival. The Main Street businesses play a softball game against the resort owners in town. It's sort of an end-of-the-season reminder of a fabulous summer, and it's a big deal. We've been practicing for a couple weeks now, but you could join us tomorrow as a member of the Mains."

"You're a member of the Main Street team?"

"The church is just a block away. And we have a fantastic pitcher—she used to play fast-pitch for WU. Do you play baseball?"

It was a good question, and certainly he should have an answer, and probably one better than, Um, I think maybe I do…so, "Yes. Yes I do."

Didn't every American kid play baseball?

"Excellent. Practice is at the rec center Saturday morning."

"Donuts!" Raven's voice singsonged through the open room, halting work. She came in carrying two huge boxes of donuts. Behind her, a woman with a handkerchief tied around her pink hair and wearing an oversized shirt that said Happy's Donuts carried two thermoses of coffee.

Caleb headed for the donuts, and Mack moved to follow, but as he did, a giant crash sounded in the far end of the building as someone jumped off their ladder, jostling it and sending it careening to the ground. The noise bulleted through the room, a cacophony of violence that echoed into Mack's bones and soul.

The memory rushed him.

He was in an apartment with cement walls, a tile file, and it seemed he was young, because he was scared.

No, not just scared, *terrified*. Fear, like a cold rush of water filled his entire body, his throat, his mouth, drowning him.

With a whoosh, he saw three men wielding metal pipes, beating someone who lay prone on the floor. The pipes clanged against the cement floor.

His breaths released hard and fast, and he turned and practically fled toward the scorched kitchen.

Anything to not unravel in the middle of the pub.

The memory followed him, adding screams and the tinny smell of blood, and he hung on to the charred doorframe to the back office where he'd rescued Jethro. Sweat ran down his spine, and he might pass out.

The world swirled around him, tilted—

Something touched his back. Then a voice. "Mack?"

He *knew* that voice. It stopped his world from tilting, and he turned, hard, fast, staring at her.

She jerked away from him. Held up her hand.

Oh. The brunette. Sydney.

His heart raced. "Sorry." He hadn't a clue why he'd acted that way. Still, she'd rattled him.

Concern filled her blue eyes and she reached out again, this time grabbing his arm. "Are you okay?"

Her voice sounded so familiar. He looked at her. "I don't know. I...I think so."

She glanced back toward the pub, then to him again, and cut her voice low. "We're alone now, so you can talk to me if you need to."

He just stared at her. Was she making a pass at him? Suddenly, what Jethro had said about him being blind to women rushed at him. Maybe—

"This reminds me of the smell of a Russian train station. Doesn't it? Like gritty and dirty, the smell of smoke."

His mouth opened. "I, I don't know. I've never been to Russia."

She drew in her breath, and he wanted to add, *Have I?* But then, as if she hadn't heard him, she said something in a foreign language.

"*Pravda? Ya ne veryo tebe.*"

She paused then, as if her words might mean something.

"I don't understand."

She sighed and caught her lower lip, and for a second, he thought her eyes filled. But then she blinked and nodded. "Okay, then. Um, wow. Are you sure you don't want to talk about it?"

Yes. Yes, he was very sure he didn't want to talk about the fact that he thought he'd just seen somebody murdered in his memories. And he was quite sure he was involved or—*please no*—even to blame. So, no. Not at all. "I'm fine."

"Right," she said softly. "Okay. Sorry to bother you." She walked away, back to the pub.

He watched her go. She was pretty. *Real* pretty, the kind of pretty that would stay with a man, make him remember her.

Shoot, did he know her? But if he did, why didn't she say anything? And how could he know her if she was a member of the congregation?

Maybe he was just so desperate to find anything familiar he

was now assigning meaning to random moments. He needed to calm down and start settling into the fact that he was Mack Jones.

Mack Jones, who belonged here now.

The old Mack had died in that car crash.

This Mack would rebuild with sturdier stuff.

And even if the past wanted to find him, he wasn't going to let it.

———◆———

It wasn't him. It *couldn't* be York.

RJ climbed up the ladder, holding the long brush, trying not to breathe in the chemicals of the cleaning solution.

Her eyes burned. She wanted to blame the burn on the chemicals, but really…

Her disappointment was a hot ball in the pit of her stomach.

Mack looked *exactly* like York, even with the thick beard. She couldn't see the scar on his neck to confirm, but his profile, his physique, even the way he held himself as he'd talked to the pastor, his shoulders wide, his hands on his hips—all the York she'd known.

And Mack weirdly possessed the same toe-curling accent, that delicious British accent from York's time overseas, learning English in Russian schools.

But clearly, it was just a coincidence.

Still, she'd been so sure.

She couldn't stop herself from coming up to him when he walked into the building. She'd nearly—oh, so nearly—called him by his name.

Instead, just in case he was undercover, she'd played his game.

He'd just stared at her, then gasped. And for a split second, she thought…and then Raven had walked up, put a proprietary hand on his arm, and any recognition had vanished.

Just to be sure, RJ gave him a name that he might recognize. The name that might put a twinkle in his eye and confirm to her that inside this lumberjack there lived the man who she knew and loved.

Sydney. As in Sydney Bristow from *Alias*. And he was her Vaughn. The running joke between them about how she had gotten in over her head and desperately wanted to be a super-agent.

But nothing. No twinkle in his beautiful blue eyes. No smirk to his angular mouth, no catch in his wide chest.

As if it meant nothing to him.

So she'd taken a brush and gone to work, trying to figure out what his game was.

She kept one eye on him as he talked with the pastor. She hadn't realized she'd joined a church group, but apparently it made for a good cover.

Then Raven had returned with donuts, and the guy at the end of the row dropped his ladder on the floor, and suddenly York freaked out right before her eyes.

He'd bolted toward the back room, and RJ had taken it as her chance to get him alone.

The poor man was breathing hard and shaking, as if he might be having some sort of panic attack. So *not* like York at all that the first sliver of real doubt took root.

Then RJ had touched his back, called his name, and he flinched. Whirled around so fast, a look in his eyes that had her jerking back because for a second she was on the train with him, watching his reflexes as he protected her from an attacker.

His blue eyes cut down into hers with such steely strength and hard-edged abruptness that it could only be York.

Of course it was York.

Except again, he stared at her as if he didn't know her. So she'd tested him with the little memory of the Russian train station where she'd almost been shot by an assassin. Where he'd said goodbye to her and told her that he'd find her, again, someday.

Nada. Nothing. Not even when she spoke in Russian to him.

She'd told him she didn't believe him.

He didn't even blink.

He didn't know her.

Or, and she could hardly bear this thought, but any good analyst had to consider it—he was trying to forget her.

Just like her mother said.

A fresh start, leaving his past behind.

Well, Shelly, Washington, was certainly the place to do it. Quaint, tight-knit, and the members of the community had already adopted him as their own.

Especially the dark-haired one who now stood beside York-slash-Mack, laughing at something he said.

No, he couldn't be her York. She was a fool.

RJ climbed down the ladder, started on the lower section of the wall. She'd leave at lunch break, sneak away, and...

York was dead. She had to let that truth into her soul—

"Do you know him?"

She turned.

Raven stood beside her, her voice low, her blue eyes searching RJ's.

RJ shot a look at York, back to Raven. "Um...I..." Because if he was undercover, then... "I don't...no. I don't know him."

"Oh. Okay." She made a face. "I saw you go into the back, and when he came out, he couldn't stop looking at you, so I thought maybe you recognized him."

RJ kept her voice even. "He looks like someone I used to know."

Raven raised an eyebrow. "Oh, uh, really?"

RJ frowned, not sure— "Yes. But he died."

"Oh." Raven put her hands in her back pockets. "I see." She offered a smile. "My name is Raven."

"R—Sydney."

"You're not from around here."

Shoot, she'd blown her cover already?

"I heard about the fire and wanted to help."

"Huh. Well, that was nice of you." She glanced toward Mack. "He's been a huge help to my dad since we hired him. He can cook and bartend and apparently rebuild pubs too."

He could? The only memory she had of York cooking was tea he made in Moscow.

So, clearly *not* him. "You're Raven Darnell," she said, remembering her last name. "I saw you singing last night."

Raven brightened. "You heard me?"

"That cover you did from the Yankee Belles was great." She didn't want to mention that she actually knew the Belles and that, well, Raven could use a little work.

Okay, so maybe her opinion was a little tainted.

"Thanks. I love their stuff. They're supposed to be coming in concert with NBR-X in a few weeks in Spokane. I'm trying to get tickets."

And if RJ were a really good person, she might speak up, offer to help land those tickets.

But her gaze kept casting over to Mack. And the way his was casting back to her.

And the buzz she felt under her skin.

Or maybe he was looking at Raven.

Raven seemed to catch his gaze and frowned.

Quick—"Your dad was the one he saved in the fire, right?"

"Mmmhmm."

"Is he a firefighter?"

"No. Just one of our bartenders. But he's…well, he's really brave. He even beat up a guy who tried to, um, well, who was here after hours harassing me." She folded her arms. "We're sort of dating."

Wow. And maybe RJ *was* Sydney Bristow after all because she didn't even flinch, not a hint of the knife that separated her ribs, piercing her heart.

"He's a real live hero. I think he was in the military, but he won't talk about it. Has a few scars—one on his neck. I saw it before his beard started coming in."

With her words, everything inside RJ stilled.

Oh, oh…

Because York had a scar on his neck, starting at below his ear.

It *was* him. And, again, she *knew* it. She looked at Mack— *York!*—and watched as he bore down, scrubbing the soot from the cement, a fierce set to his mouth.

Yes. *So* York Newgate, action hero. A hundred and ten percent into his work…

"But that life is over. Mack is here, starting over." She folded her arms now and smiled at RJ.

Starting over.

Huh.

Either he was undercover or he really didn't know her.

The problem was, however, if she could find him, so could Damien Gustov. And the York she knew would never bring trouble to the front door of people he cared about.

Unless...and the thought hit her as she turned back to Raven.

Maybe he wasn't the York she knew. Something didn't smell right, and it wasn't just the chemicals seeping up from the cement. "We all need fresh starts sometimes, don't we? I think I'll stick around for a while too." She smiled at Raven.

Because oh, RJ was so getting to the bottom of this.

6

He could do this.

Mack stood on the sidewalk in front of the church, his heart a fist in his chest, not sure why the sight of the building—just a nondescript log structure with a bell tower and a cross on the roof—caused his breath to turn to fire in his lungs.

Just a church.

Certainly he'd been to church before.

"You comin', Mack?" Raven stopped a few feet away from him, turning and squinting in the sunlight. She wore a jean skirt, a T-shirt, her boots, and a thin jacket. The wind caught her hair, drawing it across her face. She drew her hair back and grinned at him, her eyes warm.

This is what normal people did. Went to church. Hopefully with a cute girl.

And besides, Jethro had invited him. It seemed like the polite thing for a houseguest to do.

He could do this. This could work. He could reinvent himself and become Mack Jones.

He liked Mack. Mack was a good builder—he hadn't realized that he had building chops, but as he'd talked through the renovations with a local contractor Jethro had hired, he understood all the steps—from the framing to the electrical—as if he'd heard it before.

So maybe he'd been a carpenter.

Like Jesus.

The thought lifted his mouth and gave him the gusto to take Raven's outstretched hand and follow her into the building.

He let it go at the top of the stairs because he was already giving her way too many wrong signals.

Try as he might, he couldn't get past her age. Or the fact that…well, shoot.

He couldn't stop thinking about the *other* girl.

The one who kept showing up at the building site, offering to help.

Sydney. With the dark brown hair and blue eyes and yeah, there was clearly nothing wrong with him. The red-blooded male inside him was still functioning.

Mack didn't know why—he liked Raven well enough. She was sweet and had made him a part of this town, calling him her hero and introducing him to everyone she knew.

He'd practically been MVP at yesterday's softball practice. And he didn't flinch once when the bat cracked the ball.

See, he was practically a new man.

And maybe if he could get Sydney out of his head, there might be room for Raven.

Problem was, after five days, Sydney had even found his dreams.

She was there, with him on the train. Speaking to him in that foreign language. Looking at him with those blue eyes as if he could save the world.

And heaven help him, in the dream he thought so too.

Last night, when he'd fallen, she'd reached out a hand to catch him.

It woke him up, left him feeling as if she'd actually been there, holding on to him, as if the dream wasn't a nightmare but an honest-to-goodness memory.

Had he killed someone and pushed them off a train? He shuddered with the thought.

See, this was why he needed to get her away from him. The what-ifs were gnawing at him, keeping him from stepping into a life he wanted.

This small town, normal life. A home, a family, a church…

He wanted the safe and ordinary life of Mack Jones.

"Hey, Mack, great to see you. Excellent practice yesterday."
Caleb stood in the doorway of the church sanctuary and shook
his hand as he walked in. Jethro had come early for some meeting
and now stood way, way down in front, waving.

Oh boy.

Mack followed Raven down the aisle. Sunlight streamed
through stained glass windows, rays of divine light casting into
gleaming wooden pews. A carpeted runner ran down the aisle,
but the rest of the flooring was hardwood, except for the stage,
draped in red carpet, with a plain wooden cross hanging on the
back wall behind the altar.

The fist in his chest tightened.

Maybe he'd had a bad experience in church.

Or maybe his inner man, the one who remembered what
Mack couldn't, knew he shouldn't be here.

He slipped into the pew, and someone behind him tapped his
shoulder. He turned. Jimbo, chief of police. "Glad to see you're
sticking around." He didn't smile, and Mack wasn't sure what he
meant by that. But he nodded.

Mack sat next to Raven, Jethro on the other side of him, and
tried to squelch the urge to bolt.

Especially when Caleb got up on stage and welcomed him,
personally, to church. He also welcomed a few other newcomers,
asking them to stand.

Mack looked around and for a second froze at the sight of
Sydney, seated in the back, being nudged to her feet by the woman next to her.

She was new to town? He'd thought she was a regular church
attender.

And that thought added another fist to his gut.

It got weirder when he realized he knew the songs—everybody knew "Amazing Grace," probably, but when the strains of
what Caleb called an "oldie but goodie" flashed on the screen in
front, the song practically leapt from his bones.

How deep the Father's love for us…how vast beyond all measure…that

He should give His only Son to make a wretch His treasure.

Mack reached out for the edge of the pew and wrapped his hand around it, his grip whitening as he mouthed the words.

Why should I gain from His reward?...But this I know with all my heart, His wounds have paid my ransom.

And now, crazily, his eyes filled, his heart thundering.

He was losing his mind.

The hymn ended, and his knees nearly gave out as they sat. He stared at Caleb giving announcements, hearing a different voice. *No eye has seen, no ear has heard, and no mind has imagined what God has prepared for those who love him...*

Of course he was trapped in the middle of this stupid pew, practically in the front row.

Caleb stepped behind the pulpit, his Bible in his grip. "Let's praise the Lord together that this past week Jethro's place burned to the ground."

Mack frowned, glanced at Jethro, who was just grinning at the pastor, nodding.

"We're so grateful that no one got hurt—thank you, Mack—"

Mack looked away, toward the stained glass window, just in case Caleb decided to look his direction.

"But we are also grateful for the opportunity to suffer. To die and be born again. Sorrow is part of life. It's a part of living as a person of faith—we *will* have it. And it can be either from sorrow we bring on ourselves or sorrow others inflict on us—cruelty, injustice, even deliberate evil. The point of suffering is our faith. It either shows you yourself and what you believe...or destroys you."

And what if nothing remains? Mack's question from a few days ago returned to him. Maybe he had nothing of faith to begin with.

"Suffering is the key to rebirth," Caleb said. "In fact, the Bible says in Philippians, 'I want to know Christ and experience the mighty power that raised him from the dead. I want to suffer with him, sharing in his death, so that one way or another I will experience the resurrection from the dead!'

"Suffering leads to death of ourselves because our only chance of survival is to cling to Jesus. And when we cling to Jesus, we are changed. Reborn. We become who we were meant to be because there is nothing of ourselves left."

Mack didn't know when he'd turned back, staring at Caleb, but every muscle in Mack's body stilled.

"When you have nothing, that is a perfect place for Jesus to fill you with His resurrection power. To be reborn."

And shoot, now he looked right at Mack. Just a moment, right before he swept his gaze over the rest of the congregation. "Do you have nothing? Do you want to be reborn? Do you want to discover your true self?"

An anvil lay on Mack's chest.

"Then right now is the day of your rebirth."

And we know that in all things God works for the good of those who love him, who have been called according to his purpose.

Mack was shaking. Because he didn't know who he'd been before. And frankly, maybe he didn't want to know, ever.

But he did know who he wanted to be now.

Caleb came down from the pulpit. "First Peter 1:3–5 says, 'We have been born anew to a living hope through the resurrection of Jesus Christ from the dead, and to an inheritance which is imperishable, undefiled, and unfading, kept in heaven for you.' Be reborn into living hope today. Embrace the inheritance of peace and joy and eternity offered to you."

And shoot, if Mack's legs didn't move him out of the pew, past Raven.

Moved him right up to that blood-covered altar. Gave out on him in front of the cross.

And just like that, Mack Jones bent his head and held on to the only thing that made him who he wanted to be.

Please, Jesus. I don't know who I was, but…I want to be a different man. A man who trusts You. Please forgive me for the darkness I know is in my past…and help me to live as a new man.

He felt a hand on his shoulder and opened his eyes to see

Jethro kneeling beside him, his head bent. "Bless this son of Yours, Lord. Thank You for bringing him to us. Help him find his place in Your grace."

Mack's jaw tightened.

But the fist in his chest had released, and he lifted his head and took a breath.

A full, undefiled breath.

Free.

Alive.

Anew.

He smiled and found Jethro grinning at him, his eyes shiny. "See, I knew you came to us for a reason."

Mack got up, and Caleb met him, his hand outstretched, then pulled him tight into a quick hug. "Welcome, brother."

This felt awkward, but he slapped Caleb's back before he let him go.

Raven stood in the aisle, beaming at him.

And behind her, farther down at the end of the aisle...Sydney.

Tears streaked down her face, her eyes wide on him.

What—?

The only promise you have to make to me is to not let go of the guy who saved my life.

The voice slammed through him, and he gasped.

She swallowed, nodded as if in finality, turned and practically fled the building.

"Wait!" Mack looked at Raven. "Go home without me—I'll meet you there."

Then he strode past them all and headed down the aisle. "Sydney!"

She had worked her way through the crowd in the vestibule and he barely caught sight of her disappearing down the stairs. "Sydney!"

A few heads turned, and he offered a tight apologetic smile as he pushed through the crowd, out into the open.

She was halfway out of the parking lot, fast-walking toward the sidewalk.

He leaped the last step and took off for her.

She glanced over her shoulder, hustled her pace for a second, then she turned and held up her hand. "No—*no*—" Tears streamed down her face.

What on earth? Because the sight of her crying nearly wrecked him, a strange response that he couldn't untangle.

She turned and bolted. A flat-out run—and she was wearing Cons and a pair of jeans and had some real speed on her.

Okay, so this was weird.

But he sprinted after her.

And yes, he felt a little like a predator, but he couldn't suppress the urge to talk to her. *Right. Now.*

She knew something.

He dodged a bicycler and a display of flowers outside Mystical Pizza and caught up to her just as she hit the Riverwalk Park. "Stop!"

He didn't want to grab her arm, but she wouldn't slow down, so, "Please!"

Maybe it was the *please*, because she whirled and he nearly smacked right into her.

She was still crying, but a fierceness had washed over her face, into her eyes. "What do you want?"

"What do I—you're the one following *me*!"

Her mouth opened, and oh no, he was right. She *was* following him.

"Oh—you know me, don't you?" And now he did grab her arms, pushing her back into the shadows of a towering oak. "You know me, *don't you?*"

Her blue eyes latched on him, her jaw tight. "Do you know me?"

He blinked at her. "This isn't a game!"

"I know—believe me, I know! But answer the question—Do. You. Know. Me?"

He drew in a breath. Then, slowly, shook his head. Let her go. "No. I think I should, but…I don't."

Her mouth tightened into a grim line.

"But you know me."

She nodded.

"Who am I?"

She wiped her cheeks, almost harshly, met his eyes again. "Do you really want to know?"

The question had the force of a punch right to his sternum. He swallowed. Nodded past the tightness in his chest.

"Your name is York. You're thirty-two years old. We met in a foreign country, and if I tell you any more, it'll destroy everything you've built here." She raised her hand, as if she were going to touch his chest, then dropped her hand. "It'll destroy Mack Jones." She swallowed. "Do you want that?"

He stared at her.

In the park, people rode bikes, and the wind stirred up the fragrance of the freshly cut grass mixed with the dying leaves, the loamy scent of autumn from the nearby hills. Winter was coming and he'd seen himself maybe buying a little cabin…

"Just tell me…was I a good man?"

She stared at him, her chest rising and falling. Finally, she opened her mouth.

He cut her off. "Don't bother. You've answered my question."

Then he turned and walked away.

There he went, walking right out of her life.

And she was going to let him go.

RJ watched as York—no, not York. Not anymore. As *Mack* strode down the street, away from her, his hands clenched at his sides, not looking back.

Not even once.

Do you know me?

Maybe she should have said no, let him live in the fresh start he'd so craved.

The York she knew—and loved—had so many regrets they were slowly consuming him. Grief. Mistakes. Horrible choices.

He'd done wet work for the CIA. Although he hadn't admitted it outright, she knew it by his personal grief.

And today, he'd let that all go and become a new man.

She wiped her face, then crossed the street to the B and B. A couple other patrons sat at the wicker tables overlooking the river—they'd probably seen the altercation as York had chased her across town. She kept her head down as she walked onto the porch and inside.

Darcy came out of the kitchen just as she hit the stairs. "Did you find the church okay?"

She'd asked Darcy for directions this morning. Not that she'd been entirely sure she would attend, but...

If York didn't know who he was, then he wouldn't know that an assassin was after him.

Someone needed to keep York alive.

At least that had been her working justification for sticking around after her panicked phone conversation with Coco four days ago after her first conversation with Raven.

After she'd realized that York was, well, York. Except *not* York.

When she first considered the fact that the man she loved had forgotten...everything.

"The woman said that he's staying in town, starting over."

"Take a breath, RJ," Coco had said, probably getting up from her bedside vigil of her son. "Start at the beginning."

"I found him. York. But he calls himself Mack, and he's... he's different. So different that I wasn't even sure it was him, but this woman he works with—actually she said they were dating—"

"Dating? *What*—?"

"Yes, I know. I don't know what's going on, but she said he has a scar under his beard and that the other day he beat up some guy who'd tried to harass Raven—anyway, it's York. *For sure* it's York. But he...he acts like he doesn't know me."

She'd been standing in the Riverwalk Park, staring out at the blue water, watching a boat motor past, the wind in her hair, the smells of the nearby pizza store stirring her hunger.

She would have liked to join the group for pizza for dinner—a suggestion by Caleb, the young, handsome pastor. But frankly, her head was buzzing from watching York interact all day like he might be the local handyman or even the owner's son that…shoot, she had to walk away.

Untangle her mind.

"What do you mean, doesn't know you?"

"I spoke to him in Russian. I called myself Sydney, just in case he was undercover. Not a blip of recognition. I'm sorry—he's good, but certainly, if I was somehow blowing his cover, he'd ask me to leave."

Silence.

"Coco?"

"What if…and I know this sounds crazy, but what if he was so injured in the car accident that he lost his memory?"

And that's when the idea had locked in. *I think he was in the military, but he won't talk about it.*

Ding, ding, ding. "You think he has amnesia?" she'd voiced to Coco. "I know it sounds like something that only happens in soap operas, but I was reading this article about this guy in Arizona who fell in the bathroom and lost twenty years of his life. It happens. And often, from trauma."

Amnesia.

Coco had nothing, so RJ had spent the night googling it and forming her own hypothesis, one that included a fall, probably hippocampal damage, retrograde amnesia, at least of the past few years, and finally nothing that offered a real cure.

Maybe with time, and perhaps exposure to past memories via smell or music or photographs, he might…

He might be York again.

But in some cases, it never resolved.

Which meant he might never know he was in danger.

So, she'd stuck around, showing up every day with her scrub brush and even joining the handful of helpers for lunch, not sure what to do.

At night, she'd stayed until he got into Raven's car. And waited until they turned the corner before she let herself cry.

She'd even shown up at the baseball field yesterday, at loose ends with herself, standing in the shadows in case any Russian thugs showed up.

Sheesh, she'd turned into Tate, the bodyguard.

But it was just an excuse, a way to hang on because York was so very, very capable. He'd swatted a couple pitches into left field like he might be Babe Ruth. And when they put him in center field, he scooped up at least two fly balls, fielding the others.

The man did everything well.

Including sweat. He came onto the bench with a line of exertion down his back, pulled off his hat, and it left all that beautiful blond hair a mess of tangles. He hadn't cut it in weeks, and now it lay longer than she'd ever seen it, golden and kissed by the sun. He still hadn't shaved either, the sun picking up the bronze in his beard. He'd worn a shirt with cutoff sleeves and a pair of jeans and Converse tennis shoes and looked so utterly not York, it had made her realize what an all-around American kid he was at heart.

Or at least had wanted to be.

If he hadn't grown up in Russia, witnessed the murder of his parents, and been raised by his grandparents in Wisconsin.

Probably he'd played baseball there—which of course he couldn't remember—so seeing him play made her realize just how close York was to being the man he'd probably dreamed of being.

Before he joined the Marines.

Before he transferred to the security detail of the American ambassador to Russia.

Before he married the ambassador's daughter on the sly.

Before he lost his job and started working for the CIA.

Before his wife and son were murdered.

Before he killed the man to blame.

And before he entered, as he put it, the "transportation" business.

Oh, yes, and that was before his girlfriend was killed by the same assassin who tried to frame RJ for murder.

But all of that would not have changed her answer, if he'd let her give it after he chased her down. After he forced the truth out of her.

Just tell me…was I a good man?

Yes. Absolutely.

The kind of man who deserved a fresh start.

So yes, York had a lot of reasons to want to forget his past and become Mack Jones, and if she loved him, *really* loved him, she'd let him.

Right?

"I really enjoy Caleb's preaching. It always hits the mark." Darcy's comment brought her back to the moment, and RJ turned.

"Yes, it was good. Life changing, really."

Darcy raised an eyebrow.

"I'm going to check out today. Thank you."

Darcy smiled at her. "Tired of our town already?"

"No. I love Shelly. But I don't...well, I got what I came for."

"The scenery?"

RJ nodded, unable to speak through the thickening of her throat. Then she turned and headed up to her room.

She should have left earlier, but this morning...well, she'd needed something. Needed to lean in to the only thing that had ever made sense...

Because for the first time in her life, she felt very, very alone. And normally, in the past, her father would have shown up with wisdom.

So she'd come down to breakfast and asked Darcy for directions to the nearest church.

She never expected to see York sitting near the front.

Opening the door to her room, she went straight for her carry-on and tossed it on the bed. Swept the clothing from her drawer into the bag. Went to the bathroom to fetch her toiletries bag.

Stared at her reflection in the mirror. Reddened eyes, a hint of a tan, her dark hair tangled around her face. *Do you have nothing? Do you want to be reborn? Do you want to discover your true self?*

She had discovered her true self—or at least she thought she had—with York. With him she'd been brave and strong and capable and...

Maybe she didn't have to have York to be all those things, right?

She ran water and dampened a washcloth, pressing it to her face.

Breathed, hearing her thundering heart.

Then right now is the day of your rebirth.

She couldn't believe it when she saw York rising, saw him scoot out of the pew, saw him walk up to the altar and bend to his knees. Bow his head.

Saw his shoulders shake.

And right before her eyes, he became reborn. Free.

It wrecked her.

She couldn't imprison him again with his past. Not just his pain, but with the fear of it roaring back. She couldn't leave him looking over his shoulder wondering when it might hurt the life he wanted.

She'd find Gustov on her own and make sure he never destroyed Mack's world.

But somehow, she had to figure out a way to tell Mack about his past...something that didn't destroy him but enough to let him in on the danger of Gustov.

Then again, Gustov hadn't shown up yet, and if Mack could stay out of the news, the likelihood of Gustov tracking him to this little town...

Yeah, he should know.

Maybe she could write him a note. Just tell him to watch out.

Grabbing her toiletry kit, she dropped it into the carry-on bag, then closed it up. She could probably bunk with her mother at Wyatt's place tonight in Seattle. Resume the search for Gustov with Vicktor in the morning.

Yes.

She stood in the silence of the room, pressing her hands to her face.

God, I know I don't pray enough, but...please, help me to let him go. And protect him.

She blew out her breath, turned, and scooped up her baggage.

Opened her door.

Mack stood in the threshold, one hand braced on the frame. He looked at her, his blue eyes stormy. "I don't believe you."

She hitched her breath. "Uh—"

He took a step toward her, backing her into the room. "I don't believe you."

"What don't you—"

"That's what you said to me five days ago. In Russian, at the pub, wasn't it? I. Don't. Believe. You."

Oh. She nodded.

He closed the door. "Start at the beginning."

7

None of her crazy story should make sense. But deep in his gut, in the core of his chest, Mack—er, *York*—knew she was telling the truth.

Or most of it. Because there were parts that didn't quite fit together.

"Stop, wait. Let me understand this." He turned to her on the bench where they sat, the afternoon sun falling behind them.

They'd started the conversation in her room. With him on the chair, her pacing.

She made him a little seasick, watching her figure out how to tell him that he was an…well, she didn't say it aloud, but she'd alluded to the fact that he'd killed people. For a living.

Which, in his book, sounded like an assassin.

What the—?

He'd needed some fresh air then and dragged them outside.

"You're saying that you were framed for the attempted murder of a Russian general by some mafia thug. And I helped you get out of the country?"

"Yes. You are—were—connected to a guy named Roy. That's how I found you. Or rather, you found me." She looked up at him, those blue eyes holding so much of his past, and said, "You saved my life, York."

York. Not Mack. Still, they sounded alike. So maybe that's why the name Mack slid so easily into his mind and soul.

"And when you say *saved*—"

"You helped get me out of Russia. And since then you've been hunting for the Russian killer, a man named Damien Gustov. He tried to kill my sister, Coco—your friend Coco. And we think he followed you to America."

He drew in a breath, met those eyes. "And why did I come to America?"

She swallowed, and there it was.

He might still have whatever instincts that he'd cultivated doing whatever dark things he'd been doing because he could spot a dodge when he saw it.

"Sydney—"

"RJ. My name is Ruby Jane. But sometimes you called me Sydney."

He frowned.

"After Sydney Bristow, a television show—never mind." She looked away. "You came to America to bring my nephew, who is half Russian, to the hospital. He has leukemia."

Oh. Huh.

Yeah, no, he still didn't believe she was telling him the entire truth.

"*Ya ne veryo tebe.*"

She looked at him, frowning.

"That's what you said. It came back to me like a slap right about the time I returned to the church. I was standing in the parking lot and just like that, I heard your voice, clear as day, in Russian. And I understood it." He leaned forward, his elbows on his knees. "I debated not coming back, but it occurred to me that someone who had taken the time to track me down all the way to Shelly, Washington, might be someone I need to talk to." He glanced at her. "And yet, you were leaving. Why?"

She sighed. "Because of what happened today, in church."

Yes. That.

He could still feel the crazy rush of freedom, the fresh breath, the sense of clean that saturated his body.

He felt new. And even her crazy story didn't seem to diminish it. Probably because he was finding it very hard to see himself as the action hero-slash-007 spy she painted him as.

Or maybe he just wanted to disbelieve it, because there was the tussle with Teddy…

"You said to me more than once that you'd like to start over, begin again, and…well, here you had your chance. And I didn't want to take it away from you."

So she was going to leave him to restart his life. Maybe he had been reading too much into their unspoken past. His own strange attraction to her.

"Then why did you find me in the first place?"

She looked over at him. "Because I was worried about you. You vanished, and everyone else thought you were dead. But I…I couldn't accept that."

A tentative smile slipped up her face. "I knew you were alive."

He studied her. She'd been crying, her eyes reddened, but that didn't diminish the very down-to-earth beauty she possessed. The breeze tossed her hair, and she wore a floral shirt, jeans, and her Converse tennis shoes, and yes, at first glance she might have reminded him of Raven.

But this woman had a determined fix to her countenance that made her appear capable. The kind of partner a guy might trust.

"Are you a spy?"

She laughed. "No. But I do work for the CIA, as an analyst. Even then, I wasn't able to find you until you made the news after the fire."

Oh, that.

"You just can't break free of your own heroism, can you, 007?" Her eyes twinkled, and for a second, he really, *really* wanted to understand her joke. To land with her in the sweet memory behind that smile.

It fell. "Nothing, huh? What do you remember?"

He stared out at the river. "I woke up on the side of the highway, wounded, my head on fire, completely confused."

"Wounded?"

He leaned back and pulled up his shirt to reveal his again-healing wound.

"That looks deep."

"Jethro stitched it up. I didn't want to go to the hospital. I'm not sure why—instincts, probably—but I thought if I went in, they might report this as a stabbing, which would only bring the police, and I couldn't shake the idea that I was a criminal."

"You're not a criminal, York."

She said it softly but met his gaze, as if she knew he needed to hear it said with surety. "You're one of the good guys."

Shoot, the words nearly took him under and his stupid eyes burned, and he looked away because he couldn't speak either.

She touched his arm. "You had to do things for the sake of your country. But you're a man of honor, a man who cares about the people around him."

He nodded. Blinked.

"You had a wife and a son once."

He looked at her, the heat from her hand bleeding through his arm, solid, comforting. "What happened?"

She shook her head.

"Divorced."

"No."

Oh.

"It was a long time ago. But another reason I didn't want to drag up the past."

He rubbed his hands together. Stared out at the water. "You were leaving because you didn't want me to remember."

She said nothing.

"But I am remembering, RJ. I started remembering the moment you walked into Jethro's." He glanced at her. "You're in my dreams."

She stilled, her eyes widening.

"Yes, it's exactly how it sounds. Because you're in my dreams, and we're kissing. And then suddenly—"

"You're attacked."

He froze.

"And you have to fight someone."

"I throw him off the train, and I'm about to fall, too, but you grab me…"

"You didn't fall off the train."

Oh. "But I did kill someone."

"A member of the Bratva."

His gaze hadn't moved off her face, and now it traced down to her lips, then back. "And we *were* kissing."

She swallowed. Looked away.

"RJ, do I love you?"

Her breath caught. She closed her eyes.

He touched her cheek and gently moved her face back to his. "Do you love me?"

Her eyes glistened. "It doesn't matter, does it? You're with someone else now, and you have a new life—"

"It matters very, very much," he said, his voice low. "I'm not with anyone else, and if someone loved me, then—"

She pushed his hand away. "Then she'd let you have the life you wanted."

She met his eyes, and a tear spilled out.

He couldn't move.

Because he saw her—flashes of memory really—but yes, there she was. Kissing him in the darkness of a Russian park, then trembling beside him as he gasped for air next to her, even clinging to him in the darkness of an alleyway as he pressed her against the wall, his hands buried in her hair, as he kissed her. *I could find you when this is over.*

"You'd better stay alive, Bristow."

Her eyes widened. "You remember—"

"I just remember this." Then he cupped his hand on her face, leaned in, and kissed her.

And everything that had lain dormant, all the desires and emotions he'd been trying to light for Raven, simply ignited, flashing over into a rush of longing, almost painful. RJ tasted like...like his. Like he'd come back from a very dark, foreign place to find home. She smelled of comfort and desire, and when she wrapped her arms around him and pulled him close, he very nearly cried.

He didn't know her, but he *knew*, yes, oh yes, every hidden part of him *knew* he loved her.

Pulling her tight against him, he deepened his kiss, nudging her mouth open, drinking in the sense of coming back to himself, to finding the lost pieces. To wholeness.

She made a sound, her body trembling, and he let her go, suddenly— "Why are you crying?"

She caught his face between her hands, looked at him. "Because I missed you so much it hurts. But I...I don't want you to come back with me, York."

He frowned. "I don't—"

"You have a life here. The one you always wanted."

"Did I? I mean...yes, but..."

"I met with Crowley. You probably don't remember him, but he was the ambassador to Moscow, and you married his daughter. He works for the CIA now, and you always feared he would retaliate if you ever came stateside, but...you're wrong. You're forgiven. He...well, he said he was wrong about you."

York just frowned at her. "But I thought you said the CIA took me in Seattle."

"That's what we thought. But now, we don't know." She pushed away from him. "But I'm going to find out. And when I do—"

"I'm going with you, RJ."

She drew in a breath.

"Just because I don't remember anything doesn't mean I can't help. That I don't have a responsibility—"

"You have people counting on you here. And...well, it's safer."

He made a face.

"You're not a killer anymore, York. I mean, you never were, but..."

"But that is a part of me that isn't useful to you anymore."

"You're safer here."

"I think I can fend for myself."

"Stay here. Be free." She rose, took a step away. "Be Mack Jones." But her voice wavered.

"Aw, RJ. No way. I'm going with you—"

"No, you're not." The voice came from behind him, and he turned. Jimbo was striding toward him, out of uniform but flanked by two officers.

York stood up. "What's going on?"

Jimbo came up to him and gave him a grim look. "I'm sorry, Mack—or rather, York Newgate. But you're wanted for questioning in the kidnapping and murder of Jason Mack."

———————◆———————

"He didn't murder anyone." RJ stopped in the lobby of the Shelly police station, tired of sitting on the chairs, and posed her statement to the big man named Jimbo, in his *Magnum, P.I.*–style Hawaiian shirt, who had arrested—okay, not arrested—but dragged York into the station.

The place had the charm of a used car office—a bare clock, a couple desks, and a wilting plant that sat by the window, plotting its escape.

Jimbo held up his hand. "I didn't say he did. Calm down—"

"If you add a 'sweetheart' after that—"

He held up the other hand. "Never. But you need to keep your voice down. No one is accusing him of murder, but there is a BOLO out for him, and when I ran his prints, it pinged."

She wanted to like Jimbo, despite the fact that he'd—illegally, she might add—grabbed York's fingerprints off a soda can and ran them, in hopes of adding background to the stranger in their midst.

Not that she could blame him, a hometown police chief looking after his own. And he wasn't a jerk about it. He didn't cuff York or grab him or even march him to the car like a felon. Just asked him to join him at the station.

He did use a this-isn't-a-request voice.

But he'd offered her coffee as she waited in the lobby and even let York come out and talk to her. *It's going to be okay, RJ.*

In what world? Because if the chief had alerted the law enforcement system to York's whereabouts, wouldn't someone—anyone—who might be nefarious and watching for his name to ping—let's say, the rogue CIA group who'd taken him last time—hop in their car and show up to *finish him off*?

Oh, she'd left calm miles behind in the rearview mirror.

Now RJ followed the chief to his cluttered office. "He doesn't remember anything. I'm a bigger help to you than he is."

"I'm aware that he has 'lost his memory,'" Jimbo said, but he finger quoted it, so how compassionate could he be? "But it's really out of my hands. People are coming from Seattle tomorrow to question him."

"People? Which 'people'?" And she finger quoted *that*. "Because I've met *people* before, and that's how he got into this mess."

"Sydney."

York's voice behind her made her turn. He stood in the lobby, wearing a smile, Jethro beside him.

Where had he come from?

"Let's go," York said.

Go?

She looked at Jimbo. He gave her a tight smile. "See you tomorrow."

She still didn't—

"I'm being released," York said. "Under Jethro's custody."

"Don't run away," Jimbo said, and it didn't sound like he was kidding.

Oh, for cryin'…although with his warning, a plot was forming. What if they did run? They'd done it before, and then York could go into—

"No." York reached out his hand and caught hers, and her eyes widened. He pulled her out of the building, holding the door open for her.

"No what?—"

"I could see what you were thinking."

"No, you couldn't."

He grinned, something sparking in his eyes. "Listen. I might not know you, but somewhere in here, honey,"—he touched his chest—"I know you."

"Then, pumpkin, you know that running is our specialty."

Jethro had walked ahead, so maybe he hadn't heard them, but York slowed her down anyway.

"What?"

"I'm tired of running. And hiding. And not knowing who I

am. I'm going to stick around and talk to whoever is showing up here tomorrow, and then…we'll see."

She touched his chest then, felt his heartbeat, steady and warm under her hand, and wanted to weep again, still tasting his lips on hers, the way he'd kissed her, like, indeed, he loved her. *I just remember this.*

He hadn't forgotten her. Deep in his heart, he'd kept a place for her.

"I know you, York. I know you wouldn't murder some passerby. Some *kid*."

He put his hand over hers, on his chest. "Thanks. But it freaks me out just a little that the only name I could remember when I found myself bloodied on the side of the road was Mack."

"That does feel unsettling."

He raised an eyebrow.

Jethro had rounded back and now came up to them. "Let's get you home, Mack. Raven has supper on."

York walked toward Jethro's truck. Stopped at the door, his fingers still entwined with RJ's. He took a breath and looked at her, back at Jethro. "So, my real name is York. And this is RJ."

Jethro looked at them, said nothing. Then gave a short nod.

"I need to ask you a favor. I'd like to ask if RJ can stay with you—"

"York! No, I'm fine."

His hand tightened on hers and he glanced at her. "No. This whole thing has me…anyway, I don't know what to think and until I can get my head around—"

"Of course she can," Jethro said. "Although I liked the name Sydney." He winked and got in.

They stopped by the B and B and picked up her bag, then RJ got in her car and followed them out of town.

She could imagine that York was filling Jethro in on their conversation.

She was trying to sort out who might have put a BOLO out on York, a dead man.

Maybe she should call Crowley, give him an update, let him do some sleuthing.

She pulled up behind Jethro's truck into a gravel driveway. Trees bordered the long drive, but as they drew closer to the lake, the road opened up, and she spotted other homes in the dips and valleys along the lakeshore.

Jethro's home was a single-story cedar-sided cabin with a wraparound porch that overlooked the lake. A little piece of paradise tucked away.

She got out and York was waiting for her. "Listen, so, uh, I probably need to have a conversation with Raven. She has a little crush on me…"

"A little one? Hello, Mr. Oblivious."

He smiled. "Fine. Gimme a second."

She nodded and followed him onto the porch but sat in an Adirondack chair as he went inside.

She couldn't hear the conversation, and Jethro came out and sat beside her.

"That's not pretty in there," he said and glanced over at her. "I tried to warn my daughter that Mack had his secrets. But he's a hard guy for a young girl to ignore."

She sighed. "For the record, I didn't come to town looking to break hearts. He's been missing for over a month, and everybody else thought he was dead."

"He looked dead when I found him in the park. Beat up, bleeding, his wound was starting to get infected. He looked like an escaped convict, except he was wearing a dark leather jacket, blue jeans, and dress shirt, which made me think he might be a PI running from a client."

She laughed.

He met her smile. "So…who is he?"

Oh. Uh. "He…he used to work for the CIA." Sure, that much she could tell without giving him away.

"And what happened?"

"He was arrested…except not really because the people who took him were…well, they weren't who they said they were, and that's all we really know. York has the rest."

"He's ex-military."

"Marines."

Jethro grinned. "Yep. Thought so. Semper fi."

The door squealed on its hinges and York walked out. Glanced at Jethro. "You sure you don't mind us staying here? Just for tonight? Because I'll bet tomorrow I'll be...well, who knows where I'll be."

"Son, you can stay as long as you'd like. And so can your girl." Jethro patted her shoulder. "I'm going to chop some wood." He got up and headed off the porch.

The sun had bled red into the lake, a fiery ball of orange hanging just over the horizon. It bathed York's face in dark shadows.

"I'm going to clean up. Raven said she'd make you a bed in the other downstairs guest room."

"I'll get my stuff." She got up as he went inside, retrieved her bag from the car, and returned to the house.

Raven stood at the counter, chopping onions, sniffling.

"Raven?"

She looked up, her eyes red. "What?"

"Are you—"

"Guest room is downstairs."

Right. RJ headed for the stairs, ruing the feeble battle she'd waged.

"So you lied to me then."

She froze, grimaced. Turned.

Raven still held the knife, and RJ raised an eyebrow.

"That day at the pub when I asked you if you knew him. You lied."

"Actually, when you asked, I wasn't sure. And then...well, I didn't know what was going on. I didn't know if he wanted to be found. I didn't know he'd lost his memory until after that."

"And you still stuck around." Raven took a breath.

RJ set her bag down, took a step toward her. "I'm so sorry. I know you like him. And why not—he's a great guy. He doesn't even know how amazing he is, but you can see it, can't you?"

Raven nodded.

"Me too. And I told him that he could stay here, be Mack, and he still can, if he wants. But...right now, he's in trouble and

I need to stick around to help him get out of it."

"What are you, his bodyguard?"

Huh. "Well, York can fend for himself, but right now, yeah, maybe I am."

Raven put down the knife, her mouth pinched. "He made me feel safe."

"He does that."

Raven sighed. "He didn't want me, did he?"

"Oh, uh, I don't…"

"It's okay." Raven looked up again and reached for a napkin, wiping her tears. "Stupid onions."

Yeah. "I hate onions."

"Can't blame a girl for trying, though, right?"

"Never."

Raven gestured with her chin. "Bed is made, towels are on the bed. York is right next door." She winked.

Oh, uh… "It's not like…I mean—"

Jethro came through the door and she scooped up her bag and carried it down the stairs.

The basement was small, carpeted, and looked out to the lake under the massive deck. She put her bag in the tiny, paneled room with the single bed. Through the wall, she heard the shower going and…

Humming? No, singing.

York Newgate was singing. And he had a voice that could tunnel under her skin and turn her body to fire.

Even if he was singing a hymn.

High King of heaven, my victory won,
May I reach heaven's joys, O bright heaven's Sun!

Never in a billion years would she have thought that York would know her father's favorite song.

Yeah, that felt weird.

She changed clothes and by the time she emerged, the shower was off. She headed upstairs, where Jethro had built a fire in the black wood-burning stove. Raven was pulling lasagna out of the oven.

The family room overlooked the lake, now turning dark with the deepening twilight. Two overstuffed leather chairs flanked a leather sofa, a worn coffee table. A round table sat to the side, in the kitchen area, and it was set for four.

Never in her wildest dreams did she see this day ending with her at Jethro's table.

Or finding herself at the receiving end of a smile from the most attractive man she knew.

And this man, the one in the clean jeans, a blue button-down shirt rolled up past his elbows, and flip-flops, she knew. Gone was the lumberjack, the bearded hipster. York had shaved his glorious beard, revealing his square jawline and the scar that ran from his ear halfway across his neck.

He'd never told her the story behind it, but she'd become so accustomed to seeing it, it had disappeared into the fabric of the man she knew. Strong, brave, a survivor, the kind of man she could count on.

The man who showed up when she needed him—twice.

He grinned at her and slid into a chair beside her. For a guy who didn't remember her, he was certainly stirring old memories.

"That smells amazing, Raven," he said as she set the lasagna on the table.

She smiled at him. "Thanks."

Bless her heart, she was trying.

Raven added salad and bread, and York made all the appropriate noises as he savored her dinner. Sweet.

RJ tried not to think about the fact that tomorrow he might lose his freedom. Especially if she couldn't figure out how he'd gotten wrapped up in the death of an innocent bystander.

So this might, indeed, be his last supper.

And now, she'd lost her appetite.

They finished and she helped Raven clear the table, Jethro washing dishes, and York drying.

It all felt so normal.

The kind of life they might have had if they'd met years ago. Without the shooting, the running, the threats...

Oh, who was she kidding—she'd never wanted this life.

And maybe York never had either. After all, he joined the military straight out of high school.

But it was a nice moment, the calm, maybe, before the storm.

She stepped outside after dinner, onto the deck, watching the stars wink against the vault of night.

"You okay?" York said as he stepped out behind her.

"I was just thinking...what if we never went back?"

He leaned on the railing, facing her. "I stayed Mack and you stayed Sydney?"

She laughed. "I guess so. Do you think we'd be happy in a small town like this? Making lasagna for dinner?"

He drew her over to him and parked her between his legs. "I don't know. I mean, I don't really..."

"Know me."

He nodded. "I mean, I do...I feel like..." He took her hand. "I know you, RJ. My heart knows you. It did the first moment you showed up in the pub. I took one look at you and I couldn't breathe."

"It sort of felt that way when we first met too."

"How did we first meet?"

"You chased me into an alleyway, grabbed my hand, and told me to follow you if I wanted to live."

"Sounds very Terminator."

"You were scary."

He grinned, his eyes shining. "And yet you followed me."

She sighed, palmed his chest. "I'd still follow you."

"How did you end up in Russia?"

"I followed a lead—"

"No, I mean, why did you become an analyst? Where are you from?"

Oh. "Montana. I have five brothers—four of whom you know. Knox, Tate, Ford, and Wyatt."

He shook his head.

"Probably for the best. But I grew up trying to keep up with them. All the Marshall boys are spectacular. My brother Reuben was a smokejumper, Knox was a bull rider, Tate is a bodyguard, Wyatt is an NHL goalie, and Ford is a SEAL."

"So, underachievers, then."

She laughed. "And then there's me."

His smile fell and he searched her eyes. "You don't think you're an underachiever, do you?"

She lifted a shoulder. "I didn't want to be. But…well, I wasn't brave growing up."

He frowned.

"Ford and I got trapped once in a cave, and we nearly died because I was too afraid to be left alone."

"How old were you?"

"Twelve."

His mouth made a tight line.

"I know, I should have been braver."

"Are you kidding me? I think you're being too hard on yourself."

She looked away. "The problem was, my father blamed Ford—or at least I thought he did—for getting us into trouble, and I think he sort of told my brothers to look after me. It always made me feel as if—"

"As if you had to prove yourself."

"Yeah."

"Mostly to yourself."

She met his eyes. "For a guy who doesn't know much—"

"I know about regret. And wanting to be someone you're proud of." He touched her face. "I think you're plenty brave, Sydney Bristow."

"You remember."

"I googled it."

His hand slid behind her neck, his thumb running along the soft skin at the well of her throat. "Thank you for finding me."

He leaned forward and pressed his lips to hers, softly, testing, as if kissing her in the park had been a fluke.

As if not sure he was welcome.

She slid her arms around his neck, sinking into his embrace.

The door opened, and she pushed away from him as Jethro came out onto the deck.

"Oops. Headed out for more wood."

"Let me help."

"No, that's okay, son. Carry on." Jethro grinned and headed off the deck, and RJ wanted to melt into the boards.

York laughed and reached for her, pulling her against him. "Everything is going to work out, RJ. You'll see."

She didn't want to tell him that this was the first time ever she'd heard him say this. So maybe he had changed.

She liked the new and improved York. Even if he couldn't remember her.

A shout from the woodpile broke through the darkness.

"Jethro? You need help?"

Nothing, and RJ pushed away from him as he straightened. "Jethro?"

Silence, and York started for the edge of the deck.

A man appeared out of the darkness, ax in hand, swinging so fast RJ barely registered it.

York spun away. The ax embedded in the wall.

York jerked the back of his elbow onto the guy's neck.

The man grunted, turned, and slammed his fist into York's back.

York stumbled, caught himself on the rail, and whirled around just in time to duck the second fist.

He sent his own into the man's jaw and, in a swift follow-up move, caught the man's arm, trapped it with his own.

The man punched York in the throat.

York stumbled, fighting to catch his breath.

The assailant smacked York in the chest hard and he went down.

RJ screamed.

The man was big—bigger than York, and balding, square jawed, *I-hurt-people-for-a-living* written in his cold eyes as he headed for her.

She scrambled back.

York tangled his legs into the thug's and the man went down

to his knees.

Emitted a curse word.

In Russian.

York rolled, his legs around the Russian's beefy body, his arms around his neck, a rear naked choke hold.

The Russian writhed back, slamming York into the railing, dislodging him.

Raven appeared at the door and screamed.

RJ scrambled to her feet.

And when the Russian stepped toward Raven, RJ threw herself in front of her, pushing her back.

Russki grabbed RJ around the neck, lifting her off her feet.

Her world turned splotchy as she scraped at his arm, kicking.

"Get off her!" York shouted.

Her turn. She slammed her fist down, hard, between the Russian's legs.

He dropped her, snarling.

She fell to her knees.

He whirled and unloaded his fury into York's face.

York fell against the railing.

Russki reached for the ax.

"Drop it!" a voice said.

The Russian ignored him, turned toward York, the ax raised.

RJ screamed again.

A gunshot cracked the air.

Russki stumbled, and York met the ax handle with his outstretched hand.

"Don't move!"

York grunted, put another hand on the ax, staring at the Russian.

Then, abruptly, the Russian let go and took off down the deck and away from their shooter.

York whirled to follow, then grabbed the railing, hard, wobbling.

The shooter ran onto the deck, into the light.

Not Jethro.

Jimbo looked at RJ. "Are you okay?"

She nodded, and he turned to Raven. "You?"

Raven stood with her hands cupped to her mouth, eyes wide. She lowered her hands. "Where's Daddy?"

"He's over here," said Jimbo. "And he's hurt."

No. But as Raven ran past her, RJ looked at York.

Blood ran down his face, from his nose, his mouth, and he'd collapsed back against the railing, his eyes wide, his chest rising and falling fast as he stared toward the darkness.

Looking very much like he might be having another panic attack.

"York?"

But his eyes were empty, looking past her, all the way to yesterday.

8

Just. Keep. Breathing.

Tate stood in the family room of the house overlooking Wapato Lake, the late morning sun streaming in to cascade over the leather sofa, the worn leather chairs, and the four victims trying to make sense of last night's attack.

One of those victims was his *sister*.

RJ still had bruises on her neck, and he could barely look at her.

Another was York, who looked, at best, unraveled. Because apparently he didn't know who he was or why a Russian thug might want to kill him. And *that* was a story Tate still couldn't quite wrap his brain around.

The third was a woman who looked uncannily like his sister, although younger. Raven wasn't exactly sitting on the sofa. She kept sitting on the arm, then getting up to pace, then sitting again, her gaze always going to the man in the recliner.

Jethro Darnell, her father, sported a killer hematoma over his eye, a mild concussion, and not a little frustration that he'd been taken out by a hard swing to the head by one of his own logs.

But that's how the Bratva worked. They were scrabblers. Resourceful.

Relentless.

Because, according to RJ's description, the man who'd attacked them happened to be Tate's old, out-of-prison-too-soon nemesis, Slava.

131

Enforcer for the Vegas Bratva.

And the man, just months ago, who'd tried to kill him with his fists.

Yes. Just. Breathe.

Tate wrapped his hands around the back of a chair, leaning onto it. "Describe him again."

"Balding. Tall. Broken nose. Spoke Russian," RJ said.

"He swore in Russian. I'm not sure that counts as fluent," York said.

The man looked rough—swollen eye, broken lip—and he moved as if his bruises went deep. Tate really wanted to get him alone and dig into this amnesia game he was playing. But right now, "You're just lucky you're not dead. If this guy is who I think he is, he's one of the Bratva's most lethal enforcers."

"How do you know him?" The question came from Vicktor, who stood with the chief of police for Shelly, Jimbo Reynolds. Vicktor had put a BOLO out on York a month ago when he disappeared. It apparently popped up in the system when Jimbo ran York's prints. So RJ's instincts about York being alive had been correct.

Apparently, she had chops as a CIA analyst. If Tate ever went missing, he hoped she was on the case.

"It's a long story," said Tate to Vicktor. "The short version is that I had my own up-close-and-personal with Slava about six months ago."

"He's the one who beat you up?" RJ asked, her eyes wide.

"Yep."

"What's he doing out of jail?" she asked.

"I don't know anything about that. But I do want to know how he found you. And why."

York was leaning forward, his elbows on his knees, his head hanging. "My memories are still choppy, but if I remember correctly, I met him in Russia a month ago when I was trying to get Coco out of the country. Actually, it was in Moscow." He looked up, a tight set to his mouth. "I should have killed him when I had the chance."

The room went silent and York drew in a long breath, looked

away.

York didn't look any happier with the statement than Tate was. Or RJ, whose mouth flattened into a dark line.

"He and another guy jumped me while I was searching Damien Gustov's place. Tried to get some information out of me, but I was able to get away."

Tate's gaze went to RJ as York spoke, saw her jaw clench.

"So, Slava is connected with this Russian assassin," Tate said. "Which makes sense, if they're both controlled by the Bratva."

"Gustov must have found York and sent Slava," RJ said. She drew in a breath. "And I think it's my fault."

York glanced at her, frowning.

"I called him."

Now, York turned. And all of Tate's residual doubt that this was really York—although a leaner, more confused version—disappeared with his hard-edged, steel look of fury. "What?"

"I didn't mean to—I got a number off the information I found from my boss's journal, and I…I called it." She looked at Tate. "Ford hung up, but it might have connected, and maybe Gustov pinged it and followed me." She pulled out a phone. "I also called Coco a few days ago from here."

Tate glanced at Vicktor, then back to RJ. "Coco has been tracking down the number you gave her. The phone was purchased with a credit card—the same one used to secure the room at the hotel where Randall was murdered."

Vicktor came around the island. "We thought it was stolen because it had been canceled. But we were able to track the company—Imagine, Inc., a subsidiary of a charity organization called Jackson Global Trust."

When Vicktor had told him on the drive to Shelly of Coco's findings, something inside Tate had turned into a hard ball. He heard Glo's voice on the phone from a few nights ago. *I had this crazy dream that Sloan found you and killed you.*

That had been hard to shrug off, right after seeing Sloan's picture at the hotel where Sophia Randall had been killed.

Somehow, this was all connected, and he needed to figure out how.

"A couple days ago, I was able to identify the man who we think killed Randall," Tate said. "He was caught on a security camera going into the back entrance."

"Who?" RJ asked.

"A guy named Sloan Anderson. He used to work for Senator Jackson."

And yes, that sounded bad. Because either Sloan had used the Jackson family charitable foundation for his own evil schemes, or…

Or Glo's family wasn't exactly the good guys.

"I know Sloan, from when he worked in DC as a lobbyist," RJ said. "And I think he even helped out the CIA with information. But I don't understand. Jackson Global Trust is Senator Jackson's organization, right? They're heavily involved around the world with humanitarian aid—medical supplies in Africa, clean water projects in the Middle East, orphanages in Africa and a couple Eastern European countries. I think they've even donated funds for disaster relief around the world."

"Yes," Tate said quietly. "That's all true."

"So, why…I mean—"

"Sloan used to be her assistant campaign manager," Tate said. "So maybe he set up the account. But Coco did track down an address for Imagine, Inc." He took a breath. "In Vegas."

The room went silent.

"Tate. You're not thinking of going there, are you?" RJ said softly.

Tate turned and walked out, needing air.

He stood on the deck of the cabin, staring out at the lake. Storm clouds had gathered overhead, the air pregnant with doom, casting a pallor over the pellet-gray lake.

Vicktor followed him out. Stood beside him. "What's in Vegas?"

Tate glanced at him. Looked away. "My past."

Vicktor had become a sort of friend over the past few days. He'd even taken Tate home to meet his wife, Gracie, and his two sons, ages nine and ten.

Tate leaned over, rested his forearms on the deck. "I was an

FBI informant against the Russian Bratva."

Vicktor said nothing.

"It started a couple years before that, when I went to Vegas. I'd separated from the military after an injury and…well, some dark stuff that went down. And I wasn't in a good place. I didn't set up to get involved with the mob. I was actually working cleaning pools. One of the clients was this Russian guy, and he had a girlfriend named Raquel. He was pushing her around one day while I was there, and…well, we got into a tussle. Unfortunately, the guy fell and hit his head and died. This guy named Yuri showed up and told me that if I worked for him, he'd cover it up. I…" He looked out over the darkening horizon, blew out a breath. "That was the wrong choice, but for a couple years, I was Yuri's man. I showed up, made some threats. Never really hurt anyone, but I didn't like myself. I was dating Raquel and trying to figure out a way out when the FBI approached me. They wanted details on Yuri's weapons dealing…"

He scrubbed a hand over his face. "Yuri found out and I returned home one day to find Raquel, um…" He swallowed, glanced at Vicktor. Shook his head. "It was bad. I gave the FBI what they wanted and ran. Yuri died in prison but left orders to kill me if I ever showed up in Vegas again."

"Slava delivered on those orders?"

"He would have killed me if my brother Knox hadn't shown up."

Thunder rolled across the sky. Tate gave a wry laugh that had nothing to do with humor. "My fiancée had a dream a few nights ago that Sloan killed me. I didn't tell her what we found… so yeah, that's creepy."

"You can't go back."

The voice turned him and he saw RJ standing in the threshold, her arms around her waist, her blue eyes fierce. "I know you think you need to hunt down Sloan and this Slava guy, but Tate— you can't—"

"Slava tried to *kill* you," Tate snapped. "You think I'm just going to sit back and let him come at you—or the rest of our family—again?"

She glanced at York inside, then stepped out onto the deck, lowering her voice. "You think he was after *me?*"

"I don't know who he's after," Tate said. "But I can't help but think that Sloan and Slava are connected. And if we find Sloan, we find Slava."

"And if we find Slava, maybe we can find Damien Gustov and end this," RJ said.

It scared him a little when she talked like that. "RJ, this isn't your fight—"

"It absolutely is, Tate. I started this mess by going to Russia in the first place. And now it's found us here. Why, I don't know, but I'm going to figure it out. So, you can bet I'm going to Vegas to do…well, whatever it is we're doing."

Tate glanced past her, inside to York. He sat with his head in his hands. "And him?"

"I don't know. He's been acting strange all night since the attack." She ran her hands up her arms. "He lost his memory, and I fear that, well, it might be coming back."

"Oh my."

"Yeah." She blew out a breath. "I'm not so sure he'll be joining us."

That, Tate completely understood.

Please stay out of trouble, Rambo.

Glo was so going to kill him.

York's entire body ached. Everything. His brain throbbed from the barrage of images and memories that washed over him like a wave, gobbling him up, drowning him. His bones hurt from pacing all night and the shock of so many memories buzzing under his skin. His heart ached from the onslaught of loss that felt at once raw and fresh and eviscerating.

But what hurt most was his soul.

What had been washed clean, fresh and new and whole, was now littered with horror. His past had poured destruction and filth onto clean soil, shards of dark memories that told him just who he'd been. What he'd done.

York wanted to run. From himself, for sure, but definitely from RJ.

Because she knew—*knew*—who he'd been. Or at least enough of it, and she'd *lied* to him.

You're one of the good guys.

Not. Even. Close.

She'd stayed with him while he'd sat, almost catatonic, in the throes of sheer panic after the dark part of him had recognized Slava.

He'd wanted to curl into the fetal position—instead he'd walked out to the lakeshore, watched the moon, fractured by clouds, break light upon the water. The cold breath off the surface crooked a finger at him, tempting him to walk in and let the water bury him. To erase from this earth the man he'd been, the anger, the grief, the fury, the frustration…the *hatred*. Oh, the hatred.

It embedded his heart like claws, and he'd forgotten its grip until it rushed back in, and he'd nearly cried out from the abrupt force of it.

The other memories came slower—trickling in, taking their time to find footing. Most of them were still jumbled up like a box of puzzle pieces dumped out on the table with no form or linear fashion, just snapshots and images…

"How are you doing?" RJ walked in from the deck where she'd been convening with her brother, worry in her eyes. She'd slept on the sofa all night, awake when he left for the lake, awake when he returned—so maybe she hadn't slept at all.

York hadn't recognized Tate—not right away. His presence was more of a thumbprint on a familiar bruise. But it came to him slowly that Tate had been there when he'd been arrested. He didn't remember much past that, however.

RJ sat down next to him. "How's your head?"

"It feels like I got run over by a locomotive." He gave her a wry grin.

He knew she blamed herself for alerting the Russian to where he was, but who knew, really. A guy with his past could have any number of people looking for him.

York gave her a dark look, bracing himself. "Who is Jason Mack? Did I kill him?"

She drew in a breath. "Oh, York…no, I'm sure—"

"Are you, though? Because how did I come out of the crash with his name stuck inside me?"

When Vicktor had told him the story of the crash—none of which York remembered—and the missing kid who just so happened to have the name he'd come to town with…well, that, coupled with his sharp-edged memories, had York wanting to retch.

What kind of terrible man had he been? He couldn't bear to know any more.

But he'd have to, probably, because the past certainly wasn't interested in staying put. Not when it sent Russian thugs after him.

"I don't know, York. I just know you're a good—"

York held up his hand, cutting RJ off from more lies and platitudes. "What does your brother think we should do?"

A beat, then, "He thinks that we should go to Vegas. He thinks Slava and Sloan are working together and that if we find one, we might also find the other, and then some real answers." Her blue eyes pinned to his. "But I think you should stay here."

He frowned. "These guys were after me. I should go and finish this."

"What do you remember?"

"Snippets, mostly, but I do remember being with you on that train in Russia."

"Oh," she said and gave him a thin smile.

Probably because part of that memory included them kissing. He did remember that very, very much.

But he also remembered the man who attacked him and what York had done to get rid of him. So, in truth, he just couldn't look at RJ. Not without seeing the darkness of his own heart.

"What else do you remember?" RJ asked.

"I remember meeting you in Moscow. The alleyway. And a pool."

"That was at Coco's father's place. Do you remember…well, who he is?"

"Yes. Boris Stanislov. A Russian general, one of the troika—the command at the top."

"And the one that I was blamed for trying to kill."

There were other things that he remembered, but he didn't say them because most of them involved things that he himself wanted to forget. All over again. Like his hands wrapped around someone's neck—a woman's, he thought—and…yes, RJ should stay far, far away from him.

He got up and walked over to the window. "I remember that you're still in danger. If anyone's going to Vegas, I am. And if anyone's staying away, it's you." He turned around and looked at her. "I dragged you into an old-time feud. I know Damien Gustov and I go back because that name is written into my soul."

"He killed your girlfriend a few years ago. Ran her over in the snow in January."

She said it without tone, but he still flinched.

"I think I remember that." He scrubbed a hand down his face. "The memories are coming back, but only in bits and pieces, and nothing feels easy or in the right place. I have a hazy memory of my wife and child, but I don't recall how they died." He braced a hand on the window sill. "Maybe I don't want to. Maybe that's just my brain repressing the things that still hurt."

"Maybe," she said softly, "but that tells me that you're in no condition to leave. I think you should stay here in this town and recover. Get your memories back if you need to or…not." She stood up. "York—Mack. You're a different person now. One you've always wanted to be. You don't have to finish this."

He winced, then turned to her. "Not if there's going to be more people who show up on Jethro's doorstep. I might not know everything, but I know I have to put the past to rest before I can have another life. I don't have a choice. I'm going to go get my stuff."

"York—"

He ignored her and headed down to the lower level, to his tiny guest bedroom.

Went in and closed the door behind him. Sank down on the double bed, his head in his hands.

A soft knock broke through the quiet. "Mack?"

Jethro.

Thankfully the man hadn't been seriously injured—more blood than wound when they shined the light on him.

"Come in," York said, getting up. He didn't really have anything to pack except a toothbrush. Hopefully he could take the clothes on his back, but...

"Taking off?"

He couldn't even look at Jethro, at the massive goose egg on his forehead.

"Apparently I have some unfinished business with the man I used to be." He didn't mean for it to sound so dark, so jaded.

"That's the key—the man you *used* to be. Not anymore."

Jethro pulled a duffel bag from the closet and put it on the bed.

"Apparently the man I am is just a fake. The guy I was—"

"Is dead." Jethro walked over to the dresser and opened a drawer. "He died when you went forward in church yesterday."

Jethro scooped out a handful of T-shirts and put them in the duffel.

"Jethro, you don't know what I did, I mean...I—"

"Regardless of who you were in the past, Mack, you are a new person today. When you gave your sins to Jesus and received forgiveness, He made you new. The past is dead. Now the question is, what are you going to do with your new life?"

Jethro pulled out another drawer. Jeans.

"It feels like I was just, I don't know, playing a role. Wanting something so much that—"

"That God gave you a chance to have it. To see what it felt like to be free, to be whole, to be forgiven." Jethro put the pants in the duffel bag. "You would have never stepped foot in a church in your previous state, I'll bet."

York considered him. "Probably not."

"And yet, your soul yearned to be clean, to be new. And God, in His mercy, knew it. So, He gave you a clean slate. A fresh start.

The opportunity to be the man you wanted to be."

It wasn't a question, but York nodded.

"So what that you were a killer in your past."

York's eyes widened. "You know—"

"I'm not stupid. I was a Marine. I know the look in a man's eyes when he's been through war—"

"I haven't been through—"

"We're always at war with good and evil in this world. No one escapes it. It's how we see it, how we recognize it that engages us in battle. And if it's not externally, then it's in our flesh. In our soul. War is all around us. And sometimes…well, sometimes we find ourselves doing things in war that we would never do in times of peace."

"Jethro. I really…I remember killing people."

"Me too."

York looked at him. "You were awarded the Medal of Honor. That's vastly different."

"Is it? Because here's how I see it—I was asked to do a job by my country. We came under fire, and a couple of my fellow soldiers, as well as my platoon leader, were wounded and left in an exposed position. I was a medic. There to pull my men away from the battlefield. But out of sheer panic, I took command. We assaulted the position of the hostiles and killed them. Then we took out another position, during which I killed four men and took out an anti-tank weapon." He zipped up the duffel bag. "One was a kid—maybe seventeen. But we rescued our platoon leader and those soldiers, and they gave me a medal. I wasn't even doing my job—I was simply reacting. Am I more of a hero than the next guy? Maybe. I don't know."

He handed York the duffel bag. "What isn't in the citation is that after the shooting stopped, after we evacuated our guys, after we got back to our positions, I found myself a corner and emptied my gut. I saw myself do things in the heat of battle that I would have never thought I could do. But that moment doesn't define me, even if they gave me a medal. What does define me, tells me who I am? How I live every day. So you need to go and do what you need to do, but you do it as a new man. As a man who is not his own anymore but in the service of a new commander. The Lord God Almighty. Who, by the way, says, 'I will fight for you. Your victory is already won.'"

York stood there, holding the duffel bag.

"What are you waiting for, kid? I'm going to say the same thing I said to Ace…God made you the way he did for a reason. Go, be awesome."

York's throat tightened, but he met Jethro's hand. "Maybe I'll be back."

"We'll be waiting for you."

York wasn't talking to her.

And RJ didn't blame him.

It wasn't like he was giving her the silent treatment—sure he was talking to her, like, *I can get a hotel room, RJ. I don't need to stay with your family.*

And, *I really think you should stay in Seattle, let Tate and me handle this.*

That sort of thing.

But what she really longed for was a private conversation. One that told her that he didn't regret knocking on her door, asking her to tell him about his past.

A conversation that might ease the clench around her chest that said she'd wrecked his life.

Or at least the life he'd hoped to have.

RJ stood on the balcony of Wyatt's loft overlooking the Sound, staring out into the darkness. The Ferris wheel cast twinkle lights into the velvet sky, and out in the middle of the dark water, deck lights from ferries and dinner cruises glowed against the blackness.

The scents from Pike Place Market rose—bakery, exotic spices, even the faintest hint of fresh fish from today's mongers. Of course Wyatt had to have the nicest place on the block—a loft with exposed beams, wood floors, copper counters and fixtures, hand-tufted rugs, deep coffee-brown leather sofas, and a table that seated fourteen. Three guest bedrooms were all accessed by sliding barn doors, and a master bedroom loft overlooked it all.

The place probably cost a cool three mil, but who was counting? RJ was just thankful to have a place to hide out, regroup.

Figure out how it had all gone so wrong.

She slid her phone into her pocket, her conversation with Crowley fresh in her mind.

"You found him," Crowley had said. "And?"

"He lost his memory. We're not sure what happened, but it looks like he had some head trauma in the crash. He ended up in a small town in Washington State. I found him, and he is piecing things back together, but...we were attacked."

Crowley had listened to the altercation, and then she'd outlined their plan to go to Vegas. She'd asked him to use the vast resources of the CIA to check into the connection between Slava and Sloan.

He promised to look into it and told her to keep in touch before they hung up.

"Uh oh, I know that face." Her mother stepped onto the balcony, set down one of the wine glasses she carried, then closed the sliding door behind her.

RJ looked at her mother.

"Reminds me of that day you decided to ride Wyatt's bike. That ten-speed was way too big for you. But you were determined to ride it, even though we warned you not to."

"As I remember, I wiped out, and good."

"And your father—oh, he sprinted all the way down the road—couldn't get to you fast enough."

"I felt like a baby when he picked me up and carried me. I was *ten*."

"You were his daughter. And he was your father. Of course he'd save you."

She smiled, her eyes blurry. "Yes, he would."

Her throat filled.

"Are you okay?"

She sighed. "No."

"Here." Her mother handed her a glass of red wine. "Tate

told me about the attack." She touched the bruise on RJ's neck, and her mouth tightened around the edges. "Good thing York was there."

"He would've never gotten attacked if I hadn't been so stupid to make that phone call and then follow him to Shelly. I should have just left him alone to remake his life." She sipped the wine, then set it on a teak patio set. "He was fine until I got there."

"Oh, stop fooling yourself. He had no memory, RJ. And I don't care what York has done in the past, a person can't live too long with not knowing himself."

RJ shook her head. "You didn't see him, Ma. He was…he was at peace. And then I walked back into his life."

She glanced behind her. The lights were on in the main room, illuminating the crowd. Tate was on the phone, pacing in the bedroom, the door open. Coco sat at the long table on her computer, of course. Wyatt was home, too, and sitting on one of the leather sofas next to Mikka, his son. They were playing a video game on his phone. Knox had also shown up briefly, then taken off again, apparently to pick up his fiancée, who'd been hanging out with Glo at some vacation place in Cannon Beach.

"Honey, peace isn't about our circumstances—it's about our state of being. York was *not* at peace."

She turned to her mother. "He went to the altar at church."

"Really."

"Ma, I swear he was a new man when he got up. I saw his face…I'd never seen him so, well, at peace. And I destroyed it."

"RJ. He was at peace because he was forgiven. He's still forgiven. Now he just knows from how much."

RJ drew in a breath, rubbed her hands on her arms. Turned and looked back at the Sound. "I'm worried he's going to end up hurt—or killed—because of me. I should have never gone to Russia."

"Oh, now we're back to that?"

"If I hadn't gone to Russia, then York wouldn't have had to rescue me, and Ford—well, he nearly got killed. And then Wyatt got into the mess with Coco, and somehow I brought a serial assassin to America to kill the VP hopeful."

"Wow, I didn't realize you were that cunning." Her mother set down her wine glass on the railing, running her fingers up and down the stem.

"Ma."

"No, you listen. Every single person on that list had a choice. York didn't have to come running to your aid, and neither did Ford. Wyatt was just waiting to find Coco, and if some killer wants to take out the VP candidate, well, you're hardly responsible for that."

She drew in her breath. "I just feel like...well, like the troublemaker in the family."

"No, honey, that's Tate."

"Ma."

Her mother smiled. "Actually, you all do your fair share of getting in over your heads. That's why I came out here—I can't listen to any more of Tate's plotting to break into a hotel room of a man who tried to have him killed." She shook her head. "If I could, I'd wrap you all up and take you home, feed you cookies, and read you bedtime stories."

"No, you wouldn't. You were worse than Dad about telling us to go out and live our great adventures."

She grinned. "Maybe with you. I needed to balance out your father. Your dad liked to protect you, especially after we almost lost you in that cave with Ford."

RJ winced. "I still remember the way he yelled at Ford. Told him that he shouldn't have gotten me in over my head. But it wasn't his fault, Ma. He told me where to swim, but I was curious. I wasn't a good swimmer, but I didn't think anything would happen, so I got too near the rapids. Ford had to go after me. And then I refused to let him rescue us." She shook her head. "I'm so tired of my brothers feeling obligated to help me."

She glanced over her shoulder. "And I think York feels the same way. Obligated. Because if I'd left him alone, he'd be sitting under the stars with a sweet girl named Raven, who wouldn't drag him into some conspiracy to kill the VP candidate."

"RJ. No one is obligated to help you. Or be with you." Her mother put her arm around her shoulder. "Or love you."

RJ's jaw tightened. "I'd just like to know that maybe I was loved by choice, you know? Not just because they're family and have to."

"York had a choice—he didn't have to rescue you."

Poor man.

If she could, she'd go back to that day that York had made her run away in an alleyway in Russia, leaving him behind, and she'd stay. Fight her battle instead of calling for help from her brothers—any of them. She wasn't a kid. She didn't need to be carried or protected.

"*Stand back and see what I will do*," her mother said.

RJ looked at her mother blankly.

"It's what God said to Moses when he faced the Israelites. And then again when Jehoshaphat faced the Moabites. In fact, in that battle, all the people of Israel had to do was praise the Lord. He did all the fighting for them. See, sometimes we get so wrapped up in what we think we need to do to make something happen, we forget that God is actually the one orchestrating it all. Fighting our battles. God will show up even when we've made a mess of things. Even when it's our fault—*He will show up*. Because that's who He is—He loves us by choice, not because we deserve His help. There's no if...just when. And His timing is perfect."

She kissed her daughter on the cheek. "Oh, and if you want to use my little 9-mil pistol you can. It's still in my purse."

"Ma—"

"I have a conceal and carry. I'm legal."

"Last time you shot the gun you nearly took York's head off."

"I missed on purpose. If I wanted to shoot someone, I would. Not saying I want to, though."

RJ shook her head.

"Listen to me, Ruby Jane. God put you in York's life—and you in his—for a reason. Go be that reason."

RJ said nothing as her mother went back inside.

But yes. God had clearly put them together. Over and over.

And their story wasn't over.

She was going to go to Vegas and do what she'd gone to

Russia to do in the first place…stop an international assassin. And then…and then they'd have a private conversation about what life York wanted to live.

And with whom.

9

See, everything was going to be just fine.

Perfect, in fact.

Tate had said *Set a date*. So Glo had set a date.

And last night on the phone, Tate hadn't so much as hiccuped his hesitation at her ten-days-from-now announcement.

So maybe Glo's fears really did reside only in her head.

Maybe everything was going to work out, she'd marry the man of her dreams, her singing career would skyrocket, her mother would be elected as VP, and they'd all live happily ever after.

After all, Glo had even won the showdown with her mother. Sure, she'd caught the senator in-flight, on her way to an event in Ohio, and her mother probably had her current speech notes in one hand, a cup of coffee in the other as she spoke to Glo on her earpiece, but her only concern was, of course, "We'll have to make a media announcement immediately and offer up the contract to sell the photos. I'm sure *People* Magazine will want them."

Right. Oh, Tate would be thrilled with the idea of his face in every grocery store.

Oh, and, "It'll have to be on Friday night—Saturday I'm due in Minneapolis."

"Friday night is fine," Glo had said. "I'm thinking just a small event at the house in Nashville. By the pool. Just the band, a few friends, and the Marshall family."

"Whatever you'd like, darling."

What? Glo had never heard those words emerge from her mother's mouth before.

It was much more expected coming from Tate. "Whatever you want, babe, I'm in."

So, yes, Glo had probably dreamed up all her fears—literally. Because after that night, a week ago when she'd talked to Tate, her nightmares vanished.

Now, it was just a matter of finding the right dress.

"I've got you set up for a private fitting." Her friend Cher held the door open as Glo, Dixie, and Kelsey entered Nora's, a private bridal shop in the Green Hills district of Nashville. "Nora said she'd work with you personally. She works with designers, and I know you'll probably need an in-stock dress, but that doesn't mean you can't get a one-of-a-kind sample."

Cher wore a green maxi dress and gold sandals, her red hair caught back, and large gold hoop earrings. Glo felt spectacularly underdressed in her faded jeans, a white tunic, and flip-flops. But she had just gotten off a flight from Seattle, during which she'd approved a catering menu of brie and apple beer soup, a pumpkin seed and fig vinaigrette salad, filet mignon with a demi-glace, and butternut squash ravioli.

Cake tasting was later on today's schedule, again, courtesy of Cher, who had contacts she'd used before during the book launches of her handful of best-selling authors. Apparently, being an acquisitions editor for one of the largest Nashville-based publishers had its advantages.

"She's picked out a few dresses similar to the samples you pinned on your Pinterest board."

"I think Kelsey pinned most of those," Glo said and glanced at her friend who was stopped in front of a lacy A-line dress worn by a faceless mannequin. And Dixie had stopped in front of a mermaid dress that would only add va-va-voom to her already tall and willowy figure.

"Are things getting serious with Elijah Blue?" Glo asked her as Dixie turned away and followed her into the suite. Dixie had been secretly dating their drummer for the better part of three months. Or maybe not so secretly because even though they hadn't mentioned it to their bandmates, Dixie and Elijah shared a look that hid nothing.

Dixie blushed. Lifted a shoulder. "We're here for you."

"This place is magical," Kelsey said as she followed them to two long, pink velour sofas that faced a dais and three massive mirrors.

A gold chandelier hung from the ceiling, dripping a kaleidoscope of lights onto the white carpet. Chamber music played overhead, and on a tufted gold ottoman, a charcuterie tray held cheeses, meats, crackers, grapes, and fluted glasses of champagne.

Glo was really getting married.

She stepped up on the dais and looked in the mirrors. Oh, she looked tired, bags under her eyes, her white-blonde hair held back by a white bandanna, wild in the back. Maybe she was rushing things, maybe—

"Gloria Jackson. What an honor to fit you with the perfect dress." The voice came from their hostess, Nora Kleinfeld, mid-fifties, petite, with pixie short, curly dark hair and thick red glasses. She wore a pair of billowy black pants, platform heels, a tight white tank, and a slew of bangles on both arms, which she opened as she stepped up on the dais. She gathered Glo into a hug, then kissed her cheek and pulled back. "Your mother must be so thrilled. Will she be joining us today?"

Oh, wouldn't that be a boon for the shop? To have Reba Jackson's entourage camped outside, the senator herself in the private fitting session.

"No. Sorry. She's still on the campaign trail. But I told her I'd send pictures. And, of course, we'll let everyone know where I got my dress when the press release is written."

"Oh, whatever. Of course." Nora waved her words away. "And who do we have with us today?" She turned to Glo's group, neatly hiding any disappointment, clasping her hands together like they might be a kindergarten class.

"These are my Yankee Belle bandmates, and of course you know Cher. She roomed with me at Vanderbilt, and she'll be my maid of honor."

"Delightful. Cher sent me a number of designs, and I have matched them with some one-of-a-kind gowns from our recent trunk show. I think we can find something you'll like. You ladies settle in to the viewing lounge and we'll get Glo started."

She gestured with her head toward the dressing rooms. Glo walked into the hallway and found her room. Inside, three dresses hung on high hooks, shimmering white, flouncy, lacy, and honestly, Glo didn't know where to start.

"I suppose getting married in my jeans and T-shirt wouldn't be right."

Nora swept in behind her. "Not for the daughter of Senator Reba Jackson, darling. Now, I think we should start with some undergarments, don't you?"

Under— "Like a girdle?"

"We prefer *shapewear*. I'll be back with a sample." She closed the door, and Glo examined the dresses. A strapless ball gown glittered with a sheen of tiny sparkles throughout the entire dress. The second was a vintage A-line with a sheath of embroidery over a V-necked top. But crazily, it was the short one that made her catch her breath. White silk taffeta with an organza overlay bodice, a sweetheart neckline, and a satin waistband. She dug her fingers into the deeply ruffled skirt that looked like roses. The dress would fall right above her knees.

Outrageous, gorgeous, and completely her.

With a pair of white leather snip toe cowboy boots inlaid with crystals, it would be perfect.

A knock came at the door.

"Come in."

The door opened.

"I found my dress," Glo said.

"Perfect."

It wasn't Nora, but a man's voice who answered, and Glo froze. Turned.

Sloan closed the door behind him, locked it, then turned, his dark brown eyes on Glo. "Please don't scream. I come in peace. And I need your help."

He wore a suit, his hair neatly clipped, was clean shaven and didn't look at all like a criminal.

Or the man who'd tried to have Tate beaten to death.

She backed away. "I will scream if you come any closer."

He held up his hand. "Not a step."

She cut her voice low, barely able to hear it over the rush of her heartbeat. Oh, Tate was going to kill...well, her. Because she'd told her protection detail—Swamp and Rags—to grab lunch or coffee or whatever they needed after their long flight.

"How did you find me?"

"Cher. Apparently, you didn't tell her about...well, how things ended between us."

"How things *ended*? Sloan, you tried to have my fiancé killed—"

He held up a hand. "No, actually. I didn't. I'm being set up."

She stared at him. "What?"

"I never sent the Russian after Tate. I don't know who did, but it wasn't me."

Glo cocked her head. "I don't believe you. We figured it out, Sloan. We know you knew about the attack and told my mother about it even before it happened."

"Shh. When Tate sent his goons after me, and I knew no one wanted to hear my side of the story—"

"Which is?"

"Someone inside your mother's organization is working with the Russians. And they're trying to make it look like it's me."

"What—are you crazy?"

He took a step toward her, but she held up her hand.

"Fine. Listen. I got a call from this woman from the CIA not long after I left the campaign. She said she was hunting a rogue group inside the CIA who wanted to reignite the Cold War. She was looking into possible connections to Senator Jackson's staff and wanted to meet with me. I set up a meet in Seattle, but she never showed. Then, about a month later, I get a call and it's her—she says to meet her at a hotel in Seattle. But when I get there, I find the door open and her—dead."

Glo drew in a breath. Because she knew the rest of the story—how RJ and York had also found the body. "Tate thinks she was killed by a Russian assassin."

"See?"

"No, I don't see. Who would want to set you up? My mother's people are loyal—"

"I was loyal. And then I got thrown under the bus—"

"Talk to Tate. He'll straighten it out."

"Are you kidding me?" He shook his head. "Tate would take me apart the moment he saw me."

Yes, probably. She sighed. "So, who do you think it is?"

"I don't know. Maybe her campaign manager, Nicole Stevens."

"We've known Nicole for years. She's run all my mother's campaigns, starting when she ran for mayor."

"I don't know, then!" He blew out a breath. "I just know that I'm a walking target. I've been trying to lay low, but…I'm scared, Glo. These are powerful people."

In truth, she'd never seen Sloan like this. Despite his grooming, his voice shook, and a sweat had broken out across his forehead. So far from the childhood friend, band groupie, and, later, assistant campaign manager that she'd briefly, regrettably dated.

"What can I do?"

"Set up a meeting with your mother."

"What—Sloan, there's no way I can do that."

"Of course you can. Tell her she's in danger. Someone is conspiring against her. Tate can be there too—as long as he doesn't hurt me."

Her mouth tightened. "I don't know…"

"Please—"

"Okay." She held up her hand. "I need to talk to Tate first, and he's not with me right now. He's looking into the attempted assassination in Seattle."

"When will you see him next?"

She gave him a look. "Sloan…"

"Glo. I wasn't responsible for hurting Tate. I promise. And I need your help." He drew in a breath. "You used to trust me, once upon a time. I'm still that guy. The one who went to your shows, the one who cared for you. I would never do something to hurt you."

Oh Sloan. They did have history. And she never wanted to believe that he'd tried to hurt Tate. "I don't know where he is, but I talked to him last night and he said he was following a lead into the attack. He asked me about my mother's organization, Imagine, but I don't know much about it. I don't know what he's up to, but I can ask him to talk to you. No promises though, okay?"

"Yes. Thanks, Glo."

"How do I contact you?"

He shook his head. "I'll find you."

She gave him a look. "Please not at my cake tasting."

A smile slid up the side of his mouth. "Vanilla with strawberry filling was always your favorite."

A knock sounded on the door. "Gloria, are you okay in there? I have the shapewear."

Sloan cocked his head, raised an eyebrow. "Your shape looks pretty good to me," he whispered.

She glared at him, then raised her voice. "I'm fine. I don't think I need them. And I found my dress…I'll meet you in the other room."

"Are you sure you don't need help?"

Sloan's eyes widened.

"I'm fine, thank you."

Footsteps walked away, and she turned to Sloan, her voice low. "Get out of here."

He nodded, reached for the door.

"Sloan—are you going to be okay?"

He drew in a breath, something painfully vulnerable on his face, and the months of fury in her heart faded away.

Maybe he *was* being set up.

"Yes. I think so. Thanks, Glo." He slipped out.

She blew out a breath, tasting again her heartbeat.

Clearly, she'd been wrong about Sloan.

Either that, or she was about to get the man she loved killed.

York did not want to be a man who harbored murder in his heart. Who let anger and vengeance seep in and lurk in the dark corners of his mind. But his dreams—*oh his dreams.* They woke him with such ferocity and then settled like residue until the only thing he could think of was the feelings they left behind.

Like grief. And fury. And an insatiable need for justice.

People in his life had been murdered, and it left an urge to… well, pay back in kind.

But, no. He didn't want to be that man anymore.

He still couldn't look at RJ. Not after the memories flooded back—at least the ones with RJ, from watching her run after the near assassination of General Stanislov, to rescuing her in an alleyway in Moscow, to falling for her as they tried to escape the FSB, then finally following her to America where, for a fraction of a moment, he'd actually thought they could have a happy ending.

She was right. He should have stayed dead—at least then his past wouldn't have tracked him down and suddenly put her in danger again.

As soon as he found Damien Gustov, as soon as he ended it, York would walk away from her again, and this time without a trace. Because how else was he supposed to protect her from whatever demons decided to rise from the past to haunt him?

Knowing RJ, she wouldn't give up until she found him. The woman was as stubborn as her annoying brother Tate, who was laser focused on finding this man Sloan whom he was sure had murdered the woman York and RJ had found in Seattle.

Sophia Randall, RJ's boss.

Which meant it could have just as easily been RJ, and that thought kept York awake staring at the ceiling or pacing the balcony in Wyatt's apartment. York had never been so happy to get on a plane to Vegas.

Good thing Coco, aka Coco, his go-to hacker, still knew how to contact the right people. She'd snagged him a new ID. Twenty-four hours in Seattle and by Wednesday he was officially, illegally Mack Jones.

He hadn't a memory of Vegas, but the place seemed too shiny, too bright, and way too hot, even in October. Tate booked them into a two-bedroom suite with an adjoining room in a downtown hotel—Tate and RJ in the suite, York next door. Apparently, big brother wasn't about to let RJ out of his sight either.

"This place has a shark tank," RJ said now as she came down the stairs from her bedroom in the loft upstairs.

"You can stay behind and hit the pool," Tate said, coming in off the balcony overlooking a banana-shaped pool curled around a large aquarium.

The place smelled slightly of cigarette smoke, and York didn't want to imagine the parties that had gone down in this place. It made him long for the tiny bedroom at Jethro's, despite the short amount of time he'd spent there.

Tate wore a suit, so York had purchased a pair of dress pants and a jacket. Although he was grateful for Jethro's gift of Ace's clothing, it still felt weird to wear the hand-me-downs, and he needed a suit to keep up with Tate's suggestion that they should be prepared for anything when they walked into Imagine, Inc.

York knew that Tate was hoping he might walk in and find Sloan eating a turkey sandwich, just waiting, apparently, for Tate to show up and start demanding answers.

Probably not likely, but Tate seemed to believe that if they found Sloan, they'd find Slava, and since York didn't know where else to start looking for the Russian thug, it sounded like as good a plan as any.

RJ wore a light blue sun dress that did amazing things for her eyes, a pair of flat sandals, her dark hair back in a loose bun, and for a second he wanted to be anywhere but here.

Anywhere else, and someone else, with her.

Mack Jones and Sydney Bristow, starting over. *Do you think we'd be happy in a small town like this? Making lasagna for dinner?*

Maybe.

Then her blue eyes met his and he had to look away.

"Let's go," Tate said.

They had no weapons, but in the middle of the day probably they wouldn't find trouble, even if they did manage to run into Sloan.

Please. Still, as he held the door open for RJ, "Are you sure you don't want to stay here?"

The look she gave him shut his mouth.

They took the elevator down—fifteen flights—and headed past the lobby, the smoky casino pit with its dinging slot machines, and out into the heat.

Oh, the heat. It poured over him, and sweat slithered down his back. He rued his long hair, even if he had shaved.

"It's only two blocks away," Tate said and quick-walked toward Fourth Street.

He pointed to a building next to the US Bank building, a six-story, all-glass office building across the street from a US government office and a four-story parking ramp.

Please, God, don't let any of them get hurt.

And funny that the prayer—if that was what it was—even emerged because York had been too embarrassed to talk to God since…well, since he'd realized just how absurd it was that he'd even stepped foot at the altar.

God had to have been laughing at his audacity.

As York entered the cool air of the sleek marble lobby, Jethro's words threaded through him. *Your soul yearned to be clean, to be new. And God, in His mercy, knew it. So, He gave you a clean slate. A fresh start. The opportunity to be the man you wanted to be.*

Maybe, someday, he could be again.

Until then, York had unfinished business.

Tate read the lobby information. "Imagine, Inc. is on the fourth floor." He took the stairs up. York and RJ followed him.

They emerged into an elevator area and a short hallway. Imagine, Inc.'s name and logo—a swash with ocean colors—were affixed to a door at the end.

"Huh," Tate said. "I thought for sure we'd find an empty building." He walked down the hall and opened the door.

"And you'd be right," York said, coming in behind him. Because although the logo hung on a wall behind a built-in reception desk, nothing else remained of a functioning office but some spilled shredded paper in one of the rooms.

Tate headed over to a window in one of the vacant offices

and looked out onto the street below, maybe hoping he'd see Sloan slinking away in a moving van.

RJ crouched in front of the shredded paper in the second office, running her fingers through it, picking up some of the bigger pieces. *Good luck with that*, York almost said, but his darkness didn't need to bleed out onto her, so he went into the third office, at the end of the hall.

Stared out at the parking garage.

"Maybe they knew we were onto them," York said.

"You think?" said Tate as he walked out of his room. "Only, how?"

RJ held a couple fragments of paper. "These are financial reports, but they're too small to piece together."

Tate made a face, his mouth a grim line, and shook his head. "Let's get back to the hotel and call Coco. See if she's been able to ping Sloan's number."

Tate had his collar unbuttoned by the time he reached the street. RJ didn't speak, her gaze far away, as if she might be thinking.

York kept his head down, not sure he shouldn't just say goodbye to RJ and vanish.

Maybe lure Slava off their trail.

"York, are you okay?" The question came from RJ as she fell in beside him. Tate was ahead, nearly to the light.

"Yeah," York said.

"No, you're not. You've barely spoken to me since we left Shelly. I don't know what I did."

"You didn't do anything." He grabbed her elbow as they came up to the light, a weird reflex he didn't know he possessed. She didn't shrug away, but he dropped his grip.

She knew how to cross the street, for Pete's sake.

In fact, maybe he was simply overreacting. After all, she was still here, wasn't she? Clearly tougher than she looked, and if she knew everything about him before he'd lost his memory and still went looking for him, then certainly...

No. He'd seen his nightmares. And he didn't know how much of them were true, but they made him want to run from himself, if he could. Despite the screaming in his heart, he couldn't drag RJ back into the life he'd left.

In fact, he wanted to strangle the other York who'd thought it might be a good idea to follow her to America.

They crossed the street and returned to the cool air of the Golden Nugget Hotel.

Silence surrounded them as they entered the elevator. Tate punched their fifteenth-floor button on the elevator with more gusto than he needed. A couple of women, clearly inebriated, got in next to them. Pool water dripped at their feet. The women wore thongs, their tops too small, and one of them grinned at York through the mirror on the wall. He smiled back, nodded, not sure what else to do.

RJ got off first, glanced at York, and then shook her head. "What?"

"Nothing." She took out her key card and slid it into the door, let herself in. She was up the stairs before Tate closed the door behind them.

"Why is she angry?"

Tate glanced at him. "I don't know. Maybe because she thinks you're giving her the silent treatment. And now smiling at other women."

"I'm not…" But he sighed. "Listen. Your sister deserves better than me—"

"That I can agree with," Tate said. "Or at least the guy I see right now. The one I met a month ago, who'd do anything for her? That guy I liked." He dropped his key card on the bar.

"Yeah, well, I've changed. I'm not sure I can be the guy she knew. Or want to. I kind of hoped I'd left him behind. And now I'm not sure I want to find him again."

Tate looked at him. Nodded. "I get that." He looked out the window. "I was a different man before I met Glo. She made me a better person, for sure. But sometimes, like now, I need the other guy, the guy I was before I met Glo, to show up and do what needs to get done." He looked at York again.

"But the York I met a month ago knew what he wanted and why. He knew the happy ending was worth fighting for. He looked past the things he did to a better tomorrow. To hope. I think that's the guy she misses. Frankly, so do I." He turned and headed toward his room on the main floor.

York went to the window, staring out at the pool below.

Sometimes we find ourselves doing things in war that we would never do... But that moment doesn't define me...

He heard a captured breath and turned. Stilled.

Slava—or at least the man York recognized as the one he'd grappled with on the porch—had a hand around RJ's neck, a gun pressed to her head. He was walking her down the stairs.

RJ's eyes were wide, her jaw tight, and shoot, but he knew it. Deep in his gut where his fears and vengeance and darkness lived, he'd just known something like this was going to happen.

And then, just like that, a flash of memory spurred into his brain, nearly sending him to his knees.

A woman, staring at him, her eyes wide, a man wearing a black nylon mask over his face, his hand around her neck, forcing her down.

He held a thick metal bar, raising it over her.

Run, York!

"I don't want her," Slava said, snapping him back to now. "But if she has to die because you're stupid, that's okay."

York held up his hands. Breathed out. "Don't hurt her."

RJ's eyes glistened. "Sorry. He was in my bathroom."

Out of the corner of his eye, he spotted Tate, just a shadow behind his door.

Slava must have seen his quick glance because he pushed RJ down to the bottom of the stairs and turned her, his back to the window. "Come out, Tate, hands up. One move, and she dies."

Tate came out of the bedroom, his jaw tight, hands up, eyes fierce. He glanced at York, back to RJ.

One of them had to jump Slava, get him away from RJ.

Even if it meant getting shot.

A quick shout should do it—something to distract Slava while the other tackled RJ.

He swallowed, glanced at Tate, who drew in a breath.

Please let the guy be reading his mind because once upon a

time Tate had been spec ops and York had no doubt he wasn't going to sit around and let RJ get hurt.

York shouted and lunged for Slava.

As if RJ and he were in sync, she slammed her fist back, hard, aiming for Slava's groin. He was onto her and dodged, but she slammed her foot into his instep, then twisted out of his grip.

Tate launched himself at her.

A shot went off, the sound muffled with the silencer screwed to the end but still bright enough to galvanize York as he took down Slava.

The shot missed him. But he didn't look to see where the bullet went, too busy dodging Slava's fist to his face.

York deflected it, then grabbed Slava around the neck. The man had a good three inches on him and was clearly used to grappling because he rolled and slammed his body onto the floor, landing on York.

York's breath whooshed out and he lay there like a fish.

Slava whirled around. His fist came at York like a locomotive.

RJ whacked Slava with a lamp, jerking him off course. The blow landed on York's shoulder, and pain seized him.

He gulped for air, wheezed hard, but in that second, Slava hit his feet and rounded on RJ.

Where in the world was Tate?

Slava grabbed the lamp away from her as if she might be a small child. She took one look at him, turned, and fled up the stairs.

Slava turned to follow her, but York hooked his foot around him and tripped him.

York found his breath, the air coming in hard just as Slava scrambled to his feet. The man was a freakin' prize fighter the way he came at York, and he had a memory of the man in Moscow stringing him up and using him like a hanging bag.

Just a quick, dark flash, but fury ignited him.

York launched at Slava, ducking his fist, sending his own into Slava's midsection.

Slava grabbed him around the throat with both hands, cutting off his air.

York hit him again, this time in the face. Drew blood.

Slava's grip tightened.

York's eyesight was getting blotchy. His next punch pushed the big man against the window.

His fingers dug into York's neck. The room shadowed.

A shot shattered the glass.

York broke away, falling.

Slava swore and turned.

RJ stood on the stairs holding a tiny handgun, her aim shaky. "Let him go!"

Slava glanced at York, blood on his face, in his eyes.

York was a dead man.

Another shot.

Slava jerked hard, blood exploding from his chest, and he fell forward, to his knees, one hand out to catch himself.

He was dead before he landed.

York was on his feet, staring up at RJ. "You shot him."

"No—I didn't. I didn't!" She came down the stairs. Her hands still shook, and York took the gun from her.

Checked the clip of the 9mm.

Full, except for one.

"Then—how—"

"Get down!" Tate said from somewhere behind them. "The shot came from the other building!"

York grabbed RJ's wrist and pulled her down, practically landing on top of her behind one of the leather sofas.

Then he covered her body with his, his hands over her head.

"York, I'm fine."

"Stay down," he growled.

Silence, just his heartbeat as he waited.

Nothing but the wind against the drapes.

Tate made a sound, something of a grunt, and he looked up. The man was shrugging off his jacket, his teeth gritted, his arm bloodied.

RJ, too, had looked up. "Tate! You're hit!"

She tried to push York away, but he wasn't moving.

"Sorry, but there's a shooter out there."

"My brother is shot!"

"I'm fine, RJ—"

"Get off me, York."

But he couldn't move, suddenly paralyzed by the fact that—well, that this—*this was his life*. He'd moved with instincts, not a shade of fear as he leaped for Slava. Not a shade of fear and *every intent* on killing the man.

Murder in his heart.

Jethro was wrong. Violence wasn't just a moment but was *embedded* inside him.

With that thought, York practically jerked away from RJ. She scrambled over to Tate, who had crawled behind the bar.

"York, get some towels!"

He ran to Tate's bedroom and pulled a couple towels from the bath. Returned with them to the bar.

RJ ripped the arm from Tate's shirt. A ragged tear scraped across his arm.

"I'm fine."

"You need stitches," she snapped.

Tate looked at York, a quick shake to his head. Stitches meant a hospital which meant questions which probably meant a gunshot reporting. And then there was the dead body in their suite.

Not the first he'd left in a hotel room. "Let's get out of here," York said. "RJ, I'll get your stuff."

She hadn't yet unpacked, her bag open, and he had it zipped shut in moments. Tate just had a backpack, and he grabbed that too.

RJ had wrapped a towel around his arm, and now Tate pulled his suit coat over his shoulders to hide it. "Are you sure we should leave?"

"Yes," Tate and York said, almost simultaneously.

Then Tate added, "We'll call Vicktor and have him contact the police here. And give him our contact info. But I'm worried there's a shooter out there waiting for a clean shot."

York's thought exactly.

They took the stairs down, all fifteen flights, and York grabbed Tate's good arm the last few, just in case he decided to take a header.

York drove them in the rental to a motel outside the city limits, something small, with an inner courtyard that overlooked a peanut-shaped pool. Something he could pay cash for and sneak Tate into.

York settled Tate onto one of the double beds of their adjoining rooms and took a look at his wound. "I'll go to a drugstore and get some antiseptic, topical antibiotic, and superglue. Maybe a bandage so you don't wreck any more shirts, okay?"

Tate nodded. RJ pinched her mouth tight. But as he got up to go to the door, she came after him. And in a voice that wound around his heart asked, "Are you coming back?"

Frankly, she probably read him better than he had himself, because suddenly he wanted to say *no*. That now that Slava was dead, he planned on skipping out on them and leaving this life far behind.

But her beautiful eyes found his, and maybe the man Tate had described wasn't gone. *He knew the happy ending was worth fighting for.*

Or maybe he'd simply merged with the one he wanted to be. The one who had a taste of redemption, of hope.

"I'll be back. I promise."

Tate's pride hurt more than his arm.

Although, in truth, his entire body burned every time he moved his arm—funny how something so superficial could burn through to his bones.

Or maybe it was more about the fact that he'd turned down Glo's calls, twice now. Once last night, right before he'd taken off to Vegas, and one today, while York was patching him up.

She hadn't left a voicemail either.

Tate had to call her back with something that resembled a good reason for declining her calls, probably right after he finished his current call with Vicktor.

RJ closed the motel room door behind her, carrying a cold can of grape soda from the machine down the corridor. She popped the tab and set it on the bedside table between the two double beds, pushing away the box of pizza, now closed, as she sat on the opposite bed.

He put his finger to his lips—pointed to the call, on speaker.

"According to my contact, they've already picked up the body and it's heading to the coroner. I've asked him to keep me in the loop when ballistics comes back," Vicktor said.

"It could be the same guy who killed Kobie at the wharf in Seattle." Tate reached for the soda with his good arm.

"Your Russian friend Gustov."

"How did he know where we were? And why did he kill Slava?"

"Maybe he missed."

Right then, Tate knew he should take the cop off speaker. But his hand was holding the soda and the other arm was bandaged and useless and he wasn't fast enough—

"Maybe he was aiming at you."

RJ's eyes widened.

Shoot. Tate made a face, shook his head as he met her eyes and spoke into the phone. "We don't know that. And if he is, then he's a terrible shot—"

"But you're the only constant in both events."

Except, and he hated to say it, but, "And York. He was there too."

RJ caught her lower lip between her teeth.

York had gone outside after returning to bandage Tate up. He'd done a decent job, his hands practiced as he glued the wound's edges together, added antibiotic ointment, and covered it with a bandage.

But York hadn't even looked at RJ when he left, and Tate wasn't entirely sure he was coming back. The man seemed particularly silent, almost broody as he'd driven them to the semi-seedy motel with lime-green walls, ancient carpet, and a painted fish over the beds.

If Tate was going to die, he would have preferred the presidential suite, but York was probably right to move them and lie low.

"Yes, right," Vicktor said, agreeing that York might be a target. "Clearly Slava and whoever he's working for know that York's alive. But his position on the wharf was a considerable distance from Kobie's. You were the closest probable target. Especially given your other run-in with Slava and the Russian mob six months ago."

Thank you for that, Vicktor.

RJ got up and began to pace, her hands wrapped around her waist.

"If you give me the number of the detective, we'll give our statements tomorrow," Tate said.

"I'll text it to you, but he's already expecting you."

Tate paused, then, "And I'm just confirming this, but Slava really is dead, right? No more sudden appearances in hotel rooms?"

"Yes. Chest shot, through the heart."

Tate didn't want to cheer, but maybe he could stop looking over his shoulder for the shadow of the Russian mob. Except, "Only problem is, there goes our connection to Sloan. We can't question a dead man."

"I'll keep looking. Hang tight. I'll be in touch," Vicktor said and hung up.

Tate set his soda can down. Picked up his phone. Blew out a breath.

"And that's the look of a man who knows he's in trouble," RJ said. "I don't need to be an analyst to figure that out."

"Glo called. Twice."

"Oh."

"She doesn't know I went after Slava."

RJ raised an eyebrow.

"I just thought…well, the less she knew, the better. But when she hears I got shot—"

"Yes, bro, you are in deep trouble." She walked back over to the other bed. "This might help." She pulled a phone from her pocket and set it on the table between the beds.

Tate stared at it.

"It's Slava's."

166

"What? How?"

"When York was helping you out of the flat, I searched the body."

"Why didn't you say anything?" He nearly leaped for it.

She slammed her hand over it. "Not so fast there, Slick. You want this phone and the information on it, you need to keep me in the loop. I know you and James Bond out there are freaked out, but I am *in this*. All the way to the bitter end. No matter what happens."

"Sis—"

"Stop protecting me, Tate."

"Stop being so freakin' stubborn! Protecting you is my job—"

"You're fired."

"Funny. I can't be fired from being your brother."

"You got shot! He could have just as easily hit something more vital than your arm."

"That's my choice."

"It is, you're right. But just because you want to protect me doesn't mean I have to stand on the sidelines. This is my investigation. I started it, I get to end it."

He looked at her, his chest rising and falling.

She raised an eyebrow.

"Fine. You're in. Now give me the phone so I can call Coco."

"Not until you call Glo."

"What is your problem?"

"She doesn't need protecting either."

His jaw tightened. "She very much needs protecting."

"From whoever is trying to kill her mother, yes. From you, no. She's all in, Tate. And you need to let her be."

"She has enough on her plate right now." He made a face. "Besides, she actually had a dream that Sloan shot me."

Her mouth made a round O.

"So imagine how she's going to feel when she finds out she was right."

"It wasn't Sloan," RJ said.

"I still got shot."

RJ sighed. "I think you need to trust her with all of you, Tate.

Not just the things that you want her to hear. Or see. You're the guy who steps into the line of fire. And she knows that. Give her the benefit of the doubt."

"This sounds more like what you'd like to say to York."

"It's reusable."

He gave her a small smile. "Okay, I'll call Glo. Then, can I please have the phone?"

She lifted her hand.

He glanced toward the door. Back to her. "Give him space. He'll come back to you."

She shook her head. "I can't help but feel that I should've never tracked him down. I just brought danger back into his life. But now that I have, we need to finish this. And then…well, then York can be free."

He frowned, but she turned away and headed out the door.

He picked up the phone and dialed Glo.

His fiancée answered on the first ring. "Hey, Rambo."

"Hey," he said. "Sorry I couldn't take your calls. I was talking with Vicktor." He eyed the phone RJ had found. "I think we have a lead on Sloan."

Glo was quiet. Then, "Really?"

"Well, I hope so. I…I have to tell you something."

She drew in a breath. "Me too, but…you can go first."

If it was about the wedding, yes, he needed to go first. Because then she could spend the next hour talking about the wedding and he'd listen and by the time they were finished, he could be the hero again.

Oh, he hoped.

"I'm still in Vegas."

A beat, then, "And? Did you find what you were looking for?"

"Not so much."

A pause. "What happened?"

He took a breath.

"No secrets, Tate."

Oh boy. "I came here to find Sloan. We have a lead that he might be connected to the Russian mob. I didn't find him, but…I did run into Slava."

Silence. Then, "The man who beat you up?"

"I got a few licks in—"

"Whatever—*why on earth* isn't he in jail?"

"Actually, he's dead."

"*What?*"

"He was killed today in my hotel room." And oh, he was so skimming across the surface, but he just didn't want—

"Your *hotel* room? Oh, Tate, did he—he didn't ambush you again, did he?"

Shoot. He should have rephrased that. "Yes—no, sorta—he ambushed RJ."

"RJ? Is she okay?"

"Yes, she's fine. She shot him."

"RJ *killed* Slava?"

"No—he was killed by a sniper—"

"A *sniper? What*—"

"Calm down. Everything is fine. I was hit, but it's just a nick—"

"*You were hit!*" Nothing in her voice said calm.

Maybe she should have gone first.

"Glo, I'm fine."

But her breath was catching and she sounded like she might be trying not to cry.

"Babe, I'm fine. York superglued it shut, and we have a phone from Slava so we can track down Sloan's whereabouts—"

"*I know where Sloan is!*"

His heart thumped. "What?"

"I know where Sloan is. Or was, at least. He came to see me yesterday."

"*What?*" And now his voice had hit higher decibels. "Where?"

"In my dressing room at the bridal shop—"

"In your *dressing* room?"

"I was fully clothed, but here's the important part—"

"Where was Swamp?"

"I sent him to lunch."

"He's a dead man."

"Tate! Listen to me. Sloan is innocent."

He had nothing, just his heart slamming against his chest wall. "No, he's not."

"He wasn't the one who told Slava where you were."

"That doesn't make sense. Of course he was—"

"He said he didn't."

"And now we'll never know, will we? Because Slava is *dead*."

"Sloan didn't kill him."

"How do you know?"

"Because—I don't know. He's not a sniper? He's a politician?"

"Same thing."

"Tate."

"Fine. But listen to me, Glo. Sloan is not innocent. He's up to his eyeballs in this thing. I saw him on camera at the hotel where Sophia Randall was murdered."

Nothing, so he continued. "When I was visiting Vicktor's office, I saw a picture of Sloan, caught on a security camera. He was at the hotel and very possibly the killer."

"I know he was there, Tate."

"What?"

"He told me that he was being set up. That someone had called him and told him to go there, but when he got there, he found her murdered."

"He's lying."

"You should have seen him—"

"I'd like to see him, believe me. In person. Preferably alone, in a closed and locked room."

"Tate. Please."

"No, Glo. He's using you."

"He wants to set up a meeting with my mother and you, to tell his side of the story."

"You've got to be kidding."

"Not even a little, Mr. I-Got-Shot-Today!"

He drew in a breath. "I'm sorry. I should have told you I was going to Vegas."

"You *think*?" And now she was crying. "I had a dream, Tate. A dream that you were going to get killed."

"By Sloan, not Slava—"

"It doesn't matter! Don't you think, for one second, you might have thought twice about hunting down someone who had tried to kill you? And nearly succeeded. I'll never forget sitting in that hospital, watching you try to breathe. Try. To. *Breathe.* Do you have *any* idea what that feels like? To fear that your next breath will be your last?"

"Glo—"

"It *shattered* me, Tate. I still have nightmares about it. I can't...I can't go through that again. Ever."

"Glo. I'm not going to die."

"Don't even—"

"I'm fine!"

Silence.

He waited for a response, anything, but the line was painfully quiet. "Glo? Are you there?"

He looked at his phone.

She'd hung up.

What the— He pushed Redial and it went to voicemail.

Nice, Glo. But he waited for the voicemail to pick up. "You'd better be just mad at me and not suddenly dodging a bullet or something. Text me back, tell me you're okay, or I'm on the next plane to Tennessee."

He hung up and waited.

And waited.

And when the text finally came in, he wanted to throw his phone across the room.

I'm fine. But we're not.

The wedding is off.

———◆———

RJ just couldn't escape the feel of York's body covering hers, his legs bracketing her hips, his arms around her shoulders, his breath against her neck, protecting her with his body.

And sure, the word *sniper* hung in the air, but still, even after she'd told him she was fine, he hadn't moved. As if reluctant to let her go. And oh, she hoped it was more than fear but something deeper that made York hang on to her.

The thing that had made his heart remember her even when his brain couldn't.

She spotted him, a dark shadow sitting by the pool on a lounger, staring at the water. He didn't even move as she came up and sat down on a nearby lounger.

For a long while, she said nothing. Because Tate had probably been right when he suggested giving York space. But despite Vicktor's words, she had no doubt that that shot had been aimed today for York.

Not Slava. And certainly not *Tate*—that was crazy.

Damien Gustov was after York, she knew it in her bones.

"Who is Martin?"

The question jerked her out of her thoughts. She looked over to the man who had changed into a T-shirt and a pair of cargo shorts, flip-flops.

He looked very much like the Mack Jones he'd left behind.

But given the look on his face, Mack was long gone, replaced with someone dark, brooding.

Broken.

"Why?"

"I keep seeing this face. Tough guy, dark hair, square jaw. And I hear myself call him Martin. But it's just a puzzle piece that doesn't fit anywhere."

"You used to work with him in Russia. When you were in the CIA."

"So I trusted him."

"I'm not sure. You did seem surprised to see him."

He nodded. "That's what I feel when I think of him. Surprise."

"Crowley said he thought Martin might have been the one to blow your cover with the Bratva, but he wasn't sure."

York looked over at her. "Blow my cover? I worked undercover?"

"That's how your wife and son were killed. Your informant turned on you—"

"Please don't tell me any more."

She closed her mouth, her throat tightening as he sank his

face into his hands. He was so strong, it undid her to see him unraveled. "York, that was a long, long time ago."

Oh, she longed to touch him. To climb onto the back of his lounger, wrap her arms around him, and pull him against herself. Help him hold on as he faced his past.

"I'm so sorry I tracked you down."

He looked up then, his eyes hot. "Are you kidding me? What if Slava had found me first and killed Jethro? Or Raven? Or you?" He got up from the chair, pacing hard away from her. "At least you gave me warning."

"Or led him right to you."

He rounded. "He would have found me. That much I know. And killed people I care about." He took a breath. "Like you." He bent over and grabbed his knees. "It still makes me sick to think how close he came today."

She too found her feet. "I'm fine. And so are you, and even Tate. And we're going to find Gustov and stop him from hurting anyone else."

He stood up. Then, crazily, he walked over to her and pulled her to himself.

Just held her in a grip so tight it nearly knocked the wind from her. "I can't watch you die, RJ."

She put her arms around his waist, unnerved. "You won't."

"Please go home."

She stilled. Pushed away from him. "No, York. And I'm not having this fight with you. I already had it with Tate and won, and FYI, we had this conversation in Russia and there is no way, not a chance, I'm leaving you again, so—"

He swore. Something so crisp and raw and dark it startled her, her mouth opening. His gaze pinned her. "Don't you get it? I watched my mother die right before my eyes. I watched someone beat her to death! And I can't…" He held up his hand. Turned and walked away from her.

She couldn't move. *What*—? Because he'd told her his parents had been killed, but… "Are you sure, York?"

He stood with his back to her. "Yes. No. I don't know. I think so." He turned. "I keep having this recurring nightmare of

watching a woman getting beaten and yelling for me to run." He
ran a hand over his mouth. "And I can't shake the feeling that it's
my fault."

"No, York." And even the warning in his eyes couldn't stop
her from walking over to him. "That wasn't your fault. York, you
did *not* get your parents killed!"

He drew in a breath, met her eyes with his. "How do you
know that?"

She opened her mouth.

"Because I'm a *good man*?" He finger quoted the words. "Yeah,
right. You said that before, and I made the mistake of believing
you." He shook his head. "Not again, sweetheart."

He was morphing right before her eyes into the jaded, angry,
hard-edged man who'd scooped her off a Russian street because
he had to.

Not because he wanted to.

Her chest burned, tightened. "York, listen to me. You *are* a
good man. I know you—better than you know yourself right
now. All your memories lack context."

"I'm a murderer."

"You were a…transporter."

He stared at her, something of horror on his face. "What
does that even mean?"

"Um, well, uh…that's what you called it."

"I'm a real piece of work."

"York, c'mon—"

"The answer is yes, RJ." He looked up and met her eyes.
"Yes, I think I could be happy in a small town, eating lasagna for
dinner."

Oh.

"I want to be done with this life. But…I don't think you do."

She stilled.

"Could you be happy in a small town, shaking the dust off
the life you've built?"

She drew in a breath. "I…I don't know."

He nodded. "I get it. I'm not the man you met in Russia."

"I liked the man I met in Shelly. The man who went to the

altar."

He blinked, his chest rising and falling. "I don't think I'm that man either."

Her eyes burned at the shards in his voice.

"I guess I don't know what's left."

She stepped closer, and he didn't move, not even when she pressed her hand to his chest, right over his heart. Then she touched his face, met his eyes, drew her thumb down along his cheekbone. "Remember what that preacher said? That when we cling to Jesus we're changed. That we become who we were meant to be because there's nothing else left. I believe in the man who's left, still in here. The one clinging to Jesus."

Then she rose up on her tiptoes and kissed him.

He didn't respond. Not at first, but after a moment, he gentled his mouth and kissed her back. Something filled with longing.

Maybe even hope.

Then she stepped away and met his gaze. "I'm not afraid to find out who you are, York Newgate."

And for the first time since leaving Shelly, he smiled. Something slow, like the dawn over the lake, illuminating its depths. "Okay, Sydney, you win. Me either."

10

Cher wore the expression that Glo felt. And her words voiced her own disbelief. "Wait, what happened? Because maybe I haven't had enough coffee, but I thought I heard you say that you and Tate *broke up*."

Glo sat on a high top chair in the kitchen of her mother's sprawling Nashville-area estate in an over-sized T-shirt she'd stolen from Tate, a pair of jammie bottoms, and a short kimono with flamboyant pink flowers. She'd pulled her hair back in a headband, letting it curl out in every direction, and wore nothing of makeup.

Not that it would help, because her eyes felt like sand. Glo stared at her yogurt, stirring her spoon through it, not really hungry.

She didn't have much room left anyway after consuming most of a freezer-burned carton of Moose Tracks last night.

"Yep," she said and put the yogurt down on the granite countertop. Outside, the sun shone bright on the pool, but it only stirred up memories of when Tate had shown up after she'd driven him away with her stupidity and he told her he loved her.

Said that he'd never leave her.

"We had a fight," Glo said now to Cher's question.

"So what?" Cher set her bag, filled with wedding magazines, on the counter. "You don't break up every time you have a fight."

"Oh, if we broke up every time we had a fight—no, no, this was...it was different." She scooted off the high top, the travertine cool on her feet as she went to the fridge. Something in there should make her feel better. "He got shot."

Silence behind her and, seeing nothing in the fridge except carrots, she closed it and turned back to Cher.

Her friend was staring at Glo, wide-eyed. "*Shot?*"

"Yeah." Glo put her hands on her hips. "While in Vegas."

Cher sat back on one of the chairs. "What on earth was he doing in Vegas? Last time he was there, the Russian mob hunted him down and nearly killed him."

"I remember. And so did he, which is why he didn't tell me about it. Hashtag trust. Hashtag what-else-is-he-doing-that-he-isn't-saying?"

"Wait—stop. What was he doing there?"

Glo grabbed a browning banana off the counter. "Looking for Sloan."

A beat.

"But why?"

Glo looked at her. "Well, see, he thought Sloan was—is—in league with the Russian mob."

"*Sloan?*"

Glo peeled the banana and broke the top part off. "Frankly, I might agree if he hadn't shown up at the bridal shop the other day."

Cher just stared at her. Glo popped the banana in her mouth. Nodded.

Finally, "He says he's being set up. That he had nothing to do with Tate getting hurt. And apparently, he's also being linked to a murder in Seattle."

"A *murder?* No, that can't be right. Sloan is...well, he's a little arrogant, but he's harmless."

Glo dumped the rest of the banana in the garbage. "I know, right? But Tate doesn't agree, and when he found out that Sloan talked to me, he completely freaked out." She poured herself another cup of coffee. "Never mind that he was sitting in some sleazy hotel, bleeding. He could have been killed."

She turned, her hands wrapped around the warm mug, her eyes glazing again. "I can't live like this, fearing for his life every time he's not with me. He's…"

"A hero."

"Scary."

"Oh, Glo. I thought you worked through all this. You told me that you would rather have Tate in your life the way he is than not at all."

"And I thought so!" She put her coffee down, whisked away the tear across her cheek. "I thought so. But then I had this crazy dream about Sloan killing him—"

"You had a dream that Sloan killed him?"

"Yes. And then he started lying to me, or at least keeping things from me—and we have a rule…no secrets."

"Girl!" Cher smacked the counter. "He's still trying to protect you! Of course he's not going to tell you that he's walking into your greatest fears."

Glo narrowed her eyes. "You're supposed to be on my side."

"I am. Tate. Hello. The man is crazy about you. And you're crazy about him. And you're going to have to trust him a little."

"I do trust him."

Cher's voice softened. "Then what's the deal?"

The sunlight was pouring into the room in long, glorious beams of gold. Glo walked over and stood in it, staring out at the fresh-cut grass, the blooming goldenrod bushes that flanked the pool area. Sighed. "I'm too happy."

"Glo. What?"

She couldn't look at Cher if she wanted to tell the truth. But it had sunk like a ball into her gut the moment she'd voiced it to Dixie and Kelsey, and now with Tate's injury… "You know my mother always loved my sister best. She doted on her, and when we lost her, my mother just…she could hardly bear to look at me."

Cher, behind her, didn't say a word.

"When I met Tate, I felt like I was at the center of his world. He made me feel seen, and more than that, brave and pretty and…well, like I mattered. Of course I fell in love with him. And when he asked me to marry him, I was so happy it was nearly painful."

She walked back to the counter and slid onto a high top. "And then the shooting in Seattle happened, and Tate became consumed with finding the shooter and suddenly…I started to think maybe I was *too* happy. Even selfish to want to be the center of Tate's world. And that probably all this was designed to put me back in my place. To remind me that no one gets to be that happy." She took a sip of coffee.

Cher was frowning at her, as if Glo had lost her mind.

Maybe. But, "It's not about my fear of him dying, although that's true. It's about feeling like I can't trust the happiness. I'm pretty sure all this happiness, all these good things are a fluke and someday it's all going to blow up in my face."

"Why would it blow up in your face?"

Glo lifted a shoulder.

Cher slid off the stool. Took her by the shoulders. "No one is perfect, Glo. We all have our flaws and our issues and our regrets. I know one of those is that you couldn't help your sister. That she died even though you gave her a kidney. But it doesn't mean that you don't deserve love and happiness."

"I don't know, Cher. Maybe it's not about deserving it or not. Dixie said that the sun shines on the good and the bad. So maybe it's not up to me. But if it's not, how do I live with the fear that it could all end?"

"So instead, you end it yourself?"

Glo looked away, her eyes sheening again.

"That's called self-sabotage. Making yourself miserable simply because you're afraid of being miserable."

Glo looked at her, made a face.

"Just speaking from personal experience," Cher said. "I'm afraid to ping the cutest guy on my dating app because I just know he'll reject me, so I go out with the guys I know won't make me happy so if they do hurt me, I can tell myself I didn't want them anyway."

She pulled Glo into a hug. "Or I break up with them when I like them too much because I'm sure I'm the one who's going to get hurt."

Cher let her go.

Glo drew in a breath. "I am afraid of losing him."

"Of course you are. But is that fear worth pushing him away?"

The doorbell sounded into the house.

"I have flowers coming," Cher said. "I need you to pick out a bouquet."

Glo headed toward the front door. "But the wedding is off—"

Glo opened the door.

Tate stood on the step, such a fierce, exhausted, drawn expression on his face it looked as if he'd waged a small but brutal war on his way to her door. He wore a blue T-shirt with the words Shelly Lions on the front, a pair of baggy jeans, dress shoes, and his suit coat. His hair was unkempt, his eyes red, and he took one look at her and stepped across the threshold into the room.

"Our wedding is not off," he said as he shut the door behind him. Then he wrapped his arm around her waist, backed her into the wall, and without a word of hello, kissed her.

Not a sweet, I'm so glad to see you kiss, either, but one of possession. Of desire and hurt and fear. He tasted like cinnamon, as if he'd chewed gum on his way here, and smelled like freshly applied deodorant, but his unshaven whiskers, his worn shirt, and scent of salt on his skin told her that probably he'd taken a red-eye.

Maybe the moment she'd hung up on him.

And that only shattered the hard ball of anger inside.

Tate.

The man is crazy about you.

Indeed.

And yes, she was just as crazy about him. What had she been *thinking?*

She slipped her arms up around his neck and sank into him and slowed them down, gentling his mouth, and his heartbeat settled down from the terrible thunder against her. She wrapped a leg around his, holding him tighter. Deepened her kiss. *Hello, tough guy.*

No, the wedding was most certainly not off.

He finally let her go, pushing back from her, touching his forehead to hers.

"Hi," she said.

"Hi." His mouth was a grim line.

"Sorry," she said.

"Me too, babe. Me too."

She just stared into his blue eyes, lost, found. Happy.

"We are getting married," he said as he drew away, then caught her hands. "But not here. And not next week."

She raised an eyebrow.

"We're catching a plane for Montana. We're getting married on Saturday. Let's get this done."

"That's in two days."

He glanced over at Cher, who had returned to the kitchen but was still close enough to hear. "Cher?" he said, raising his voice.

"I can make that happen!" she called back.

Glo laughed. "All right then."

He smiled, and it was a blast of pure light right to her soul.

"Hungry?" she asked.

"I could eat a rhinoceros."

She took his hand and walked him through the family room.

He stopped, staring at a wall of family pictures, candids, and other shots. She and her father fishing, her mother on a horse in her youth. A family safari trip with the foundation. She hated that picture, the one posed with her near a dead elephant.

"Where is this?"

"Africa. We were on a safari hunt sponsored by our foundation. Brought a few of the biggest donors."

He pointed to a man near the front holding a rifle. "Is that—"

"Sloan? Yes. He was the one who shot the elephant."

Tate drew in a breath, looked at Glo, the ferocity back, this time with a hint of fear. "Pack your bags. We leave in an hour."

———————◆———————

RJ was going to prove to York he wasn't a bad guy. That his dark memories were simply shadows. That he wasn't the man he feared he was.

She just needed to get them someplace safe while she figured out how.

"This place is breathtaking, RJ." York sat in the passenger seat of the rental car they'd picked up in Helena and stared out at the rolling, pine-dotted hills of west central Montana. In the distance, the black hump of the Garnet Range glistened with the smallest rim of white, snow already finding the mountains.

"How many acres does your family own?"

"Around nine thousand. We have about twelve hundred head of beef cattle, but Knox started raising prize bucking bulls after my father died, so he poured all the money into that. I'm not sure what direction Reuben is taking the ranch—he took over a couple months ago."

York had changed into a pair of jeans, a gray T-shirt, and tennis shoes and appeared so, well, normal, she just couldn't wrap her head around the guy who seemed actually nervous to meet the rest of her family.

"They like you," she said, resisting the urge to take his hand and squeeze it. "You met them already. You just don't remember it."

"I remember some of it. Like Ford jumping me in Russia—that was Ford, the SEAL, right?"

"Yes. But he didn't know who you were."

"I think Wyatt nearly got me shot, too, if I remember—"

"The rest of them are really nice. And no one is going to get shot way out here."

And it was *way* out here. A hundred miles from Helena, the closest town, Geraldine had a population of thirteen hundred. Cell service was sometimes spotty, and it wasn't unheard of to see a cowboy on horseback riding fence or herding cattle. With the blue sky arching high over the land, the pine-laced wind stirring the evergreen trees that dotted their property, it seemed a land lost in time, right out of the Wild West.

But to RJ, it always felt like one place she could relax.

Even hide.

"What river is that?" York pointed to a lazy silver thread that wove through the foothills.

"The Geraldine River. There's a falls that you can see from a point behind the house. We used to swim in it."

"Is that the river—"

"The one with the cave where Ford and I got lost? Yes."

York trimmed his mouth into a thin line. "A lot of memories here."

"Most of them good," she said. She pulled up to the Triple M Ranch gate sign cast in iron and hanging between two soaring log braces.

"I'll get it," York said and got out before she could stop him. He unhooked the gate, opened it, and waited as she passed through. Then he relatched it and got in.

"You're a regular cowboy."

"Please. I'd fall right off a horse." But he smiled.

Oh, how she liked it when he smiled.

The ranch house came into sight as she topped the first hill. It sat in the notch of a second hill, a dark log-sided, two-story house with a stone front porch. Her mother's flowerpots, flanking the red door, boasted orange and red chrysanthemums, and blankets hung over the two rocking chairs. Almost as if waiting for her.

"This is gorgeous, RJ."

"You forget about it when you're gone, but yeah. Every time I drive up here I realize what I have to come home to."

He reached over and took her hand, squeezing.

Such an odd, affectionate gesture for York, but perhaps not for Mack.

She rather liked this new, merged version.

She parked near the barn, noticing the unpainted new wood on the back where Reuben had rebuilt it after the fire earlier this year. And in the corral, Gordo, Knox's prize bull, watched with glassy dark eyes as she got out of the rental.

A couple of baby goats ran out of the barn.

"Catch them, RJ!"

The voice accompanied her brother Reuben, who barreled out after the two bony goats. He wore a pair of jeans, work boots, a grimy flannel shirt, and a baseball hat.

York scooped one up, held it in his arms.

Reuben caught up with the other and slung it up on his hip. "These rascals are forever escaping. Hey, sis." He leaned over and kissed her cheek.

Reuben was the tallest, the oldest, and the one she knew least. He'd left the ranch before she was even a teenager, and before then, he spent most of his time playing football or hanging out with their father, learning the ropes. She barely remembered the infamous family fight that had driven him away but clearly remembered his return and the day he made amends with Knox.

Set Knox free to pursue his dreams.

It seemed that maybe Reuben, too, had found his happy place, tending the ranch, his wife, Gilly, expecting their first child.

He turned to York. "Hey. I'm Reuben. You must be the man RJ calls 007."

York offered a feeble chuckle. "York." He met Reuben's outstretched hand.

"I guess you're here for the big party," he said.

RJ laughed. "If you mean Tate and Glo's impromptu, I-have-to-marry-her-now wedding, then yes."

Reuben stared at her. "Uh…" He glanced at the house. "What?"

"So, you'd better talk to Ma."

She frowned, and Reuben reached for the other goat. "Good to meet you, York."

York fetched his duffel bag and RJ's suitcase from the back seat and followed her in.

She always equated the ranch house with the smell of chocolate chip cookies, scones, and baked bread.

Her mother didn't disappoint. The smell of cinnamon rolls beckoned her inside as she opened the door, and she spotted her mother standing at the large granite kitchen counter, oven mitts in hand, talking with Coco, who sat on one of the high top stools.

"Wow," York said, following her in, and she guessed he meant the soaring two-story stone fireplace, the polished logs, the deep, worn leather furniture, and the magazine-perfect view of the mountains through the two flanking windows. "You guys don't do small, do you?"

"RJ!" Her mother set her mitts down and came around the counter with her arms open. "I didn't expect you two so soon."

Gerri pulled her into a hug. "You okay?"

She nodded, not sure exactly how to tell her mother about the events in Vegas.

"Did you find the man you were looking for?" Her mother pulled away, glanced at her, then York. "Where's Tate?"

"Yes and no, and he's with Glo. And he's on his way here. Didn't he call you?"

She shook her head as she reached for York. His eyebrows went up as he hugged her.

RJ shrugged. Maybe she should have warned him, but he'd get used to it. Her mother adopted everyone.

"He's coming here with Glo. I think they're hoping to get married this weekend."

Her mother's eyes widened. "Oh dear."

"What?"

The oven timer buzzed and her mother returned to the counter and picked up her mitts. RJ walked over and hugged Coco.

"When did you get here?"

"Yesterday. We left right after you all did. Wyatt wanted Mikka to see the ranch and get some fresh air, and...well, I guess our timing is perfect because...um..." She looked at Gerri.

She pulled a tray of rolls out of the oven and now set them on a rack to cool.

"Kelsey and Knox eloped."

"What?"

"Yes. They called, and they're on their way, and we're having a family party this weekend."

Oh.

"Tate didn't even call?" RJ slid onto a stool. Her mother was right. "Oh boy."

"What's going on, honey?" her mother said, loading another tray of risen rolls into the oven.

"Oh, Tate is so in the doghouse. He was supposed to invite you to his wedding next weekend."

"Next weekend?" Her mother looked at Coco, who had drawn up one leg and now shrugged.

"But after he was shot in Vegas, Glo completely freaked out and he had to fly down there and calm her down. And he figured the only way to do that was to get married, immediately. But he doesn't want to do it in Nashville, so he's bringing her back here."

Her mother just stared at her.

York set his hand on RJ's shoulder. "He's fine, Gerri."

Oh. Whoops. She'd blown right by that first sentence.

Her mother drew in a breath. "How bad is it?"

"It was just a graze on his arm. York glued it shut," RJ said.

"Glued."

Wyatt had shown up, carrying Mikka over his shoulder. "It's a great way to mend wounds on the fly. My coaches used to do it all the time." The little boy was all smiles, despite being pale and thin. "We're going out to the barn to chase baby goats," Wyatt said. "But maybe we should just have one big wedding. What do you think, Coco?"

Coco's eyes widened and she looked like he might have suggested they skydive. "What—this weekend?"

"Why not? A big Marshall family wedding."

"Go away, Wyatt," his mother said.

"What?"

Coco had blushed as Wyatt bounced Mikka out of the house.

"We *are* engaged," she said, turning back to them. "I was just waiting until Mikka was further along in his treatment. He's in remission, but we're starting stage two, and I just think we need to wait longer…"

"For life to get easier?" Gerri said. "Less complicated? There will always be something that demands your attention. You and Wyatt have waited five years to be together—with heaven's blessing. How much longer do you want to wait?" She turned to York. "You can bunk in Tate and Ford's room. Wyatt is in Knox's room. I'll put Knox and Kelsey on the pullout in the den. Reuben and Gilly have taken his old room."

York looked confused with all the shuffling.

"I'll show him, Ma." RJ went to reach for her bag, but York

picked it up. She led the way upstairs and walked by Knox's room, the one he once shared with Wyatt. When Wyatt had moved out, Knox had turned it into a single room. Wyatt's gear was dropped near the bed.

"This is mine." She noticed Coco's belongings were already piled on her twin bed. York dropped her suitcase on the other one. "Yours is the next one down."

He nodded.

"York?"

He turned back.

"Are you okay?"

He nodded, but something in his expression...

"What?"

He sighed. "It's just...you've got a great family, RJ. And it makes me wonder what kind of family I had."

"You don't remember?"

His mouth tightened around the edges.

Right. "Okay, so you lived with your grandparents in Wisconsin after your parents were...after they died. And I know you had an uncle who was in the Marines. That's what made you go into the Marines, so it must have been good."

York nodded. "I have some patchwork memories of a small yellow house, a woman with white hair...but frankly, I'm afraid to try too hard. I feel as if I got all the bad memories and none of the good. I don't know if I can take remembering anything else."

She walked over to him, touched his chest, his heart a steady, warm beat. He hadn't shaved and his whiskers had come in golden, returning him to the rough-edged lumberjack look. "You have good memories, York. But maybe yes, you've remembered enough. Now it's time to make new ones."

He touched her face, something sweet, maybe hungry in his blue eyes. "Thanks, RJ."

Her phone buzzed on her bed and he went down the hallway.

She picked it up and closed the door as she answered. Pitched her voice low. "Thanks for calling me back."

"How is he?" Crowley said. "Are his memories resurfacing?"

"Not all of them." She walked to the window. "He has these

memories of his parents being murdered. And the crazy sense that he's somehow to blame. I was wondering if you had anything on that, maybe, from when you vetted him?"

"I can look into it, if you'd like."

"Please, yes." She watched out the window as an SUV drove up. "Did you find out any connection between Sloan and Slava?"

"No. But we did discover something else concerning."

"Yes?" The SUV pulled up by the barn. The door opened and Knox got out. It warmed her heart to see Reuben pull his brother into a hug.

"We got the forensic reports on the three bodies from the crash. One was a twenty-year-old named Jason MacDonald."

Aw. She was hoping, despite Vicktor's investigations, that Mack would have shown up, maybe just lost in the woods.

"The other two bodies were inconclusive. We pulled DNA, but there was no match with anyone in our system."

She stilled. "So, what about Martin?"

"He's still in our database, but according to the DNA taken, there is no match."

She watched as Kelsey and Knox came up the walk holding hands. Sweet. Knox deserved his happy ending after he'd done so much to hold the family together.

"So Martin could still be out there."

"Does York remember anything about why Martin wants him? Anything that would incriminate Martin?"

She heard York's voice from another time, another place. *I have a feeling that if the CIA knew I was here, I might be in trouble. I have too many secrets.*

"No. I don't think so."

The greetings of the newlyweds rose from the room below.

"Then you have to help him remember, RJ. Because if Martin is still alive, he is probably looking for York. And then you're both in danger."

She closed her eyes.

No. Her entire family was in danger.

According to Tate, they'd found their shooter.

Problem was, it just didn't sit right in York's gut.

Tate and Glo had shown up, with their small entourage—her bandmate Dixie, their drummer, Elijah Blue, and Cher, her maid of honor—about an hour after Kelsey and Knox.

The guy needed to work on his tact, however, because after he'd congratulated Kelsey and Knox, Tate broke the news that he wanted to get married too.

This weekend. As in two days.

But apparently Glo's friend Cher and Coco, Glo, and Gerri had it under control. Like a well-oiled operative team.

Which left Tate available to pull York aside and give him an update. The ballistics report on Slava had come in—and it matched the bullet that took out Kobie, the shooter in Seattle.

From a Remington 700 SPS tactical rifle.

The same kind of gun Tate had apparently seen Sloan holding in some picture hanging in Glo's mother's house.

Means, motive, and opportunity, and Tate had the case sewn up and had moved on to solving the problem of the broken tractor.

Nope, it just felt all kinds of wrong. Maybe it was simply because York was miles and miles out of his element.

The Marshall brothers, minus Fast-Fists Ford, who York now remembered from their altercation in a Russian alleyway three months ago, were congregated in the barn, gathered in concerned conversation around a very ancient green tractor, the name Oliver 2255 written on the side. The seat was ripped, the chassis rusty, and the paint was chipping off like leaves in autumn.

York stood a little back from the group, not saying anything, watching the brothers assess it like it might be a wounded animal. Reuben had the side hood open, had taken out a spark plug, and was cleaning it with a rag.

Knox was on his knees, looking at the tires. "It has a hydraulic leak on the left-side brake."

Tate had walked around the machine and kicked the tires. "When did the floorboard fall off?"

"About a year ago," Knox said. "It needs to be welded back

on." He got up and dusted off his hands.

York didn't remember Knox from when they'd met a month ago, but Knox seemed familiar. He had a sturdy, solemn get-'er-done aura about him, and the first thing he'd done after filling in the family on his elopement was to go outside and check the stock with Reuben.

Reuben, too, felt like someone he'd met before, although according to RJ, he hadn't met the former smokejumper. Reuben had a military-esque bearing about him, a big guy with big shoulders and a big smile. It didn't surprise York to hear that he'd been a sawyer on a firefighting crew.

Wyatt was leaning against a stall, drinking a soda, watching. "I always hated that thing," he said. "We'd be out in the middle of the field, and it'd die on us, and Dad would make me walk all the way back to the barn for some stupid tool. And then when I got back, he already had it fixed. Stupid. I say junk it."

"Zip it, Wy," Knox said. "This thing was Dad's pride and joy. It just needs a little more TLC."

Frankly, York was with Wyatt and nearly pronounced it a goner when another man walked into the barn.

All the men looked up and over at him. Reuben set the spark plug on the top of the tractor. Knox grabbed another rag and started wiping his hands.

"Hey, Hardwin," Reuben said and shook his hand.

Hardwin. The name sounded familiar. Over six foot, he wore a pair of pressed jeans, boots, a jean shirt, and a leather cowboy hat over gray hair. His leathery face suggested hours outdoors, but he was clean shaven and smelled as if he might be going out on a date.

Oh. Right.

Hardwin was the man dating RJ's mother.

See, York could remember good things.

Although, by the way the posse gathered, maybe it wasn't such a good thing.

"I hear congratulations are in order," Hardwin said to Knox.

"Thanks," Knox said. "We've been talking about it for a while, and we were thinking of running off to Hawaii but...I couldn't wait." He smiled, glanced at Tate, winked.

And for some reason, it only stirred a desire inside York.

Since she'd kissed him at the motel, his feelings for RJ were flooding in—everything from sheer panic to admiration to frustration to the desire to dig his hands into her hair and pull her to himself and kiss her.

Really kiss her. Because when he was with her, he felt...well, maybe not like the man he barely remembered, but also not like Mack, the man he didn't really know. And he didn't feel confused or lost or even angry.

He felt right. As if it didn't matter who he was or wasn't, but with her—like last night by the pool—he was exactly who he wanted to be.

A man who could be trusted. A man who would protect. A man who wanted to be better.

Yes, that's what it was. She made him feel like he was better.

He could admit that he needed RJ.

And maybe that meant, too, that he loved her.

He just couldn't remember, exactly, what that felt like either.

"I understand that, son." Hardwin dropped his hand. Cleared his throat. Smiled. "Actually, that's what I was hoping to talk to you about. And since you're all here...um..." He took a breath. "I'm going to ask your mother to marry me."

This was probably where York should sneak out.

"And I was hoping to get your blessings."

Yep. York edged toward the door.

Silence filled the barn, and suddenly he wasn't sure if Hardwin needed backup. Because York might be on the receiving end of those quiet, dangerous expressions someday if...

What? He asked to marry RJ?

Did he *want* to marry RJ? *Yes, I think I could be happy in a small town, eating lasagna for dinner. Could you?*

"You want to marry Ma," Tate said.

"I do," Hardwin responded, his deep voice unwavering. "She and I have plenty of good years left, and even if we don't, I love her. She is...well, she brings sunlight to my life after a very long darkness. And I think I do the same for her."

York had paused by the door, caught in his words.

Sunlight in darkness. That was exactly the sense he had when he first met RJ, as Sydney, back in Shelly. A light trying to break through his layers of shadows.

"When my wife first died, I tried to hang on to all the memories we had. And I think that got in the way between your mother and me. But she's...she taught me that I don't have to say goodbye to all my memories to embrace new ones. And neither does she. I'm not here to replace your father—I could never do that. But I'm hoping to be someone who could make your mother happy in this new season."

York slipped out, walking away from the scene, pretty sure that Hardwin was going to get a yes.

But his words wrapped around York. *I don't have to say goodbye to all my memories to embrace new ones.* RJ was right. Not all his memories were bad. Maybe he simply remembered the good ones and went forward into a new season.

He stopped by the corral, resting his hands on the top rail as he watched the bull in the yard. Wide shoulders, a ring in his nose, the bull snuffled through hay.

"That's Gordo, my brother's prize bull," RJ said, coming up next to him. She'd changed into a pair of jeans and a flannel shirt, looking very cowgirlish in her cowboy boots. "He lost Hot Pete in the bombing in San Antonio, but apparently, Gordo sired another upcoming champion. And he still has some good straws in him."

"Straws?"

"Seeds. You know..." She grinned at him, waggled her eyebrows.

Oh, right.

She put one foot on the lower rail. "So, have you remembered anything more about Martin, the guy you recognized when he arrested you?"

He looked at her, frowned. "No. Why?"

She drew in a breath. "I don't know. Just, you know...trying to figure out why they would want you."

He looked back at Gordo. "I don't care anymore. I just want

to leave it behind. I know enough to know that life is over. And I'm grateful to have been given a second chance. And no, I don't want to be Mack—but I do want a new season." He looked over at her. "A lasagna season."

She raised an eyebrow. "Lasagna, huh?"

"I'd eat turnips if it meant you were with me."

And he didn't know where that came from, but it felt right, even when she swallowed hard but didn't look away.

So, "I think I love you, RJ."

She closed her eyes, drew in a shaky breath. He touched her cheek, ran his thumb down it.

Then he leaned over and kissed her. Gently, as if for the first time.

She didn't step toward him, but she softened her lips, kissing him back.

Pouring sunlight into his soul.

He heard voices emerging from the barn and drew away, his gaze in hers. She smiled ever so slightly.

"So, when are you going to ask her?" Wyatt, walking up beside Hardwin. "Because, you know, we could have a big Marshall family wedding."

"Ask who, what?" RJ said to York.

"Oh, you'll see," he said.

The Marshall family knew how to put on a celebratory spread. Smoked ribs, homemade rolls, a feta-orange-arugula salad, cheesy potatoes, and chocolate cake. Knox told the story of how, after hearing York's tale of losing his memory and nearly his life, he got in his car and drove to Cannon Beach, picked up Kelsey, and refused to wait another second to marry her.

RJ kept looking at York across the table, probably replaying his words in her head. And he kept glancing at Hardwin, who spent most of the night with a crazy smile pinned to his face as if by betraying any other emotion he might give himself away.

Only, all the guys knew, and that meant they, too, kept looking at him and wearing stupid smiles, and finally, Hardwin stood up.

"You all know that I love your mother," he said, looking at Gerri, whose face had paled. "I never thought I'd find someone who I could love again, but I do, and I know she feels the same about me."

Gerri took a quick breath, her eyes wide. And then Hardwin turned to her and pulled out a velvet box. "Gerri. You brought light into my world when it was dark. You make me a better man, every day. And I want to spend the rest of my life making your life bright and safe and better too. A new season for us. Will you marry me?"

York looked at RJ, trying to read her expression. She drew in her breath, put a hand to her mouth.

Gerri's chair banged as she rose. Gave Hardwin a terrible, pained look, and then turned and fled from the table.

The entire family sat in stunned silence.

RJ got up and followed after her mother, and Coco followed after RJ, and Gilly got up and started clearing plates, along with Kelsey and Glo and...

"Was that a no?" Hardwin said, sitting back down.

And he looked so defeated, so wrecked, York had to look away.

"That was a bomb," Wyatt said.

Tate glared at him.

York carried his plate to the kitchen, then walked out to the back porch. The sun had exploded into a firebomb of red, gold, and orange, leaving a flaming trail along the horizon as it fell into darkness.

He stood there, unable to move. Unable to breathe, his chest aching.

Because he'd finally figured out why Martin wanted to kill him.

11

P ut the cupcakes into the fridge to cool," Gilly said. "And then we'll frost them."

Her mother had said nothing about last night's debacle with Hardwin, but RJ caught her looking out the front window occasionally, as if waiting for him to show up while they baked for Glo's wedding.

Certainly Hardwin wasn't giving up, was he?

But RJ got it. She really did.

Understood completely why her mother had gotten up and practically fled from the table at Hardwin's public proposal.

Why she'd locked herself in the bathroom, even when RJ and Coco came to her door and sat outside it.

Why she'd been crying when she opened it and let them in. Stood at the window and watched as Hardwin left the house, got in his truck, and drove away.

RJ got it, because she felt the same way.

What did you do when you loved someone but they wanted a different life than you did?

"I don't know if I want a new season," her mother had said, finally turning from the window to sit on the edge of her jetted tub. She'd taken a towel to wipe her face. "That poor man. I completely eviscerated him. He didn't deserve that."

RJ sat on the closed toilet. "Ma. Even I could see Hardwin's proposal coming a mile away—didn't you know he was going to propose?"

"I…I thought he might, but I kept trying to dodge it. I just…"
She sighed. Looked up at RJ, at Coco. "After your father died, I
was…I was completely wrecked. We built this life together—this
ranch, this family, a world I loved. And then it was gone. It's
taken me five years to get back on my feet and…now I like my
life. I paint and garden and bake. Help Reuben and Knox with
the ranch. I go on your adventures with you." She looked at RJ.
"I love Hardwin—I do. But being married means losing a little
bit of yourself, merging it with another, and I…well, maybe that's
selfish, but I'm not sure I want to lose myself again."

RJ frowned. "Mom, you always told me that marriage is an
addition, not a subtraction."

"Yes, it is, RJ. For sure. A good marriage is. And your father
and I had a good marriage. But he was…he was larger than life,
and his dreams were big, and I willingly put mine aside for his.
Now…I don't have to."

York's words, his question rounded back and sat in RJ's heart.
*I think I could be happy in a small town, eating lasagna for dinner. Could
you?*

No.

And that truth burrowed in like a coal, searing through her.

She loved the ranch. But she didn't want this life. She wanted
the life she'd built—working for the CIA. Using her gift of analysis to stop international evil, and sure, maybe her dreams were
fueled by too much time binge-watching *Alias*, but probably it
only ignited the very real action-adventure heroine inside.

After all, she was a Marshall.

And that's why she got it. "Ma. You don't have to marry
Hardwin. You can say no."

Her mother closed her eyes. "But I love him." She opened
her eyes, met RJ's. "I really do. He's a good man. Kind. Patient.
Wise. And I do get lonely, sometimes."

That just about broke RJ's heart. She squeezed her mother's
hand. "I should call more."

"Oh, honey, it's not about you calling more. It's about having
someone to share your life with, the big and the small moments.
Like when I see a sunset and want to turn to your father and say,

'Orrin—isn't God amazing?' Or when I watch Wyatt save a goal and I can share a grin with your dad. *Those* moments. I had so many of them with your father. And I'd like to share them with someone again."

Her mother shook her head. "Oh, I don't know my own stupid heart!" She got up. Took a breath. "But I do know that Glo and Tate are getting married. In two days. And we have work to do."

Right.

But RJ couldn't get out of her mind the image of Hardwin walking down the step, getting into his truck, and driving away in a cloud of dust.

Reminded her way too much of Clancy McGiven.

Coco must have remembered it too, because she brought up RJ's failed prom date that night as they tucked into their beds. Coco was looking at the solitaire ring that Wyatt had given her, finally, a couple days ago, spinning it on her finger. "Wyatt was the reason I didn't date anyone in high school," she said, almost out of the blue.

But not really, since RJ could practically read her mind.

"But you, RJ, had a thing for Clancy since our freshman year." Coco looked over at her. "I remember the day he showed up to ask you to prom. Knox was still living here, and I think Wyatt was home for the weekend. And of course Ford. And wasn't Tate back from the military already?"

"Yeah. Full house of brothers," she said. She grabbed her pillow, leaning back on the headboard. "I'd been so hoping he'd ask me to prom, even dropped him some hints at school, so when he came to the door, I was so excited. I was up here, and I came out into the hallway and heard stupid Knox answer and when Clancy asked to talk to me, Knox asked why." She looked at Coco. "Just...*why*? And of course it wasn't any of Knox's business, but you know my brothers. It's like they were born with an extra protection gene when it comes to me. And frankly, it's only gotten worse since Dad died, but Knox just stood there, and the next thing I know, Clancy is turning around and walking away. Walking away! He didn't talk to me once for the rest of the year."

"He took Sheila Jensen to the prom."

"Yes, he did."

"Sorry about that."

"If a guy can't stand up to my brothers, then maybe he's not the one, but…still, they treat me as if I need protecting—"

"Um—"

"Stop. I get it. And I'm grateful that I have brothers who watch my back—I really am. But they need to trust me, too, right? When I get married, I want a partner—someone who'll join me in my adventures, and yeah, watch my back, but maybe let me watch his back too." She got up and went to the window. "I thought I found that in York. Sure, he had to rescue me in Russia, but I rescued him right back in Shelly, or I thought I did, but… he's not the same man I knew in Russia." The moon stretched out across the rolling pastures, haunting in its wan light. "And in truth, I liked the guy I saw in Shelly too. I guess I just want both the man who loves Jesus and the man who loves justice."

"And the man who won't walk away."

RJ nodded. Coco drew up her legs, encircled them with her arms.

"Wyatt is sure cute with Mikka," RJ said.

"He's adorable. Never leaves his side unless he has to."

"Sweet."

"Marriageable." Coco smiled. "He keeps mentioning having a big Marshall family wedding."

RJ's eyes widened. "Really?"

"I can't do that to Glo. But maybe…well, your mom is right. There will always be something that demands my attention, but I don't want to wait any longer. I've found the one who makes me better, as Hardwin said."

RJ sat down on the bed. York made her better, or at least the old York had.

I think I love you, RJ.

And she loved him, didn't she?

The question rattled around in her head now as she helped Gilly make cupcakes for Glo's wedding. Not a big event—just the family—but of course, Senator Jackson was flying in tomorrow

198

morning, which meant her security people would also be here. Tate had vetted and rented out a private vacation rental on a nearby lake for the group, and he and York had spent the morning setting up security around the lodging.

Frankly, York needed something to do. He'd gotten up early this morning and gone for a run—she didn't know the guy worked out, but yeah, that made sense—and when he came back, he'd been distant with her. Or maybe just caught in thought, but he'd greeted her as she and her mother and Glo pored over cookbooks, searching for the right menu, then headed upstairs to shower.

She couldn't help but notice the way he'd pulled off his shirt, probably in the middle of the run, and hung it over his shoulder. The wicked scar from the accident burned a deep red line across the muscles in his abdomen, but he hadn't lost any of his lean form over the last month, probably from working at the pub, both before and after the fire. His blond hair was slicked back but curled at the ends, and he still hadn't shaved, his beard shiny with gold and red flecks.

Yes, she liked the lumberjack look.

Paul Bunyan was gone when he'd returned wearing a white oxford, a pair of suit pants, his whiskers gone to reveal a strong jaw and that scar she rarely noticed.

Still a handsome man. The two sides of York Newgate.

Okay, if she were honest, she liked them both.

York had grabbed a cup of coffee, then headed out with Tate to check on the vacation rental.

Again, he'd barely looked at her, gave her just a quick hello.

What if he'd remembered something he didn't want to tell her? The thought itched RJ as she blended the maple cream cheese frosting, following one of Gilly's super-secret family recipes for pumpkin cupcakes. Her family owned a cupcake shop in Ember, a tiny town in upper west Montana.

"How does it look?" Gilly asked and came around behind her, bumping her extended tummy into the counter as she slowed the mixer. She poked her spatula into the mix, drew it out, and touched her pinky to the creme. Tasted it. "Oh, that's perfect."

Her mother had retrieved a batch of over-sized yellow pumpkin cupcakes from the oven and set them on a board to cool.

Cher and Kelsey had gone to a store in town to pick up groceries.

Coco was sitting at the counter, putting together a floral order from a couple magazine pictures Cher had cut out and given her. RJ had spotted a computer window open that displayed wedding gowns.

Hmm.

Glo was acting strange as she finished gluing lace to a white vintage hat Cher had found. RJ had seen the dress—a frilly, short strapless stunner that would show off Glo's curves along with her legs.

Apparently, the bridesmaids—Cher, Kelsey, and Dixie—were wearing dresses they'd found off the rack in some high-end wedding shop, all in deep purple.

Glo kept looking at her phone, then the door, barely listening to the conversation.

When the door finally opened and Tate walked in, she visibly relaxed.

"Smells good in here," Tate said and walked over to his mother, giving her a kiss on the cheek. "Thanks for pulling this together." He went over and gave Glo a kiss. "Your mom is on her way. I got a text from her security detail."

Glo wrinkled her nose. "She's mad, isn't she?"

"It's our wedding. She'll smile for the pictures, I'm sure."

York walked through the house to the back porch.

RJ followed him. "You okay?"

"This doesn't feel right," he said quietly.

She frowned. "What—the wedding?"

He glanced at her. "No. No—that's fine. The house is safe. Tate's security team met him there, and they're going to be at the wedding tomorrow." He looked back to the horizon. "But Tate seems to think this is over. That he's found his shooter—Sloan Anderson—and as soon as he's in custody, he can put this threat to bed. Apparently, he told Jackson's team his reasons and they agreed. The secret service is tracking him down right now."

York turned to her, leaning a hip against the post. "But I don't think so."

"Why?"

He had the expression he wore when he didn't want to tell her something, when he knew it would only lead to trouble, and the realization that she knew him that well, maybe better than he did, rippled through her.

See, they were good together. "Just tell me."

"I remembered Martin."

Oh. And his grim expression told her it wasn't one of the good memories.

"I know why he wanted me dead."

"Why?"

"Because I think he was a member of the rogue branch of the CIA you talked about, and if you're right, they've been working for a long, long time to create a new kind of war, the kind that would close Russia's borders and ignite another Cold War."

He took her by the elbow and walked off the porch, as if he didn't want anyone to hear them.

"After Claire and my son were killed—and yes, I do remember them now—I left the CIA and became an independent contractor. I did—well, let's call it odd jobs for various groups."

"I know what you did, York. You don't need to hide it."

"Maybe that's for my benefit," he said, and his mouth slid up to the side.

Right.

"Anyway, do you remember the Moscow subway bombing about eight years ago?"

"Yes. It was blamed on a couple of Islamic terrorists, women I think."

"What if it wasn't them? What if they were just convenient?"

She shook her head, frowning.

"I was in that attack." He pointed to the scar under his ear, halfway across his neck. "Nearly died in it. But the thing was, I saw the bomber, and it wasn't a woman."

They'd reached the fire pit and she sat down on a bench beside him.

"I got on the stop before Lubyanka Station and I spotted Martin on the train. He was in the next car down. I hadn't seen him in a year or so. He worked with me at the CIA, but he'd left too, or I thought so. I was surprised to see him. I think that feeling of surprise I had whenever I thought about him was from the bombing in Russia, not the arrest in Seattle. Maybe. Anyway, he saw me too. He was carrying a duffel bag, I remember that, and I started to work my way down the car toward his car. But if you remember Russian metros, they're usually packed, and we got to the next station before I could reach him. He looked at me through the glass, sort of gave me a smile and a nod, and then got off. I never did talk to him. But, as he walked away, I noticed he didn't have the duffel bag over his shoulder anymore."

"Oh no."

"The train blew up before the doors closed. If I'd made it to his car, I would be dead. As it was, I nearly died."

"And you think Martin was behind it."

"I'm sure of it. But I was in a Russian hospital for a couple weeks and by the time I got out, more so-called suicide attacks had happened in Moscow, and a jihadist group in the Dagestan region, near Chechnya, claimed responsibility."

"But you think it was this CIA faction."

"Think about it. Blow up a train. Cause unrest. Violence. And more violence would lead to a greater need to protect, which would create more police force, which only leads to more control, and eventually they're back to a police state, right? Hello, Stalin."

"I suppose it makes sense, right?"

"It gets worse. Do you remember the name Viktor Ginkut? He was a high-ranking officer in the Black Sea Fleet."

"No."

"Well, by the time of the bombing, he'd left the Navy and was commissioned as General Boris Stanislov's head of security."

She raised an eyebrow at the connection.

"Ginkut was killed in the attack."

The realization slid over her like a cold hand. "He was replaced by FSB Colonel Natalya Smolsk, the woman who tried to kill you and Coco."

"After setting up the assassination attempt on Stanislov and trying to pin it on you."

RJ stared at him.

"It's just a guess," York said.

"A terrifying one that suggests that this is a very long game this group is playing. But why would this jihadist group claim responsibility for the attack?"

"Maybe they're working together. Remember, Arkady Petrov, the man poised to take Stanislov's place, is a member of the Russian mob. Which has very long arms. Even into Chechnya."

"And America," RJ said, and her mind was webbing out to all sorts of possibilities. Like the Bratva manipulating elections by murdering candidates so they could create more unrest on this side of the world. More arms. More money.

More power.

And maybe not just for the Bratva.

"When you were in Russia, you couldn't cause problems, but the minute you brought that information home to America…oh, York, you need to call Crowley."

He blinked at her. "Tom Crowley? Claire's dad?"

"Yes. The former ambassador to Russia—the one who now works for the CIA. He needs to know what you just told me about Martin."

"I'm sure he already knows. And besides, Martin is dead."

She made a face, shook her head. "No, he doesn't know. And…Martin might not be dead."

York's expression went blank. "What—? How do you know?"

But she never got a chance to explain because a shout lifted from the house, carrying across the morning air.

"No, Tate! Stop—no! *Don't kill him!*"

───────◆───────

Somewhere in the back of his head, Glo's voice registered, but Tate reacted on pure adrenaline, pure fury when Glo opened the front door to let a murderer into his home.

Where his *family* lived.

It took him less than two seconds to cross the room, grab Sloan by the throat with one hand, use the other to grab his hand and turn it out, forcing Sloan to his knees.

With everything inside Tate he wanted to put a knee to Sloan's smug face, but he refrained and simply forced him to the ground, put a knee in his back.

"Tate! Let him up!" Glo shouted, her hands pulling on his shoulders.

"Not. A. Chance."

For his part, Sloan wasn't resisting—but how could he? His cheek was being smashed into the front porch, his body twisted under Tate's force. Still, the man just kept his voice calm, breathing through what had to be pain.

Oh, Tate hoped it was pain.

"Get off me, Tate, I come in peace."

Hardly. "What are you doing here?"

In the back of his head, where he'd partitioned Glo's screaming, he knew that the likelihood of Sloan showing up on his front doorstep to turn himself in was close to nil. "Are you *crazy*?"

"Yes, clearly! I knew I couldn't get close to you if you were traveling with Jackson, and Glo said you'd listen if I showed up to talk, and somewhere in my brain, I believed her."

"Glo said—?" And this was when he looked up at his fiancée.

She had covered her mouth with her hands, her eyes wide. And shoot, she was nodding.

"Glo. What the—"

"He's telling the truth, Tate. I believe him."

"What do you believe?"

"That he's being set up. That he didn't try and kill you in Vegas!"

"*Which. Time?*" Because right now Tate's wound had started to really hurt, and he might have ripped open the glue, and yeah, that was a pretty picture.

Sloan still wasn't struggling. His arrogant jaw was gritted, though, and a sweat had broken out across his pretty face.

"Were you in Vegas Wednesday?"

And although he expected it—it was like asking a dog if he

ate the leftovers—Sloan shook his head. "No, I was in Nashville!"

"He was, Tate. I told you—he came to see me in my dressing room on Tuesday—"

And now, again, Tate just stared at her. "And *Wednesday*, we showed up at Imagine, Inc., it was cleared out, and someone shot the only connection we had to Sloan. Do the math, Glo—there's plenty of time to get to Vegas after seeing you in your underwear."

"I was clothed! Sheesh, Tate."

He knew that, but still—

"I wasn't there, man!"

Yeah, sure.

Now others had joined him—York blew in from the backyard, standing beside him. Knox and Reuben had come in from the barn, covered in grease, clearly still wrestling with the tractor. Coco had gotten up, gone around the island to stand with Ma. He hoped Mikka wasn't around.

But it was RJ who made him ease off Sloan. "Let him up, Tate. Let's hear what he has to say. Because I think this thing is bigger than just Sloan Anderson and his jealousy."

She stood with her hands on her hips, that sort of tone her voice took when she knew what she was talking about.

Like the time she'd zinged him for his not-so-hidden need to keep up with his brothers. Which of course wasn't at all true, except maybe it was, sometimes, and…okay, she could usually sift through the facts to find the truth.

It was weird that Sloan had shown up. Either he was stupid, he was using Glo, or he had something to say. "He doesn't leave my sight," Tate said and hauled the guy up.

Sloan shook out his arm. "Hey, Glo." He went to hug her but Tate stepped in the way. "Are you kidding me?"

Sloan drew in a breath. "Right. Okay. But really, Tate, I wasn't the one—"

"Zip it, pal." He caught him around the back of the neck and pushed him toward the den. "RJ, York, you're with me."

"And me," Glo said.

Aw, he didn't want Glo anywhere near Sloan Anderson and their little *talk*.

Because in his heart, Tate knew the guy wasn't innocent. And he wasn't sure what he'd have to do to get the whole truth out of Sloan, but he didn't want Glo around to see it.

Although, maybe that's why she stepped into the room, her arms folded, as Tate pushed Sloan down onto the sofa.

"Why did you run in San Diego when we tried to find you after the bombing?"

"Seriously? You sent Swamp and Sly after me—I saw them coming and I knew you'd pinned the beating in Vegas on me."

"Because you were the one who told them where I was!"

"No, I wasn't." Sloan folded his arms. "Fine. I was the one who dug up the information on you. I was the one who knew your connection with the Bratva. And I was the one who told Senator Jackson you were both in Vegas and might be in trouble. But I wasn't the one who got you beat up—you did that all on your own, Rambo."

Tate took a step toward him without even thinking, but York clamped him on the shoulder. It felt like razors going into his lungs. "Take a breath, Tate."

"Listen," Sloan said. "I'm the victim here. I was fired from my job for no reason. And then I get set up for the murder of a CIA agent—which I didn't do."

He was talking about Sophia Randall. Interesting. "I saw you on the security video."

"I was there—but I didn't do it. Certainly you could look at the time stamp and compare it with her time of death."

Tate glanced at Coco, who'd come into the room. She nodded. Yes, they could do that.

"Talk to the Senator—she'll vouch for me."

"No, buddy, she won't," Tate said, and that took a little wind out of Sloan's sails.

That's right, hotshot, your sins will find you out. "What about the gun?"

Sloan blinked at him.

"The Remington 700 Sps tactical rifle you used to kill Alan Kobie in Seattle. The same gun that killed Slava in Vegas."

"I…"

"I saw you posed with the same rifle in a picture at Glo's house."

He frowned.

"The one in Africa, when we went on safari," Glo said. "The one you used to kill that beautiful elephant."

So maybe Glo *wasn't* a liability here.

"Seriously? That's not my gun. I used it, yes, but…that gun was provided by the directors of the safari. It's not mine."

Tate narrowed his eyes.

"The safari was sponsored by the Jackson Foundation," Glo said. She turned to Tate. "But my mother is against guns."

"Hard to go hunting without a gun," York said quietly.

Sloan swallowed and for the first time, looked a little pale.

"How long have you worked for the Senator?" RJ asked.

He looked at her. And took so long in answering that Tate was toying with the idea of asking Glo to leave. "Um, nearly seven years. I was an intern during her freshman term. My father got me the position."

"In all that time, did she ever take a trip to Chechnya?"

"What—RJ, what are you saying?" Glo said, unfolding her arms.

"Let him answer, babe," Tate said. Because suddenly he was rounding back to Kobie and his crazy accusation that somehow Jackson was involved with a Chechen warlord.

And then, further back, to the words of former POW soldier Graham Plunkett right before he'd taken a header from four-stories in San Diego at the national convention. Words about being at war with Russia if Jackson won the presidency.

Crazy talk.

But, something inside him curdled when Sloan said, "She's been over there three times during her public service."

"To *Chechnya?*" York said.

"Humanitarian aid trips to visit refugee camps."

Tate looked at RJ. "What are you thinking?"

"That this is a conspiracy theory gone crazy!" Glo said. "My mother is a patriot. She loves this country."

"Calm down, Glo," Tate said. "No one is accusing her of

anything."

Sloan was shaking his head. "I agree with Glo—it's not Jackson. It's inside her staff. She has connections—"

"To the CIA," RJ said and looked at York. "As a member of the Armed Services Committee, she'd be privy to—maybe even oversee—certain elements of the CIA."

Glo stared at her. "What does that mean?"

Out of the corner of his eye, he saw York give the smallest shake of his head.

Yeah, he needed an answer to Glo's question. But maybe… maybe not with Glo in the room. "Babe—"

"Oh, don't you *babe* me!" She rounded on him. "Let's not go back to twenty-four hours ago, Mr. I'm-Shot-but-I'm-not-Going-to-Tell-My-Fiancée!"

He drew in a breath. "Glo, we need to find out what's going on, and if it's only going to make you angry—"

"I'm beyond angry. The gall of all of you—especially *you*—" She pointed at RJ. "After my mother cleared your name of your stupid behavior in Russia—hey, if we're going to accuse people, maybe we should take another look at RJ and what she was doing in Russia!"

"Glo, that's enough," Tate said quietly. "We all know RJ is innocent."

"Just like *my mother* is innocent." Tears whisked her eyes. "Can't you see the circumstantial evidence—"

"I'm just asking questions, Glo," RJ said. "No one is blaming your mother for anything."

"We have to ask, however, if it wasn't Sloan shooting at Wyatt in Seattle and presumably, Senator Jackson, then who was?" Coco said. "And why?"

Her question shut the room down.

"Have you ever heard the name Damien Gustov?" York asked quietly. "Or better yet, Alan Martin?"

Sloan's eyes widened. "I know Martin. He was on a list of people who accompanied the Senator overseas. Protective services, I think."

"To Chechnya?" York asked.

Sloan nodded.

"When is the last time you saw him?" RJ asked.

"I…I don't know. Maybe a few months ago—yes!" He looked at Tate. "He was on the plane the night you were attacked in Vegas."

Tate frowned, looked at York. "Who is Martin?"

"I think he might be behind this entire thing."

Sloan nearly came off the sofa. "See? I told you—it's someone inside her organization."

"Sit down, Sloan," Tate said.

Glo refolded her arms over her chest. "See?"

"Do you see?" RJ said. "Because if Martin works for the Senator and he's our shooter, then he was shooting at Wyatt or Kobie—to *shut them up.*"

Glo just looked at her, her eyes wide.

RJ stared back. "Um, you have to ask *why?*"

Glo's mouth opened. She closed it. Looked away, tears sheening her eyes.

"Because it's true," Tate said quietly. "Because the Senator is in bed with the Russians somehow."

Glo shook her head, closed her eyes.

"Babe," he said and wrapped his arms around her. "Shh. It's okay."

"She's a patriot," Glo said softly. "She wouldn't do this."

"Maybe it's just Martin. Maybe we're reading too much into this," Coco said. "Maybe Damien Gustov hasn't been after us all this time. Maybe all of this is just a string of strange coincidences."

"I saw him in Russia. He *kissed* me! And said it was so he could play games with York," RJ said, her voice shaking. "And he attacked Wyatt."

York put his arm around her. "It doesn't mean he's here and still stalking us," he said.

"You're saying it was Martin who shot me in Vegas?" Tate said.

"Or Sloan," Coco said.

"Hey."

"You're done talking," Tate said to Sloan. "Unless you have

an alibi for where you were on Wednesday, around lunchtime."

Sloan's jaw tightened. "I was at home."

"Sleeping."

He lifted a shoulder.

"Okay, we need to find a place to stash him until I can straighten this out," Tate said.

"Stash sounds awfully close to kill—" Sloan said.

"Pipe down, no one is going to kill you." Tate turned to York. "We're going to hide him in plain sight. If Jackson is in on this, we'll know by the way she reacts when she sees Sloan."

Sloan started to shake his head. "Tate—"

"You wanted to talk to Jackson? You got your wish. You're going to a wedding, pal."

This just might be the longest night of York's life.

The house was quiet, the dishwasher humming, and Glo and her girls were upstairs in the bedroom he'd been kicked out of when the entourage showed up. Apparently, Tate wasn't letting Glo out of his sight, either, so Tate and York were on the sofas downstairs.

But right now, Tate had Sloan locked in a bathroom at the end of the hall. Tate had rigged a rope around the handle, tacked it to another door handle.

Sloan wasn't thrilled, but Tate gave him a blanket and a pillow and suggested he bunk in the tub.

Coco had retired with Mikka to Wyatt's room to read a book, and Gerri had left to pick chrysanthemums out in the back garden for table decorations.

Meanwhile, Tate and his brothers were outside, under the glow of the barn light, shooting hoops while York sat with RJ at the table, dissecting theories.

York kept getting distracted by the way RJ's hair fell out from where she kept latching it behind her ear, the way she worried her lip when she worked, like she did now, bent over a piece of paper, her computer open on the table.

He'd wanted to cheer for her the way she'd unraveled her theory today. Wow, she was smart.

After the interrogation in the den, she'd called Vicktor and checked out Sloan's story about his visit to the hotel. The time stamp put him just outside the probable time of death of Sophia Randall.

York remembered that day in clarity now, the way he'd come into the room, thinking RJ had sent him a text asking him to meet her there. The smell hit him first, and then, as he'd rounded the corner, Gerri had nearly taken his head off with a shot.

But most of all, he remembered the rush of emotions as he spotted RJ. Beautiful RJ standing in the middle of the room, horror on her face. He'd simply grabbed her, pulled her to himself, so much relief pouring out of him that it could still turn him weak.

Yes, he loved her. Then. Now. And the sense of it sharpened him, turned him focused.

He wasn't going to lose her like he'd lost Claire.

Because he remembered that too. His young, cocky self thinking his wife and child would be safe from the evil he was fighting.

As if.

Frankly, he'd like to walk away, right now. Let Tate figure out who was after the VP candidate. But York was neck-deep in this—especially with his information about Martin. And with Gustov still on the loose…

No, he had to stick around.

But as soon as it was over, he was gone. Mr. and Mrs. Mack Jones, maybe.

"So here is what we have," RJ said, yanking him out of his dreams for their house tucked back in the secluded woods or countryside, preferably overlooking a lake.

She moved her notebook over to him.

The web she had woven chilled him to the bone.

She'd written a number of names and dates on the paper, with lines drawn between them. And Jackson's name, circled in red, in the middle.

"We know that ten years ago, while she was still a freshman senator, Jackson went to Chechnya on a humanitarian aid mission. We also know that during that time, a half-Russian, half-Chechen warlord named Pavel Tsarnaev was in the region. Tsarnaev has connections to the Bratva.

"A couple years later, you see Martin plant a bomb in Moscow. The bombing gets blamed on a rebel group in the Caucasus region, including Chechnya."

"They claimed responsibility."

"So, Tsarnaev may or may not have been involved. But fast forward a few more years to Tasha."

Tasha? He looked at her. "Wait, what? How is *Tasha* involved?"

"Coco said your girlfriend was a videocaster, right?"

He nodded. "She called it the October Review. Debunked conspiracy theories, that sort of thing. Wait—we actually met Tsarnaev at a resort on the Black Sea in Ukraine. She was doing research. I was working as an information courier for the CIA and didn't give him much thought."

"Coco said that Tasha was looking into a scandal involving a Russian politician who had an American mistress."

"How does that fit in?"

"What if the man wasn't a politician, but a warlord named Tsarnaev, and the mistress was…" And her pencil landed on Jackson's circled name.

His mouth opened.

"I know it sounds crazy, but just listen. You said that you got the name of Tasha's assassin from Roy, right?"

York hadn't said that, specifically, but of course she would have figured that out. He nodded.

"Roy said that Gustov had picked up the contract. But what if Roy was wrong? What if *Martin* killed Tasha?"

He stilled. And the question was a knife to his chest. "I always thought it was because of her politics. Are you saying she died because of *me?*"

She gave him a look of horror. "No! Because Martin was working for *Jackson* and wanted to keep the affair quiet. And Tasha had figured it out—or at least a connection between them."

212

Oh.

"Not everything is your fault, York."

He gave her a wry smile but looked away, his chest tight.

She put her hand on his cheek. "You. Are. Not to blame. You did nothing wrong."

He looked back at her. "Aw, RJ. Let's be real here. I've done a lot of things wrong. And a lot of wrong things."

Her thumb ran down his cheek, and he just wanted to close his eyes and lean in to her touch.

After.

Please, let them have an after.

"So, Tasha was killed because she was smart," York said. And that statement didn't do anything to make him feel better, but RJ took her hand away and nodded.

"Meanwhile, Jackson gets reelected and pops up the food chain and is given a position on the SASC—the Senate Armed Services Committee. She then builds a relationship with Russian General Boris Stanislov."

"Maybe that's who she was sleeping with," York said.

"Stop. That's Coco's father. And it's disgusting."

"It's disgusting any way you cut it."

"Let's hope that part was just a rumor. But while Jackson is on the SASC, she takes a couple more 'humanitarian' trips to Chechnya." She finger quoted the word *humanitarian*.

Oh, RJ was cute when she worked. And he respected the work, but he just wanted to push a strand of that dark hair behind her ear, let his touch linger...

"And somehow—what?—gets into a relationship with Tsarnaev?" She made a face. "Okay, maybe I'm dreaming all this up. Glo is probably right—her mother is a patriot. Nothing about this makes sense."

"You had a pretty good head of steam there. Let's attack this from the other side." He took the paper and wrote Arkady Petrov at the top. "Communist. Hard-liner. Wants Stanislov's job. Is affiliated with the Bratva, whose main source of money is trafficking—drugs, women, and guns. More war means more guns, which means more money. So, if they can cause a cold war between America and Russia, that's good business.

"Petrov and the Bratva have been trying to oust Stanislov since the bombing of the metro, putting in place their own informant and setting up an assassination, maybe even a coup. So, the Bratva hires Gustov to shoot Stanislov…and the shooting goes south, thanks to you." He held up a fist.

She grinned and bumped it.

And he nearly followed it with a kiss.

But she took up the analysis. "If Jackson is working with the Russians, of course they're going to protect her. Kobie and Plunkett, our bombers, are the real patriots, trying to stop her because Plunkett saw her working with Tsarnaev."

"Right. Because Graham was a POW at a camp in Chechnya," York said.

"That checked out, with both the facts and her time line," RJ said.

"But we still have the gap." He picked up the pencil and drew a line between Jackson and the Bratva. "Why?"

RJ sat back. "Jackson is a moderate. Hates guns and, until four months ago, was in an entirely different political party. I still can't figure out why she aligned with Isaac White. He's conservative, a former SEAL, and is pro-gun rights."

Cher had come downstairs, and now stood at the end of the hall. "Reba Jackson has wanted to be president as long as I've known Glo. So, my guess is that she'll do anything to win, even if it means switching parties." She'd spent most of the evening creating Glo's floral arrangement from the flowers Gerri had Coco order from a florist in Geraldine. She was pretty—red hair, tall, and wore a red-and-black kimono and leggings as she headed toward the fridge. "You don't think your mom would mind if I find a snack, would she?"

RJ shook her head.

York pushed thoughts of kissing RJ out of his.

But, "Why did she have to switch parties?"

Cher opened the fridge. "Rumor is she was low on money. Being the VP isn't a terrible position for a woman to have. Our first female VP in the man's world of politics." She took out a bag of baby carrots. Stood at the counter, pulling one out. "And of course, imagine what would happen if White died…"

"Oh my—" RJ said. "She'd be president."

But York was thinking of something else. "Imagine, Inc."

RJ looked at him.

"Imagine, Inc. It's a subsidiary of the Jackson Foundation, right?"

"Yes."

He pulled her computer over and typed the name in the search bar. A page of listings of articles popped up. "They're all over the world."

"Oh, sure," Cher said. "The Jackson Foundation is huge. They build schools and dig wells and fight the AIDs epidemic—"

"So why is she out of money?" York asked.

Cher retrieved another carrot and put the bag back into the fridge. "By the way, I know you guys have Sloan locked in the bathroom, but I still think it was really nice of Tate to invite him to the wedding. Sloan really had a thing for Glo." She headed back upstairs.

RJ was looking at York, trying to repress a smile.

"Yeah, really nice of Tate," York whispered. "Because if we're right, it's Sloan who'll need protection."

"I'm still not sure how I feel about that. If I'm right, then we've uncovered an international conspiracy two weeks before a national election."

"And if we're wrong, then we locked an innocent man in the bathroom."

"There's worse places to be imprisoned. Like, I dunno, gulag?"

York laughed, her words stirring memories of their escape from Russia. He met her eyes, saw the same memories in them. Her hand curled around his on the table, and suddenly he felt his heartbeat turn to a fist in his chest.

He'd even go to gulag if he could be with her.

He nearly gave in to the impulse to lean in and kiss her.

"So, Imagine might have been a shell company with a fake office front," RJ said, cutting off the impulse. She let go of his hand.

"What if the Jackson Foundation has other shell companies?"

"Maybe we should get Sloan out of the tub," York said, aware of his hand still on the table. "Do some more Q & A."

"Not without Tate. He'd killed us. And right now, he's just trying to keep Glo calm and get her down the aisle."

"If it were me, this wedding wouldn't be happening."

"Why?"

"It just doesn't feel right. It feels too rushed." He shook his head. "I'm tired of all this. I wish…"

"You wish you were back in Shelly."

"No. But I can tell you that as soon as this is over—" And he wasn't sure he was ready to say it, but his hand still tingled from her touch. "I want us to disappear."

Her eyes widened. "What?"

"I keep thinking about what Hardwin said. About your mom being light in his dark world." He caught her hand again. "You're that for me, Syd."

"Oh, York." Her breath caught, something tender on her face. "I—"

And he couldn't stop himself. He leaned forward and kissed her.

She tasted sweet, of late-night coffee and the teamwork between them.

Except her breath caught. And then she put her hand on his chest. Pushed. He leaned away, a little surprised. "What—"

She made a face. "I…I don't know if I'm ready."

He stared at her, the words not forming.

And that's when her expression crumpled. "York…"

Just like that, his world ended. "Oh. I see."

"No, you don't—"

"Yes, I do. I've changed too much. I'm not…"

"I love the man I see!"

Oh.

She stood up, whisked the tears from her face. "But the man I see—this amazing man—he doesn't want what *I want* anymore."

Um, "What *do* you want, RJ?"

Her expression betrayed pain. "I don't want a life in Shelly.

Or on my ranch in Montana. I was built for something different. Something—" She looked at her notebook.

"Something more exciting," he said quietly.

"Yes." She swallowed, nodded.

He stood up too, his throat tight, burning. "I can't live that life, RJ. Because my memories are back—all of them. I remember how my wife died. I remember my son floating in the bathtub. I remember how it turned me jaded and angry and I was filled with hate with every cell in my body. I pushed it down, and by the time I met you in Russia, I'd learned to live with it or dodge it, but it was always inside me, a burning ember. And then...then my memory was wiped and I became Mack. And yes, I remember the darkness now, but the one thing that took, with Mack, was the forgiveness. The moment at the altar when everything—all of the darkness and pain and grief and hatred—vanished. Washed away. I could breathe for the first time in...well, I can't remember how long."

She was staring at him, nodding. "I know. I saw your face."

"Then you know that I can't be the old York again and survive. I need to let him die."

"York. I want a man who wants to know and follow Jesus. But I..."

"Loved the old York."

"I love the new one too. I just don't think he wants this RJ. And this is the only one I have." A tear dripped off her chin.

He couldn't breathe through the claws in his chest. She didn't want the life he dreamed for them.

"I'm so sorry, York."

His jaw clenched, and he blinked hard, his eyes burning. "Yeah. I get it."

They stood there in silence, a gulf between them.

"I'll go get Tate so we can question Sloan," RJ said quietly, wiping her cheeks with her hands. She got up and headed for the door to fetch Tate from the barn.

And he just wanted to punch something. "I'll get Sloan."

He went down the hallway to the tiny bathroom. He unwound the rope securing the door.

"Sloan, I'm coming in, but you jump me, and you'll regret it." Apparently, he still had old York in him somewhere.

But when he opened the door, Sloan wasn't standing on the toilet with the soap dispenser, waiting to clobber him.

And he wasn't under the sink or even behind the door.

But York had the sneaking suspicion he was somewhere beyond the tiny open window, out into them thar hills, running for his life.

12

Her groom was going to have a heart attack before she even got him to the altar.

Glo couldn't decide whom Tate blamed the most for Sloan's escape—Sloan or himself for thinking Sloan couldn't squeeze through the tiny bathroom window.

But he'd nearly lost his head when RJ came running out of the house with the news of Sloan's escape.

Glo had been upstairs writing out her vows—things about loving Tate through every season and how she'd never let her fear push him away—and that's when she heard him shout.

By the time she looked out the window, he'd galvanized his brothers in a search.

Reuben took the ranch truck, Knox on one of the horses, Tate in the four-wheeler, and Wyatt came into the house.

York had taken off into the backyard on foot.

Tate had found Sloan in less than an hour, near the road, hiding in a ditch. Glo didn't mention the facial bruises on both of them when he hauled Sloan back to the ranch. It made Sloan look beat-up—but only toughened Tate's hard-edged expression as he threw Sloan back into the bathroom, boarding up the window with plywood.

He retied the door shut, then grabbed a sofa pillow and sat on the floor, just down the hall from the door.

"Seriously? The night before our wedding?" She hunkered down next to him. "You need a decent night's sleep." She handed him a bag of ice for the bruise on his cheekbone. She'd already given one to Sloan right before Tate locked him away.

"I won't sleep," Tate said. "I can't believe I was so stupid to fall for his lies."

Glo nodded. "I even believed him. I didn't want to, but—"

"He's a lobbyist. A politician. Of course he'd twist things to make us believe him."

She wound her fingers through his and leaned against his shoulder. "Do you think he wanted to talk to my mother so he could hurt her?"

"I don't know. Maybe. But don't worry—that's not going to happen."

"So, it's over."

He nodded and kissed the top of her head.

And sorry, but that wasn't enough. She pressed her hand against his cheek and kissed him. The kind of kiss that said exactly what she'd written in her vows—that she trusted him. Loved him, even when she was afraid. Believed in him.

Believed in their happy ending.

He made a sound deep in the back of his throat, unlatching his hand and winding his arm around her, pulling her against him. As if he might be vowing to her the same things.

He tasted of the night, his whiskers scraping her face, his grip tight, and tomorrow couldn't arrive fast enough.

Especially when he deepened his kiss, right there in the dark hallway of their house.

Oh, Tate, I love you too.

He finally broke away, breathing a little hard, and met her eyes. "Go to bed, Glo. We're pretty safe here in the hallway of my house, but the fact we're getting married tomorrow is playing a game in my head, and I need you to walk away from me."

By the heat in his eyes, he wasn't kidding. She caught his face in her hands, gave him one last quick kiss, and got up. "Please don't spend the night in the hallway."

He gave her a smile. "Everything is going to be okay. We're going to have an unforgettable day tomorrow."

"Okay, Marshal Dillon, have a good night."

She left him there.

And resisted the urge to return to him all night long.

But maybe he was right because she woke to glorious blue skies, the sun arching over the eastern horizon, the wind sweeping the scent of lodgepole pine and prairie grasses into her open windows. Gerri had generously given up her master bedroom for Glo and Cher. Dixie and Elijah Blue had found hotel rooms in town, and her mother and her security team, as well as her father, had arrived last night at the vacation house Tate had rented.

Tate wanted to clear the air with her mother, but of course her mother was innocent. RJ was weaving a conspiracy theory out of mid-air.

And, the last thing Glo wanted was her fiction darkening her wedding day.

Cher had hired a minister from Geraldine who'd agreed to the hasty ceremony. Glo's mother wasn't thrilled with the family-only event, but she wouldn't have been happy with anything less than a star-studded gala on the lawns of the Jackson estate, Glo in a ball gown and tiara.

Hardly a production they could pull off with only two weeks before the election.

Besides, Glo wasn't a ball gown and tiara kind of girl.

Her wedding dress hung from a hanger on the closet door, the short, gauzy veil with the vintage white cap hanging nearby, and her crystal-studded white cowboy boots in a bag on a third hanger.

Cher hadn't been able to rent a tux for Tate, so he was wearing one of his suits. Not her first choice, but Tate would look amazing in a burlap bag, so Glo didn't care.

In fact, the only thing she wanted was Tate, at the altar, his hands in hers, saying *I do*.

I do and will forever and ever, amen.

Yes, she'd been silly to be so afraid of some kind of disaster destroying her day. Her future.

You have to believe that no matter what happens, you're going to be okay. That God's grace is enough. Dixie's words. Glo was determined to believe she was right.

She found the kitchen abuzz with activity when she came downstairs in a bathrobe, her hair back in a bandanna.

Cher and Kelsey sat at the table winding twine around chrysanthemums to affix to the folding chairs Knox had picked up from their small church in town. Gerri was marinating the chicken and beef for the kebabs while Gilly finished loading a two-tier tray of cupcakes.

Outside, Glo spotted Swamp and Rags, two of her security detail. They'd spent the night at the vacation house, so a good bet was that her mother was nearby. And hopefully her father, although he'd probably be out in the barn or somewhere on the ranch in conversation with one of the guys.

Reuben was on the porch cleaning the grill.

RJ was chopping zucchini for the kebabs, her expression one of disapproval.

Probably because Sloan was sitting at the kitchen island, drinking a cup of coffee and eating a cinnamon roll, York watching him with those scary blue eyes, his expression grim. Tate hadn't let RJ or York talk to Sloan last night, refusing to let him spin any more lies about her mother.

Thank you, Tate. Glo didn't want to hold anything against RJ, but the woman had conspiracy theories floating around her analyst brain.

Then again, that was her job—to root out nefarious plots.

Glo could hardly believe that the traitor inside her mother's organization was Sloan. But it made sense. She'd even talked it over with Kelsey and Cher last night.

"He knew where Tate was in Vegas, both times," Kelsey said after hearing the story.

"And let's not forget he was insanely jealous of you and Tate," Cher added. "I'm sure your mother asked him to vet Tate when he first joined your band. So he knew all about his past, especially his involvement with the Bratva."

"I just never thought he would try and *kill* him." Although, maybe she really didn't know Sloan.

"And he was at the hotel where that woman was killed," Kelsey said. "RJ's boss."

222

"Sophia Randall. Right. Which puts him in Seattle for the shooting at my mom's rally."

"Maybe Tate *was* the target," Kelsey had said.

And that had sent a tremble into Glo's bones.

But Sloan was under watch now, and he couldn't hurt anyone.

Still, it unnerved her to see him sitting at the island as if he might be a guest. He looked at her. "Good morning."

She frowned. "Yeah."

"Don't worry, honey, he'll be back in the bathroom soon enough," York growled.

"No, he won't." Her mother emerged from said bathroom. She wore a black dress with full, lacy arms, her hair down around her shoulders.

"Black, Mom, really?"

"Sorry, honey. I came right from a charity gala and didn't have time to pick up a new gown. I decided this was better than a white pantsuit, right?" She kissed Glo on the cheek, then turned to York and held out her hand. "We met in Seattle."

"Ma'am," he said and shook her hand. "I appreciate your compassion, but Sloan—"

"Is innocent," Her mother said.

Silence as all motion in the kitchen stopped.

"See?" Sloan said. "I knew your mother would vouch for me."

Her mother held up her hand. She knew how to command a room, knew how to find exactly the right expression of disdain and confidence. "I didn't say he hadn't made mistakes. Clearly what he did to Tate—"

"Ma'am!" Sloan started, but her mother gave him a look and he closed his mouth.

"Let's say, for argument's sake, that he was behind the attack on Tate. It still doesn't make him guilty of murder. My team took a look at Tate's information, and Sloan has satisfactory alibis for each event."

Where was Tate? Glo had expected him to be sitting in the kitchen watching Sloan like a bulldog. Except maybe he'd been up all night, so perhaps he was getting some winks.

Or maybe he was executing his usual prowl around the perimeter.

"Of course he won't be allowed to leave, not until the proper authorities can verify his story. I've called the FBI, and they're sending a team out to secure Sloan. Until then…" She turned to Sloan. "You've been a valuable member of my team for many years, and a friend of the family. You can join us at the wedding."

"Mom!"

Her mother turned to Glo. Took a breath. "You're right. It's up to you, honey."

Really? Glo stared at her, a little speechless. Out of the corner of her eye, Sloan was looking away, something pained on his face.

Oh, maybe her mother was right. Her mother had vouched for him.

"Fine. Okay."

Her mother nodded. "That's my girl." She kissed Glo on the cheek again. "Oh, and your father is outside with Tate, giving him the talk, but he'll be in shortly."

The talk?

What talk?

But neither Tate nor her father mentioned it when they came in from whatever father-son chat they'd had out near the corral.

Tate nearly went ballistic again when Glo summed up her mother's verdict, but when York said he'd watch Sloan, he consigned himself to the fact that the senator had the last say.

For now.

Really, it didn't matter.

Again, the only thing Glo wanted was Tate, at the altar, his hands in hers, saying *I do.*

And maybe for nothing disastrous to happen. Like a sudden snowstorm or perhaps a nuclear bomb detonation.

"Hey, Glo-light," her father said as he grabbed a cup of coffee. He wore a pair of gray pants, a white shirt, a vest, and a bow tie. And, of course, his black Cons.

"You're looking very history professorish today."

"At least I don't have chalk in my hair." He kissed her cheek. He'd cut his long hair for a big fund-raising dinner four months ago, but now it was curly again around his ears.

"Working on that man bun I see."

"School's already started. I feel like a hockey player without a beard."

She laughed. Leaned close. "Wanna tell me what you and Tate talked about?"

"Just the usual. If he hurts you, I'll kill him, that sort of thing." He winked.

And somehow, right then, the day turned perfect.

See, she had nothing to worry about. Especially when she stood at the threshold of the porch some three hours later, the sun a glorious chandelier to their afternoon wedding. A white runner down the aisle of grass was framed by red, yellow, and orange chrysanthemums in mason jars.

And at the end, past the smiling faces of their small congregation, stood Tate.

Glo could barely breathe. He wore a black suit, a silver bow tie at his neck, and a pair of shiny, black cowboy boots. He'd shaved and now stared at her with such a look—yearning, admiration, love—it was a good thing she could hang on to her father's arm.

Except it wasn't an unknown minister standing at the end of the aisle, but…Hardwin?

She looked at Cher standing beside her. "What?"

"The minister couldn't make it. Gerri said that Hardwin was licensed to perform weddings in Montana—he'd done one for his daughter a year or so back. We checked, and his license was still good…see, everything is going to be just fine. No disaster waiting. And you look gorgeous, by the way."

Yes, maybe, by the look in Tate's eyes as she glanced toward him. Her groom was flanked by Knox, then Reuben and Wyatt. Too bad his brother Ford couldn't be here, but that was military life.

Cher handed her the bouquet of dark purple calla lilies as Dixie began playing "A Thousand Years" on her violin.

Not even the sight of Sloan standing two chairs down from her mother could mar the day. She ignored him, her gaze on her groom as she headed toward him.

Overhead, a hawk cried, the sound piercing through the music.

She slowed, but Tate didn't take his eyes off her. Just gave her a slow, warm smile.

Held out his hand when she reached him.

"Hey," he said softly. "I thought you'd never get here."

Oh, Tater.

Hardwin smiled at her, nothing of the embarrassment of his failed proposal in his expression. She didn't have time to wonder at that because he dove in to the ceremony with greetings, a prayer.

"I wanted to say a few words about marriage," Hardwin said, and just for a moment, his gaze cut past them to the audience.

She didn't have to guess who his target might be.

"Marriage is meant to be a taste of heaven. A taste of that amazing union of the church—the Bride—and her Savior. See, we were made for eternity. For much more beyond this life. But we can't see eternity, can't taste it, and we have to live on faith that it's out there. And so God, in His kindness, gave us glimpses here. The beauty of this world, the laughter of our children, friendships and support of our family, and the love of our spouse. Even our suffering gives us a taste of heaven because it drives us into the arms of our good, good Father."

Tate looked down, away, and it occurred to her that his own father wasn't here. She squeezed his hand.

"And that's what I want you to remember as you walk into this new life together. Lean in to each other, but lean also in to God. Remind yourself, through everything, who He is. God is good. He is our rescuer, the tearer downer of strongholds, our forgiver and provider, and most of all, the victor. When all else is done, God is enough, everything, and always. Let not your hearts be troubled. Believe in God. Believe also in Jesus. Trust Him to give you what you need. And in this, you will find what you truly hunger for—peace for your souls. Let's stand and pray, and then we'll ask Tate and Glo if they want to be married to each other."

Tate looked at her, his eyes a little reddened. Nodded.

You have to believe that no matter what happens, you're going to be okay.

That God's grace is enough.

Yes, yes it was, no matter—

A crack sounded, a distant roar that dissipated into the sky.

Tate jerked, and in a second, he wrapped his arms around Glo, enfolding her to himself.

What—? "Tate, let me go!"

Another crack, and this time Tate brought her to the ground.

"Is someone *shooting* at us?"

Maybe, because screams erupted along with the shouts of the security team.

"Everybody down!" Maybe York's voice, maybe one of the brothers, she didn't know.

She just knew that Tate's body covered hers, his breath in her ear. "Don't move."

And then he got up.

She grabbed him, her hand in his jacket. "Where are you going?"

He looked at her and when another shot sounded, braced his body over hers, his mouth close to her ear. "Let go of me, Glo. I think your mother's been shot."

———◆———

It happened so fast, RJ had trouble sorting it out.

One minute she was standing beside her mother, tumbling Hardwin's words through her head—*When all else is done, God is enough, everything, and always.*

And then, the shot. At first, it sounded like the kind of shot she'd grown up hearing occasionally on the range. Usually a rancher shooting a critter, or maybe a hunter after a deer.

But then Senator Jackson screamed. Someone nearby her took her down, and she curled into a ball, still screaming.

And in that second, the case RJ had built against Jackson exploded. Clearly, *she was the target*, and RJ had conjured up a conspiracy theory of epic proportions when, instead, they should still be looking for a shooter.

Probably Damien Gustov, in league with the Bratva, who

wanted to derail the conservative party's candidates and weaken America when they put Petrov in power.

Then the second shot sounded, and RJ hit her knees.

Only then did she realize that the man who'd landed on the senator was Sloan.

Wait—*what?*

She scrabbled toward the woman, but Tate was already there. "It's Sloan! He's trying to kill the Senator!"

She didn't know who shouted it, but, wrong again, because Sloan lay still, slumped over the woman, who was hitting him, still screaming. "Get him off me!"

"Ma'am, don't move," Tate was saying as he pulled Sloan away.

RJ spotted blood pooling on Senator Jackson's body, center mass.

They needed to stop the bleeding. RJ climbed to her feet, but York yanked her down so hard she fell in the grass next to him. "Stay down!"

"The senator!"

"It's not my blood—it's not mine!" Jackson shouted.

And that's when RJ realized why Sloan had fallen.

Maybe to protect the senator, maybe not. But someone had shot him through the heart.

Sloan was very, very dead, his eyes already glassy, his chest sopping blood.

RJ's brain was scrambling that fact through her head when Glo screamed and crawled over to her mother.

Tate caught her. "Inside the house, Glo," he said and got up, his body around hers, and took off for the house.

A couple of the senator's security personnel had raced in to cover Jackson.

"Let's get inside," York said. He'd crawled over to hover beside RJ, studying the activity around them, his face grim.

And then his face paled, horror bleeding into his expression. He looked back at RJ.

"What—?"

She turned.

And screamed.

Her mother lay on the ground, moaning, writhing. Knox and Reuben kneeling on either side of her, Reuben's hands on her chest trying to stave a flow of blood that leached out around his grip. Knox was tearing off his shirt, wadding it into a ball, visibly shaking. "Get help!"

Wyatt took off for the house, not even bothering to duck. Coco had grabbed Mikka, and now he ran behind them, protecting them, his back to the shooter.

York clamped his arms around RJ, a vise that, for the moment, kept her from shattering. "It's okay, she'll be okay—"

RJ couldn't stop screaming.

Knox shoved his shirt over the wound and took over the pressure as Reuben got up. Gilly was still crouched on the ground, her hands over her belly. "We'll get the plane warmed up," he said to her, and she nodded as he pulled her in tight next to him and took off for the house.

"You'll never get to the hospital in time," Hardwin said. He was also crouched next to Knox. "Let me call a friend—he's got a rescue chopper and a medical team." He was already on his cell phone, his hands shaking.

He covered his mouth and turned away.

The shooting had stopped.

"Get in the house, RJ," York said.

"I'm not leaving my mother!" She tried to wrestle out of his grip, but he wasn't letting her go, his hold tightening.

"Okay, okay. Just breathe."

Breathe. As her mother bled to death. But she stopped trying to shake away. Instead she wound her fingers around his strong forearms and hung on.

Kelsey crouched next to Knox. "Elevate her legs or she'll go into shock."

"Get in the house, Kels," Knox barked. "Right now."

Even RJ was afraid at Knox's shattered, terrified tone.

Kelsey got up and ran.

The security team had hustled Jackson in too, which just left Sloan's dead body, her mother, and the handful of people trying to save her life.

"Chopper is on the way," Hardwin said. He took Ma's hand. "Don't you die on me, Gerri Marshall. Even if you won't marry me, I'm not going anywhere. I love you."

Oh, RJ might throw up, right there, and she simply gave in to York's arms around her, turning her face away. "God, please, please don't let her die."

"She's still breathing," Knox said. "Ma, stay awake."

"Let's get her inside," Reuben said, running back to them. He scooped up their mother as if she weighed nothing. Knox pressed his hands on her chest and they headed toward the house.

RJ held her breath, unable to move.

Still, no more shots.

"Let's go," York said and took her hand.

Inside, they put her mother on the kitchen floor. Kelsey and Coco had retrieved towels and now pressed them against the wound. RJ had taken a look—it seemed the bullet had hit somewhere on the right side of her chest—probably missing her heart, but certainly her lungs had to be damaged.

Her mother wasn't breathing well, making tiny, pained noises. "Hang in there, Ma."

Knox hit his feet. Turned to Hardwin. "Your chopper isn't going to make it—we gotta take her by plane."

"They'll have medical equipment and EMTs."

"We can fly her to Helena," Reuben said. "Gilly's already getting the plane warmed up."

"Kalispell has the number one trauma center in Montana," Hardwin said, his voice terribly, perfectly calm. "And it's just about the same distance."

And in that moment, he reminded RJ so much of her father, it nearly buckled her legs. Calm. And completely committed to saving their mother.

But not the same, either, because he was standing back, letting the brothers care for their mother.

Then again, he wasn't her husband.

Yet.

Oh please, Ma. Because her mother had found a true man in

Hardwin. A man who wouldn't walk away.

A man to share all the moments with her—*please* let her have more moments.

And maybe RJ had found a true man, too, because York still had a hold of her hand. He wasn't running around like crazy Tate trying to save the world.

York was just right here, with her, saving hers.

Even though she told him they couldn't be together.

But as she stared at her mother trying to breathe, blood pooling on the kitchen floor, she realized—

She wanted York more than she wanted a life that—well, that could explode in her hands at any moment. What had he said? *I'd eat turnips if it meant you were with me.*

Yeah, turnips for her too. Because she would rather be with him for all the boring moments than without him for the big ones.

Forever and ever, amen.

But now wasn't the time to tell him that.

Hardwin walked out to the porch, again on his phone. This time, RJ heard shouting.

Tate came charging back into the room. RJ wasn't sure where he'd gone—maybe to see Jackson and her crew off back to the vacation house.

Glo sat on the sofa in the family room, her arms wrapped around herself in her beautiful, now grass-and-blood-stained wedding dress, her knees scraped from when Tate tackled her, tears streaming down her face.

RJ felt bad for her. And now replayed their conversation in the den in her head.

Glo was *so sure* her mother was innocent.

Except…and amidst all the chaos and horror, as Tate and her brothers packed their mother's wound with ice and bandages, it came to RJ—what if *Sloan* had been the target?

What if everything he said had been true? He hadn't been a traitor but had indeed been framed. A scapegoat for someone else's actions. Because why else would he leap on the senator, trying to protect her?

Hardwin came back inside. "Let's get her down to the plane. They're on their way, but they might not get here in time."

"We need a stretcher," Knox said.

Wyatt walked over to a kitchen drawer, took out a butter knife, and started to remove the hinges on the pantry door.

Tate helped him.

"What if Sloan was the target?" she said to York and maybe anyone else who was listening. "What if he was silenced because—"

"Oh, not this again," Glo said, jumping up. "Seriously? Someone just tried to *murder my mother* and you're going to bring up your crazy conspiracy theory?"

"Glo—c'mon!" Tate was saying as he brought over the door. "Not now." He looked at RJ with a glare.

"But—if he was the target, why would he try and save her life?"

"He didn't try and save her life!" Tate shouted. "The shooter missed!" He turned to Reuben. "Let's lift her onto the board."

"Did he? What if this was intended to silence—"

"Shut up, RJ!" Wyatt said, crouching near their mother, lifting her shoulders with the rest of his brothers. "Just *shut up.*"

His tone rocked RJ back, but no more than the look he gave her after they settled their mother on the door. "You got us all into this freakin' mess—if you hadn't gone over to Russia with your stupid overactive imagination—"

"Hey!" York said.

"No, you hey," Knox said, getting up. "Step back, York." He looked at Wyatt. "This isn't the time."

"When is the time, Knox?" Tate said. "This is crazy, RJ! Sloan escaped so he could connect with whomever his shooter was— probably this Martin guy you talked about."

"Martin is dead," York said quietly.

"Really?" Tate said. "How do you know?"

"Really." York let go of RJ's hand, took a breath, and stepped toward Tate. "Because I killed him."

And the entire room went quiet. Tate just blinked at York, and Knox blew out a breath. Reuben ignored them all, motioning to Wyatt to pick up the other end of the door.

But Wyatt was looking at RJ. "Nice. So now, whoever is after you is after *us*." He lifted the door, his gaze on RJ. "You brought an assassin into our lives and now Ma is dying."

And if there was any air left in the room, Wyatt's words sucked it out.

York's not an assassin, she wanted to say, but the words wouldn't emerge. Because, actually, well…

RJ's eyes filled and she turned away, pressed her hand to her mouth.

"Let's go," Hardwin said, but behind his words came the distant hum of a chopper.

He ran out to the backyard, waving his hands.

Tate didn't look at RJ as he held open the door for Reuben and Wyatt, as they carried their mother to the chopper, Knox still pressing on her wound.

The blue-and-red chopper landed in the yard, and the door opened. A couple of EMTs came out, a man with long brown hair tied back, the other a taller man, the copilot. A woman sat in the cockpit, kept the rotors turning.

The two EMTs transferred her mother onto a gurney and loaded her into the chopper, securing the gurney to the floor. Meanwhile, the brothers waged a loaded conversation, hidden under the roar of the chopper, as to who might ride with her.

Reuben won.

He got in and the doors closed, and RJ stood with her hand to her mouth as the bird rose into the blue sky. *Stay alive, Ma.*

Silence descended as the brothers came back inside. No one looked at her. Knox went to the sink to wash his hands.

"The Cessna holds five passengers" Knox said, grabbing a towel.

"I'll stay here with Mikka," Coco said, her arms around her son as they sat in a leather chair. The boy looked spooked. "Wyatt, you should go."

"I'll stay too," Kelsey said. "Knox. Go be with your mom."

Glo's mouth tightened as she looked at Tate, her eyes filling. But she nodded.

Tate closed his eyes, looking pained. Then sighed, opened them, and nodded. "I'll get Swamp and Rags over here."

"I'm sorry, but RJ isn't going anywhere without me," York said quietly, and RJ looked at him. "So, if we need to take the truck—"

"You're going on the stupid plane," Tate growled. "Let's go." He too had washed his hands and now threw the towel in the sink.

York took her hand again.

As they left, she realized that Hardwin's truck was already gone.

She'd never endured a more miserable flight. They touched down at the airport, took a cab to the hospital, and arrived just as her mother was going into surgery.

Still alive.

Hardwin arrived twenty minutes later. He sat away from them, and RJ couldn't help but feel sorry for the man.

But she was afraid to say anything. Because maybe they all were right.

Maybe this *was* her fault.

She finally got up and headed out into the hallway, stopping by the big windows that overlooked the mountains to the north. The sun had sunk to just above the ragged horizon, tipping the early season snow a blood red, the backdrop a bruised magenta.

She pressed her hand against the pane.

"They're wrong, you know."

She didn't expect the voice that followed her.

"Just because people do bad things doesn't mean we're responsible for their actions," Hardwin said softly. "You're just like your mother. She's smart and brave and she would have done the same thing if she had to."

"What, go to Russia and get in way over her head?" RJ turned, her eyes filling. "And bring trouble home to her family?"

Hardwin had taken off his Stetson and now ran his fingers along the rim. "She would have done what was right, regardless of the cost. Because that is the core of who your mother is. And who you are, RJ. Who you *all* are. And I guess it's because of your

234

father, also—you're like him too. You have his heart."

"What if she dies?" Her voice trembled.

Hardwin reached out and pulled her into a hug.

She covered her face with her hands, letting her fears shake out.

"Shh," he said. "It's going to be okay."

"My brothers hate me."

"No they don't. They're scared, just like you, and they want someone to blame when life feels out of control."

"They refuse to listen to me."

"Yeah?" He leaned back. "Well, your man York is having it out with them right now."

Her eyes widened.

"He's got your back, kiddo."

Huh. She wiped her cheeks. "Are you going to ask my mom to marry you again?"

He gave her a crooked smile. "If she wants me to. And if she doesn't, then I'm going to stick around anyway. Because I love her. Now, I'm going to get some coffee. You want some?"

She nodded.

Hardwin left her there and headed down the hallway.

York is having it out with them right now.

And then the words York said in the kitchen came back to her.

He'd killed Martin. Or at least *thought* he did. But Crowley said Martin might be still alive...

And finally the last of the puzzle pieces fell into place.

There was only one person who tied everyone together, who knew what York knew, who had been there at the beginning, and now at the end.

Who knew all the players, the big picture, and probably the end game.

This *was* all her fault.

She turned and headed down the hallway, back to the waiting room.

Her phone buzzed, however, and she pulled it out. Didn't recognize the number.

"Hello?"

"You just can't obey orders, can you?"

Her breath caught.

"It's been you all along."

"You're too smart for your own good."

"Clearly not smart enough. I should have guessed this was personal."

"Very." He hung up.

She stilled, looked at her phone. Then, oh, *York!* He had to know—

But from behind her, a hand covered her mouth, an arm pulled her against a hard male body and dragged her into the stairwell.

She kicked at him, but a hard prick into her neck, the cool rush of liquid told her that the fun and games had just begun.

RJ's brothers looked like they wanted to take him out, each one, separately.

Yeah, well, let's go.

That's what York wanted to say. Because it twisted him up inside to see RJ hurt, to see her reddened eyes.

To watch her walk out of the room.

"You guys were way too hard on her."

Right about then Hardwin had walked out, and York had the sense of being the lone dog amongst wolves.

Tate gave him a look. "York, I get that you want to protect her—"

"Of course I do. I love her. But I also know she's right." York didn't raise his voice, just kept it even, calm.

But with enough threat to let them know that Tate wasn't the only alpha dog in the group.

He didn't want to throw down with RJ's brothers, but he would, if he had to. "You need to listen to me. RJ is smart, really smart, and she's figured this thing out."

Tate was shaking his head.

"I know it sounds crazy"—and he held up his hand to Tate—"but RJ has drawn a line between Reba Jackson and everything that's happened."

"I think the more you persist with this, the more we waste our time," Tate said. "You had me thinking it was Sloan, and all my attention was on him and not on the fact that there was a shooter in my backyard!"

"Then do your freakin' job better!"

Tate took a step toward him. "If I hadn't suspected Sloan, I would have set up a perimeter—"

"Just stop, you two," Reuben said. He stood by the window, looking out. "This is exactly what evil wants—us fighting each other." He turned. "It drove us apart before, and…well, the last thing Ma would want is our family yelling at each other."

"He's not my family," Wyatt snapped.

"But he probably will be." The voice came from the doorway and York turned to see Ford standing there, dressed in his civvies, holding hands with Scarlett. His hair bore a fresh clipping, and he came into the room looking travel weary, a strain around his eyes.

"Ford? What—"

"Sorry I'm late—our plane in Helena just landed and Hardwin called me on the way to the hospital." Ford walked in. "How's Ma?"

Knox leaned forward, his hands on his knees. "Tough shape. The bullet collapsed her lung, and she has quite a bit of internal bleeding."

Ford nodded, his jaw tight.

York glanced at him, a little surprised at his unlikely ally. The last time he'd seen Ford the man had left a few bruises.

Ford came over to him. "So you're not dead after all."

York looked at him, but Ford smiled. "RJ refused to stop looking for you. She believed that you're apparently superhuman."

He wanted to smile at that. But Ford's words raised the prayer that kept rattling around inside him. The one he'd spoken nearly a week ago at the altar in Shelly. *Please, Jesus…help me to live as a new man.*

For a week he'd been trying to figure out what that meant—a

237

new man. Sort of thought it meant starting over, far away from his old life.

But something Hardwin had said kept ringing through his mind too. *When all else is done, God is enough, everything, and always.*

What if living as a new man wasn't about changing his location or his name or even his skill set—but what Caleb had said… just him, clinging to God?

Just him and God, nothing else between them. No hate, no anger, no fear—

And we know that in all things God works for the good of those who love him, who have been called according to his purpose.

Maybe his purpose wasn't a mission or a name or even a location but a surrender.

What if he was just supposed to do and be who God told him he was?

Trust Him to give you what you need. And in this, you will find what you truly hunger for—peace for your souls.

He hungered for peace. For home. For RJ.

And maybe a small town. Lasagna. Baseball.

But not today. Not yet.

Because he also hungered for justice.

Which felt like something that was very much on God's list also.

"I'm not superhuman," he said now to the Marshall brothers. "But I do have a certain set of skills that might help you catch the person who shot your mother."

Tate looked at him. Then he gave a slow nod.

Wyatt too.

Knox sighed. "Thanks, York."

Ford clamped him on the shoulder.

Hardwin walked back in, carrying coffee. Looked around. "Where's RJ? I got her a cup of coffee."

York frowned. "I'll go find her."

But as he was starting to leave, the surgeon came into the room. He wore scrubs, a tall man who introduced himself as Dr. Wilson. "She's out of surgery and doing well. We have her in recovery, but she'll be in a room in a bit—you can see her then."

York could nearly feel the collective relief from her sons as he exited the room. He looked up the hall for RJ.

Found the vending machines. Came back. "Did you see her, Hardwin, when you went for coffee?"

"Yes," Hardwin said and frowned. "We talked. She got a call just as I was leaving."

Huh.

York exited again and this time headed downstairs to the lobby. Sometimes with calls, reception was spotty in a hospital.

He lifted his own burner phone, the one he'd picked up in Vegas, from his pocket. Dialed RJ's number.

Got her voicemail.

And now he was worried.

He called again. "RJ, call me when you get this." Texted the same message.

She wasn't outside in the parking lot.

The hair started to rise on the back of his neck.

He returned to the waiting room, hoping she'd beat him back. The brothers were just starting to leave to visit their mother.

Ford gave him a frown.

"I can't find RJ."

Ford turned to Scarlett. York recognized her from the alley-way in Russia, the woman who had crossed an ocean with Ford to find his sister. "Can you check the ladies room?"

Thank you, Ford, for being worried. "It's weird, right?"

Ford nodded. Reuben, Knox, Tate, Wyatt and Hardwin followed a nurse down the hall toward Gerri's room. Ford waited with him.

Ford looked at him. "We never, um...so..." He shoved his hands in his pockets. "Thanks for watching RJ's back in Russia."

"Thanks for getting her home."

"I'm glad you're not dead."

"Thanks."

Scarlett returned, shaking her head.

And now York was starting to freak out, a fist in his gut. RJ—

His phone vibrated in his hand. The only one who knew his number was RJ. "Hey. Where are you? Are you okay?"

"Da," said the voice. *"Vso Horosho."*

York stiffened, the Russian like an old shoe he'd slipped on and was still trying to work out the kinks. Because the voice stirred up a dark, age-old threat, one he'd tried to forget.

And, he understood the words perfectly.

Of *course*. He closed his eyes, his jaw tight. "Where is she?" he said in Russian, glancing at Ford, then walking to the window. He looked down three stories to the parking lot, scanning it. He switched to English, his voice emerging in a growl. "You'd better not have hurt her."

"She'll be just fine, York. All I want is you."

He didn't even pause. "Deal. When and where."

He got a location. Hung up.

Ford had followed him. "That wasn't RJ."

"No. But we're going to get her back." He pocketed the phone. "Don't tell your brothers what's going on. I need to finish this. But I promise—RJ will be coming home." He strode past Ford.

The SEAL stopped him with a hand to his chest. "You're not doing this alone."

York moved his hand away. "He just wants me. And RJ would kill me if any of you got hurt."

"RJ believes you're a good man, worth fighting for. And I'm inclined to believe her."

York considered him, a little moved by the words. Yes, he would have wanted to be in this family. He moved away from Ford. "Thanks. But RJ's wrong. I'm not a good man. Not today, at least."

13

His mother could have died and it was all his fault. Tate wanted to put a fist through the arrogant visage in the mirror. Why hadn't he listened to RJ?

Because in his heart he didn't want her to be right. Didn't want to believe that he'd spent the past six months helping a traitor. Believing in someone who had no regard for the safety of their country.

The one his Ranger brothers had died for.

Frankly, Tate still didn't know what to believe, especially with RJ's words sticking in his head like a burr—*What if this was intended to silence—*

Wyatt shouldn't have snapped at her—Tate knew that—but they were watching their mother bleed out, and RJ's obsession with her conspiracy theory was the last thing they needed.

Although, what if she was right? Now that he'd seen his mother and called Glo and also Swamp, just to make sure the house was on lockdown, Tate had a second to process.

To breathe.

Either he'd completely dropped the ball on his job or...or RJ was right, and this hit wasn't for Senator Jackson but Sloan.

Either way, he stared at the face in the mirror and shook his head. "You're an idiot."

Because, as usual, he'd failed everyone.

The memory of his mother's rasps as she'd gulped for air on the kitchen floor could still send a razor through him, serrate his

241

insides.

His last clear memory before that was looking at Glo's beautiful eyes as Hardwin told them to pray, Hardwin's words stirring in his head.

Lean in to each other, but lean also in to God. When all else is done, God is enough, everything, and always. Trust Him to give you what you need.

Tate needed truth.

He needed to know that he hadn't killed his mother, hadn't completely screwed up.

Hadn't let an innocent man die.

The door to the bathroom banged open, and he turned to see Ford come in.

"Hey," Tate said. He grabbed a couple paper towels and scrubbed his face, wiped his hands. No need to let his brother know he was completely unraveling.

"We have trouble," Ford said.

And it was the way he said it that had Tate looking over at him. "Oh no—is Ma—"

"She's fine, bro." Ford took a breath. "It's RJ. York just got a call—I think someone took RJ."

"What—?"

"York said he's going to get her back, but—"

"*Where is she?*"

"I don't know. York took off a few minutes ago. He told me not to tell you what's going down—that he was going to finish this, but yeah, right. We gotta help him."

Finish this. And right then, York was in Tate's head with his words, *Martin is dead. Because I killed him.*

He'd said it with such cold, dark precision it'd sent a chill through Tate.

Tate had been a soldier, so he understood what it took to kill someone. And, he supposed, York had been trying to defend himself from whatever was going down in that SUV.

Still, Tate agreed with Wyatt. He wasn't so sure he wanted York in his sister's life.

Except for *now*.

Because if anyone could find RJ and get her back, it was the man who'd kept her safe in Russia.

"Was it Gustov?" Tate asked.

"What about Gustov?" Wyatt came walking in.

Tate made the mistake of giving Ford a look.

"Aw, c'mon! I met him. Fought him. Hurt him. So, guess what, I get to know what's going on."

"We gotta go," Tate said. "York got a call, told Ford that RJ had been taken—"

"Taken? As in kidnapped? And you're *still standing here?*" He started moving toward the door.

"We don't know where he went—"

"We can find out. Sheesh." Wyatt shook his head as if he were talking to a couple rookies. "He went to find RJ. And we can track down RJ, right?" He had his hand on the door.

Tate had stopped, frowned.

"Coco put a tracker on her phone, genius. We can find her and intercept him. Or at least back him up."

Ford raised an eyebrow as he started for the door.

"Don't start. I went to Russia, I found my girl, and I brought her home. Hello."

"Fine," Tate snapped.

"I'm calling Coco," Wyatt said and left the bathroom.

Ford looked at Tate as he caught the door. "He's going to get hurt."

"What are we going to do, sit on him? Tie him up?"

"I agree with Wyatt. We need to help York," Ford said. He stepped inside, let the door close.

"No doubt, Rambo. But are you armed? Because I didn't wear my shoulder holster to my wedding. I know, what was I thinking—"

"No," Ford snapped. "But I'll bet York isn't either."

"Oh, that's fun." Tate scrubbed his hands down his face.

"You okay—?"

"No, I'm not okay! I need to think. We can't just run out of here like we're on fire!" And maybe Tate should have schooled his voice. But he was just so— "I should have known better. I should have listened to her." He wanted to punch the mirror. "Okay, just...I need to figure this out..."

"At the risk of getting hit—my team leader used to call me the lone wolf. Said I never asked for help." Ford glanced at the door. "But I'm not the only one. Wyatt. Knox. You. Even Reuben went for years without coming home. We all work on teams, but we never seem to..."

"Work together," Tate said. "I know. I've spent my whole life trying to be—"

"As good as your brothers?"

Tate looked away. "I guess."

"Get in the freakin' line," Ford said. "But I nearly died this summer, and I'm tired of being the lone wolf. Remember that time Dad took us hunting for that wolf that was threatening the cattle?"

"He armed us with tranq guns and we sat in a snowbank for two days," Tate said.

"Coldest I'd ever been," Ford said. "But he was caught because he was alone. Separated from the pack. We're Marshalls. And we are not alone."

Tate looked at him. *God is enough, everything, and always. Trust Him to give you what you need.*

His family.

"Let's get our sister."

Ford reached for the door but pulled back as it opened.

Knox stood in the entrance. "What is Wyatt doing?" He came in. "I heard him on the phone. He's tracking RJ?"

Tate looked at Ford. "RJ's gone missing. And York's gone to find her."

"What—*what?*" And there was no schooling Knox's voice. "Are you *kidding me?*"

Tate gave him a look. "Totally— *No!* Of course not!"

"Calm down!" Knox growled. "So, what are we going to do?"

"What we're not going to do is stand around in the bathroom—" Ford said. "We need a plan."

He made to push past Knox, but his brother stopped him with a hand to his chest. "This is not hard. How many times did

244

Dad take us on roundup?"

"I hate roundup," Tate said.

"I love roundup," Ford said.

"Yeah," Knox said, grabbing the door. "Roundup is our plan."

He opened the door.

Reuben stood on the other side, flanked by Hardwin. "You were shouting," Reuben said. "What's this about roundup?"

———◆———

RJ should have listened to her gut back in Moscow when it said *run*. Before the shots were fired that took down General Stanislov. Before she stepped up into the glow of the lamplight for CCTV to capture her and connect her to an international crime.

Probably even before that when her boss's contact, Roy, tried to contact her boss regarding the information about the possible hit and she'd decided it might be a grand idea to meet him in Prague and stop an international catastrophe.

In fact, if she were going back to her regrets, maybe it was thinking she could be some sort of superspy. Thank you, Sydney Bristow.

Because if RJ had listened, she wouldn't be lying on a cement floor, the night descending around her in bruised shadows, a chill seeping in through the fabric of her dress. The dim hue of faraway lights, along with the smell of fresh-poured cement, dirt, rebar, and woodchips suggested she was in a skeletal shell of a building. She made out the skyline and realized she was at least two stories, maybe three, from the ground. It had started to rain, the patter light upon the cement and the dirt and raising a breath of grimy mist into the air.

Her hands were taped behind her, a rope scraped her neck, nearly cutting off her air.

She gasped as the full weight of her capture bore down on her.

She was alone—no one knew where she was.

"Stop struggling, RJ. It'll be over soon. We're just waiting until your boy gets here."

RJ lifted her head, the world spinning slightly, probably an aftereffect of the drug she'd been given.

Footsteps echoed, coming closer, and hands grabbed her arms, setting her upright. "Let's get you up so he can see you."

He. Your boy. *York?*

Oh no. "I led you right to him."

"Thank you for that. When you said he was still alive, I didn't dare hope. But you are tenacious, RJ. You would have made a good analyst." He stepped around her, and for the first time she confirmed what she already knew.

Director Tom Crowley. He wore suit pants, a dress shirt, which he'd rolled up to the elbows, as if reluctant but willing to get his hands dirty.

And right then, she knew she was going to die. Because there was no way that Director Crowley was going to let her live after she'd figured him out.

Crowley, the leader of the rogue faction that wanted a new cold war. Crowley, who'd been the ambassador to Russia, seen the corruption taking over New Russia, and wanted a return to the old ways.

At least then, Russia would be labeled the threat they still were.

This was RJ's working theory as she wrestled with the tape around her wrists. "I am a good analyst. And so was my boss— she put the pieces together, didn't she?"

Probably RJ should shut her mouth, just like Wyatt said. But if she was going to die, she wanted all of it. "You had her kidnapped, then killed." Shoot—she hadn't even considered looking at the source of the other numbers on Sophia's call log.

"She just didn't play well with others," Crowley said. He reached over and picked up the end of the rope, cutting off RJ's air. "And neither do you." He threw the end of the rope over a girder above them. "But it doesn't mean you weren't helpful."

He pulled on the end, drawing up the slack, yanking her up to her tiptoes. She whimpered.

And selfishly wished York might show up. Tears pricked her eyes.

No.

"This isn't about the senator, is it?" she rasped.

"This is about the safety of the world." He dragged over something, the metal scraping against the cement as he stepped back in front of her. A metal sawhorse. "Up we go, now."

He grabbed her arm with one hand, the noose with the other, and tugged, cutting off her air until she acquiesced. She climbed up on the narrow sawhorse, no more than six inches wide, and stood there as he took up the slack, again pulling her up to her tiptoes.

"Why are you doing this?" she gasped.

"Did you know that my daughter was tortured before she was killed? By the Bratva. They brought her to an empty building where her screams couldn't be heard, and…well, her body was nearly unrecognizable when the militia found her."

"This isn't just about politics. This is personal. This is about York."

He spoke from behind her. "York brought this on himself."

"By marrying your daughter. By getting her killed." RJ shook her head. "Only it wasn't his fault. He was betrayed."

"It's always York's fault, sweetheart. And now York deserves to hear you scream. Watch you die."

She searched the darkness, not sure if she should pray he'd be there or not.

"You had Martin kill Tasha, didn't you? Or was it Damien Gustov?"

He laughed. "Tasha knew too much."

"She knew about the affair between Jackson and…who? Tsarnaev? Stanislov?"

"Oh, sweetheart, you know too much too. You should have left well enough alone, let Sophia answer her own calls."

"So that was your plan—send Sophia to Russia, let her take the fall for the assassination. Start an international incident. But she was onto you."

"She didn't know what she was onto. And neither do you."

"I know you're trying to influence the election—"

"This is way bigger than the election or you or York."

She drew in a ragged, burning breath. "This is about money. About power."

"Money *is* power."

"No, truth is power." And probably she shouldn't have said that because he set his foot on the sawhorse. Pulled a handgun out of his belt.

She was already struggling to breathe. "You're not going to get away with this. York will find you." And with her words, she knew it in her bones.

York *would* find him.

And kill him.

And never escape the past, become the new man he longed to be.

Her eyes filled. *I'm sorry.*

Wyatt was right. She had gotten them all into this freakin' mess—and they'd probably all come running to save her. Except, of course, they had no idea where she was, so there was that.

And maybe her mother was already dead, too, because RJ heard her now, showing up to whisper in her head. Her heart. *God will show up even when we've made a mess of things. Even when it's our fault—He will show up.*

Right. *Please, God. Show up.*

He was your father. Of course he'd save you.

Her eyes blurred.

Because that's who He is—He loves us by choice, not because we deserve His help.

"I'm counting on it," Crowley said to her threat.

"Tom."

And even though she expected it, even though she knew in her bones that York would show up, seeing him emerge from the shadows turned every muscle weak, her body longing to dissolve into a puddle of relief.

There's no if…just when. And His timing is perfect.

"York," she gasped.

He still wore the suit from today's wedding, his jacket shed, and in the glow of wan light from the moon looked exactly like the man she first met in Moscow. Dangerous. Confident. *If you want to live, follow me.*

Anywhere, York. Across the world, even to Small Town, Washington State.

He glanced at RJ tied up, balancing on the sawhorse, and something flickered in his eyes, just a hint of the fury igniting deep inside. "Let her go, Tom. This is between you and me."

Crowley trained the gun on York and moved around behind her. "Do you ever think about how she died? Ever think about her screams echoing off the cement? How she probably called your name?"

York didn't move.

"They hung her after they finished with her. Left her in the darkness—"

"I know," York said. "I found her body."

RJ looked at him. He hadn't told her that part.

And now he was here to find her body too.

"You should have stayed away from my daughter, hot shot," Crowley said. "Get on your knees."

"No—!" RJ shouted

The sawhorse wobbled and she gasped, the rope burning her neck. She was a fish, gulping for air.

"Stop!" York held out his hands. "I'm getting down." He lowered himself to his knees, his hands behind his head. "Just let her go."

"Oh, there's not a chance of that, son. The question is, who will die first—you or her?"

Then Crowley kicked the sawhorse. It wobbled for a second, then went over.

And she dropped.

"No!" York leaped for RJ, catching her and holding her up. "It's okay. I got you—I got you!"

He was holding her with one hand, prying at the tape around her hands with another.

And that's when she spied Crowley behind him. "York!"

Her voice came out strangled, but strong enough for York to

brace himself as Crowley swung at him with a two-by-four.

He hit him broadside across the back, and York grunted. "Stop!"

Because she got it now. Crowley would make him choose— hold her up to let her breathe or protect himself.

And in her heart, she knew what he'd choose. Because he was a good man, the kind of man who would gladly sacrifice himself to save her.

Crowley hit him again, this time in the legs. York stumbled— "Hey, you!"

The voice came from behind her, but she jerked, recognizing it.

Knox!

Crowley backed away, his gun out, aimed at York. "Stay back."

"Sorry, bud, no can do."

Reuben!

Crowley pointed the gun at RJ. "I said stay back."

"Probably not." The voice came from ahead of him. Wyatt.

They were herding Crowley, or at least confusing him.

Because Tate was out there, too, hidden in the darkness.

Only, not Tate but *Ford* exploded from the other side of the building, jumping on Crowley like he might be a calf in need of branding. He swept the tall man's feet, jerked his gun away, sent it spinning across the floor, and took Crowley down so fast he was bouncing on the cement.

York set up the sawhorse, climbing up beside her, fighting to loosen the noose. The tension locked it tight.

RJ got her hands loose. She put her hands on York's shoulders, pushed up, and he yanked the noose from around her neck.

The movement took out the sawhorse, already precarious, beneath them.

RJ went sprawling, hitting the cement hard.

She didn't know where York had landed, but she rolled to her knees, her head spinning.

York must have gotten his hands on the gun because she heard his voice. "The thing is, if you pull your weapon, you have to be willing to use it. Ford, back off him."

She found her feet and saw York with Crowley's gun trained on the man.

"York," she said quietly. She took a step toward him, put her hand on his arm. "York. You're not this man anymore."

He drew in a breath, shook his head, his eyes hard. "I'll always be this man, RJ."

"The man who shows up. The man who believes in justice, yes. The warrior God created, yes, but not this man, who kills out of revenge. This is not you. This has *never* been you."

He looked at her then, swallowed.

Lowered his weapon. Took a breath.

A shot pinged off the cement girder behind her.

"Get down!" York turned to grab her, but she'd already hit her knees, scrambling away toward the shadows.

A hand grabbed her hair. "I told you we were going to have fun."

Her breath caught.

Because for a moment, she was on a train station platform, a man's face caught in the glow of the platform lights right before he kissed her. Just a peck, but enough to sour her gut and make her want to retch with the memory.

His arm went around her neck and the cold press of a gun barrel screwed into her neck.

"Gustov." York's voice, not far from her. "Let her go."

"It's time, don't you think, for us to end this game? Gun, down."

Her fingers clawed into his arm. "I should have guessed you two were working together."

York put down his gun, held up his hands.

Crowley rolled over. "What took you so long?" He climbed to his feet, breathing hard, picked up his gun, and pointed it at Ford. Raised his voice. "Any of you try anything and I will end him."

A crash sounded in front of them and Gustov jerked.

Another one, this time behind them. Gustov stepped away from the sound. "Stay back."

She glanced to the side and spotted Wyatt in the shadows.

He pressed a finger to his lips.

Then he shouted. "Remember me?" Wyatt stepped out of the shadows. "Let's have another go."

Gustov jerked her around, pointing his gun at Wyatt, then York. Back.

She wasn't sure where Tate came from, but in a second he materialized and swung a two-by-four at Gustov.

York lunged for her.

Ford rolled away from Crowley's aim.

A shot fired off, a howl, and then she couldn't see anything with York's arms around her, dragging her away.

Another shot and it pinged off a metal girder.

"Neutralize him, Wyatt!" Ford yelled.

She spotted Wyatt just as Gustov slammed his gun into her brother's head. Wyatt staggered back, fell. Tate was scrambling to his feet, growling, clearly injured.

Gustov pointed his gun at Tate.

And right then she knew it.

Gustov was going to kill them. Tate, then Wyatt. And probably Ford, and maybe even Knox and Reuben as they rushed to save her brothers.

Her.

And she would have led her entire family to their deaths.

"No!" She jerked away from York. "No!"

Tate glanced at her, frowned.

And then, before she could move, follow the impulse inside—York rushed Gustov.

To her rising screams, he grabbed Gustov around the waist, took two more steps—

York tackled the Russian over the open side of the building, sailing out into the darkness.

And was gone.

———————◆———————

Roy hadn't called York the Bird for nothing.

York tasted the night air, bold and ripe with the smell of pine and the decaying loam as he sailed out into the blackness.

Free.

Forgiven.

The kind of man he always was and would be.

A warrior, a man who loved justice. And Ruby Jane Marshall. All the way to eternity.

The thing was, York didn't think it through. Not really—he just saw Tate on his knees, spotted Wyatt groaning, and didn't stop to think about anything past Gustov putting a bullet in Tate's head.

Right in front of RJ.

Yeah, no, that wasn't happening.

York was armed with nothing but his bare hands and the crazy urge to end this. To take Gustov out even if he had to die doing it.

If ever he needed a little divine help, it was now.

Please, Jesus. Help me finish this.

So he'd launched himself at Gustov. Locked his arms around him.

Took him over the edge of the building.

The ground came up quicker—and softer—than he imagined, and even as he lost his breath, he realized—

He'd landed in a massive pile of wet sand.

And on Gustov.

York rolled off the man, down the mound, over and over, until he lay on the ground, his hand on his chest.

Still alive.

His breath wheezed in through his constricted lungs.

But, yes, *alive*. And so was RJ and Tate and—

Gustov landed on him. Cuffed him across the face, put another fist in his gut.

And that was just *enough*.

York was tired of evil winning, of its relentless pursuit, its unfair games, its no-rules tactics. Tired of running, tired of looking over his shoulder.

No more.

He kneed Gustov hard and flipped the man over his head.

He found his feet, and ducked just as Gustov swung a shovel at his head.

Nope. York charged him, slammed him into the ground.

Gustov punched his fist into his kidney, and the pain spiked through York. He rolled off, coughing. He might have serious damage after Crowley's battering. But as Gustov tried to scramble up, York grabbed him back, trying to wrestle Gustov into a choke hold.

Gustov jabbed an elbow into his ribs, writhed, but couldn't dislodge York's hold, especially when he wrapped his legs around him. Rain pelted his eyes, blinding him as he held on.

"York!"

The sound found him through the sudden roll of thunder. RJ.

He needed to end this before she got here.

This is not you. This has never been you.

Gustov went limp. Unconscious.

Not dead.

But a few more moments...

And his prayer lifted, a ghost inside him. *Please, Jesus. I don't know who I was, but...I want to be a different man. A man who trusts You. Please forgive me for the darkness I know is in my past...and help me to live as a new man.*

"York!" RJ ran up, a figure in the darkness, standing over him. He stared at her, dripping wet, her blue eyes holding his, like he could save the world.

God made you a warrior, York. Like David. A man after God's own heart—and a man of battle.

The man who was left when he clung to God.

Today, starting now, he was on God's side. The side of justice and truth.

And he couldn't kill Gustov. Not anymore.

Evil wouldn't win today.

York pushed the man off him into the mud and climbed to his feet. "Let's find some rope. We need to secure him."

He stepped away, breathing hard.

"You okay?" RJ said, reaching out to touch him.

Gustov came alive.

He grabbed RJ's leg, and pulled her down. Rolled on top of her, pinned her arms with his knees and raised his hand, gripping a chunk of jagged cement block.

"No!" York was scrambling hard, trying to find purchase in the mud—

Someone flew by him holding a shovel and slammed it against Gustov's body as if taking a shot on goal.

Wyatt.

Gustov spun off RJ, lost his balance, then dropped, falling into a pit below—maybe the future parking garage. He screamed when he landed. The sound echoed into the night.

York crawled over and yanked RJ up into his arms.

A light careened up, someone running, maybe with a phone. "Are you okay?" Knox, shining the light on a sopping wet Wyatt, breathing hard.

Wyatt looked at York, then at Knox. "Yeah."

"I meant him," Knox said and looked at York.

"I'm okay." As long as it meant never letting her go.

Sirens whined through the soggy air.

Ford, too, ran up. "Where is he?"

Wyatt pointed to York, but Ford ran to the edge of the pit. "Wow."

York joined him, RJ's hand gripping his.

Gustov had landed on a spire of rebar, a pike poking through his chest, his body now still.

RJ slipped out of his grip, walking away from the scene.

"Where's the other guy?" Knox said.

"Reuben has him. And he called an ambulance for Tate."

But York didn't ask about Tate—he got up, striding after RJ through the rain and the mud.

She was moving fast.

He caught up with her next to a dump truck, grabbing her arm, and she spun, her hands curled into fists. He caught them just as they aimed for his chest. "What—"

"You shouldn't have come for me! You shouldn't have—"

"Have you lost your mind? *Of course* I came for you! Sheesh,

RJ. Haven't you figured it out? I will *always* come for you. No matter what. I. Choose. You."

He let go of her fists, pinned her face between his hands. "I know you're scared. I get it. I've never been so scared as when I saw you standing there, a noose around your neck. But I knew that nothing—nothing Crowley could do to me would stop me from trying to save your life. Even if Crowley beat me to death."

She was crying, and he ran his thumb under her eyes. Not that it helped with the storm crackling above, the deluge of rain soaking them through. "I love you, RJ. Period. And I don't care where we live or what we do—I'll follow you around the world—"

She kissed him. Fisted his shirt and pulled him to herself. She smelled like the night, and off her radiated the crazy bravery that said she believed in something bigger than herself. Maybe even him.

She wrapped her arms around his neck, and he put his arms around her waist, lifting her, practically inhaling her.

Because he got it then. God had sent her to Russia to rescue *him*. To lead him home.

He backed her against the dump truck, let her down, and braced his arms on either side of her. "I love you, Syd. Oh, how I love you."

Then he kissed her again, needing her, tasting her, wanting her, losing himself in the essence of RJ. Brave, bold, overwhelming, in-over-her-head RJ.

And he couldn't stop drinking her in until she finally pressed on his chest.

He raised his head, his lips burning, breathing hard. The rain drove down around them, cutting through the lights of the construction site, but all he could see were her beautiful blue eyes in his.

As if she could look right through to his soul.

Well, she probably could. She always probably could.

"Turnips," she said, running her thumb along his lips.

It took a second, but then, yes. His lips curved into a smile. "Turnips."

Then, like the thunder haunting the air, the voice tremored into his bones. *And we know that in all things God works for the good of those who love him, who have been called according to his purpose.*

Only, this time, the memory flashed with him, sitting at a kitchen table eating oatmeal—funny, he hated oatmeal—with a man and a woman.

She had short blonde hair. The man was darker haired, wore a mustache.

His parents. He knew it, all the way to his marrow. His father had his Bible open. The man looked up at York and smiled, something so warm in it, it nearly knocked York over. *Everything has a purpose.* You *have a purpose, York.*

He made a sound, like a whimper.

"You okay?" RJ said, frowning.

The image faded, but left behind a residue—no, a *rooting.*

Or simply, maybe, peace.

He looked at her. "Yes. I am. I think maybe, for the first time in years, I really am."

"Hey, RJ, oh—sorry." Knox came up to them, shining the light. "Um, the cops are here, and we need you to untangle this thing."

"That's all you, Syd," York said, but she slid her hand down to his and wove her fingers through his.

"I'm not sure I can untangle it all, but I'll give it a try." She walked out toward the shiny red lights.

"Maybe it can wait until we get back to the hospital," Knox said. "Because Hardwin texted. Ma needs us."

14

RJ never expected it to end like this, but the ceremony was beautiful.

Exactly how her mother planned it.

Yellow and orange cone flowers from her garden in bouquets near the front of the chapel, bright orange chrysanthemums in a spray behind the altar. Worship music instead of the traditional hymns, but it still felt right. And her entire family lined up, together, sharing this moment.

"See, it wasn't a crazy idea," Wyatt said to RJ a moment before he joined Tate and Hardwin at the altar.

Maybe not crazy at all.

After all, when the Montana Marshalls did something, they did it in a go-big or go-home way.

It was nice of the hospital to allow them the use of the chapel. And their chaplain, Scott Faris, who stood at the front, beaming as one by one the brides walked down the aisle.

Glo wore her fancy, frilly short dress, freshly cleaned, with her sparkly white cowboy boots and a vintage hat with a short veil, no fear in her eyes as she grinned at her groom.

Tate wore a blue suit, his cowboy boots, and the expression of a man who wasn't looking over his shoulder. Somehow, with the capture of Crowley, he'd been able to exhale. He leaned on a crutch, his knee still on the mend from where the bullet nicked it. He was counting scars with York these days, but he wasn't stepping down from his role as head of Glo's security.

Swamp and Rags might look like ushers, but RJ knew they carried weapons under their suits, despite hospital rules.

Coco went next, dressed in a simple white silk gown, V-necked, with a cutout back. No frills, her freshly dyed red hair a dramatic statement as she held Mikka's hand, her eyes on Wyatt. Oh, the man cleaned up well—no wonder he landed on the cover of magazines. Tousled brown hair and a broken nose only added to his tough mystique. He wore a pair of gray trousers, a white shirt, and a vest that only accentuated his athletic goalie shoulders. RJ had somehow talked Coco into a pair of heels, but she still appeared so petite next to him. The beauty and the beast.

"Are you ready, Ma?" RJ asked, squeezing her mother's hand. Her mother sat in a wheelchair but now took a breath and stood up.

"Completely," she said.

RJ had woven orange cone flowers into her mother's fluffy hair, and her mother had picked out a dress online, a simple A-line, knee-length dress with ruching under the bodice and lace on the long arms. "To hide these stupid IV bruises," she'd said, although RJ knew that Hardwin wouldn't care. Her mother could wear a pair of her dirty work jeans and an old flannel shirt and walk down the aisle barefoot as long as she said *I do*.

For his part, Hardwin had said *I do*, at least silently, through his actions the moment the family arrived back at the hospital.

He'd asked their mother to marry him again. And this time, she wanted her family's blessing before she said yes.

A resounding *hello*, and yee-haw *yes* because Gerri was done with wondering if marrying Hardwin would make her less.

Because anyone could see that Hardwin thought she hung the moon and stars and would only give her the world. With Hardwin, she was more.

Just like RJ was more with York.

More creative. More courageous. More...herself.

Somehow just knowing he was in the room to catch her made her believe in herself...more.

Reuben came up to stand beside her, offering his arm. He looked completely resplendent in a pair of dress pants and a black suit coat, the right man to lead their mother down the aisle into the next season of her life.

Gerri took his arm, leaning on it. "I'm so glad you're back, Rube. The ranch couldn't be in safer hands."

RJ thought she spotted a glistening in his eyes.

"Off you go, Ma," she said and kissed her mother's cheek as Reuben started them down the short aisle.

She felt York reach for her hand and slipped her fingers through his.

Oh, the man cleaned up well, yet another version of his amazing persona. He wore a blue suit and tie and had gotten a haircut—a high and tight, just like when she'd first met him. It only made his blue eyes devastating, especially when he turned them on her and smiled. "You okay?"

She could turn into a puddle right here. "Perfect."

Right now, at least.

The last week, however, as she'd watched her mother in pain and slowly come back to herself...

York led her into the chapel just as the chaplain began the opening remarks. They took their seats on the groom's side.

She still couldn't believe that she hadn't figured out Crowley's involvement. And the moment York went over the edge with Gustov still made her shudder, awaken in a cold sweat.

And the information Coco had quietly dug up about Imagine, Inc. still hung under RJ's skin. Namely the educational grants Imagine had given to humanitarian aid organizations in Chechnya. But maybe it was all just coincidence.

Looking at Senator Jackson now, sitting in the front row, bride's side, it seemed a little far-fetched to think she might helm an international conspiracy to reignite the Cold War. She wore a red pantsuit, on her way to yet another speech in California, her jet waiting at the Helena airport.

Apparently, she was less than thrilled to have to touch down between stump speeches to attend Glo's wedding again. But with the election one week away, no one blamed her, really.

Glo had agreed to a fancy reception in a few weeks, after the dust had settled.

The chaplain was on to the vows. First Glo's and Tate's, written a week ago. Then Coco's and Wyatt's, written last night, probably on the back of his airplane ticket as he traveled home from a game. And then Gerri's and Hardwin's, the traditional vows that included to love, honor, and obey.

Obey. She glanced at York. She might consider obeying a man who would give his life for her.

Not only that, but York had stood up to her brothers, refused to leave her, and had helped her forgive herself for calling Crowley to tell him about their trip to Vegas and their whereabouts in Montana, which had inadvertently put them in danger.

Apparently, she was very, very good at that game.

But she wasn't going to do it anymore. She had enough with her conspiracy theories and grandiose ideas of treason.

"You can exchange rings."

Kelsey and Knox sat in the pew behind the senator, beside Dixie and Elijah Blue and Cher. Reuben and Gilly across the aisle. Ford and Scarlett sat behind them.

Hardwin's daughter had driven down from Kalispell with her husband, but they were driving back later today.

And then it would be over.

RJ hadn't a clue what would happen next.

Back to DC?

And what about York?

Lasagna.

Oh, she wanted that life with him. But she couldn't deny the stir inside that this wasn't done.

Stop. No more conspiracy theories.

"You may kiss your brides."

She looked at York, and he grinned and even though they weren't at the altar, he leaned down and kissed her. Oh, he tasted good, and he smelled of his aftershave…and she could get lost in his kiss forever.

So maybe it didn't matter where they lived.

Hardwin gently lifted her mother into his arms to carry her up the aisle. Her mother laughed, a quiet, soft breath. In it, RJ heard her words. *See, sometimes we get so wrapped up in what we think we need to do to make something happen, we forget that God is actually the one orchestrating it all.*

Yes, God. You know the ending.

I trust You for it.

Tari, the chaplain's wife, had ordered cupcakes and some lemonade for them, setting up a tiny reception in a staff room. Gerri sat in her wheelchair, holding Hardwin's hand. Wyatt was sitting with Mikka, peeling the paper off a cupcake. And Glo and Tate were saying goodbye to her mother, about to leave with her security team.

Life moved fast.

But in the moment, this place, everything was perfect.

Mostly.

"Dad would be happy," Ford said quietly behind her.

She turned. He wore a white oxford, rolled up to the elbows, and a pair of trousers, held Scarlett's hand, but his gaze was on Gerri. "He'd be glad to know that she's safe. And that we're together."

She nodded, her throat thick. "I miss him."

Ford swallowed, his eyes glistening. "But this was his vision for us. To be doing what we were made to do, together. To carry on his legacy."

Tate limped over. "Are you sticking around?" he asked Ford.

"Sorry, bro. Scarlett and I are headed back to San Diego. Her little house just sold and we have packing to do."

"I thought she was staying in San Diego?"

"I like Minneapolis," Scarlett said. "And I'm going to work on Ham's SAR team too."

"Her little brother is coming for Thanksgiving, so we need to get her apartment set up," Ford said.

We? Ford could still read her mind, clearly because he grinned. "I'm still living in San Diego. And bunking with a couple of her new teammates in Minneapolis. But not for long." He winked.

Maybe they should have made more room at the altar. She grinned at him.

Knox came over to them, holding a cupcake. "These are really good."

"When does NBR-X start back up again?" Ford asked.

"A couple weeks. We have a big finale and then a three-month break. I'm not sure where we'll land…" He glanced at Reuben, his arm around the shoulders of his pregnant wife. "I think they might need a little room."

"Nashville is nice," Tate said. "Glo and I will go back to her mother's estate—at least until the NBR-X event. After that, well—"

"The White House?" Wyatt said, moving into their conversation.

"Please, no." Tate laughed. "Although, maybe if we are there, we'll get to see RJ, right?"

RJ's eyes widened.

"Yep," York said, however, and squeezed her hand.

She turned to him, frowning.

"The country needs her if they want to unravel this Crowley mess," York said, raising an eyebrow.

Oh.

"I'd like to give a toast." Hardwin's voice lifted across the room. He was holding a glass of lemonade. "To my bride. But also to her amazing family. I…" He lowered the glass, his gaze traveling over her brothers and RJ. "I wish I'd known your father. But I see the man he was through you all. I see his faithfulness to family, his courage to stand up for what's right, his tenacity for justice, and his unconditional love in all of you."

Gerri took his hand.

Hardwin's voice thickened. "I'll never be him, but I'm grateful to be in your lives. I know he would be very, very proud of all of you."

And that shut them all down. RJ's throat filled, and she glanced at her brothers. Tate looked away, Ford swallowed hard, Knox drew in a long breath, and Wyatt offered a thin grin, nodding.

"Thanks, Hardwin," Reuben said and held out his hand. "Welcome to the Marshall family."

York's hand on her shoulder squeezed.

"Hear, hear," Wyatt said next to him and drank down his lemonade. Then, "I suppose that means I'll need to send you season tickets."

"Center ice, pal." Hardwin pointed at him. His phone rang in his pocket and he fished it out, looking at the text.

RJ turned to York. "Really? You'd go back to DC with me?"

He touched his forehead to hers. "I told you—turnips."

"But what about Shelly?"

"Maybe someday, right?" He kissed her forehead just as Hardwin walked up.

"Um, can I talk to you two?"

Tate and the others had moved away from their private conversation, and now RJ looked at Hardwin, then her brothers. "Me?"

"And York." He gestured with his head toward the door.

They followed Hardwin down the hallway, then into the stairwell and down another flight until they came to the administrative area of the hospital, the general offices. He went in, and the receptionist, a woman in her midfifties, simply pointed down the hall.

He stopped at a closed door and knocked.

The door opened to a suited secret service officer. He stepped aside to let them pass. A few other suited men with ear pieces stood around the room, and two men stood at the window. One was younger—midthirties, brown hair, the build of a warrior. He stood with his back to them, hands clasped as if in parade rest, staring out at the mountainscape to the west.

The other had turned upon their entry and bore the good looks and build of George Clooney, with dark hair, graying at the sides, deep blue eyes, and the winning smile of a politician.

RJ would recognize him anywhere—presidential candidate Senator Isaac White.

"Hardwin!"

She stood there, her mouth agape as White pulled her stepfather into a hug. "Congratulations! I couldn't believe it when Reba's people texted me with the news."

He let Hardwin go, gave him a slap on the shoulder.

"Yes, well, thanks for flying in, Isaac," Hardwin said. "I know it's a bit unorthodox, but I thought you should hear RJ's entire story."

What—?

"I read your briefing, thank you. And I agree."

His *briefing?* Her mouth opened.

Hardwin turned to her. Smiled. "You're not the only one with secrets. And, by the way, in case you're wondering, your mother knows that I have a little side job serving my country." He put his finger to his lips. "But keep your brothers out of it, okay? We all know how intense they can get."

She stared at him. "I thought you were a bank president."

"Yes, you did," he said, winking.

"Right. So, are you still in the game?"

"I'm mostly retired. But still around enough to know that you're onto something. And here's where I'm going to step out." He walked past her, but not until he put a hand on her shoulder. "Your father would be very proud of you, RJ."

He closed the door behind him.

The senator walked over and shook her hand, then York's. "Hardwin has filled me in on most of the last five months, as well as your theory."

"My *theory?* But how did he—?"

"I might have told him," York said. "We were sitting up late one night last week, and I told Hardwin the entire story, from the moment you decided to go to Russia to the death of Gustov. And I threw in the information about Kobie and Graham and the bombings."

"And Hardwin called me," Isaac said. He pulled out a chair and gestured to it. "RJ, I'd like to ask you for a favor."

RJ sank into the chair.

York took the one behind her.

The senator motioned to the man standing by the window and he joined them. White set his hip on the table.

"This is special agent Logan Thorne. He's my director of special investigations, a position we're keeping on the down-low. But he's going to head up the investigation."

"What investigation?" RJ asked as she shook Thorne's hand.

"The one that you'll assist him in. You and York. The one

that looks into the treasonous ties between Reba Jackson and Russia."

Her mouth opened.

"But…I work for the CIA. So won't I already be doing that?"

"If Senator Jackson is in any way involved in this," Thorne said, "we need to make sure she doesn't get a whiff of your activities. So, we'd like you to not return to the CIA. But you'll still have top-level clearance and everything you need to run your investigation."

Oh.

"I'd like you to lie low and start working that brain of yours." White looked at York. "Both of you. With your international skills, York, you're exactly the man I need to help unravel this."

York nodded, his expression stony.

White glanced at Thorne. "You'll be under the purview of Director Thorne, answering to him. And him to me." He sighed and crossed his arms. "We're one week out from the election. I can't pull Jackson from the race. But if she's a traitor, I can't have her serve with me either."

And according to the polls, they were slotted to sweep the election.

"So that means I need to know ASAP if she's involved in any way. And I need you to keep it quiet. Off the radar."

RJ looked at York. "What if we were to set up in a small town? Maybe somewhere unexpected, tucked away and secluded."

York smiled at her. "I like how you think, Syd." He turned to White. "I'm in if she is."

"Hiding in the mountains, solving an international conspiracy?" With the man of her dreams, part small-town, part spy? "As my twin brother would say, hoo-yah."

White smiled, shook her hand, then York's. "I'll be in touch after the election."

Senator White and Thorne left the room. RJ and York followed and rode an elevator back up to the reception.

York took her hand and leaned back against the elevator wall, pulling her with him, nestling her between his legs, his hands at her waist. "So, lasagna?" His blue gaze traced her face.

She ran her hands behind his neck. "Bartender makes a good cover."

He grinned. "I don't suppose you'd consider being a waitress."

"Not even a little." Then she kissed him.

"Hey—whoa, seriously?" The voice behind her made her push away. York still had a hold of her as she turned.

Ford stood outside the elevator with Scarlett, Glo, Tate, Knox, and Kelsey. He looked at York. "So, you ditched us to go make out?"

York gave them a smirk. "Something like that."

"Where did you go?" Tate asked, his arm catching the door before it closed.

"Why?" RJ asked. "Is this the posse trying to hunt me down and rescue me?"

Ford look at Tate, who looked at Knox, then back at RJ. And he smiled. "Naw. Not anymore. That's what you got him for." He nodded to York.

"That's right, boys," York said and tightened his hold.

Tate took his arm away. "I think we'll take the next elevator." The door closed.

"I might end up liking them," York said. And then he pulled her to himself and kissed her like the spy-slash-lumberjack he was—full of mystery and danger and exactly the right kind of man to disappear with into the woods.

York hadn't expected coming home to feel this good.

Especially in a town he'd only lived in for a month, with people whose names he barely knew.

The folks at Caleb's church treated him as if he'd returned from war. Short a parade, he had people thumping him on the back and offering to buy him pizza or root beer down at the still-renovating Jethro's.

He'd been back for less than a week and he'd already rejoined the baseball team.

Something about listening to RJ scream his name in the

stands—*Great hit, York!*—but he'd kept the name Jones for the purposes of their undercover sleuthing—did something to his spirit.

Rooted him, maybe, into a place and time that he'd thought he'd never find.

Home. Happily Ever After.

And now he was turning into a sap, but as York sat in a red booth at Mystical Pizza, watching the election returns with Jethro, RJ, and Raven, with people still welcoming him "home," it felt a little surreal.

Very, very surreal.

As if, without him even trying, he'd become…

Himself.

The man he'd crafted in his head, the one he'd longed to be but was too afraid to really voice.

A man with friends. With family. A woman who loved him.

A man of faith.

And when we cling to Jesus, we are changed. Reborn. We become who we were meant to be because there is nothing of ourselves left. Caleb's words from weeks ago, but they pinged inside York now, even as he watched the pastor carry a large Firecracker pizza to his table of youngsters.

He'd gone off that building clinging to Jesus.

He'd landed in grace, risen a new man.

A warrior, like David, pursuing God's heart.

Justice.

Faith.

Grace.

And second chances.

Mack and York, a merge of both sides of his heart.

"White took Ohio," said Jethro across from him, watching the flat-screen over York's shoulder.

"That's it, then," Raven said. She sat next to Jethro, but her gaze had been on Caleb all night long.

Interesting.

Jethro and Raven had asked few questions when he pulled up with RJ in her mother's old pickup. York would have to get them new wheels, pronto.

Right after they found a place to live. Jethro had offered his digs for now, but RJ needed her own place to set up her vast computer equipment.

And although he bunked at Jethro's for now, York didn't want to let her out of his sight.

So, on that list was a marriage proposal also.

And somewhere in there, a permanent job. In the meantime, Jethro had offered him a position leading the reconstruction of the pub.

Yes, it made for good cover.

Because he agreed with White.

RJ was smart. And if anyone could root out the truth, it was his own personal spy sitting across the table from him, dressed in a blue *Isaac White for President for a Safe Tomorrow* T-shirt. She wore her hair up in a ponytail and looked so darn small-town he just wanted to grab her, drive out to the lake in their pickup, spread out a blanket, turn on some Yankee Belles on the radio, and watch the stars fall from the sky.

How had Ford put it—ditch everyone and go make out.

He smiled, thinking of pulling out that ponytail, twining his fingers through her hair…

"Hey, York." Jimbo came by the table and held out his hand, wearing a smile. "Glad to see that Jethro has some help. Try and stay out of trouble." He winked.

York didn't know what to think about the man. But he had saved York's life, coming out to check on them, following what he termed a catch in his gut.

"Did you hear that the Yankee Belles are playing at the celebration party?" Raven said, watching another screen, this one of the live feed of the White–Jackson campaign headquarters. "I can't wait to see them in Spokane." She looked at RJ. "Thanks."

York couldn't wait to tell her that RJ had also secured a meet and greet, including a tryout for a backup singer position. But that was his girl—always thinking ahead.

"You're welcome," RJ said, winking.

No, he would have never fallen for Raven. Because there was

no one like RJ, and she had already imprinted on his heart, even when his mind couldn't remember her.

"The opposition is conceding," Jethro said just as a waitress came by to grab their pizza remains. "I'm heading home."

"I think I'll stick around for a while," Raven said, getting up with him.

"I'll give you a ride home," York said.

"No, thanks, Mac—York. I can find my own way."

She headed over to Caleb's table.

"She likes him," RJ said, beside him.

A crazy, protectiveness stirred inside him. Like she might be his sister. Huh.

"Let's go," he said. But RJ wasn't moving.

"Not yet," she said. And he thought she might be watching the screen.

But not. She was looking toward the door, and his gaze drifted down from the television to the man standing there. A big guy, maybe six three, with salt-and-pepper hair worn military style—high and tight. He wore a jean jacket, his hands shoved into the pockets, a pair of jeans, and work boots and stood, scanning the place, as if looking for someone.

Recognition slid through York like warm caramel, the smell of a bonfire after a football game, and the scent of loam in the morning air.

He stilled, his breath caught.

"He's here," RJ said and turned to York. "Just…stay here."

He couldn't move anyway, his heart an anvil in his chest, slamming against his rib cage.

RJ went to the door and talked with the man. He looked over at York.

Smiled.

And for a crazy, horrible moment, York wanted to cry, like he might be a small, pitiful child.

He swallowed hard and slid out of the booth as RJ returned with the man.

"York, I'm not sure if you remember—"

"Uncle Jack," he said and held out his hand.

The big man smiled, such warmth in his eyes York had trouble registering what he saw with what he knew.

Uncle Jack, the decorated Marine.

Uncle Jack, who had shown up in Russia to fetch him after the murder of his parents.

Uncle Jack, who'd brought him to Wisconsin to live with his grandparents.

Oh, how he'd wanted to be just like his uncle Jack.

The man yanked him into a hug, wrapping his arms around York.

He was going to dissolve into tears like a freakin' baby if he didn't—

Jack pulled away and ran his fingers under his eyes. "Shoot, kid. Now you have me blubbering."

There was no going back. York just nodded, letting himself tear up. "Shoot."

Uncle Jack laughed, the sound of it sweet and familiar and *healing*. The kind of healing that reached into old wounds and sealed them over.

"I never thought I'd see you again," Jack said. "Until your girlfriend called me a few days ago and asked if I wanted to come out and see you."

RJ did that? But of *course* she did.

She knew how to find people.

And she knew *him*.

"She said you got beaned on the head and have a few gaps in your memory." Uncle Jack slid into the booth where Jethro had sat earlier.

"It's a very long story," York said, sliding back in. RJ joined him and he reached under the table and took her hand, weaving his fingers through hers.

Squeezing.

Oh, he was going to marry this woman, and soon.

"I...I can't remember how..." He looked out the window, drew in a breath. Looked back at Uncle Jack. "How did my parents die?"

Under the table, RJ had a firm grip on his hand.

Jack looked at him, frowned. "Oh, York, are you sure you want to know this?"

And shoot—he knew it. Just *knew* it. He swallowed. "I'm to blame, aren't I? Something happened, something that I did that—"

"Are you kidding me?" Uncle Jack said, his voice quiet. Then he leaned over the table. "*Are you kidding me?*"

York drew in a shaky breath. Shook his head.

"Aw, York. You were still pretty young. And it was traumatic. Of course you wouldn't remember, I guess, but..." Jack motioned to a waitress who came by. "Can I get a water?"

She nodded and left to retrieve it.

"Ten years sober," Jack said. He pressed his hands on the table. Met York's gaze. "Your father and mother were missionaries in Siberia. A city, so it wasn't remote, but there were gangs and mafia and just a handful of expats. They believed in putting you in Russian schools so you'd learn the language because their intent was to live among the Russian people and share the Gospel with them."

"I have a memory of sitting at our kitchen table, reading the Bible with my father."

"Oh, he was a real zealot. And you were just like him. You knew your Bible verses like you might be a revival preacher." He looked at RJ. "The kid could recite entire passages of Scripture."

"And yet he can't seem to remember to fill up for gas," RJ said.

"My mind was wandering," York said, but she bumped him with her shoulder.

Jack's smile faded. "We're still not sure how, but on March first, nineteen years ago, around noon, three men broke into your flat. You were home with your mother. Your father was not. She did everything she could to protect you from them, standing between you and them even as they beat her. They forced her to the floor—"

"And she shouted at me to run," York said, his voice thin.

"You had nowhere to go. You were on the top floor of a nine-story apartment building, and they were guarding the door.

So you ran to the kitchen and pulled out a knife. And then you came back to the room to protect your mother."

York drew in a breath. "I don't remember that."

"That's good. Because that's when your dad came home. They were going after you, and according to the police, he jumped between you and them. He took the knife away from you and told you to run."

York stared at him. "I ran."

"Yes. You somehow got past them and ran down the stairs—all nine flights—while your father kept them busy."

"I got away."

"You got *help*. You were screaming, and someone found you and called the militia. But when they got there, your parents were…they were gone. And the attackers had lit your flat on fire."

"I can smell it. The smoke in the stairwell. I can hear the screaming echoing down the stairs."

RJ's hand tightened in his. "York, it's over."

He nodded. Met Jack's brown eyes. "But that's why I thought I killed them. Because I had the knife."

"Maybe. But they would have killed them anyway, and you, if you hadn't run. You did *exactly* what your father wanted you to do."

York shook his head.

"York. Your father loved you so much he gave his life for you. But you are not to blame. He gave it of his own free will."

York looked away.

"And he would be very proud of you."

He made a face. "I don't think so."

Jack said nothing. Took a breath. "Your father had a favorite verse—"

"Romans 8:28. I know. It keeps pinging around in my head. 'And we know that in all things God works for the good of those who love him…'"

"'Who have been called according to his purpose,'" RJ said. "My father loved that verse also."

"Then you both know that the darkest part is never the end of the story. Even the middle, when we see the light—that is not the end. There is still victory ahead. It was one of your grandpa's favorite sayings—'In time, we will see the victory of the Lord.'"

The waitress returned with his water.

"Thanks," he said. Took a drink. "Listen, we've all done things…believe me, I get that. But that's why God sent Jesus into the world—to pay the price for our sins. Willingly. Freely. So we could have eternity. And that purpose we've been called to? Redemption. Grace. Truth. All this time, York, you've been living out your story. I don't know what you've been up to, but I do know this. God had you in His hands, whether you knew it or not. And whether you were cooperating with Him or not. Your story is not over—it's all led to right now. This moment. Grace. Truth."

York looked at him. Heard Jethro's voice. *Bless this son of Yours, Lord. Thank You for bringing him to us. Help him find his place in Your grace.*

Grace. Truth. The purpose of his story.

"When I look at you, York, I see a warrior. A man fighting evil. A man seeking truth. Your father died fighting evil, to save the lives of others. I see that in you. I know he would be proud of you because *I* am proud of you."

York's eyes burned.

Jack made to slide out of the booth. "Son. Heaven is still ahead, and victory awaits. Evil will *not* prevail. We must keep our eyes on that vision, whatever happens. I'm going to grab a slice of pizza, I'm starved."

He headed toward the counter.

"It looks like you come from a family of preachers," RJ said, her smile soft.

"So it seems," York said. He blinked away the burn, drew in a shaky breath. Then he turned to her, his voice broken. "How did you know…well, that I needed to talk to Uncle Jack?"

She touched her hand to his face. "Analyst, darling."

"I'm going to have a hard time keeping up with you, aren't I?"

"I'll make sure I don't run too far ahead. I need someone to catch me, after all." She winked, then leaned forward and kissed him.

Applause erupted on the screen and through the pizza joint, and York broke away to see President-elect Isaac White taking the stage.

Vice President elect Reba Jackson stood beside him.

"For all your smarts, I really hope you're wrong about Jackson," he said, pulling her against him.

RJ sighed, her hand on his chest. "For the first time in my life, I hope I am too."

She fit perfectly and yes, he'd have to propose very, very soon. Because York–Mack Jones–Newgate had a past.

But, as he lifted her chin, met her eyes and kissed her, he realized that it didn't matter who he'd been yesterday.

His future was every day from now when he got to be the man he saw in the eyes of the woman who had brought him home.

What's Next?

Want More? Check out The Way of the Brave, in stores January 2020!

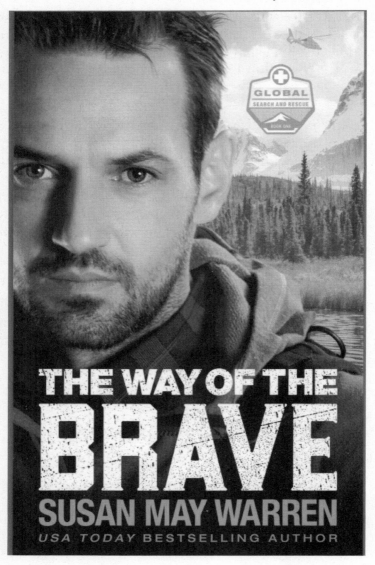

Former pararescue jumper Orion Starr is haunted by the memory of a rescue gone wrong. He may be living alone in Alaska now, but the pain of his failure—and his injuries—has followed him there from Afghanistan. He has no desire to join Hamilton Jones's elite rescue team, but he also can't shirk his duty when the call comes in to rescue three lost climbers on Denali.

Former CIA profiler and psychiatrist Jenny Calhoun's yearly extreme challenge with her best friends is her only escape from the guilt that has sunk its claws into her. As a consultant during a top-secret mission to root out the Taliban, she green-lighted an operation that ended in an ambush and lives lost. When her cathartic climb on Denali turns deadly, she'll be forced to trust her life and the lives of her friends to the most dangerous of heroes—the man she nearly killed.

Her skills and his experience are exactly what's needed to prevent another tragedy—but in order to truly set Orion free from his painful past, Jenny will have to reveal hers. They'll have to put their wounds behind them to survive, but at what cost?

Leap into action with this
high-octane, breakneck new series
from bestselling author
Susan May Warren.

The Way of
the Brave

~ Excerpt ~

H e should have never left Alaska.
Sure, in Alaska Orion woke to his breath in a hover
of mist over his face, his fireplace having simmered to a
low flame, the room lit in gray, the sun denting the eternal night.
But he belonged in all that cold and darkness, under the shadow
of unforgiving Denali, buried under a numbing layer of ice and
snow.

There, his anger couldn't break through, couldn't ignite with
the injustice of the daily news.

Couldn't consume him with helplessness.

It was better to be cold.

The vast aloneness of Alaska allowed him to breathe, despite
the stinging cold in his lungs. Allowed him to scream without
anyone knowing.

"I hate New York City," Orion muttered now, just below his
breath, but loud enough for Ham to hear as they boarded the 4
train.

"You just need coffee," Ham said.

"Vats of it." Orion tried to ignore the man who knocked into him, bumping him into the subway pole.

Orion wanted to blame his dark mood on the ache in his bum knee, the fact that his body should still be sleeping, the static in his brain evidence of his jet lag. Maybe he should attribute his general sour attitude about humanity at large on the fact that his buddy Ham had insisted they route through Memorial Park to spend a few moments staring into the acre-wide footprint of the North Tower.

Orion had fisted his hands into his canvas jacket, the wind bullying him, the sun glaring off the glass of One World Trade Center and watched as the waterfalls stirred up a mist into the brisk April air.

He couldn't escape the thud in his chest.

The start of the War on Terror, right here—a war that still hadn't been won, despite the casualties, the sacrifices, the personal losses.

All of it put Orion into a humdinger of a stormy mood.

Then he spotted the punk kid with the look of a thug slide through the closing doors of the subway car.

He didn't know why, but all the hackles rose on the back of his neck.

White, midtwenties, rail thin, the young man wore a grimy Knicks jersey, a pair of ripped jeans, and the fuzz of a few nights on his chin. He radiated an odor that suggested a night or two spent in the same clothing.

Maybe the guy was homeless—Orion shouldn't be so quick to judge. Clearly he'd watched one too many episodes of Law and Order during his months in rehab. Orion had probably looked the same way when he arrived at LaGuardia, freshly out of hibernation at his homestead under the loom of Denali.

Orion dismissed the kid and hung onto the bar overhead as the train pulled away from Fulton station. "We could have walked to Foley Square," he muttered to Ham, who leaned his shoulder against the pole, clearly used to the jerk and roll of the New York metro.

Ham's gaze was tracking Knicks as he moved halfway down the car.

So Orion wasn't the only one whose instincts fired.

"You're limping," Ham said, not looking at him. He sounded as grumpy as Orion. "And we're late. The rally has already started."

"I'm not an invalid. My knee just doesn't like eight hours on a plane." He watched as the guy nudged up behind what looked like a college student, brown hair, fuzz on his chin, clean-cut, a black backpack with a purple NYU logo on the flap hanging over his shoulder. "I hope White has answers."

"If anyone can track down Royal, it's Senator White. He's on the Armed Services Committee."

Orion glanced away, toward the other side of the car. A couple women sat with their bags clutched on their laps. Another woman stood, her bag over her shoulder, scrolling through her phone. A man in a suit coat and satchel was reading the paper, folded in half in his grip.

Behind them a young man wearing a black hoodie, earbuds affixed, bobbed his head to music. He caught Orion's eye, then looked away.

"You should have told me that you went to rescue Royal and Thorne," Orion said, looking at Ham.

Ham met him with a frown. "It wasn't my information to give."

Orion's mouth tightened. "I wasn't thrilled when Logan Thorne landed on my doorstep last summer, very alive and packing a conspiracy theory."

Ham turned to face him, as if ready to share answers as to why a former Navy SEAL who'd been taken by the Taliban in Afghanistan some three years ago had appeared alive, although shot, and in the backwoods of Alaska. Thorne surfaced with stories of an off-the-books rescue mission, a CIA cover-up, and the desperate fear that someone was still out to get him.

Thorne's story sat in Orion's gut and chewed at him until, some five months later, he finally contacted former SEAL Hamilton Jones.

Ham invited him to NYC to tell his story to Senator Isaac White, who served on the Senate Armed Services Committee and had ties to the CIA. If anyone could find Royal, it was the people who'd been behind his disappearance. Besides, they owed Orion answers about a number of things. So yes, he'd emerged from the woods for a face to face with White.

Ham had been bugging him anyway to join his private international SAR team, Jones, Inc.

Hello, no. The last thing Orion wanted was to dive back into the world of spec ops and medical tragedies. He'd barely survived last go-round.

Had left behind buddies, pieces of himself, and a broken heart.

"Listen, that rescue mission blew up in everyone's faces and got a good man killed, so no, my first thought wasn't to call you," Ham said. "Besides, if I remember correctly, you were still in Germany—"

"Knock it off."

The sharp voice turned both Ham and Orion. Knicks had jostled NYU enough to get a rise out of the college kid. "Step back."

Knicks, however, came up on him, gave the student a push. "What? You got a problem with me?"

Ham stiffened.

NYU moved away, hands up. "I don't want any trouble."

What he said. Orion's jaw tightened. Please don't let the kid be armed.

The car swayed as it screamed through the tunnels. Orion glanced at the next stop on the map above the door—Brooklyn Bridge–City Hall station, still three minutes away.

A couple people pulled out their phones.

A ripple of fear silenced the subway as Knicks took another step toward NYU. Then he got in his face with a string of expletives that even Orion hadn't heard before. And he'd been in spec ops boot camp, a special kind of H-E-double-hockey-sticks.

Yikes.

Orion's code of honor made him glance, almost in apology, at the women standing in the back of the car and—wait, what?

Knicks and the man in the hoodie might be working in

tandem because, hoodie slipped past one of the women with what looked like her wallet disappearing into his front pocket.

Aw, shoot. The last thing Orion wanted was to get tangled up in other people's trouble.

On the other side of the car, the altercation erupted. Knicks cornered the pale, yet angry NYU student who was trying to bump past him.

When Knicks shoved the kid against the door, Ham moved.

Orion should have expected it. Ham wasn't the sit-around type—even when they were serving at their base in Asadabad, Ham got to know the locals, as well as everyone on base. The man was the base party coordinator—he'd fashioned a basketball hoop and nailed it to a pole, even dragged in music.

He'd also started a prayer meeting, but that was Ham, the rescuer of lost souls.

Probably why the man wouldn't stop hounding Orion about leaving the woods and joining the living.

No, thank you. Mostly because Orion had nothing left to give, the rescuer inside him all tapped out.

Truth was, he just wanted to mind his own business.

Not with Ham around. The former SEAL took four steps and didn't break stride as he slammed into Knicks. At six foot three, Ham could be imposing when he wanted to, and part of the PR for his small empire of GoSports gyms meant a regular workout.

Knicks hadn't a prayer.

In a second, Ham had his arm around Knicks's neck, pressing into his carotid artery and jugular vein, cutting off the air.

G'night, pal.

Knicks clawed at Ham's arm, stumbled back, and Ham brought him down gently, letting him go when the man slumped into unconsciousness.

For a second, no one moved.

Then, clapping erupted through the car, even as Ham stood up and put a foot on the man's chest. "Stay down," he said, not raising his voice as the kid rose to consciousness.

The train started to slow.

Orion glanced at Hoodie. He'd moved toward the door, his head down. The only one, it seemed, not watching the debacle at the front of the train.

Aw, shoot.

Because Orion really didn't come here to make trouble, find trouble, or even insert himself into the middle of trouble.

And yet . . .

He couldn't live with himself. No way Hoodie was getting away.

Orion stepped up in front of him, blocking the door as the train pulled into the station.

Hoodie looked up. Dark eyes, a hint of dark whiskers, and his eyes narrowed.

"Give it up," Orion said and held out his hand.

Hoodie frowned.

"The wallet." He didn't take his eyes off the man. "You're not getting off without returning it."

"Get out of my way," Hoodie said as the car rolled to a stop.

The doors opened.

Sure, Orion could have moved. Could have given in to the life mantra he'd that he'd embraced with two hands, clutching it to his chest after the tragedy in Afghanistan—it wasn't his problem.

But he was tired of evil winning, or at least winning the battle, and maybe God had put him right here to save one hardworking woman from having to spend the day fighting identity theft.

Not that that he actually believed God intervened anymore, but apparently Orion still did, so— "I don't think so, buddy."

Hoodie tried to move around him, but Orion grabbed his shirt and slammed him back against the pole. Glanced at the woman from whom Hoodie had lifted the wallet. "Check your bag, ma'am."

She stared at Orion in horror, then searched her bag.

Hoodie grabbed his wrist, but Orion jerked his hand, turning it, and in a second, he had the thief turned around in a submission hold.

"It's gone."

Yep. He knew it. "Give it up and I'll let you go," Orion said to Hoodie.

"Ry, what's happening?" Ham came over dragging Knicks by the shirt.

"Meet the dynamic duo," Orion said. "The old sleight-of-hand trick."

Hoodie was struggling, swearing, kicking out at Orion.

Sheesh, he didn't have time for this. With everything inside him, he just wanted to put the guy on the floor, put his knee in his back.

Okay, and maybe school the jerk about old-fashioned right and wrong.

But he was trying not to be that guy, despite the stir of anger in his chest, so Orion reached around him and grabbed the wallet from the pouch in his sweatshirt.

He released his hold just enough for Hoodie to turn.

The kid slammed his foot into Orion's knee.

Pain spiked up his leg as his leg buckled.

Just like that, Orion landed on the deck, his hand gripping the wallet. Hoodie took off running.

Orion bit back a word.

Knicks shouted, and Ham must have let him go because he nearly stepped on Orion on his scramble away from the car.

"Are you okay?" The woman knelt next to him. He felt like a fool, trying to gulp back a whimper.

But, holy cannoli, he wanted to let out a scream. "Yeah," he said, his voice strangled. He handed her the wallet.

"You're a hero," she said, "Thank you."

He wanted to respond, to shrug her words away, but it was all he could do to catch his breath.

Ham was helping him up, and heaven help him, Orion let him do it, trying desperately to fix a smile on his face.

"No problem," he finally managed. His voice sounded like a fist had closed around his lungs, and it felt like it, too, as he limped out, the doors closing behind him.

He leaned against the wall.

Ham stood behind him. "Well, that was fun."

"I need that coffee," Orion said. He ground his teeth, pushing up, finding his balance.

Ham hesitated. "Or, maybe you need one more second?"

Orion sucked in a breath. "I thought you said we were late." He limped out, trying not to wince and failing.

They took the escalator up to freedom—not a hint of Knicks and Hoodie. He did see their victim, NYU, however. The kid's pack hung over his shoulder, his head down as he all but fled the station.

Poor kid. It never felt good to have to be rescued. Humiliating, really.

Orion worked out the pain in his knee as he climbed the stairs to Centre Street into the heart of New York's court district. Protesters stood on the steps of the New York State Supreme Court building. The scent of hot dogs and gyros seasoned the air, and his gut growled. "I'm stopping in the Starbucks," he said to Ham. "I'll meet you at the rally."

Orion glanced over to the plaza crammed with spectators. From a distance he could see White standing on a platform, half hidden by campaign signs. Orion knew the man by reputation only—apparently, Ham had served with him during his early days as a SEAL. Conservative, not easily ruffled, the man was rising quickly out of the stew of political contenders.

He didn't care what stump speech Senator White delivered— if he got onto the presidential ballot, Orion would vote for him.

"Text me. I'll find you," Ham said and headed toward the crowd.

Orion crossed the street and entered the Starbucks, painfully aware that his knee burned deep with every step. As he stood in line, he eased off it. It had started to swell.

Next time he had the bright idea to get on a plane, he needed a good bang over the head. A reminder of the fact that his family had set down roots and stayed in Alaska for a reason. He didn't know why the need to find Royal ground a hole through him, but he couldn't pry it out of his mind. Answers—that's all he needed, maybe. Answers to the question of how he and his other Pararescue Jumpers—PJs—had been ambushed on that mountain, in the back hills of Afghanistan. And not just the cosmic, survivor's guilt kind of question, but the specific one—namely who in the CIA had pulled the trigger, armed with lousy intel that had sent two SEALS and two PJs to their graves.

Left two to be captured and tortured by the Taliban.

That question burned him awake in the long nights of the Alaskan winter, fueled an anger that he couldn't seem to douse.

Maybe if he could find Royal, bring him home . . .

Orion ordered a Venti Americano and by the time he stepped back out into the brisk air, he felt almost human, the caffeine sloughing off the adrenaline, along with the dark edge of frustration. Across the street at the rally, a band played—a country music group that roused something home-grown and patriotic inside him. And, from deep in the well of his memory, stirred a voice, soft, light. "How do I live without you? I want to know. . ."

A simple song on the radio, sung by the girl he couldn't forget on a base deep in the Kunar province. For a dangerous second, he let the memory light the darkness inside and stepped out onto the street.

Honking jerked him back. A taxi nearly sideswiped him.

Yeah, he hated the city.

The taxi driver flipped him off.

And people, really.

Orion waited with the crowd until the light changed then crossed over into the concrete park, searching for Ham. The crowd was still packed, the supporters not quite ready to give up the day, and Orion stood at the edge, scanning the crowd. His gaze landed on a familiar backpack—NYU. The college student he'd seen on the subway stood next to an abstract black granite sculpture. As Orion watched, NYU took off his pack and sat on the edge of the circular fountain, wearing a stripped, pale expression, a line of sweat streaking down his cheek.

The kid might be going into shock. The former trauma medic in Orion gave him a nudge.

Fine. He took a sip of his coffee and ambled over to the kid.

NYU abruptly got up, drew in a breath, and walked away.

Clearly, the kid was rattled because he'd left his backpack behind. Orion jogged up to it and lifted it. "Hey kid! NYU! You forgot your backpack."

The student turned, glanced back, eyes wide. Stopped.

Orion tossed it toward him.

NYU's mouth opened, and he grabbed the pack, clutching it to him as if it might be explosive. If possible, his face had gone even paler. "Thanks," he shouted.

Orion had the strangest urge to follow him, put his hand on his shoulder, make him sit down, breathe.

He knew what it felt like to barely escape with your life, and sure, the kid hadn't exactly been in mortal danger on the subway, but maybe his heartbeat hadn't figured that out yet.

Poor kid should take the day off. Go back to his dorm.

Hide in Alaska . . .

As if reading his mind, NYU turned, walking away fast.

Orion let him go.

Turned back to the crowd.

His phone vibrated in his pocket and he pulled it out. Ham. Meet me behind the stage, at the tour bus.

Orion texted back and moved around the crowd, working his way toward the large bus with Isaac White's handsome mug plastered along the side.

Ham stood, hot cocoa in hand, talking with a couple security guys in suits who guarded a roped-off area. Wind raked his dark blond hair, lifted the collar of his leather jacket. He blew on his cocoa and nodded toward Orion when he spotted him.

One of the security guys walked over and let him in. Shook his hand. "Ham says you had a little scuffle on the subway."

Orion shrugged. "No big deal. A couple thugs. We didn't save the world or anything."

The man laughed and Orion smiled as he walked over to Ham. Okay, it felt good to pull out the old warrior, dust him off. "You're a hero."

Not really. Not anymore.

The tour bus door opened, and a man walked down the stairs.

Orion had watched a few news clips of Isaac White but hadn't expected the immediate charisma that radiated off the former SEAL. Graying hair, blue eyes, he took Orion's outstretched hand with a two-handed grip. The man possessed the kind of smile that made Orion feel like he was in the presence of a movie star.

George Clooney, maybe.

"Senator," Orion said, wishing he'd cleaned up a little better than his canvas jacket and a pair of jeans.

"Ham said you needed my assistance." White angled Orion over to where Ham stood.

Orion's mouth went weirdly dry. Fueled by anger for so long, it had suddenly abandoned him in the face of White's seeming willingness to help.

Ham must have seen his stripped expression. "We're looking for a teammate who went missing in the debacle in Afghanistan," he said. "Operator Royal Benjamin. He was one of the two SEALS captured in the attack. And one of the two—"

"Who were rescued in your rogue op." White looked at Ham. "I know."

"Then you know that something isn't right," Orion said, finally finding his voice, a little more oomph to it than he probably needed. But the anger was returning. "The other SEAL, Logan Thorne, showed up on my doorstep last summer. He told me a story about the CIA trying to cover up what happened in Afghanistan—and, trying to kill him."

White held up his hand, lowered his voice. "Not here, not now—"

Orion's mouth closed, and the heat stirred in his chest. He should have known—

"Mistakes were made, for sure," White said. "And the CIA knows it. But before you start throwing accusations around, let me do some digging."

"C'mon, Senator—"

Ham shot Orion a shut-up look, but White talked over him.

"I'm not sure where your friend is, or if he's even alive, but if you want me to find out, I'll need some time." He clamped a hand on Orion's shoulder. "And patience."

Orion wanted to believe him and his smile, but—

"Sir, we need you come with us right now." One of the security agents stepped into the conversation. "There's been a bomb found in the square." He pushed White away from them, toward a waiting SUV. Ham jogged after him, Orion limping quickly behind them.

He caught up to the second agent. "What kind of bomb?"

The agent looked at him. "I don't know. We found a backpack near the fountain. The bomb squad is on their way, and the police are evacuating the square. It could be the same kind of bomb that took out the San Antonio rodeo arena a couple weeks ago."

San Antonio arena? Orion hadn't a clue what he might be referring to.

That's what he got for living off the grid.

Still, a fist had grabbed his gut, squeezed. "What kind of backpack?"

The man flashed his cell phone toward him.

Black, with a purple NYU stitched on the back pocket.

Orion slowed, stopped, watching as the agent climbed into the front seat.

Ham hung back and joined Orion.

"What?"

"That kid with the backpack."

"Seriously?"

Orion finished his coffee and tossed the cup into a nearby trash can. "I'm going back to Alaska where I can stay out of trouble."

Get your copy of The Way of the Brave!

Author's Note

"Behold, I make all things new." (Revelation 21:5)

Do we really believe it?

Do we believe that God is a God of the impossible? That he can take brokenness and make it whole? That he can forgive any sin, heal every hurt, restore what was lost?

It's hard to sit back and wait upon God for that answer. Because in our hearts, we wonder...can he? Does he? Maybe he needs my help!

The minute I introduced York, with his shady, dark past, I wondered...how was God going to redeem this character. I mean, I know God can redeem anyone, but frankly how was he going to save a man who was too disgusted by his own actions to reach out for grace, forgiveness?

York didn't want to be saved. Or rather, he didn't even see it as possible.

So, I had to take his memory away. Show him who he could be, without the past. Show him what could happen if he went to the cross and let salvation wash him clean. When I wrote the scene of York's salvation, I wept, knowing all he had been forgiven of, even if he didn't know.

That's why I had to put Ruby Jane in the audience—so she could weep for joy with me.

God can do the impossible, and believing it is the biggest

challenge of all. Trusting Him for the best outcome. Believing Romans 8:28 with everything inside us. *And we know that in all things God works for the good of those who love him, who have been called according to his purpose.*

But there's an even bigger truth here—not JUST that God can do the impossible, but he can do the impossible even when we don't believe it. Even when our faith is nothing.

I looooove it when God says to Moses, and then Jehoshaphat, *"Stand back and see what I will do."*

Just stand back and praise the Lord as he does the fighting for us. Even when—no, *especially when*—we don't deserve it.

York needed to get out of his own way to be set free and God did exactly that by taking away his memory. Extraordinary means to get to the heart of the matter—that York was his son, and he wasn't letting him be imprisoned by his sins any longer.

He's not going to let you live in darkness, either. Even if he has to do something extraordinary to get you out of your own way.

As for RJ, she was a woman who felt she had to prove herself. But God says—*you don't have to prove anything to your real Father. Your heavenly Father. Don't you see—I choose to save you.*

When I conceived of the Montana Marshalls series, I used the hymn *Be Thou My Vision* as my thematic guide. I wanted, in the end, for the family to see that though they'd lost their earthly father, they still had their Heavenly Father, and most importantly, that was the legacy their father had left them. I wanted them to gain a new vision, one that they could never lose.

It's the vision I hope you, my reader, has too. You're loved. You're worth fighting for, and God will go to extraordinary means to save you.

And, when all else is done, God is enough, everything, and always.

Heart of my own heart, whate'er befall
Still be my Vision, O Ruler of all!

My deepest gratitude goes to my team, those amazing people who have helped me bring the Montana Marshalls to life. My writing partner, Rachel Hauck, for her endless wisdom and creativity. Alyssa Geertsen, my key beta reader, Barbara Curtis, for her amazing editing. Really, she's so fantastic. Rel Mollet, who keeps me on schedule, makes me sound good, and takes the time to help me bring the story deeper. Thank you to my talented cover designer, Jenny @ Seedlings Design Studio, and my fabulous layout artist, Tari Faris. Thank you also to my wonderful proofreaders (any mistakes are all mine!) Lisa Jordan, Lisa Gupton, Bobbi Whitlock and Laurie Stoltenberg. You guys are just such a huge gift to me!!

And, I'm thankful to the Lord, who is always and forever telling me He loves me. That he will do extraordinary things to set me free, and that He is my good, good father.

Finally, thank you, awesome reader friend, for reading this series! I hope you enjoyed reading it as much I loved writing it!

Susie May

Susan May Warren is the USA Today bestselling, Christy and RITA award–winning author of more than seventy novels whose compelling plots and unforgettable characters have won acclaim with readers and reviewers alike. The mother of four grown children, and married to her real-life hero for nearly 30 years, she loves travelling and telling stories about life, adventure and faith.

In addition to her writing, Susan is a nationally acclaimed writing teacher and runs an academy for writers, Novel.Academy. For exciting updates on her new releases, previous books, and more, visit her website at www.susanmaywarren.com.